# SHALADOR'S
# LADY

# ANNE BISHOP

# SHALADOR'S LADY

A *Black Jewels* Novel

A ROC BOOK

ROC
Published by New American Library, a division of
Penguin Group (USA) Inc., 375 Hudson Street,
New York, New York 10014, USA
Penguin Group (Canada), 90 Eglinton Avenue East, Suite 700, Toronto,
Ontario M4P 2Y3, Canada (a division of Pearson Penguin Canada Inc.)
Penguin Books Ltd., 80 Strand, London WC2R 0RL, England
Penguin Ireland, 25 St. Stephen's Green, Dublin 2,
Ireland (a division of Penguin Books Ltd.)
Penguin Group (Australia), 250 Camberwell Road, Camberwell, Victoria 3124,
Australia (a division of Pearson Australia Group Pty. Ltd.)
Penguin Books India Pvt. Ltd., 11 Community Centre, Panchsheel Park,
New Delhi - 110 017, India
Penguin Group (NZ), 67 Apollo Drive, Rosedale, North Shore 0632,
New Zealand (a division of Pearson New Zealand Ltd.)
Penguin Books (South Africa) (Pty.) Ltd., 24 Sturdee Avenue,
Rosebank, Johannesburg 2196, South Africa

Penguin Books Ltd., Registered Offices:
80 Strand, London WC2R 0RL, England

First published by Roc, an imprint of New American Library,
a division of Penguin Group (USA) Inc.

First Printing, March 2010
10   9   8   7   6   5   4   3   2   1

ROC REGISTERED TRADEMARK—MARCA REGISTRADA

Library of Congress Cataloging-In-Publication Data:

Bishop, Anne.
    Shalador's lady: a black jewels novel/Anne Bishop.
        p. cm.
    ISBN 978-0-451-46315-9
    1. Witches—Fiction.  I. Title.
    PS3552.I7594S54 2010
    813'.54—dc22            2009036065

Set in Bembo
Designed by Ginger Legato

Printed in the United States of America

FOR

NADINE, MERRI LEE, AND ANNEMARIE

AND FOR

NEELA

# ACKNOWLEDGMENTS

My thanks to Blair Boone for continuing to be my first reader, to Debra Dixon for being second reader, to Doranna Durgin for maintaining the Web site, to Rick Kohler for making the map pretty, to Pat Feidner just because, and to all the friends and readers who make this journey with me. And a special hello to Nikki and Sloan, the humanitarian vampire princesses I met on an Alaskan cruise.

# Dena Nehele

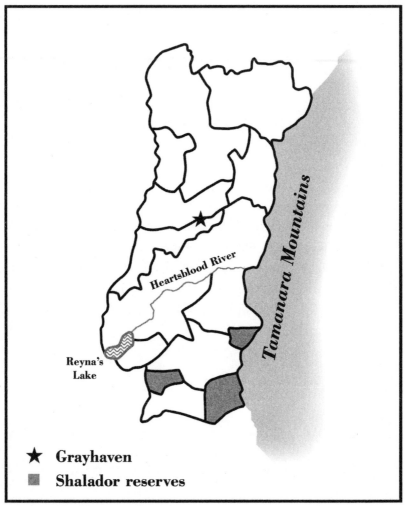

★ Grayhaven
▨ Shalador reserves

Note: This map was created by a geographically
challenged author. All distances are whimsical
and subject to change without notice.

# JEWELS

WHITE
YELLOW
TIGER EYE
ROSE
SUMMER-SKY
PURPLE DUSK
OPAL★
GREEN
SAPPHIRE
RED
GRAY
EBON-GRAY
BLACK

★Opal is the dividing line between lighter and darker Jewels because it can be either.

When making the Offering to the Darkness, a person can descend a maximum of three ranks from his/her Birthright Jewel.
Example: Birthright White could descend to Rose.

## AUTHOR'S NOTE
The "Sc" in the names Scelt and Sceltie is pronounced "Sh."

# BLOOD HIERARCHY/CASTES

MALES:

landen—non-Blood of any race

Blood male—a general term for all males of the Blood; also refers to any Blood male who doesn't wear Jewels

Warlord—a Jeweled male equal in status to a witch

Prince—a Jeweled male equal in status to a Priestess or a Healer

Warlord Prince—a dangerous, extremely aggressive Jeweled male; in status, slightly lower than a Queen

FEMALES:

landen—non-Blood of any race

Blood female—a general term for all females of the Blood; mostly refers to any Blood female who doesn't wear Jewels

witch—a Blood female who wears Jewels but isn't one of the other hierarchical levels; also refers to any Jeweled female

Healer—a witch who heals physical wounds and illnesses; equal in status to a Priestess and a Prince

Priestess—a witch who cares for altars, Sanctuaries, and Dark Altars; witnesses handfasts and marriages; performs offerings; equal in status to a Healer and a Prince

Black Widow—a witch who heals the mind; weaves the tangled webs of dreams and visions; is trained in illusions and poisons

Queen—a witch who rules the Blood; is considered to be the land's heart and the Blood's moral center; as such, she is the focal point of their society

# PLACES IN THE REALMS

## TERREILLE

*Dena Nehele*
TAMANARA MOUNTAINS
GRAYHAVEN—BOTH A FAMILY ESTATE AND A TOWN
EYOTA—VILLAGE IN THE EASTERN SHALADOR RESERVE

*Ebon Askavi* (aka the Black Mountain, the Keep)

*Hayll*

*Zuulaman*

## KAELEER (THE SHADOW REALM)

*Askavi*
EBON ASKAVI (AKA THE BLACK MOUNTAIN, THE KEEP)
EBON RIH—VALLEY THAT IS THE KEEP'S TERRITORY
RIADA—BLOOD VILLAGE IN EBON RIH

*Dea al Mon*

*Dharo*
WEAVERS FIELD—BLOOD VILLAGE
BHAK—BLOOD VILLAGE
WOOLSKIN—LANDEN VILLAGE

*Dhemlan*
AMDARH—CAPITAL CITY
HALAWAY—VILLAGE NEAR SADIABLO HALL
SADIABLO HALL (THE HALL)

*Nharkhava*
TAJRANA—CAPITAL CITY

*Scelt*
MAGHRE—VILLAGE

HELL (THE DARK REALM, THE REALM OF THE DEAD)
*Ebon Askavi* (aka the Black Mountain, the Keep)
SADIABLO HALL

# CASSIDY'S COURT

SHIRA—BLACK WIDOW/HEALER
VAE—WITCH; SCELTIE
REYHANA—SHALADOR QUEEN

*Warlord Princes*
ARCHERR
BURNE
HAELE
JARED BLAED (GRAY)
RANON—TALON'S SECOND-IN-COMMAND
SHADDO
SPERE
TALON—MASTER OF THE GUARD
THERAN—FIRST ESCORT

*Princes*
POWELL—STEWARD OF THE COURT

*Warlords*
BARDRIC
CAYLE
RADLEY

# KERMILLA'S COURT

*Warlords*★
ASTON
BARDOC
FLYNTON—MASTER OF THE GUARD
GALLARD—STEWARD
JHORMA—CONSORT
KENJIM
LASKA
LIEKH
RIDLEY
TRAE

★There are two more Warlords in her court, but they are not mentioned in the story.

# SHALADOR'S
# LADY

*As tales of the new Queen's heart and courage spread through the Territory of Dena Nehele, the Black Widows felt something tremble through the land. But when they spun their tangled webs of dreams and visions, what they saw gave them little comfort.*

*Many saw honey pear trees, heavy with ripe fruit, growing out of rotting bodies that had been left on the killing fields. A few saw a new beginning that was draped in the colors of sunset. Nothing they saw offered clarity—only the certainty that something was coming that would change Dena Nehele forever.*

*In Ebon Askavi, the Sanctuary of Witch, another Black Widow studied the dreams and visions in her tangled web—and saw more than the other Black Widows ever could.*

*Tears fell from her sapphire eyes, but even she could not have said if those tears were born of sorrow or of joy.*

# CHAPTER 1

## TERREILLE

Ranon stepped out on the terrace behind the Grayhaven mansion, closed his dark eyes, and raised the wood flute to his lips. Then he hesitated while a lifetime of caution warred with the hope he felt because of Lady Cassidy, the Queen who now ruled the Territory of Dena Nehele.

Because there was hope, and fledgling trust, Ranon took a breath and began to play a greeting to the sun—a song that had not been heard outside of the Shalador reserves for many, many years. Even there, it had not been played openly.

His grandfather had taught him this song and every other song the Tradition Keepers had held on to since the Shalador people fled the ruins of their own Territory generations ago and settled in the southern part of Dena Nehele. The people had thrived there and put down roots, respecting the traditions of Dena Nehele but never forgetting their own—and hoping, always hoping, that someday they would have a Territory of their own again.

It had been good land once, and a good place to live when it had been ruled by the Gray-Jeweled Queens. Then Lia died, and Dena Nehele's decline began. Queens who were backed by Dorothea SaDiablo, Hayll's High Priestess, gained control within a couple of generations. Dorothea hated the people of Dena Nehele for holding out against her for so long, but she hated the Shalador people even more because of Jared, the Red-Jeweled Shalador

Warlord who had been husband and Consort to Lia Grayhaven, the last Gray Lady to rule Dena Nehele.

Because Dorothea hated Jared's people, her pet Queens ground away a little more of what was uniquely Shalador with each generation. The boundaries of the reserves where the Shaladorans had settled were whittled away until now they struggled to grow enough crops to feed themselves. The Shalador traditions were forbidden. The dances, the music, the stories—all were taught in secret and at great risk.

His paternal grandfather was a Tradition Keeper of music. A strong, quiet man, Yairen had been—and still was—a respected leader in Eyota, the village where Ranon had grown up. He was also a gifted musician who believed it was his duty to teach the young how to play the songs that had shaped the Shalador heart.

The Province Queen who controlled that reserve broke Yairen's hands as punishment for teaching the forbidden—and then broke them twice more. When they healed the last time, Yairen could barely hold a flute, much less play one. But he still taught his grandson, and he taught him well, despite the crippled hands.

So this music had been a secret for most of Ranon's life. Even when he admitted to playing the flute, he never played within the hearing of anyone he couldn't trust—and even then, he rarely played the songs of Shalador.

Did the Queen he now served understand how much trust was required for him to stand here and play the music of his people? Probably not. Lady Cassidy had recognized his reluctance to play, but not even Shira, the Black Widow Healer who was his lover, understood how deeply fear and hope had twined in his heart these past few days as the flute's notes floated on the air and became a part of the world. Yes, he was afraid, but the hope of something new and better was the reason he stood here, in a place that had been a stronghold for the twisted Queens, and played music that had been forbidden.

As one song followed another, Ranon let his heart soar with the notes and fill with a joyful peace.

"How long do you have to spend serenading the little green things before you can have breakfast?"

He opened his eyes and lowered the flute. The peace he'd felt a moment before vanished as Theran Grayhaven stepped out on the terrace.

He and Theran didn't like each other. Never had. But he detected nothing in the question except polite interest.

"A quarter of an hour." Ranon glanced at the hourglass hovering in the air next to him. Judging by how much sand was in the bottom of the glass, he'd played twice that long. "Gray says it will help the honey pear trees grow."

"Does he really think they'll wilt and die if you don't stand out here playing music?" Theran asked as he studied the thirteen pots that were sheltered by the raised flower beds that formed the terrace wall.

Ranon's heart gave a hard bump at the thought of any of the little honey pear trees dying, but he wouldn't admit to anyone how much the living symbols of the past meant to him.

Jared had brought six honey pear trees to this land. One of them had been planted here at Grayhaven for Lia and had remained in the gardens long after it died as a mocking symbol of the Gray-Jeweled Queens who had once ruled. But that dead tree had hidden thirteen honey pears, carefully preserved. Lia had hidden them; Cassidy had found them as the first step to locating the Grayhaven treasure. Because of that, those little trees were a thread of shining hope that linked the past and the present.

"Doesn't matter what Gray thinks," Ranon replied. "It is the Queen's pleasure that I play the flute each morning for the honey pears, so I play."

He knew the phrasing was a mistake the moment he said it.

"Well, we all play for the Queen's pleasure in one way or another, don't we?" Theran said. Then he glanced at Ranon and added with a touch of malice, "Better play faster or there won't even be porridge left by the time you get to the table, let alone meat and eggs."

*I guess we're not trying to get along anymore,* Ranon thought. Since he made no secret of it, everyone in the court knew he hated porridge. Which meant Theran had said that in order to jab at him. Why? Because they didn't like each other, and the effort to be civil rarely lasted for more than a few minutes at a time?

Hell's fire. Grayhaven had been running hot and cold since Cassidy found the treasure and proved she was meant to rule here, but they were all committed to working together for the good of the land and the Queen.

For the good of the land, anyway. The other eleven men who made up the First Circle knew Theran didn't feel the same commitment to Cassidy that they felt. Serving in her court was part of the agreement Theran had made in order to bring a Kaeleer Queen to Dena Nehele. That didn't mean he *wanted* to serve her, despite his recent efforts to work with her instead of opposing her.

"Tell you what," Theran added. "I'll save my share of the porridge for you."

An edge of temper. A slash of heat in the air between them. And an unspoken invitation to spill some blood.

"You're twenty-seven," Ranon said coldly. "I'm thirty. We're both too old to indulge in a pissing contest over porridge."

Theran jerked back as if he'd been slapped. Then, snarling, he took a step forward.

Using Craft to vanish the hourglass and flute, Ranon instinctively took a step to the side to give himself more room to maneuver.

He wore an Opal Jewel; Theran wore Green. They were both Warlord Princes, aggressive predators born to stand on the killing fields. If they unleashed their psychic strength against each other, they could destroy the Grayhaven mansion and kill many of the people living here before anyone else knew there was danger. Even without using the power that made the Blood who and what they were, they could cause a lot of harm to each other with just muscle and temper.

But if either of them was damaged so badly he couldn't serve, the court would break, and Ranon's hope for the Shalador people would break with it.

Remembering that, he backed away from the fight, indicating with a subtle shift of his body that Theran was the dominant male. Which was true, as far as the Jewels were concerned. But only as far as the Jewels were concerned. And that, too, Ranon conveyed with that subtle shift.

Fury flashed in Theran's green eyes. Instead of accepting that Ranon had yielded, he took another step forward. Then . . .

*Theran? Theran!*

*Saved by a Sceltie,* Ranon thought as he watched Theran's hasty retreat into the mansion moments before the small brown-and-white dog bounded up the terrace's steps.

"Good morning, Lady Vae," Ranon said with more courtesy than was required.

The little bitch growled at him.

Glancing at the Purple Dusk Jewel half hidden in her fur, Ranon offered no challenge. Vae was kindred—the name given to the Blood who were not human—and he'd seen her pull down a full-grown man in a fight. His caste outranked hers, since she was only a witch, and his Jewels outranked hers. On the other hand, she had speed, strong jaws, and sharp teeth.

*You are not usually so foolish as other human males, so I will not nip you this time,* Vae said.

"Thank you, Lady. I appreciate that."

He also appreciated the implied threat that the next offense would earn him more than a nip.

Vae trotted into the mansion, no doubt intending to administer her own brand of justice on the other foolish male.

Ranon sighed. He'd come close to spoiling something that was as delicate as the honey pear seedlings growing in their pots.

*Give her the best you have, Ranon,* the Shalador Queens had told him when they left yesterday evening. *Show her that Shalador's heart and honor are worthy of such a Queen.*

Cassidy was a Rose-Jeweled Queen from Dharo. A tall, gawky woman with red hair and freckles, she was nothing like the image of the beautiful, powerful Queen that Theran had painted when he'd told the surviving Warlord Princes about his plan to save Dena Nehele.

But when Ranon saw her that first day, he had felt the bond between Warlord Prince and Queen grab hold of his heart and gut, had felt the *rightness* of handing over his life to her will. In the few weeks since her arrival, she had shown herself worthy of that trust, and in the wake of all she had done in the past week—fighting against a Warlord and his two grown sons to defend a landen family, as well as discovering the treasure that had been hidden on the Grayhaven estate—even the Warlord Princes who had been disappointed when they had first seen her were reassessing the Queen behind the long, plain face.

He didn't like Theran. He never would. But because he was grateful for Cassidy's presence—and because he knew how he would have felt if he'd been required to serve a Queen he didn't believe in—he would do what he could to keep peace between himself and Theran.

And to bring back a little of the peace that had been spoiled, he called in his flute and played a while longer.

Theran paused in the dining room doorway and took a moment to watch the people around the table. Despite their commitment to serve, the men who made up the First Circle of Cassidy's court had been wary of her. They had seen too much brutality done at the command of the twisted Queens who had ruled here. And no matter what they said, he knew they had been disappointed in their Queen's lack of beauty and power.

Then Cassidy found the treasure that had been hidden by Lia and Thera, the Black Widow who had been Lia's closest friend. Not only did that discovery restore the Grayhaven family's personal wealth, it had uncovered journals and portraits that gave him and the other men in the First Circle a glimpse of the past that had helped to shape them—because the people in those portraits had known what it meant to have honor. And Cassidy, by her actions, had shown herself to be a Queen of the same caliber as Lia.

Because of those things, he had made the choice to be Cassidy's First Escort in more than name, to serve her as if he felt the bond that the rest of the First Circle felt. But he didn't feel that bond, and despite his best intentions, serving her scraped at him. He was grateful for what she had accomplished so far, but he still believed that if Cassidy could do this much, the kind of Queen he had wanted for Dena Nehele could do so much more. The Blood who saw Cassidy had to get past that plain face and Rose Jewel in order to consider if she had anything to offer the land or the people—and most of the Blood would be disappointed enough not to bother.

*Her contract to rule Dena Nehele is only for a year,* Theran thought as he walked over to the table and took a seat. *I can put up with serving her for a year. And it gives me time to find the right Queen for Dena Nehele.*

The right Queen wouldn't stick a Shalador Warlord Prince in his face every damn day. His only excuse for his behavior this morning was that Ranon's presence scraped at him even more than Cassidy's. He'd spent his whole life being *Grayhaven,* the last descendant of the Gray Queens' bloodline and the man destined to become *the* male leader—the Warlord Prince the other men would follow. Until he brought Cassidy to Dena Nehele and she formed her court, that was exactly who he had been. Now people looked at the dark hair and golden skin that proclaimed Ranon's heritage. Then they looked at *him,* and instead of seeing Grayhaven, they saw *Shalador.*

Worse than that, when men saw him with other members of the First Circle, they responded to him as *a* leader, but not as *the* leader. They acted like the Grayhaven name no longer meant as much now that Cassidy was here.

Feeling spiteful and pissed off at everyone, he started to help himself to a double serving of steak, eggs, and potatoes—taking Ranon's share as well as his own—but as he stabbed the second piece of steak, Cassidy held out a clean plate and smiled at him. Noticing how sharply the other men around the table were watching him, he had no choice but to give her half of everything.

When she set the plate in front of herself and didn't eat, resentment bubbled up. If she hadn't wanted the food, why had she prevented *him* from having it?

*At least Ranon is still stuck with the porridge.* Then Theran glanced at his cousin Gray and remembered another reason to try to get along with Cassidy.

Gray had been damaged in body and mind by the Queen who had captured and tortured him when he was fifteen. Now, twelve years later, Gray was finally changing emotionally and mentally from boy to man. A boy couldn't be Cassidy's lover, and that desire, that *need* was the force driving Gray's transformation.

The proof of that was a simple thing: When they had first come back to Grayhaven, Gray had been too afraid of being inside the mansion to eat with them. Now he was here, sitting beside Cassidy, talking about . . .

"What?" Theran almost dropped the coffeepot. "We're doing *what*?"

"Going to the Shalador reserves," Cassidy replied calmly. "The Shalador Queens invited me. They want me to see the land their people are subsisting on, want me to see the truth of their concerns."

"It's not safe," Theran said. It had been his automatic response to all of Cassidy's attempts to get out among the people, but this time he really was concerned about her safety and not what people would think about the Queen who now ruled them.

He poured his coffee and began to eat because he needed to fill his belly.

"Then it's up to Talon as Master of the Guard and Ranon as his second-in-command to make it safe," Cassidy said.

"If we were going to the southern or western reserves, I would agree with Theran," Shira said. "They border other Territories, and the people there are as desperate as we are when it comes to repairing their lives and land."

"What are you concerned about?" Cassidy asked Shira. "That they'll try to abduct me?"

"Yes."

Silence around the table. A sharpening of psychic scents as the Warlord Princes who served in the First Circle put an edge on tempers that were always well-honed.

"You underestimate your value, Lady," Shira said. "You don't know how much a good Queen is worth in Terreille. Especially now."

"An abducted Queen isn't worth anything," Cassidy countered. "You can't force her to rule."

"But abducting a Queen could start another war."

Cassidy leaned back, clearly startled by that possibility.

"Ranon's home village is in the eastern reserve, far enough away from other Territory borders to be safe, and it's backed by the Tamanara Mountains," Shira said. "Protected on all sides."

"But not protected from what's inside," Theran said.

"The Shalador people have no reason to wish Lady Cassidy harm," Shira said coolly.

"Prince Grayhaven, you can debate this all you want, but my decision is made," Cassidy said. "Five days from now, I'll be staying at the Shalador reserve. You, Powell, and Talon will discuss what needs to be done in order to accomplish that."

She would have backed down a fortnight ago, Theran thought. She would have respected that he knew more about what Dena Nehele needed than she did—and the other Warlord Princes who served her wouldn't have opposed him.

*A leader, but no longer the leader.*

He felt as if he'd lost something too elusive to name, but the sense of loss was real.

"In that case, I'll get started on the plans," Theran said, pushing away from the table. He picked up his plate and coffee mug. "If you'll excuse me, I'll finish my breakfast while I work."

He barely waited for her nod of dismissal, but he waited because Protocol required it. Then he walked out of the dining room to finish his meal away from the woman he'd brought into his land.

Cassidy might do some good during the year she was contracted to rule here. But letting the Shalador people think they were more significant than the rest of Dena Nehele wasn't going to help anyone.

That was Ranon's doing. He never let anyone forget that the Shalador people had borne the brunt of the cruelty that Dorothea's Queens had heaped on the people of Dena Nehele.

And Ranon never let *him* forget that if his family name had been anything but Grayhaven, Theran would have been living the same desperate life on one of the reserves as the rest of the Shalador people.

Which implied his life had been easy, and that wasn't true. As the last of the Grayhaven line, he'd grown up in the rogue camps that were hidden in the Tamanara Mountains, living among men who would fight to the death and beyond rather than serve a Queen who wanted them to whore their code of honor. He'd been trained by Talon, a Sapphire-Jeweled Warlord

Prince who had been demon-dead for almost three hundred years—and who had been a friend to both Jared and Blaed, the Warlord Prince who had helped Jared elude Dorothea SaDiablo's guards and get Lia back to Dena Nehele.

Not an easy life by any measurement, but other men had survived worse. Gray, for one.

It was only for a year, he thought as he ducked into a room to finish his meal. Not *that* much could change.

As he ate, he ignored the little whisper telling him that a great deal had changed already.

The only thing left on the table was porridge.

Ranon suppressed a sigh and took a seat beside Shira. That put him across from Cassidy, who had a full plate of steak, eggs, and fried potatoes.

"Coffee?" Shira asked, holding up the pot.

"Thanks." He scraped what was left of the porridge into a bowl. It was food, and he was thankful to have it.

That didn't mean he had to like it.

As he dug in, Gray turned to Cassidy and asked, "Will you be coming out to the garden to work?"

"Not this morning," Cassidy replied. "I'm going with Shira to check on the landen girl who was injured."

Ranon tensed. So did every other man who was still at the table. But no one challenged that statement, which was a welcome change since Theran was always yapping whenever Cassidy wanted to leave the estate.

Archerr, an Opal-Jeweled Warlord Prince, said, "Prince Spere and I have escort duty this morning. If you think the First Circle should show a stronger presence, I can ask Prince Shaddo and Lord Cayle to stand as escorts too."

Archerr kept his eyes on Cassidy, but Ranon knew the question was directed at him as Talon's second-in-command. He tipped his head in a subtle nod. Additional escorts weren't needed to ensure Cassidy's safety during this visit, but it didn't hurt to remind the townspeople that the Queen was served and protected by strong men.

Then Gray said, "Perhaps Lady Vae would be willing to join you."

"I don't think any of us could stop her," Cassidy said.

Ranon snorted softly. Before Cassidy's arrival, no one here had seen a Sceltie. Vae had been an education for all of them.

Powell, the Prince who was the Steward of the court, pushed away from the table. "With your permission, Lady, we'll leave you to begin the day's work."

Cassidy nodded. "When I return, I'll stop at your office to review anything that requires my attention."

"Certainly. Ranon? When you have a moment, I'd like to discuss the Lady's visit to your home village."

"I'll join you shortly," Ranon replied.

"Lady Shira and I will be ready in half an hour," Cassidy told Archerr.

"I'll see you later," Gray said, brushing a fingertip over the back of Cassidy's hand.

*He's come so far so fast,* Ranon thought as Gray and the rest of the men left the dining room. *Now he's acting more like the Warlord Prince he should have been.*

When the last man left the room, he pushed aside the half-eaten bowl of porridge—and Cassidy pushed the full plate of food in front of him.

"Lady," he protested.

"I ate," Cassidy said. "But we've agreed to live lean and not cook more than we need for each meal. You were out with the honey pear trees, and I had a feeling that there might not be anything left by the time you got here."

Living lean. In the reserves, winter was called the Season of Hunger, so he knew about not wasting food. And he knew the unspoken rule of this court: Once everyone was served, what was left could be eaten by anyone who wanted more. The Blood's bodies needed more fuel than landens', and the darker the Jewel a person wore, the more food that person needed in order to remain a healthy vessel for the power that lived within. So everyone was willing to eat another helping when it was available.

Because he'd been late, and because of Theran's remarks, he hadn't expected to get more than porridge that even hunger barely made tolerable.

"If you have no objection to a solitary meal, Shira and I really should be going."

"I've no objection," he said. He touched his fork to the edge of the plate. "Thanks for this."

He waited until Cassidy and Shira left. Then he began eating with enthusiasm. As he poured the last of the coffee from the pot, it occurred to him that Cassidy had not only saved some food for him, she had used a warming spell on the plate so the food wouldn't get cold.

A small thing, perhaps. A simple courtesy. But when simple courtesies came from a Queen, it said a great deal about how she would treat her people—and, hopefully, how she would treat his.

# CHAPTER 2

## KAELEER

Lying facedown on the large bed, Daemon Sadi groaned with relief as his wife's skilled hands coaxed his back muscles to relax. The warming spell Jaenelle was using to ease the tightness didn't hurt either.

"Tell me again how you did this," Jaenelle said.

A typical wife question, particularly when said in *that* tone of voice.

"Daemonar was stuck in a tree," Daemon mumbled. Then, "Oh. Right there."

"Uh-huh. That is a very nasty knot." She said nothing for a minute while she worked on that part of his back. "So we're talking about Daemonar Yaslana. Your nephew."

"He's your nephew too."

"Yes, he is. And he's Eyrien. Which means he has wings."

"He's just a little boy."

"Who has wings."

Damn. She was going to hold on to that little detail like a Sceltie herding a single sheep.

"Since he is little," Jaenelle continued. "How did he get up in the tree? He wouldn't be able to reach the lower branches to climb up like you did."

Oh, no. He knew a trick question when he heard one.

"He flew up, didn't he?" Jaenelle said. "Using his wings."

"Darling, you're starting to sound like a Harpy," Daemon said. "Ow!"

That because she dug her thumbs into his back—which he deserved for the Harpy comment.

"Why don't you just admit that climbing a tree in those shoes you usually wear instead of using Craft to float up to the branch where your erring nephew was waiting for you, and most likely giggling, was a dumb idea?"

He wasn't about to admit to anything. Especially when it *had* been a dumb idea. He'd known that when he was doing it. He'd known it even better when he watched Daemonar flutter down to find out what he was doing flat on the ground. But it had been a matter of pride. Jaenelle understood about male pride. She might find it amusing or irritating, depending on the consequences, but she understood it. So she should understand that, at that moment when the boy was looking down at him, he saw himself as the uncle who used Craft instead of muscle, who didn't participate in the physical world the way his brother Lucivar did. In that moment, he didn't want to be seen as *less* by a boy who wasn't old enough to appreciate the power and skills he *did* have.

So he'd climbed the damn tree.

Idiot.

"At least I didn't actually hit the ground," Daemon muttered. "I did remember to create a shield and use the air walking spell." Which saved him from serious injury since he landed on a cushion of air instead of hard ground, but it didn't spare him from having the wind knocked out of him—or having a back full of tight, aching muscles.

"Good for you," Jaenelle said, her voice so dry there was no question she was not impressed.

"All right. Fine. I was an idiot." Which was a story he was sure the servants at SaDiablo Hall would share for many years to come, since a couple of them had witnessed the little drama. They wouldn't share the story with outsiders, because anyone who worked at the Hall knew the private lives of the SaDiablo family remained *private*. But he could see someone like the footman Holt taking a young servant aside and telling him that story as an assurance that the powerful, dangerous, *lethal* Black-Jeweled Warlord Prince of Dhemlan could also be a man who acted like a bumbling uncle with good intentions and a shortage of brains.

"Shit." He could *feel* her smile, and the fact that she didn't need to comment was more than sufficient comment.

She kissed him between the shoulder blades, and that simple contact between lips and skin warmed him in other ways, and the next stroke of her hands down his back had him purring instead of groaning.

"Just relax," Jaenelle said. "I'm almost done. By tomorrow you'll be your usual wonderful self, and if you can remember that you're a grown-up, you should be able to get through the last day of your nephew's visit without doing any more damage to yourself."

Her hands glided over his back, more a caress than a Healer's touch.

"You're not relaxing," she said.

"I'm very relaxed," Daemon purred. Most of him, anyway. He'd been sore enough that he hadn't focused on anything besides not hurting. Now he was aware of a few other things.

"No, you're not."

He heard the concern in her voice. That meant she was looking at him as a Healer and not a woman—and he wanted the woman's attention.

"Sweetheart, you're sitting on my ass. There are parts of me that find that very interesting and don't want to relax yet."

"I am not sitting on your ass," Jaenelle huffed. "I'm straddling you to work on your back."

"You're close enough that I can tell you're not wearing anything under that shift, so I call that sitting."

"And you can tell what I'm not wearing because . . . ?"

"When you brush against me, it tickles."

A too-thoughtful pause. "You're awfully sassy all of a sudden."

"Blame it on my beautiful wife."

"Boyo, I don't think your back will take what you have in mind."

"Then I'll just roll over. Since you're already straddling me, you can give us both a ride."

She snorted out a laugh. "You're such a romantic when you're exhausted, but I'll take you up on your offer. Just to help you relax completely, of course."

"Of course."

"Hold still for another minute."

Her hands glided over his back, the warm, sensuous caress of a lover.

Jaenelle Angelline. The living myth. Dreams made flesh. The former Queen of Ebon Askavi. And his wife. His wonderful, longed-for wife.

"Daemon?"

In another minute he would roll over and touch her body. He would use a psychic thread to link with her, mind to mind, and consummate their lovemaking with more than his body, touching her in ways he had never touched another woman.

"Daemon?"

He could picture her fair-skinned hands gliding over his golden brown chest as she sheathed him in silky fire.

In just another min . . .


## EBON ASKAVI

Saetan Daemon SaDiablo, former Warlord Prince of Dhemlan and still the High Lord of Hell, set aside the current stack of books he was sorting in the restricted part of the Keep's library, leaned against the large blackwood table, and watched the son who was a mirror prowl restlessly around the room.

Not physically a mirror. Not quite. They had the same thick, black hair and gold eyes—although his hair now held wings of silver at the temples. They had the brown skin of the long-lived races, but Daemon's skin was a golden brown—more Dhemlan than Hayllian in color.

He had always been considered handsome. Daemon, on the other hand, was beautiful and moved with a feline grace that drew the eye and aroused the senses.

The foolish lusted after that body, forgetting that the man inside the skin was a powerful predator with a cold, killing temper.

Which made him wonder about the reason for this visit.

"You're here early," Saetan said.

"Went to sleep early, got up early," Daemon replied.

Back and forth. Ceaseless movement. If it was Lucivar, he wouldn't think twice about the prowl. But Daemon?

Daemon stopped moving and stared at the wall. "I think there's something wrong with me."

Fear clamped around Saetan's heart, but he asked calmly, "In what way?"

A few weeks ago, Theran Grayhaven came to Kaeleer and asked Daemon for help. Disturbed by the physical resemblance between Theran and his old friend Jared, Daemon had slipped into painful memories, confusing the past with the present. No one had known there were deep emotional scars connected to the years after Daemon helped Jared and Lia elude Dorothea's guards. No one had suspected there was anything wrong—until Daemon attacked Jaenelle.

Since that night, Daemon was quick to hone his temper when anyone questioned his mental or emotional stability, so the subject had to be approached with caution.

He understood that. When the witch Vulchera had tried to compromise Daemon's honor by playing her particular brand of blackmail games, something had snapped inside of *him,* and he'd slid into the Twisted Kingdom where his rage had found an insane and terrible clarity. It wasn't the snap and slide that had disturbed the family; it was the deliberate way he had executed the bitch that had scared them.

So the whole family was still feeling a bit raw—and Lucivar going into rut so soon after didn't help.

"In what way?" he asked again.

Daemon turned to face him. "I'm only seventeen hundred years old. I've been married for a year to the woman I love with everything in me—a woman I've waited *centuries* to be with. So when that woman indicates she wants to make love with me, I should *not* be falling asleep between the thought and the deed!"

Relief made Saetan's knees weak—and he needed every drop of his fifty thousand years of self-discipline and control to keep a straight face.

"Lucivar is in rut," he said.

"I know that," Daemon replied, sounding as if he'd like to whack his brother's head against a wall a few times because of it.

"Who is looking after Daemonar?"

Daemon frowned. "He's staying at the Hall with us. I thought you knew that."

"I'm aware of where he's staying. Who is looking after him?"

Daemon shifted his weight from one foot to the other. In and of itself, it was an insignificant movement—except that *Daemon* had done it, and Daemon rarely showed any sign of uncertainty.

"I am, for the most part. Well, Hell's fire, Jaenelle can't hold the leash on that little beast."

*Of course she could,* Saetan thought. Even now, when she no longer had the abundance of physical energy she used to have, Jaenelle was probably one of the few people who *could* keep up with a small Eyrien boy. Not to mention that Daemonar loved his Auntie J, sensed on some level that she couldn't take rough play, and now had his young Warlord Prince instincts tugging at him to protect the Queen.

"Holt is also taking shifts watching the boy," Daemon added.

"Holt?" Saetan wondered if the footman was writing out his resignation. Which would be a shame, because the man was an asset to the household.

"He's young, strong, and has the experience of having several nieces and nephews," Daemon replied. "He also gets double wages for any day he assists in looking after the boy—and an extra day off with pay."

"Generous," Saetan murmured. "If those are the terms you offered, you should have plenty of volunteers."

"Not after the first hour," Daemon growled.

*Don't laugh,* he told himself. *You know exactly what this is like, so do not laugh at him.*

But he wanted to laugh. So he gave himself a stern mental shake and cleared his throat.

The rut wasn't a laughing matter. Once or twice a year, the fierce sex drive that always simmered in a Warlord Prince intensified to a need that eclipsed sanity, and a man who could normally control his predatory nature became a danger to everyone except the woman he'd fixed his attention on—and sometimes, if she wasn't careful around him, even she wasn't safe from a temper that had no leash.

It changed when a Warlord Prince had a strong relationship with a woman, particularly when that woman was his lover. She, at least, could usually penetrate the sexual madness and provide a little control during those three days. And a Warlord Prince who was a father could usually tolerate his own children's presence when they were infants or toddlers, as long as he didn't have to interact with them.

But Daemonar had begun the transition from toddler to boy last autumn and now had the unmistakable psychic scent of a Warlord Prince. Now Lucivar saw a rival instead of a son. So the boy could no longer stay in the eyrie when his father was in rut. Which meant Daemon took Daemonar for those days in the same way Saetan had taken Andulvar's son, Ravenar, and Andulvar had taken Mephis and Peyton.

"You're taking care of a small boy who is in motion almost every moment he's awake, and you think there is something wrong with you because you fell asleep before making love to Jaenelle?"

"Well . . ."

"When he goes down for an afternoon nap, do you have sense enough to take an hour of that time to get some sleep yourself?"

Daemon's gold eyes flashed with annoyance. "I do have work to do."

"Meaning you haven't taken that hour."

His son snarled softly. "Lucivar doesn't take naps."

Hell's fire. This wasn't a competition. Or maybe it was. Except for these past few years when they had been reunited with him, the only measuring stick they had for what was "normal" for a male with so much power was each other.

"Lucivar is Eyrien," Saetan said, his patience starting to fray.

"Half Eyrien."

"Nevertheless, the Eyriens are a very physical people, and your brother is no exception. Besides, Lucivar catches quick naps throughout the day. Haven't you seen him stand perfectly still with his eyes focused on some distant spot while you're talking to him and then realize he hasn't heard anything you've said?"

Daemon shrugged, a movement full of dismissal and irritation.

"He was asleep," Saetan said.

Daemon jerked. "What? He was *what?*"

"Asleep. I'm not sure if it's something Eyrien males are born knowing how to do or if they're trained, but they can sleep on their feet with their eyes open. Just a few minutes at a time. For a warrior, being able to snatch those moments of rest can mean the difference between surviving a battle or being one of the dead." Saetan paused, then added, "Andulvar used to do that sometimes when I was talking to him. He even had the balls to tell me my voice was a soothing drone."

Daemon snorted in an effort to hold back a laugh.

"If it's any comfort to you, I know for a fact there are nights when Lucivar flops on the bed and is so deeply asleep by the time Marian comes in that she can't shift him, so she throws a blanket over him and sleeps somewhere else. A few hours later, he wakes up, realizes she isn't there, and goes and fetches her to tuck them both in for the rest of the night."

"But he didn't think something was wrong with him," Daemon muttered.

Saetan raised an eyebrow. "Then why do you think I know about it?"

Daemon blinked. Blinked again. "Oh."

He huffed out a sigh. "Is that it? Anything else? I noticed you're a bit stiff this morning." When Daemon mumbled a response, he put some paternal steel in his voice. "What?"

"I fell out of a tree."

"I see." He didn't—and he wasn't going to ask about it. But even knowing the response he was about to provoke, he decided to trespass. "How are you otherwise?"

A heartbeat was all it took for Daemon to switch from being a son to being a Warlord Prince whose cold temper could be as elegant as it was deadly.

"I'm fine," Daemon replied, a warning chill in his voice.

"And I'm your father," Saetan replied, "as well as the High Lord of Hell. I'll have an honest answer this time, Prince."

They stared at each other, assessing, measuring. Then Daemon leashed the Warlord Prince in order to be a son again.

"I don't like knowing there are places where I'm fragile," Daemon said. "I don't like admitting I can be vulnerable."

"No man does. But very few men, if any, could have survived having their mind shattered twice and come back from it. Everything has a price, Daemon. Knowing there are some things you can't do seems like a small price to pay for getting your life back." Saetan studied his son. "There's something else. What is it?"

"I'll be going into rut sometime in the next few weeks," Daemon said.

"And that worries you?"

"Yes."

"Does it worry Jaenelle?"

"No." Daemon shifted his shoulders. "Could you talk to her? Make sure she's willing after . . ."

. . . *after the attack.*

Daemon took a deep breath and let it out in a sigh. "I need to get back. Jaenelle was sure she and Holt could deal with the boy for a few hours, but I don't want to be away too long."

"I'll talk to her," Saetan said. "Soon."

Daemon nodded. "If Lucivar gets Marian pregnant again . . ."

They both sighed.

"If that happens, we'll all deal with it," he said. *And hope for a girl.*

"I don't think Eyriens created the hunting camps just to train boys to become warriors," Daemon said thoughtfully. "I think they created them to send young males away from home because that was the only way Eyrien males would have siblings other than older sisters."

Saetan's lips twitched. "You could be right. Yes, I think you could be right."


"Hello, witch-child." Saetan pushed the books aside and turned to lean on the blackwood table. He'd been expecting her. That was why he hadn't retired to his suite to rest during the harsher midday hours that were so draining for a Guardian.

"Hello, Papa," Jaenelle replied.

She didn't come to him for a hug. She didn't look away. In fact, the fingers twining around and around one another was the only sign of nerves.

The living myth. Dreams made flesh. The daughter of his soul. They had almost lost her when she purged the Realms of the Blood who were tainted by Dorothea and Hekatah. Now she was whole and healthy again, if still a bit too thin in his opinion. The golden hair, cut short while she was healing, looked shaggy now. He couldn't tell if that was a deliberate style or the result of letting it grow.

But it was the sapphire eyes that held him now as they had held him the first time he met her.

"What is said between father and son is private, and I appreciate that," Jaenelle said. "But I need to know if Daemon is all right."

"Are you asking about his back?"

"I know about his back, Saetan."

And there it was—that hint of caverns and midnight in her voice that told him he was no longer talking to his daughter; he was talking to his Queen. To Witch.

"Daemon Sadi is the most powerful male in Kaeleer," Witch said. "He's a Black-Jeweled Warlord Prince with a temper that cannot be dismissed or taken lightly. He's *your* equal."

"Actually, he's dominant," Saetan said quietly. "His power is a little darker than mine. Which makes him *the* most powerful male in the history of the Blood. I'm aware of that, Lady. What is your point?"

"He slunk out of the bedroom this morning. He *slunk out,* Saetan. I need to know why."

"He was embarrassed because he had fallen asleep before making love to you last night. He thought there must be something wrong with him."

Jaenelle's mouth fell open. She stared at him. Finally she said, "Well . . . Hell's fire. He's been chasing after Daemonar for two days. Why was he surprised that he fell asleep?"

"Because, like his brother, he hasn't taken into account that having the stamina to run other grown men into the ground is not the same thing as trying to keep up with a small, bright boy who leaps into exploring the world with all the arrogance of his race—to say nothing of having inherited Lucivar's confidence in being able to meet any challenge the world foolishly chooses to toss at him."

"Oh."

"Were you disappointed that you didn't make love last night?"

She gave him a dry smile. "Frankly, I'm not sure either one of us could have stayed awake through the whole thing if we'd tried."

*End of discussion,* Saetan thought. Except it wasn't. Not quite. "He's also concerned about how you'll respond to him the next time he goes into rut—which will be fairly soon."

The look in her sapphire eyes sizzled along his nerves. He was her adopted father, and he had never thought of her physically in any other way. But he was also a man and a Warlord Prince, and there was always a sexual awareness between a Warlord Prince and his Queen, even when there was no desire to do anything with that awareness.

When Daemon was caught in the rut's sexual madness, how much of his relief came from physical sex and how much came from the knife-edged dance of being with Witch in the Misty Place deep in the abyss—of being with the living myth when she revealed the Self that lived within the human body? The Self that was not completely human.

The sizzle faded. He had to clear his throat before he could speak. "I'll tell Daemon not to worry about the rut."

★I've never worried about the rut,★ she told him using a psychic thread.

Now he understood why she didn't.

Jaenelle closed the distance between them and hugged him. Then she gave him a bright smile. "I'd better get back to the Hall before Daemonar gets his Unka Daemon into trouble."

"I thought Daemonar had given up the baby talk."

"Oh, he has for the most part. But he likes the sound of 'unka,' and his uncle doesn't insist that he say the word correctly."

Saetan smiled. "I see. Off you go, witch-child. Try to keep them both out of the trees, will you?"

"I'll do my best."

Later, when he was alone in his suite, preparing to sleep through the midday hours, he allowed himself to remember her in that moment when she showed him a side of Witch a father would never see.

And he allowed himself one moment to envy his son—and to wish he could have been the lover instead of the father.

# CHAPTER 3
## TERREILLE

Propped up on one elbow, Ranon watched Shira's slow return to awareness after the climax that was the finale of a long, slow, intense evening of lovemaking.

Before coming together in Cassidy's court, they'd had five years of fast, furtive coupling because his interest would have drawn the wrong kind of attention to the Black Widow Healer. Five years when he'd tried to stay away from her and had been unable to resist being with her. Five years of love always being entwined with fear.

Twice that five years, actually, if he counted the years before they became lovers. He had been twenty and still adjusting to the Opal power that coursed through him after he'd made the Offering to the Darkness. She had been sixteen—a young Black Widow, born to the Hourglass Covens, who was just beginning the secret training that would hone the Craft she instinctively knew, as well as the open training required to be a Healer.

They had both been visiting friends in a village that wasn't home to either of them. They had met by chance when their companions had chosen the same dining house for the midday meal. And that meeting had shaped their hopes and dreams for the next ten years.

Now, thanks to Cassidy, he and Shira could spend time together openly, could spend the night together, could begin to build a *life* together. That alone would have earned Cassidy his loyalty. The fact that she was proving to be a far stronger ruler than any of them had expected from a Queen who wore a Rose Jewel had earned his respect and a different kind of love. Her will was his life, and he would do everything he could to help her rule Dena Nehele—and by doing so he would do more than he'd dreamed possible for the Shalador people.

"What are you looking at?" Shira asked, her dark eyes reflecting the pleasure of their lovemaking as well as amusement.

His thoughts had drifted beyond her bedroom, but his eyes had been focused on her breasts.

He lowered his head and placed one warm kiss between her breasts before saying, "A Shalador beauty."

Her response was a little snort. "I know what I look like."

"But you don't see what I see," Ranon said. He was considered a handsome man. The sharp features typical of his people gave his face a rugged handsomeness that went well with a warrior's lean body, and he had the dark eyes, dark hair, and golden skin that made Shaladorans distinct from the brown-skinned, long-lived races or the fair-skinned races like the people of Dena Nehele.

She had the look of their people, too, and many men had thought the sharp bones of her face and the curves that lacked abundance made her less appealing as a lover—and her sharp tongue and temper discouraged most men from getting close to her. But it was exactly those things about her that excited him in ways no other woman had, and he understood why Gray could look at Cassidy—whom even the most generous supporter could not call pretty—and see a beautiful woman.

Shira turned her head away from him, an evasive movement that wasn't typical of her.

He considered his words. *You don't see what I see.* Then he considered the nature of a Black Widow's Craft and felt a chill settle in his belly.

"Shira? Have you seen something in a tangled web?"

"I can't talk about it."

"Can't or won't?"

"Can't, won't. The words make no difference."

They made a difference to him. His voice went flat. "You saw something in a web of dreams and visions. Didn't you?"

"I can't speak of it, Ranon. None of us will speak of it."

The chill in his belly turned to jagged ice. "How many Black Widows have seen this?"

She sighed, a sound full of exasperation and a hint of anger.

He shifted away from her, sat up, and wrapped his arms around his bent knees. He had no right to push. If she felt he needed to know, she would have told him. Hell's fire! She was the one who had pushed him to come to Grayhaven when Theran had first summoned the Warlord Princes to talk about bringing a Queen from Kaeleer. She hadn't told him anything then, either. She'd just said he had to go.

The Hourglass didn't divulge what they saw in their tangled webs. Not very often, anyway. And not directly. But a Black Widow never made a suggestion about an action to take without a reason.

"Is it something to do with Cassidy?" he asked.

She didn't answer.

"Shira . . ." He didn't know what to ask.

Finally Shira asked quietly, "Who has your loyalty, Prince Ranon? Tell me the list in order."

His heart ached, but she had asked. Because he would give her nothing less than honesty, the words had to be said. "I love you with everything I am, but my first loyalty is to my Queen. Then you, then our people, then Dena Nehele."

She sat up and pressed a hand against his face. When he looked at her, she said fiercely, "Remember the order of that list. Hold on to it with everything you are."

Was she warning him that something might happen to Cassie when they went to the Shalador reserves?

"Hold on to it the same way you've held on to your honor," Shira said.

And that was the answer: Cassidy the Queen came before anything and everything else—his lover, his people, his land.

The visions seen in tangled webs didn't always come true. Sometimes they were warnings of what might be. Shira was telling him that his choices would make a difference. *His choices.* And she had told him, without breaking her own code of honor, what his choice had to be.

That night, while Shira slept and he lay awake staring at the dark ceiling of her bedroom, he realized that fear could entwine with hope as well as love, and all he could do was give his best to the two women who were now the center of his life.

# CHAPTER 4

## KAELEER

Daemon rounded a corner and let out a roar—which only made his quarry pump those little legs faster.

Hell's fire. He'd only looked away for a minute while he was packing up the things Daemonar would take home. One damn minute! That's all it had taken for the boy to shoot out of the bedroom like an arrow released from a bow.

Well, if this was going to be their last pissing contest during this visit, he was *not* going to lose.

He was going to lose.

When he realized the stairs leading down to the informal receiving room—and beyond that, the great hall—were up ahead, he *ran*. The boy was going too fast to get down those stairs without a bad tumble.

Almost in reach. If he couldn't stop Daemonar . . .

The boy spread those little membranous wings and launched himself over the railing.

Daemon gave a moment's thought to leaping over the railing and using Craft to make a controlled slide on air, but that wasn't an easy bit of Craft to do, despite how simple Jaenelle always made it seem, and since it wasn't something he did on a regular basis—until lately, anyway—a miscalculation could end with a broken leg. Or worse.

At least the door to the great hall was closed, Daemon thought as he pounded down the stairs. At least the little beast didn't know how to make a pass through a solid object. At least he'd only be chasing a flying boy around a contained space.

Which was when Holt opened the door—and Daemonar dove right at the footman's head. Startled, Holt dove for the floor, and Daemonar flew past him into the great hall and let out a happy squeal.

Damn! Did someone just open the front door? If Daemonar got outside, it might take *hours* to catch him.

Leaping over Holt, Daemon skidded into the great hall.

And there was Lucivar, with his arms full of happy boy.

"Hello, boyo," Lucivar said, giving his bundle of boy a smacking kiss on the cheek.

"Papa! Papa!"

Daemon braced one hand on the wall and sucked in air while he watched the reunion.

"Were you a good boy?" Lucivar asked Daemonar. He gave Daemon what might have been a sheepish look—if it had been anyone else but Lucivar.

"Guess what, Papa! Unka Daemon fell out of a tree!"

Daemon's face burned with embarrassment.

Lucivar kept his eyes on his son. "What was Uncle Daemon doing in the tree?"

Daemonar suddenly turned shy and began playing with the gold chain that held Lucivar's Birthright Red Jewel.

"What was Uncle Daemon doing in the tree?" Lucivar asked again.

Daemonar hesitated. "Falling."

"Uh-huh."

*Is Marian pregnant?* Daemon asked on a Red psychic thread.

*We won't know for a few weeks,* Lucivar replied.

*You know, you prick,* Daemon thought. And Lucivar not giving him a straight answer *was* an answer.

Lucivar's gold eyes brightened when Jaenelle stepped into the great hall.

"Hey, boyo." Jaenelle smiled at Daemonar. "Are you going home without reading one last story with me?"

"No! Put me down, Papa!"

When Lucivar didn't respond fast enough, Daemonar rammed his feet into his father's gut and launched himself at Jaenelle.

Too fast, Daemon thought as the boy winged toward Jaenelle. But Daemonar backwinged an arm's length from his beloved auntie. He dipped and wobbled, but he landed without slamming into Jaenelle.

"Excellent backwinging." Jaenelle held out her hand as she gave Daemon and Lucivar a warm, amused look. "Come on. We'll sit in Uncle Daemon's study and read a story while he and your papa have a little chat."

When boy and Queen disappeared into the study, Lucivar rubbed his belly. "Well, so much for my minute of being important."

Daemon didn't reply. He just crossed the great hall and went into the formal receiving room.

*Thank you, Beale,* he thought when he saw the tray that held a decanter of brandy and two glasses. Normally he wouldn't consider a drink before the midday meal, but today . . .

"You're looking a bit rough, old son," Lucivar said as he came into the room and closed the door.

Daemon poured himself a hefty glass of brandy and took a generous gulp. "If you got Marian pregnant, you damn well better have a girl, because if you don't, I will twist your cock off. I swear it."

When he didn't get a smart-ass reply, he turned and looked at his brother—and the look on Lucivar's face made his heart pound. "What's wrong? Is Marian all right?"

"She's fine. She's good. Father is at the eyrie now, pampering her." Lucivar made a face. "When I do something, it's fussing. When he does the same damn thing, it's pampering."

"He has a way with women," Daemon said. "Lucivar . . ."

"Was it that hard?" Lucivar asked. "I know the boy is a handful. Hell's fire, Bastard, I know he is."

"We did all right," Daemon said sourly.

Lucivar sighed. "Look, next time I'll leave him with the Eyriens and—"

"No, you will not." Daemon's voice chilled. "You and I were given a particular code of honor when we were very young—a code that isn't known by many, if any, who come from Terreille. And that is the code of honor our family will live by. So when your boy needs to spend some days away from you, he comes here. Is that understood?"

"Not all Eyriens view honor as something they can bend to suit themselves," Lucivar said cautiously.

*Falonar.* The name of Lucivar's former second-in-command wasn't spoken, but it hung in the air between them.

Then the moment, and the tension, were gone.

"Look," Daemon said, setting the brandy aside. "I'm just pissing and moaning. I fell out of a damn tree. I'm entitled to piss and moan. And I feel . . . inadequate." Hell's fire, it bruised his ego to admit that.

"You're not Eyrien, old son," Lucivar said. "You never will be."

"Yes, I know."

"No, I don't think you do." Lucivar studied him. "We knew Daemonar couldn't stay with us anymore when I went into rut, and when Marian recognized the signs and got him down to Merry and Briggs before I . . ." He raked a hand through his black hair. "The boy wanted *you.* His Uncle Daemon. Who isn't Eyrien. Who doesn't fly or fight—at least in a way he understands yet—but who knows *lots* of things. He doesn't want you to be Eyrien. He wants to be with you because he loves you."

Hearing those words relaxed the knot of expectations he'd inflicted on himself—and filled him with warm pleasure.

"I'd better get the little beast home. His mother misses him." Turning, Lucivar reached for the doorknob, then stopped and looked at Daemon. "You really fell out of a tree?"

He sighed. "I really did."

"He was up in the tree?"

"I wouldn't have climbed it for any other reason," he said dryly.

Lucivar's face was filled with baffled amusement. "Didn't you tell him to come down?"

"Of course I did."

Even more baffled. "Since you told him to come down and he didn't obey, why didn't you use Craft to haul his ass down? I would have."

# CHAPTER 5

## TERREILLE

Cassidy closed her eyes and concentrated on breathing.

Nerves and excitement. Her first official visit among the people she ruled. And the first time people outside the town of Grayhaven would see her First Circle working together as a First Circle.

She glanced at Theran. Ever since she had found the treasure hidden in the attic at Grayhaven, he had made an obvious effort to act like he wanted to serve in her court. But his forced courtesy was a daily reminder that he didn't belong to her the way the other men in her First Circle did.

In fact, his effort to serve felt too much like her previous court. They had lavished her with forced courtesy too—right before they broke her court and left her to serve another Queen.

This visit to Eyota, Ranon's home village, was harder for him to accept than it was for the rest of the First Circle. They had spent the days prior to this trip discussing the details of what was required to guard their Queen in an unfamiliar place. Theran had offered no comments, no suggestions, nothing. He had, in fact, voiced none of the concerns that a First Escort should have. Was he distancing himself because she had refused to cancel this visit—or because being on a Shalador reserve would make him look at the other side of his heritage? He was proud to be descended from Jared, but he seemed to resent having to acknowledge that Jared came from Shalador.

Then there was Gray, who was clinging to her hand despite the fact they were in a Coach that had a driver experienced with controlling a long, enclosed, furnished box designed to ride the Winds, those psychic webs through the Darkness. It wasn't being dependent on someone else's power and skill that made Gray cling to her. Captured at fifteen and given to Dena Nehele's Queen, he had survived two years of torture before being rescued. It had taken courage for him to go back to Grayhaven when Theran and Talon had announced they were going to live there with the new Territory Queen. And she knew it had taken even more courage for him to leave Grayhaven and come with her to a place that was unfamiliar and spend time among strangers.

"The boardinghouse looks shabby, but it's solid, has running water and a kitchen, and it's big enough to accommodate all of the First Circle," Ranon said.

Since this was the fourth time he'd told her that—and sounded both defensive and apologetic—Cassidy figured the Shalador Warlord Prince wasn't as calm or confident about this visit as he appeared to be. And Shira's composure had become more frayed as this day approached.

"It will be fine, Ranon," Cassidy said. "I'm sure everything will be fine." She hoped so, because the success of this visit would determine if she would be allowed to be a Queen to these people in the truest sense or only a symbol the Warlord Princes would use to try to rebuild Dena Nehele. The witch storm unleashed by Jaenelle Angelline two years ago had swept away the Blood who had been tainted by Dorothea SaDiablo, and the landen uprisings that followed had killed so many more. The survivors not only had to worry about keeping peace within their own Territory, they had to remain strong enough to stop any Blood from other Territories who might try to encroach on Dena Nehele's land and take whatever resources could be won from a fight.

"It will be fine," Shira echoed.

Noticing the way Ranon stopped himself from looking at Shira, as if a look at that moment might betray some confidence, Cassidy wondered what the Black Widow knew that could make the two Shaladorans so doubtful that anything would be fine.

★    ★    ★

They were a proud, ragged people.

Since he wasn't an official member of Cassie's First Circle, Gray stood back and watched as Lady Nimarr, the eldest Shalador Queen, formally introduced Cassie to the other Queens who ruled in the Shalador reserves. Cassie had met several of the women a few days before when they came to Grayhaven and requested an audience, so Gray figured this introduction was for the benefit of the people who had gathered to get a look at the Queen of Dena Nehele.

Then some of the Tradition Keepers were introduced, including Ranon's grandfather Yairen, who was a Keeper of Music.

Gray looked at Theran, whose face seemed frozen in an expression between stubbornness and forced courtesy, then at Ranon, who stood tall and proud—but not confident, despite his effort to appear so. Too much depended on this meeting for Ranon to feel confident of the outcome.

Gray watched Cassie talk to the Tradition Keepers. Her eyes never left Lord Yairen's face, but he knew her well enough to appreciate how much effort it took for her not to look at the old man's crippled hands. And he was certain she understood that the crippling hadn't been caused by age or accident.

The Queens wore new dresses that were simple in design. Over those dresses were finely embroidered vests—old vests that were tended carefully and probably only worn for special occasions. The Tradition Keepers had worn their best clothes too, but even skilled seamstresses couldn't hide all the mending and patches in those clothes, and Gray admired the men and women for not using illusion spells to cover one truth about the reserves.

He had lived a rough life in the rogue camps hidden in the Tamanara Mountains. These people had lived a desperate life, had endured more—and worse—than anyone else in Dena Nehele because of Dorothea SaDiablo's hatred for Jared.

Was it any wonder that Ranon felt so bitter and angry about the way his people had been treated? Was it any wonder that he took every opportunity to call attention to the way the Shaladorans lived—and what they lived without?

But was Ranon hoping for more than Cassie could give?

*    *    *

Thank the Darkness, the ceremonies were over. At least until that evening when she would be the special guest at a feast held in her honor.

*Honor,* Cassidy thought as she brushed her hair. The Shaladorans had held on to honor when they could hold on to nothing else. She saw that truth in their dark eyes, heard it in the quiet voices. Unlike Ranon, who was vocal on his people's behalf, the Queens and elders had said nothing. They didn't have to. Just looking at them, just hearing the dignity in their voices told her more than words.

The boardinghouse told her even more. Shabby? Yes. But there was a new mattress on the bed in her room, new linens. The room had been scrubbed free of every speck of dirt, although the wallpaper still showed signs of water stains. And *everything* was free of psychic scents. There was no psychic residue on the bed or linens or carpets to reveal the previous owners.

Who in the village had given up these new things in order to furnish this room for her visit?

She didn't know how much she could do for these people, but she knew where to begin—if the Shaladorans, and Theran, would let her do this much.

She looked at the door that opened into the adjoining bedroom. By rights it should have been her First Escort's room, but Ranon must have said something to the elders, and Gray had been assigned that room. His need to be close to her had been so obvious, Theran had said nothing about taking the room on the other side of hers—the room without an adjoining door. Ranon and Shira were across the hall from her, sharing a room. At some point she would ask Shira if the elders' eyes had widened because it was a Black Widow and a Warlord Prince sharing a room or just because it was unusual in the reserves for unmarried lovers to share a room so openly.

For now, she would go outside and take a look at the boardinghouse's gardens and see what she could do.

When she opened the bedroom door, there were no guards waiting for her in the hallway, there were no escorts. There were no males of any kind.

But there was a Sceltie, who took one look at her and said, *Hat, Cassie.*

"I'm just—"

*Hat.*

She fetched the brown, open-weave hat she had bought for this visit. Gray insisted she wear a hat to protect her skin, and Shira had talked her into shopping for one and had gone so far as to buy a hat too, laughingly saying it would become a trademark of the court—any Lady serving in the First Circle would wear a hat as a symbol of her service to the Queen.

At the time, Cassidy had accepted the teasing and Shira's purchase of a hat without a second thought. Now she wondered how dear the cost of the hat had been for the Shalador witch. *Her* hat had been put on the court account, and its price would be deducted from the tithe the shopkeeper owed at the end of summer. But Shira had paid for her own hat.

Prince Sadi had offered to help pay some of her expenses while she was in Dena Nehele. Would he be willing to extend the Queen's gift to a small loan so she could pay her First Circle an advance against their quarterly wages? Would she have the courage to ask him?

*Cassie?*

She plunked the hat on her head and scowled at Vae. "See? I'm wearing the hat."

*Yes.* Vae gave Cassidy a tail-tip wag. *Now Gray will not worry about your face molting.*

The image of pieces of skin fluttering to the ground like discarded bird feathers made her queasy. Kindred tended to describe things in relation to an animal, but that wasn't always a comfortable picture for humans when they were the subject of the conversation.

Vae headed for the stairs, pausing long enough to make sure Cassidy was following her.

*Gray is outside with Ranon and a young male who is a Warlord Prince,* Vae said. *He is family to Ranon, and Ranon wants you to see him, but there are worry smells too.*

"Ranon has probably spent a lot of years keeping his relative hidden from the Queens," Cassidy replied. "It can't be easy for him to bring a young Warlord Prince into the open."

*Why? You are Ranon's Queen. You are Dena Nehele's Queen. The pup belongs to you.*

*You can't claim what you can't find,* Cassidy thought. *Hide some of the Queens so there will be someone left to rule. Hide the young Warlord Princes so that another generation can survive long enough to stand on a killing field and fight for their land.*

The world was simple for Vae. Not because she was a dog, but because she had grown up in the village the Queen of Scelt called home. Even if only a few actually served in a court, a Territory Queen held the life of every person in her hands, as well as the land itself. Lady Morghann was a strong Queen and a close friend of Jaenelle Angelline, and Morghann's husband, Lord Khardeen, ruled the village of Maghre on his Lady's behalf. So Vae had no reason to doubt that praise and punishment would be given fairly—and both would be given when deserved.

Vae wouldn't hesitate to bring someone who mattered to her to the attention of the Queen she served. For Ranon to bring the boy within sight of a Queen was a huge act of trust.

Cassidy stopped at the door leading outside as she thought about this young male Ranon had brought to the boardinghouse. Brother? Or son? Was that the reason he and Shira had been acting so uneasy? Was it *their* son or just *his* son?

Neither, Cassidy decided as she rounded the side of the house and saw the three men. The boy was in his late teens—too old to be anything but a brother or cousin to Ranon.

Gray's smile was warm and open when he saw her walking toward them. Ranon's expression was somewhere between determined and hopeful. And the youngster . . .

How many friends had he seen taken away only to return broken or crippled—or never to return at all? She had no sense that the Shalador Queens had mistreated their own people, but the Shalador Queens had had little power, controlled as they had been by the Province Queens.

She stopped when there was enough distance between her and the men that Ranon could dismiss the young Warlord Prince before approaching her, eliminating the requirement of an introduction.

She watched Ranon assess the distance, and knew the moment when he realized what it meant. A moment later, he signaled the youngster and approached her.

"Lady, may I introduce my younger brother?" Ranon asked.

"You may," Cassidy replied.

"Lady, this is Prince Janos. Our father was Lord Yairen's son. Janos, this is Lady Cassidy, the Queen of Dena Nehele."

"It is an honor to be introduced to so great a Queen," Janos replied, bowing too low for the act to be respectful since his Summer-sky Jewel outranked her Rose.

*You bow too low,* Vae said. *That is rude. Sniffing female parts is rude too. That is confusing because there are good smells there, but it is something you must learn or you will get smacked on the nose. Or nipped.*

Janos's face turned dusky red as he snapped upright, making it clear that the insult had been unintentional. Ranon's coloring wasn't much better.

And Gray looked a bit too curious about female smells.

*Thank the Darkness,* Cassidy thought when the back door opened and a young woman walked out. Sixteen years old. Maybe seventeen. And beautiful in a way that made the breath catch when she moved. Long dark hair and green eyes. And a Purple Dusk Jewel.

"What are you doing here, Reyhana?" Ranon growled.

Surprised by his animosity, Cassidy stared at him. Yes, he outranked the girl, but she was a Queen and should be shown some respect unless Reyhana had done something to earn his anger.

"I asked the elder Queens if I could work here as a service to the new Queen," Reyhana replied, her voice a shade too defiant.

"You're a Queen. You shouldn't be doing servants' work," Ranon snapped.

"Why not?" Cassidy asked.

The silence was more startling than a thunderclap would have been at that moment.

"Why not?" Ranon said. "She's a Queen!"

"A Queen who doesn't know how to work is of no use to her people," Reyhana said.

"Well put, Sister," Cassidy said. Ranon looked like he'd been clobbered with a fence post, and she was sorry for what she was about to do to him, but the girl was her priority now. "My family is not aristo, Prince Ranon. We never had servants. And even though by caste I am a Queen, I am also a daughter. So when my mother pulled out the rags and mops on cleaning day, I dusted and polished furniture, and mopped the floors right along with her. And when it was my turn to clean the bathroom, I had very bad thoughts about my brother." She looked Ranon right in the eyes. "Why is it that a man can hit the center of a bull's eye at one hundred paces and yet can't manage to get all of his stream in the toilet bowl when he's standing right over it?"

Janos and Gray stood there with their mouths hanging open. Ranon, poor man, looked ready to slink away.

But it was the suppressed snort from the young Queen that told Cassidy she had achieved her goal. She'd talk to the girl later about the proper way to address a Warlord Prince when his Jewels were dominant.

She smiled at all of them. "Now if you'll excuse me, I want to take a look at the vegetable garden." As she walked away, she added on a distaff thread, *Vae, keep an eye on the males. Make sure they're still breathing.*

One, two, three . . .

*Ranon? Ranon! Are you breathing?*

There, Cassidy thought. By the time Ranon, Gray, and Janos untangled themselves from Vae's attention, Reyhana would be safely among the older women—the ones Prince Ranon would not dare offend without good reason.

When she reached the vegetable garden, she stopped.

It should have been good soil, but it was parched, almost barren, and the plants struggling to grow wouldn't yield the bounty needed to feed these people. Not parched for water; the ground was still soft, a sure sign that there had been a long, soaking rain sometime in the past day or two. No, it was parched for the connection with a Queen, for that necessary give-and-take that kept the land healthy.

Why had the Shalador Queens neglected this? Cassidy wondered as she knelt at the edge of the bed. Surely they were aware of the need. Had they been so afraid to call attention to themselves that they hadn't done this one thing that would have helped so many? Or had they stopped because they realized that if they made this land richer than the rest of Dena Nehele by following traditions, it would have been taken away? Ranon had told them that the reserves were half the size they had been when Lady Grizelle and Lia had established those parts of Dena Nehele as a place that belonged to the Shalador people.

Well, it was time everyone stopped denying one of the duties of a Queen.

She didn't turn around. If she looked at him, Gray would join her—and raise too many objections. Ceremony could come later. First she would show them *why*; then she would show them how.

Cassidy called in a short-bladed knife and made a cut on each palm. As the blood flowed, she vanished the knife and pressed her hands into the soil—and sent her Rose-Jeweled power flowing through her blood and into the ground.

So parched. So needy. So empty for so long.

Power flowed, spreading through the vegetable garden like sweet rain.

The land was the true root and heart of the Blood's power. They were the caretakers of the Realms. That was more than society and cities. It was more than music and literature, more than ruling over the landens. A connection to the land was an important part of what made the Blood who and what they were, and the Queens were the bridge because their power supported the land.

So parched. So needy. Soaking up everything she was willing to give. She could feel the land responding under her hands, wanting more. Wanting everything.

"Cassie?"

A little more. She could give a little more. Saturation would come soon, and the land would stop draining her.

"*Cassie.*"

So parched. So needy. To be wanted so much.

Then the power was draining too fast, too much. But she couldn't pull away, couldn't turn away when there was so much need.

Just a little—

"*Cassie!*"

# CHAPTER 6

## TERREILLE

The ground felt soft and smelled lightly of herbs. She didn't remember seeing herbs in the vegetable garden.

Groaning, Cassidy rolled onto her side. Her eyes felt sleep-crusted, but it was too much effort to pry them open. One hand pressed on the surface next to her head. Pillow. Was she in bed? How did she get there? What in the name of Hell happened? Every muscle ached, and she felt parched, like she had been wrung so dry she was hollow.

Quiet rustling. Movement. Then a weight settled beside her on the bed.

Had to be Shira since the psychic scent was female, but she couldn't tell anything beyond that—a sure sign that *something* was wrong with her.

"Hell's fire," Cassidy muttered with her eyes still closed. "Am I late for the evening's feast?"

"By about two days," said a voice that wasn't Shira's but held a vaguely familiar tartness.

She rubbed the crustiness from her eyes and looked at the woman sitting beside her. Short, spiky, white-blond hair. A thin face that looked a decade older than the woman's real age. Gray Jewel and Hourglass pendant. And a wicked smile that curved unpainted lips but didn't reach the glacier blue eyes.

"Lady Karla?"

"Kiss kiss."

Cassidy struggled to prop herself up on one elbow—and failed. "What are you doing here?"

"Looking after you. I was at the Keep visiting Uncle Saetan when Vae arrived howling that you were dying and needed help from a Healer who knew about Queen things. Being a Healer and a Queen, I figured I would know how to deal with whatever happened. So here I am." She paused, then added, "Lucivar is here too."

"No," Cassidy groaned. "Not Lucivar."

"Oh, he's not the worst of it." Another pause. "Maybe he is the worst of it, but he's not all of it."

Hell's fire. "What happened?"

"You were an idiot."

It was said lightly, but Cassidy heard the anger under the words.

"You let your power flow without restraint, without limit," Karla said.

"I've always done that," Cassidy protested.

"Then you missed a step in your education." Karla's voice stung like a slap. "That did you no harm in Dharo, where the give-and-take of power is done so often it doesn't take that much power to renew what had been used. But this land was *empty,* Cassidy. I don't think anyone has made that kind of offering here for generations. You were a drop of power away from breaking your Rose Jewel. Not just draining it, *breaking it.* If that Warlord Prince hadn't had the sense to pick you up and get you into the house to break the connection to the land completely, at best you would have been broken back to your Birthright Tiger Eye. At worst . . ." Karla shook her head and sighed heavily. "Well, there's no reason to dwell on that, is there? You still wear the Rose. And thank the Darkness for that."

Yes. Thank the Darkness for that.

Information began to sink in. Cassidy huffed and grunted, but she got herself propped up on one elbow. "Two days? I've been asleep for *two days?*"

Karla nodded. "We can call it 'sleeping,' which is a very generous word to use since even the deepest healing sleep usually isn't that deep—not when there's hope of the person coming out of it. I was about to call Lucivar and arrange to bring you to the Keep so Jaenelle could look at you. Then you shifted to a more natural sleep, and I decided to wait a few more hours. Which was fortunate for you—and this village."

Keep? Jaenelle? Damn. If Lucivar was here, she couldn't brush this off in her next report to Prince Sadi. And if she had been "ill" for the past two days . . .

"The First Circle," Cassidy said.

"They couldn't figure out how to declare war on a vegetable garden, so they're waiting for some indication that you're going to recover. The only reason this room isn't filled with hysterical males watching every breath you take is because I wear the Gray and outrank them all. Also, I threatened to rip the balls off any male foolish enough to enter without my permission—and Lucivar threatened to break all the bones of any man who even *tried* to enter."

"Lucivar threatened my court?"

"Court, family, village. He was too pissed off about what happened to you to be particular about whose bones were going to meet his fist."

Cassidy flopped on her back. This was getting worse and worse. Then she struggled upright again. "Family?"

"Mother, father, brother—and your cousin Aaron."

"Mother Night."

"And may the Darkness be merciful. My darling, everything has a price, and scaring the shit out of that many Warlord Princes . . . Well, how you're feeling physically is only the first part of the payment. There were so many who wanted to express an opinion about what you did, they ended up drawing straws. The two short straws get to yell at you." Karla called in a small hourglass and set it on the bedside table. "Here. A gift. Ten minutes of sand in the glass. That's how long each of them is allowed to voice his full opinion of what you did."

"Who . . . ?"

"Ranon and Gray drew the short straws. However, I'll warn you now that I don't think your father is going to hold back his thoughts on the matter. And neither is Lucivar." Using Craft, Karla floated a mug over to the bed. "Here, drink this. When you showed signs of finally waking up, I made this tonic for you."

Cassidy leaned back against the headboard and took the mug.

"You'll have the remainder of today to rest and recover. After that, darling, you face your family and court. And Lucivar."

Cassidy took a sip of the tonic and fought the desire to gulp it down. Her body craved whatever was in this brew. Craved it as much as the land had craved the connection with her.

She took another sip, then remembered the last thing she'd seen before the world had gone dark. "Gray. Is he all right? He must have been upset when I . . . fell."

A strange look came into Karla's eyes. "You woke up more than the land, Cassidy. Much more."

Ranon cautiously approached the vegetable garden. He didn't want to deal with Lucivar's thunderous temper or Prince Aaron's snarling restraint—or the worry he saw in Lord Burle's eyes. And even though the boardinghouse's grounds gave him plenty of room to maneuver, he didn't want to be caught alone with the witch who had brought Cassidy's family to Eyota. The Gray-Jeweled Queen was intimidating enough, but she had stayed inside with Cassidy. Surreal SaDiablo was a long step past scary as far as he and all the other men were concerned, and *she* had been prowling the house and grounds—and the village.

Going down on one knee, he reached out to brush a fingertip over the leaves of one little plant. A strong, healthy plant growing vigorously now. All the plants in the garden were growing vigorously now—had started growing within hours of Cassidy's collapse.

Gray had noticed the blood soaked into the ground, but the cuts on Cassidy's palms hadn't looked that deep, and Shira hadn't thought Cassidy had lost enough blood to account for losing consciousness. And *nothing* Shira or the Queens knew could explain what had drained Cassidy's Rose Jewel to such a dangerous level so quickly.

If there had been some kind of attack, why hadn't she called for help? And how could she have been attacked when he and the others had been standing right there? Gray was the first to realize something was wrong, had snatched her up and run into the boardinghouse. But they still didn't know what had happened—or why.

Shira wouldn't talk about the vision she'd seen, wouldn't confirm if this was the danger that might have cost them the first Queen to give them hope since Lia.

Was this his fault somehow? Had he failed in his duties? How? *How?*

Ranon felt the other presence, picked up the psychic scent, and knew who was about to join him.

Theran gave them all cold silence, which was understandable since Daemon Sadi was holding him personally responsible for Cassidy's well-being and Grayhaven hadn't wanted her to come to Eyota in the first place. But Gray's anger and distress was a hot, pulsing, living thing. Until they knew what was wrong with Cassidy, Gray was an unsheathed weapon, and no one knew the sharpness of that blade or how deeply it could cut.

He waited until Gray knelt beside him. Neither of them could resist coming out to this spot several times a day.

"They grew even more overnight," Ranon said, keeping his voice quiet. "We'll actually get a decent crop from this garden."

"She can't do it again," Gray snarled. "This almost killed her."

"I know that." And he did. He also knew the Queens had looked upon this garden in shock initially, then *almost* understood how this had happened. Almost.

"Company," Gray said, not turning his attention away from the plants.

Ranon looked over his shoulder and sighed. Reyhana and Janos. The young Queen had been out to look at this garden as much as he and Gray, and Janos had assigned himself as Reyhana's escort whenever she left the boardinghouse.

Then he stiffened and tapped Gray's arm before rising to his feet. "More company."

Gray sprang to his feet. Ranon grabbed one arm to keep Gray from rushing toward Lady Karla—especially because Aaron stepped out of the house and leaned against the wall, clearly not interfering and just as clearly standing watch over the Gray-Jeweled Queen who walked with a measured step that had nothing to do with dignity and everything to do with needing the support of a cane.

Whatever was wrong with her body, there was nothing wrong with her mind—or her power.

*Grizelle had been like this,* Ranon thought. *Lia had been like this.*

He'd grown up on stories of Grizelle and, especially, Lia. Had grown up fantasizing about what it would be like to be in the presence of a Gray-Jeweled Queen. He'd always thought of Grizelle and Lia as protectors of Dena Nehele—and they had been—but it hadn't occurred to him that the power that protected the land also made those women very dangerous witches. Not until Karla had stepped out of the Coach that had brought her to Eyota.

"Prince Gray," Karla said when she reached them. "Prince Ranon." She tipped her head in a silent greeting to Reyhana and Janos.

Janos hesitated, still not certain of how to respond to a Queen who wasn't from the Shalador reserves. Reyhana, on the other hand, took the greeting as an invitation to join the adults.

"Cassidy is awake," Karla said, looking at Gray. "She'll be fine. She needs to stay quiet for the rest of today."

"Can I see her?" Gray asked. "I won't yell at her yet. I just want to see her."

Karla's lips curved in a wicked smile. "Darling, her body has been working hard to regain its balance and, quite frankly, the girl smells a bit ripe. Until she has a chance to bathe and clean her teeth, you're the last person she's going to want to see."

"But . . ." Gray paused. Looked thoughtful. "Oh. Because I'm courting her? But I don't care if she smells."

Karla stared at Gray until he muttered, "Well, I *don't* care." But the stare ended that part of the discussion.

"I think Cassidy would appreciate some assistance from her mother and the court's Healer," Karla said. "And I think everyone with a penis should stay away from that hallway and those rooms for the next couple of hours. Is that clear enough?"

Seeing Lucivar come around the corner, Ranon said, "That's clear. Can you tell us what happened to Lady Cassidy?"

"Do you want it in simple terms?" Karla asked.

He nodded.

"She was an idiot."

Gray snarled and took a step toward Karla.

Aaron sprang away from the house but stopped and looked at Lucivar, who held up a hand to signal Aaron to stay back while he headed for their happy little group—slowly.

"She ignored her training and her common sense and almost damaged herself beyond repair," Karla said. "What would you call it? There was no need for what happened. In fact, there was every reason for caution and re-straint. She could have made her point without risk to herself, and without the anguish she caused all of you. It was an irresponsible thing for a Queen to do, and the Darkness only knows what possessed her to do it." Her eyes turned a colder blue as she focused on Gray. "And if you think I'm being harsh, go up to the Keep and talk to the High Lord. Having been on the receiving end of one of his verbal lashings when I did something stupid, I can tell you Cassidy is getting off lightly."

Gray took a step back. "The High Lord would have yelled at Cassie?"

"When he's really pissed off about something, the High Lord does not yell," Karla said. "He doesn't have to."

"I've heard him yell," Gray said. "Sort of yell."

"Then you heard surface temper, which is a very mild thing compared to his real temper."

"Oh."

"Could I learn to do that?" Reyhana asked, pointing to the garden.

"No," Ranon, Gray, and Janos said.

Karla looked at the men and shook her head. "Yes. I can show—"

"No," Reyhana said.

Ranon turned on the girl. Reyhana was the most promising young Queen in the Shalador reserves, and bringing her to Cassidy's attention was enough of a risk. The girl could not be allowed to challenge a Queen as strong as Karla.

Before he could say anything, Reyhana raised her chin and took a step toward Karla.

"I mean no disrespect, Lady," Reyhana said. "But if I am worthy of learning this Queen's duty, I should be taught by the Queen of Dena Nehele."

The men held themselves tense and silent as the two witches measured each other.

"From what I've been told by Prince Aaron, the last young Queen who apprenticed with Cassidy caused her a great deal of pain," Karla said. "That kind of betrayal isn't easy to forget. What Cassidy did here is important for you to learn. Vital, in fact, for the land as well as benefiting you. If she doesn't feel comfortable teaching you, then I will before I return to Glacia."

Reyhana hesitated, and in that breath between one moment and the next, Ranon saw a young Queen mature a little more.

"Is that what happened to your legs?" Reyhana asked. "Betrayal?"

Karla nodded. "I was poisoned by a member of my court. Someone who was loyal to my uncle instead of being loyal to me. I should have died from that vicious stew of poisons. Damaged legs are a small price to pay for surviving." She raised a hand, a simple gesture that ended that conversation. "Now. If the young Lady is going to learn this particular bit of Craft, you three—yes, that includes you, puppy—need to learn how to deal with a Queen. Lucivar will teach you."

"Teach them what?" Lucivar asked, finally stepping up to join them.

"Teach them what to do when a Queen is being stupid," Karla replied.

"Before or after you knock her on her ass to get her attention?" Lucivar asked.

Karla bared her teeth in what might have been a smile and said, "Kiss kiss."

Ranon blinked. He'd never heard *anyone* say that and have it mean "shove a knife up your ass."

Lucivar bared his teeth in an equally insincere smile. "Cassidy's awake?"

"Yes," Karla said, her whole demeanor changing from challenging to cautious as she studied Lucivar.

"Someone else is staying with her for a while?"

"I was about to talk to Devra and Shira about giving Cassidy a bit of company and assistance."

Lucivar nodded. "Fine. Then you can strip down and sweat a little. I want to have a look at those legs when they're working."

"I don't think—"

"Witchling, what part of that sounded like a choice?"

Gold eyes locked with glacier blue. Glacier blue looked away first.

"Prick," Karla muttered.

"Always," Lucivar replied. Then he pointed at Reyhana. "She can join you and learn a few basic moves for defending herself. And you, Gray. I'll teach you a few things that will help you strengthen those back muscles." He turned and whistled sharply. "Surreal! You're helping me with this."

Ranon felt an odd twitch in the belly. Surreal was standing in the yard, halfway between the house and their group. Open ground. Sure, she had probably used a sight shield to get that close without being noticed. Sure, Lucivar and Karla had been a distraction, but . . .

*Lucivar had known she was there.*

. . . this wasn't a witch a man wanted coming up on him without warning.

"Helping you with what?" Surreal shouted back.

"With making this lot sweat," Lucivar replied.

Surreal laughed. "In that case, sugar, I'll go hone a knife."

"What?" Ranon said.

Karla laughed and headed for the house, while Surreal moved to join her.

Lucivar gave Ranon a lazy, arrogant smile. "Show some balls, Ranon. You're not afraid of one little assassin, are you?"

"Assassin?" Reyhana squeaked. Or maybe that was Janos.

Lucivar shrugged. "Surreal is Dea al Mon. I think they're born knowing what to do with a knife."

"Mother Night," Ranon muttered—but not until Lucivar walked away. Then he looked at Gray, who was staring at the house with a strange, thoughtful expression in his eyes.

"Cassie has some interesting friends," Gray said.

*Interesting,* Ranon thought as the four of them separated for a few minutes before joining Lucivar for whatever lessons the Eyrien had in mind. Yes, the Blood from Kaeleer were certainly interesting. But he wondered if Theran was paying any attention to their visitors and the influence they were having on the people here. They were both the forge and the fire that could shape the Blood in Dena Nehele into bright steel—or leave them broken. And he wondered if, like himself, Theran was paying attention to the kind of man Prince Jared Blaed Grayhaven was becoming in the heat of that forge.

"Do you have a reason to be concerned about Karla?" Surreal asked.

"A particular reason?" Lucivar shook his head. "Her Master of the Guard works with her to help her maintain strength in her legs, and I won't step on the man's territory. But that doesn't mean I won't take an opportunity to assess her for myself and send along a suggestion or two if I think something needs more of his attention."

"Are her legs getting weaker?"

"Not yet, but the day will come when they won't support her." Considering what Jaenelle had to do in order to save Karla, the fact that Karla could walk at all was testimony to Jaenelle's skills as a Healer and Karla's strength of will. But the ever-present cane and the face aged beyond its years were a reminder that even the best Healer and the strongest will couldn't eliminate the effects of terrible poisons that should have destroyed a Gray-Jeweled Queen. "I'll help her postpone that day for as long as possible," Lucivar added quietly. Then he smiled at Surreal. "You're looking good." And since she hadn't tried to knife him, he figured she'd finally forgiven him for the time she had spent in Ebon Rih.

"I'm feeling more comfortable about a lot of things," she replied. "About myself. About this." She called in a stiletto.

Lucivar tensed—which seemed to amuse her.

"Relax," she said, vanishing the stiletto. "When I first arrived at Chaosti's clan, Grandmammy Teele gave me some old sacks. I spent the evenings embroidering your name on them, then stuffed them with rags, tied them to a tree, and stabbed them until my arm cramped."

"Shit," Lucivar said. He'd pushed her because he cared. He hadn't meant to push her so much she hated him.

Surreal laughed. "You should see your face. Breathe easy, Yaslana. I was just teasing. I would never spend that much time on embroidery."

This time he swore in Eyrien and said a whole lot of things he didn't want her to understand.

"I do recognize some of those words," she said.

"Good for you," he snapped.

She grinned at him.

He stared at the people gathering in the yard. They stared back at him and Surreal like dumb sheep facing a couple of wolves.

Dumb sheep.

Lucivar frowned. "Where is Vae?"

"Don't know," Surreal replied. "She came with me as far as Dharo when I went to fetch Cassidy's family, then continued on to Scelt instead of coming back with us."

Lucivar looked at Surreal. Surreal looked at him. They headed for their flock of two-legged sheep.

"Not our problem," Surreal said.

"Definitely not our problem," Lucivar agreed. Especially when he had a wife who wouldn't appreciate dealing with morning sickness and a small boy all by herself for more than a couple of days.

Assuming there would be morning sickness. And that *would* be his problem. And his fault. And a few other things, depending on whether Marian felt happy about being pregnant or bitchy about throwing up. So he wasn't going to wonder what Vae was doing in Scelt.

But he was certain that whatever the Sceltie was up to was going to be *someone's* problem.

# CHAPTER 7
## TERREILLE

★ *Cassie? Cassie! Are you allowed to do that?*★

Cassidy closed her eyes and counted to ten to stop herself from throwing the weeding claw at the Sceltie. All she wanted was an hour to work in the garden while she answered some of Reyhana's questions. "Yes, Vae. I'm allowed to do this. I'm *fine*."

*Gray? Is Cassie allowed to do that?*

"Isn't she supposed to listen to you?" Reyhana whispered.

"She's a Sceltie," Cassidy grumped. "She doesn't listen to anyone."

"She listens to Prince Gray," Reyhana pointed out.

And that particular alliance of Warlord Prince and Sceltie had been an unrelenting pain in the ass ever since Lucivar, Karla, and the rest of the Blood from Kaeleer left two days ago. The biggest difference between dog and man was that Vae never stopped yapping at her unless she was sitting or sleeping, and Gray wouldn't speak to her. Hadn't said one single word to her after Karla said she was well enough to leave her room in the boarding-house. But he was always nearby, watching everything she did. Judging everything she did.

*Gray? Should I nip?*

"No," Cassidy said, dropping the weeding claw and rising from the spot she and Reyhana had been weeding. "You should *not* nip. Gray, tell her!"

There was a wild look in Gray's green eyes, a look that hadn't been there before she collapsed. This wasn't the boy who had been damaged by torture and frozen emotionally and mentally. And it was more than the man Gray had been becoming since she'd met him. This was a sharp-tempered stranger who was pissed off with her but refused to discuss the reason for his anger.

Well, fine.

No, *not fine.*

"Gray, I'd like a word with you," Cassidy said, heading away from the rest of the men who were hovering in the garden, standing guard over her. When he didn't move, she snarled, "Jared Blaed, *attend!*"

*That* got his attention. His eyes blazed hot as he strode to where she waited, and it took everything in her not to back down in the face of what was heading toward her.

*Warlord Prince.* Most of the time it was easy to forget Gray belonged to that caste of males. She never forgot what kind of man she was dealing with when she was around Theran or Talon or Ranon, but caste hadn't been the dominant psychic scent when she was with Gray. Until now.

"Do you think using my real name is going to intimidate me into doing what you want?" Gray snapped. "I'm not a child, Cassidy."

She glanced at the other men. They were all paying attention to this little drama, so she kept her voice low. "I made a mistake, an error in judgment. It happens. I'm sorry it upset you—"

"An error in judgment." His voice was hard as stone. "You almost kill yourself *for no reason*, and you think it's nothing more than an error?"

He started to walk away. She grabbed his arm—then jerked her hand away in shock when he snarled at her.

"Gray, talk to me," she pleaded.

"I have nothing to say."

Her temper snapped. She could feel the heat of it rising through her body until she was sure her hair was going to stand on end like a fan of fire.

"If you're not going to talk to me, then you damn well better talk to somebody because I've had enough of your temper and your silence."

"Fine. I'll do that." As he walked away from her, Gray shouted, "Vae! You're with me."

"At least that will get both of you out of my hair," Cassidy muttered as she stomped back to the garden.

Reyhana looked away, wrestled with a weed, and swore politely when the top of the plant broke off, leaving the tap root.

"You can't pull the tap roots of those weeds out unless you do it after a soaking rain," Cassidy said, kneeling beside the younger woman. "But you can use Craft to create a slick shaft around the root so you can pull it out."

"Can you show me?" Reyhana asked.

"I can show you," Cassidy replied, then added silently, *Without those two yapping at me.*

Ranon watched Gray head right for him. Prudence and training told him he should shield when another warrior came toward him in a way that screamed aggression. But this was Gray, so he held his ground until the other man took that last step and grabbed a fistful of his shirt.

"You guard her, Ranon," Gray said, his voice so rough it was hardly recognizable. "You hear me? First Escort or not, Theran doesn't care enough about her to do what's right, so you guard her until I get back."

"Where are you going?" Ranon asked.

Gray's smile was razor-sharp. "I'm following my Queen's command. I'm going to talk to somebody."

★I will take care of Gray,★ Vae said, using a private psychic thread aimed at him.

Ranon waited until Gray rounded the corner of the house. Then he rubbed his hands over his face and sighed. After days of observing Gray and Cassidy's silent argument, he wanted to talk to someone too. But he'd have to wait until Gray returned—or until Talon rose this evening and could take over the watch. Then he would go to his grandfather's house, and Yairen would make a brew of spiced whiskey and coffee, a drink the old man only made when men needed to speak to other men about difficult matters.

He had no right to interfere between a man and a woman, but Cassidy was also his Queen, and he needed guidance in order to walk this particular knife's edge.

He crossed the yard and knelt on the other side of Cassidy, who ignored him and continued to explain to Reyhana something about drawing out the full root of a weed.

"Look," Ranon said quietly, "you probably don't want anyone with a cock within twenty paces of you right now."

"That is correct," Cassidy said, still not looking at him.

"If you promise that you'll do nothing to hurt yourself because you're upset with Gray, I'll leave you in peace." Soon after she'd come to Dena Nehele, she'd worked her hands into a bloody mess because she was distraught over something Theran had done. The court had learned a hard lesson that day, and he wasn't about to let it happen again. "Cassidy?"

"Why would she hurt herself over a man?" Reyhana said, bristling with challenge.

His temper sharpened. Reyhana wore Purple Dusk; he wore Opal. He couldn't allow a challenge to go unanswered, even if the girl was a Queen. *Especially* because the girl was a Queen.

"Sister, you're being disrespectful," Cassidy said.

"But—"

"No," Cassidy said. "Prince Ranon has reason to ask the question, and as one of my First Circle, he is within his rights to challenge me if he believes I am acting in a way that will cause me harm."

"Oh," Reyhana said in a small voice.

"Are you asking as one of my First Circle?" Cassidy asked, finally looking at him.

He shook his head. "I'm asking as a friend."

Emotions flashed in her hazel eyes, which turned tear-bright for a moment—and he wondered if anyone in her previous court had given her more than duty.

"In that case, I give you my word as a friend that I won't act imprudently because of this quarrel with Gray." She hesitated, then added on a psychic thread. *This quarrel with Gray upsets me, but it hasn't hurt me.*

He nodded to indicate he understood the difference. "Then I'll leave you Ladies to your work."

When he turned toward the boardinghouse, he froze for a moment before he strode across the lawn. With the exception of Talon and Theran, the rest of the First Circle was waiting for him.

"Is the Queen all right?" Powell asked when he joined them.

Ranon nodded.

"Is there anything we should do?" Archerr asked. "Powell, you've read those Protocol books more thoroughly than the rest of us. What do you say?"

"She gave her word that she wouldn't do anything to hurt herself," Ranon said quietly—and felt some of the tension ease in the other men.

"Can we scrounge a couple of chairs and a small table from somewhere?" Shaddo asked.

"For what?" Archerr asked.

"I noticed flagstones under the big tree," Shaddo said. "They're grown over some, but I think that area used to be a place for people to sit out under the shade."

"Ah." Powell smiled. "Chairs, a small table, cold drinks, and something to nibble. A subtle invitation to balance work and rest."

"If we start cleaning up the flagstones and hauling furniture out to the tree, won't it be obvious what we're doing—and why?" Archerr asked.

"Yes," Ranon said. "But sometimes a suggestion made by actions instead of words is more easily heard—and also less likely to offend."


## EBON ASKAVI


*High Lord? High Lord!*

"Now what?" Saetan muttered. Setting aside the book and just-warmed glass of yarbarah, he pushed out of the comfortable stuffed chair. Didn't *anyone* remember that he had retired from the living Realms? "Come."

But it was Gray, not Vae, who walked into the room. One look at the young Warlord Prince's face, and Saetan knew the reason for this particular visit.

"Lady Cassidy said I need to talk to someone," Gray said.

*I'll bet she did,* Saetan thought. Noticing the way Gray eyed the furniture and seemed ready to burst, he sent a thought to Draca, the Keep's Seneschal. ★I need some firewood in one of the courtyards now and refreshments in about thirty minutes.★

★I thought ass much,★ Draca replied. ★It iss already prepared.★

★You don't have to sound so amused,★ Saetan grumbled. Taking Gray's arm, he said, "We will talk, but first things first."

Sun and shade, Saetan thought as he marched Gray out to the courtyard. Being in sunlight would have given him a vicious headache this late in the morning, but staying in the shade would give him enough time to deal with Gray before he needed to retire.

"Watch," Saetan said. He picked up a piece of the firewood, held it over a large, wooden half barrel, released one tiny blast of Red power through his hands—and turned a piece of firewood as big as his thigh into wood chips.

Gray looked inside the barrel and frowned.

"Now you do it," Saetan said.

"Why?"

He stared at the youngster until Gray picked up a piece of firewood.

"I don't know how to do that," Gray said.

*Yes, you do.* Placing his hands below Gray's, he taught the boy how to destroy an object using power. Nothing Gray couldn't do just by following instinct. But unleashing power and letting it destroy whatever was in its path wasn't the same as unleashing it with control and purpose.

Once Gray had the sense of how much Purple Dusk power to use in order to blast the firewood into wood chips of an acceptable size, Saetan settled in the shade and watched Gray drain away the anger that had grown to the point of needing a target.

The barrel was half-filled with wood chips before Gray paused and said, "Why am I doing this?"

"Can you afford to replace furniture if you blast it into pieces?" Saetan asked mildly.

"No."

"That's why you're doing this. Chopping wood and using muscle instead of Craft works too, as long as you remember to shield before you pick up the ax. There is no reason to be careless or stupid just because your mind is chewing on a problem. In this case, you're working off some temper by changing firewood into wood chips." Saetan paused, then added, "Which, I'm told, are an excellent mulch in a garden."

Gray's mouth fell open. Then he began sputtering. "Garden? I'm making mulch *for a garden*?"

"Ironic, isn't it?"

Gray huffed. He paced. He blasted a few more pieces of firewood into wood chips.

Finally he growled, "I guess Cassie is going to have plenty of mulch for her gardens."

"I know several Queens who always have plenty of mulch for their gardens," Saetan said.

Gray stared at the barrel and sighed, the sign Saetan had been waiting for to indicate that enough of the boy's temper was spent.

"There's some water on the table over there," Saetan said. "Pour a glass for yourself. You could use it by now."

There was more than water on the table. There was a basin of warm water, soap, and a towel; a plate of fruit, cheese, and small sandwiches; and a ravenglass goblet filled with yarbarah.

He watched Gray as the boy washed up before pouring a glass of water and drinking it. Strength and scars—and the temper that made a Warlord Prince a law unto himself. And a little something more.

Gray refilled the water glass, hesitated a moment over the plate of food, then picked up the yarbarah and brought it to him.

A simple choice, but it confirmed for him why Jared Blaed Grayhaven had made the journey from Dena Nehele to the Keep in Kaeleer in order to talk to him instead of talking to Talon or anyone else in Cassie's court.

Gray had come for the same reason Khardeen, Aaron, Chaosti, and

Elan had come to him when they needed to talk out frustration caused by a woman who was a lover as well as a Queen. He had been the Dark Court's honorary uncle as well as the Steward, even before the court had officially formed. Those young men had come to him because they trusted his advice. They hadn't always liked it, but they knew they could trust it.

Using Craft, Saetan floated the plate of food over to the bench where Gray sat, drinking water and staring at the flagstones.

"Do you want to talk or listen?" Saetan asked.

Gray shrugged.

Not a surprising response. Now that the anger had dimmed, unhappiness was settling in.

"Everything is supposed to be *fine* now," Gray muttered.

"In other words, Cassidy is tired of you being angry with her."

"Yeah. So I'm not supposed to be angry anymore." Gray's hand tightened around the glass. "Well, I am angry."

"You're entitled to your anger," Saetan said quietly. "And it's your choice how long you hold on to it. But people make mistakes. Most of the time, mistakes can be forgiven. Some mistakes do enough harm to break what two people feel for each other. Sometimes the anger doesn't go away, and that means you need to walk away."

"Walk away from Cassie?" Gray looked shocked. "No!"

"Then you have to accept that she made an error in judgment."

"Because she doesn't care enough about us to take care of herself."

Saetan drank the yarbarah and let chilling silence fill the courtyard. Gray eyed him and wisely offered no other comment.

"She cares, Prince," Saetan said. "If you think otherwise, then you haven't been paying attention."

Gray hung his head. "I know she does. I just don't understand why she let the Craft go on so long that she hurt herself."

"The whip that drives Cassie was shaped before she arrived in Dena Nehele. It left scars."

Gray raised his head and looked at him.

*No,* Saetan thought, *not Gray. Jared Blaed.* Two sides of one person. Gray was the man who loved Cassie and gardens. Jared Blaed was the Warlord Prince committed to his Queen.

"Who?" Jared Blaed asked too softly.

"She's of no importance," Saetan replied. "Neither are the men who chose her over Cassidy. What *is* important is that the hurt still festers inside Cassidy."

"She's trying to prove to us that she has something to offer?"

"I think so. That's why a simple thing that Queens do all the time in Kaeleer almost turned into a tragic error."

"Just a mistake," Gray said softly.

"Yes."

"Because she cares so much."

"Yes."

Gray sighed.

*Crisis over,* Saetan thought, draining the goblet. *Until the next time.* "Eat. Then go home and smooth things over with Cassie."

Gray gave him a sideways look. Assessing. Measuring. "It would smooth things over a lot faster if Cassie and I could have sex."

Saetan said dryly, "Boyo, we're pretty sure Marian is pregnant, and she's very queasy today. Daemonar senses there is something wrong with his mama and is acting out, and Lucivar is ready to chew stone trying to deal with his misbehaving boy. Today is *not* the day to ask him about sex."

A pause. "If we had *your* permission . . ."

He laughed softly. "Not a chance, puppy. Lucivar had good reasons for setting firm boundaries for what you and Cassie can and can't do, and he'll be the one who decides when you're ready for the next stage." It didn't sound like Gray needed as much emotional protection as he'd needed a few weeks ago, but that didn't mean he had the maturity yet to be a Queen's lover.

Still, the fact that the boy was starting to question those boundaries was a good sign that Gray was growing into a healthy man instead of remaining a wounded boy. Knowing how firmly the leash needed to be held while a young Warlord Prince made the transition to adult male, Saetan added, "And from where I'm sitting, boyo, those reasons still apply."

"Oh." Gray looked disappointed, but only for a moment. Then he gave his attention to the plate floating beside him and ate every bit of food with a young man's enthusiasm.

Vae appeared on the edge of the courtyard. *Gray? Gray! Draca says it is time to go home. The High Lord will open the Gate for you. Then he needs to sleep because this is his sleep time.*

Gray sprang to his feet. "I'm sorry, sir. I didn't mean to keep you from your rest."

Saetan hesitated. In some ways, what he was about to do was a small thing, a simple choice. But the offer, and all of its underlying significance, would ripple through Dena Nehele if it was accepted. "You can call me Uncle Saetan, if you like."

The words were absorbed. The significance was understood. And one more inner layer of defense that had protected Gray the boy but hobbled Jared Blaed the man was sloughed off.

On the walk through the Keep to the Dark Altar and the Gate, Gray talked about the Shalador village and the people he'd met there. It was clear that Ranon was becoming a good friend and that he and Gray were settling into a working relationship that was typical of a strong, healthy court where the males liked and respected each other—the kind of working relationship he'd seen in the Dark Court.

What wasn't clear was how Theran was responding to any of the drama taking place in Eyota.

TERREILLE

Theran tried to ignore the sick feeling in his gut—and tried not to think about the last time Gray had disappeared. Judging by the tight expression on his face and the grim look in his eyes, Talon was trying not to think about that too.

"You're sure he's not in the village?" Talon asked for the third time.

Ranon shook his head. "We've looked. I even checked the house that accommodates unattached males. He's not here."

Mother Night. "Should one of us go back to Grayhaven?" Theran asked. "That's the only place he knows in Dena Nehele."

"He might have gone back to the rogue camps in the Tamanara Mountains," Talon said.

"Maybe," Theran said. "But he couldn't have gone alone."

"He didn't," Ranon said. "He took Vae with him."

As if speaking the name had conjured the dog, Vae rounded the corner of the boardinghouse and bounded over to them.

★Where is Cassie?★ Vae asked. ★Gray is looking for her.★

"And I'm looking for Gray," Talon growled.

Vae's tail stopped moving midwag. She spun around to face the way she had come. ★Gray? Gray! Talon is looking for you!★ Then she trotted off as if she had no more time for humans.

Gray rounded the corner, looking more relaxed than he had since Cassidy's collapse. Maybe he *had* gone to that house for sex.

Now that he knew Gray was safe, worry gave way to temper. Theran shouted, "Where in the name of Hell have you been?"

Gray didn't flinch, just gave him a steely look before focusing on Talon.

"We've been worried about you, boy," Talon said with strained control. "Where have you been?"

"I needed to talk to someone about Cassie," Gray said. "So I went to the Keep to talk to Uncle Saetan."

Ranon's eyes widened, but he said nothing.

The words felt like icy claws ripping up Theran's spine. Uncle Saetan? *Uncle Saetan?*

He glanced at Talon, not sure how to read the older man's expression.

"I see," Talon said quietly. "It would have been courteous to tell someone where you were going. These are still uneasy times. A man shouldn't go off alone without leaving a direction to follow."

"In case you need to search," Gray said just as quietly.

Talon nodded.

"My apologies, sir. I was angry and didn't think of that."

"You were all right riding the Winds?" Talon asked.

Gray nodded. "I asked Vae to go with me and show me which radial and tether lines to ride on the Purple Dusk Wind in order to reach the Keep from here."

"That's good."

Good? Theran stared at Talon. What was going on? Sure, they had to be careful. A few harsh words was all it took to have Gray whimpering in a corner, but Talon should be ripping his ass for all the hours the court had spent scrambling to find Gray while concealing his disappearance from Cassidy. Instead, Talon was almost respectful and that wasn't right. Hell's fire, Talon had *raised* the two of them, taught them, protected them.

Ranon turned his head, everything about the man on alert for a moment before he relaxed. "Cassidy, Shira, and Reyhana are back from their walk."

"Please ask Lady Shira to convey my request for an audience with the Queen," Gray said.

Already feeling off balance, Theran rocked back on his heels and wondered if the man standing in front of them really was his cousin Gray. A good illusion spell could fool the eye. Hell's fire, they had lost enough men to that kind of trickery—which should have proved that the twisted Queens who were allied with Dorothea SaDiablo had Black Widows serving in their courts.

"Lady Cassidy will meet you under the tree," Ranon said a moment later.

Gray looked at the tree and smiled. "You cleaned up that sitting area."

Ranon shrugged. "It was a way to stay close but not underfoot."

Gray shifted, as if he was about to walk away. Then he looked at Talon. "I'm sorry I worried you and the rest of the court."

"Most times it's the Steward or the Master of the Guard who is informed, but anyone in the First Circle would do," Talon said.

"Yes, sir." Gray walked over to the tree to wait for Cassidy.

All three men watched him. Then Talon rubbed his hands over his face. "Mother Night."

Turning his back on Gray and struggling to keep his voice low, Theran fixed his anger on Talon. "We spent half the day searching this village for him, and you're *polite* when he comes strolling back? Why?"

"Two words," Talon replied. "'Uncle Saetan.'"

Ranon huffed out a breath. "Yeah, that changes a few things, doesn't it?"

"It does," Talon agreed.

"Changes what?" Theran demanded.

"Gray is not a boy anymore," Talon said. "I taught him what I could. Now the High Lord of Hell will teach him the rest. Theran, no one would call *that* man 'uncle' without being invited to do so. And the simple truth is, he understands Gray better than I do."

"Then let *him* go looking the next time Gray acts like an ass," Theran snapped.

He walked away. Had to. Nothing was the way he'd hoped it would be. This visit to Eyota had shown him just how unsuitable Cassidy was to rule Dena Nehele. She had no sense of style, no sense of decorum, no *sense*. She was a handyman's daughter who, through some freak combination of bloodlines, happened to be a Queen.

He had promised to try to be a good First Escort, but every day the court had spent here had made it harder to keep that promise.

The problem was there wasn't any other choice.


She was wearing a hat. So were Shira and Reyhana, even though their skin wouldn't burn in the sun the way Cassie's did.

She removed the hat and vanished it the moment she reached the shade under the tree, which made him grin.

"You requested an audience, Prince?" Cassie said.

Still bitchy. Well, he probably deserved that.

"Does turning firewood into wood chip mulch work for female temper or just male?" he asked.

"What?" A moment's puzzlement. Then her eyes widened as if the question suddenly made sense. "Gray, exactly where did you go today?"

"I went to see—" *Uncle Saetan.* Saying that to Talon was a message. Saying it to Cassie might be bragging. "—the High Lord."

"Why?"

"You told me to talk to someone."

"I know, but . . ." She stuttered over to a chair and sat down. "What did he say?" She raised a hand. "No. Don't answer. What is said between you is private."

He was glad she appreciated that a man needed to keep some thoughts and feelings private—even from the woman he loved.

"He didn't say much," he offered, taking the other chair. "Mostly he taught me how to use Craft and power to change firewood into wood chip mulch."

Cassidy looked around. Then she shook her head. "SaDiablo Hall has acres of gardens and interior courtyards, and they all had this woody mulch I thought was wonderful. I remember asking Tarl, the head gardener, where I could find some for my mother's garden, and he asked if I had a brother. But he never explained further. You don't think . . . ?"

Gray snorted. "I filled half a barrel before the High Lord decided I had worked out enough of the temper. I think he's a practical man whose groundskeepers get a lot of help for free."

She laughed, and the sound of it eased something inside him.

"Do you want to yell at me?" he asked. He saw warmth and humor in those wonderful hazel eyes.

"I'm thinking about it," she replied.

A ritual question and answer, something that belonged to them.

He held out his hand. She slipped her hand into his without hesitation.

"We're heading back to Grayhaven tomorrow?" he asked.

Cassie nodded. "It's time. Powell will send some of the Protocol books so Reyhana, Janos, and a few others can start learning the basics."

"Janos? I thought he'd be more interested in weapons than books."

"He is." Cassie's smile widened. "But he has an older brother who has decided that he will learn Protocol—or else."

"Ranon's going to be at Grayhaven," Gray pointed out. "Easy enough to forget about the books when the older brother isn't breathing down your neck."

"Harder to forget the books when he'll be tested the next time I come to visit and his ability will determine whether or not he'll be Reyhana's escort, since she'll also come back to visit."

"Ah. Bribery." He looked at the boardinghouse. It needed attention, but he felt good in this house, in this village. As if he belonged. "So we'll be coming back to visit?"

Cassie nodded. "Hopefully I'll have a chance to meet some of the other Queens who survived the witch storm and are ruling pieces of Dena Nehele. If they don't know about siphoning power into the land, it's something I can teach them. *Carefully.*"

A psychic tap on the shoulder had him looking toward the house. "Ranon's signaling. I guess it's time for dinner."

"I guess it is."

They walked into the dining room hand in hand. Gray noticed how every man in the First Circle deliberately moved to catch his eye and offer him a nod or a smile.

Every man except Theran.


KAELEER


The study door opened without a knock or any other kind of request to enter.

Mildly annoyed at the intrusion, Daemon looked up—and annoyance gave way to warm pleasure. He pushed away from the desk and glided to the spot where Surreal waited for him.

"Welcome back," Daemon said, kissing her cheek.

"It's good to be back," she replied, hooking her long black hair behind one delicately pointed ear. "Although I may have caused a small domestic crisis."

"Oh?" Daemon raised one eyebrow. Since no one had come pounding into the study to report on the crisis, it couldn't be that bad.

"The Dea al Mon have very . . . fluid . . . ideas about what kind of greenery belongs inside their homes. When Beale escorted me up to my suite here a few minutes ago, I got so excited about not having a tree growing in the middle of my bedroom . . . Well, I hugged him."

Daemon laughed. "He'll survive. And under the circumstances, I think Mrs. Beale will forgive you."

"If she doesn't, I'm standing behind you."

Not likely. Surreal tended to fight her own battles. A feminine body that looked delicate but had sinewy strength. A lovely face and sun-kissed skin. Black hair. Gold-green eyes. And those delicately pointed ears. She got her coloring from her Hayllian sire, but her looks came from her mother's people and were all Dea al Mon.

"Jaenelle is in Halaway with Sylvia, Tersa, and Rainier. Mikal is performing in a music recital, and they're all attending," Daemon said.

"And you got out of attending by . . . ?"

"Listening to Mikal's rehearsals and figuring out twenty-seven ways of saying 'that was good but it still needs work.' I sent Rainier as my representative so there would be a male presence—and I promised my wife outstanding sex tonight if I could skip the festivities."

She laughed. "Don't you give your wife outstanding sex every night?"

"Yes, but outstanding is a bit more special on some nights," he purred.

She blinked. Swallowed hard. "Shit, I don't even want to think about that without a tub full of cold water nearby."

He kept a straight face, but it took effort. He'd been worried about her. Being trapped in that damn spooky house last autumn and the time it had taken for her to recover from the injuries she had sustained—and the fact that Rainier never would fully recover from his own injuries—had left emotional wounds.

Her time with the Dea al Mon had done her good. Physically, she looked to be in glowing health. Emotionally, he had the sense that some rough edges had been smoothed out. And there was something else about her now. Something more.

"Do you want to sit down?" He indicated the informal side of the study. "I'll ask Beale to bring in a tray unless you want a more substantial meal."

"We have something to discuss." Surreal tipped her head to indicate the blackwood desk. "But over there. Refreshments can wait."

Daemon looked at the blackwood desk, then at Surreal. "All right." He took his seat behind the desk, crossed his legs at the knees, and steepled his fingers, resting the forefingers against his chin. He watched her settle into the chair on the other side of the desk.

Formal. Official. Whatever she wanted to say would be said to the War-lord Prince of Dhemlan, not Daemon Sadi.

They sat quietly, studying each other, both comfortable with the silence. Both aware of the tension building in the room.

"Years ago, when you found me again after Titian was killed, you arranged for me to train in a Red Moon house," Surreal said.

He swallowed the anger now as he'd swallowed it then. "You were little more than a child, and you were whoring on the streets to stay alive. That wasn't the place for you. I had no right to dictate your choice of profession, but I had the means of providing you with an education that would give you more choices—and a better living."

"I wouldn't have accepted your friendship or assistance if you had tried to impose your will over mine."

He'd known that.

"The reason you gave for helping me was that my dual bloodline meant I'd live for centuries. Two thousand years. Maybe more. That might be half the usual lifetime of the long-lived races, but it's a very long time compared to everyone else." She shifted in her seat. "That didn't have much significance for me because I kept traveling all around Terreille, working in Red Moon houses and honing my skills as an assassin. It might be a decade or more before I circled back to a particular city. I saw young men who counted me as their first experience with sex turn into old men. Didn't mean much. They were a passing moment in my life."

She was working up to something, so he waited, saying nothing.

"These weeks I've spent with the Dea al Mon . . ." Surreal sighed. "Hell's fire, Sadi. I was having breakfast one morning with Grandmammy Teele, and I realized she was an old woman. Then I looked at Gabrielle—a beautiful, vibrant Queen in her late twenties—and I knew the day would come when I'd be visiting *her* and see an old woman. And Chaosti. Power-ful. Virile. Guarding his land, his people, and his Queen. Loving his wife and son. They aren't temporary people in my life. They're the other side of my family, and I'll see them grow old. I'll see them die. And even if they become demon-dead for a while, most likely they'll no longer be a part of my life."

There was a lump clogging Daemon's throat. He swallowed it before he could speak. "What's your point?"

"The visit with my mother's people helped me decide what I'm going to do with the next few decades of my life."

He raised an eyebrow as a silent question.

"I'm going to work for you."

He wasn't sure what he'd expected, but it wasn't this. "Why?"

"Because you don't have time to waste," Surreal said quietly.

The truth of those words jabbed his heart.

"Daemon, you waited seventeen hundred years for a dream. You've got, at best, a few decades to be with the love of your life. Whether you admit it or not, there must be an hourglass inside your head, and every day that ends is one more grain of sand falling to the bottom half of the glass."

"Don't," he whispered.

"You don't have time to investigate minor problems reported by Prov-ince Queens or District Queens—or time for petty shit like the game Vulchera tried to play." She smiled coldly. "For a people who keep them-selves isolated, the Dea al Mon are surprisingly well informed when they choose to be. So I did hear about the party at Lady Rhea's country house and how Vulchera foolishly tried to ensnare the Warlord Prince of Dhem-lan in a bit of sexual blackmail."

*Did you also hear how the High Lord of Hell killed her?* "What are you proposing?"

"I'm going to be your second-in-command." Something fierce and feral flashed in those gold-green eyes. "A second-in-command you can trust to guard your back."

They didn't speak the name. They didn't need to.

"I figure I'll work from the town house in Amdarh at least half the time."

"Missed being in a city?" Daemon asked mildly.

"Hell's fire, yes. Taking a bath under a canopy of leafy vines is romantic in its own way—until a large bug falls off a leaf and into the bathwater."

It was tempting to tease her and ask if it was a beetle, but that would have been unkind, and he understood the generosity of the offer she was making. He needed to work, needed the challenge of taking care of the Sa-Diablo family's estates and fortune, needed the demands of ruling Dhemlan. If he spent his time and strength on nothing but Jaenelle, he would smother her and give her no opportunity for a life beyond what they shared. But letting someone else take the burden of routine visits to the Province Queens meant being able to spend time at Jaenelle's house in Scelt—and spend time with the friends who would be only memories a century from now.

"I also plan to look for a residence here in Halaway," Surreal said. "Maybe see if Rainier would like to share a house."

Daemon narrowed his eyes. "There is plenty of room here at the Hall. And wings far enough from the family suites that they would qualify as a separate residence."

"For a man who buys property all the time, you're being dense. I want a place of my own. I want a place that doesn't belong to the SaDiablo family or you. I want a place that has my name on the deed. Since I hired Lord Marcus to be my man of business because he is yours, I figure you know well enough that I can afford just about any kind of house I want."

"Marcus would never reveal confidential or privileged information," he said with a warning bite in his voice.

"To anyone else? No, he never would," Surreal agreed. "Would he refuse to answer any question from you?" She shook her head. "That's like thinking that the firm who handles the family's investments wouldn't answer a question from Uncle Saetan about any member of this family."

True, but he wasn't going to acknowledge it out loud.

"So you know I can afford my own residence," Surreal said. "Besides, you're going to pay me an outrageously generous salary."

"I am?"

"You are."

They smiled at each other. Then Daemon's smile faded. "You've told me what I'm going to get out of this—and I'm grateful. What do you get out of this arrangement besides an outrageously generous salary?"

Her smile faded too. "I miss Rainier," she said.

"Surreal . . ."

She laughed quietly. "Relax. I know he'd rather flirt with you than with me, except he doesn't have a death wish. But he's a friend unlike any other. And love isn't always about sex. Talking to Karla about the family she formed with her adopted daughter and her Master of the Guard helped me see that. Rainier matters to me, Daemon."

"If you set up your own residence, you'll hire servants?" Daemon asked.

She snorted. "Damn right I'll hire servants. I don't want to do the cooking and cleaning by myself."

"Good. Then Mrs. Beale and Helene won't be complaining about you the way they complain about him."

"Why are they complaining about Rainier?"

"Because he keeps a room at one of the inns in the village instead of having a suite here at the Hall. Which means he isn't being looked after properly. They won't go so far as to actually criticize the cook or housekeeper at the inn since these are women they socialize with; they simply insist that it is inappropriate for the secretary of the Warlord Prince of Dhemlan to be making do with a room at an inn instead of having a proper residence and servants to look after him."

"Does he need looking after?"

He heard the concern in her voice and made a rude noise. "No more than you do, but real need is *never* the point of these conversations."

Her expression changed from concern to cautious delight. "Just how often do you get pinned to the wall because Rainier obstinately refuses to recognize this particular duty?"

"Weekly. So if you're serious about being my second-in-command, you're shouldering this particular nuisance."

Laughing, she rose and stepped up to the desk. "Done." Then she pressed her hands on the blackwood and leaned toward him, that fierce and feral *something* back in her eyes.

"One question. Does Lucivar have to worry about Falonar coming up behind him in any way?"

Ice ran in his blood, and he knew his gold eyes had turned glazed and sleepy. No one else had dared ask that question. Not even Lucivar. A few weeks ago, before she spent time with the Dea al Mon, Surreal wouldn't have dared ask that question either.

He smiled at her—a cold, brutally gentle smile—and the Sadist said too softly, "No one has to worry about Falonar anymore."

# CHAPTER 8
## TERREILLE

Gray watched Cassie from the corner of his eye and tried not to hover and fuss. Uncle Saetan had sent a note by special messenger warning him that hovering and fussing too much could turn even the most mild-tempered woman into a snarling bitch. Not that Uncle Saetan had put it in those terms, but that was the message.

It was hard not to hover when he was sitting with Cassie, Ranon, and Shira in one of the four-seat squares in the Coach. Powell had claimed one of the seats around the table so he could catch up on paperwork, the other men were split into small groups to talk or not, and Vae was sprawled on the floor where she'd be in the way of the most people, snoring lightly. Talon was in the small bedroom at the back of the Coach. Cassie had insisted he take it so he could stay inside until sunset and not be disturbed by the rest of them when they returned to Grayhaven.

It was hard not to hover when they were sitting side by side. Even harder not to fuss, but she hadn't snarled at him yet, so he figured he was keeping that tendency fairly well leashed.

Until she marked her spot, vanished the book she was reading, and closed her eyes.

"Tired?" Gray asked, trying to keep his voice casual while everything in him went on alert.

"Just feeling lazy," she replied.

He glanced at Ranon, whose attention had also sharpened.

Then Shira said, "Thank the Darkness. I wasn't sure you even knew the word."

Cassie smiled—and Gray relaxed. He slipped his arm around her and shifted them both so her head rested on his shoulder. He brushed his lips against her hair. "There's nothing to do for the next little while, so rest, Cassie. Rest."

"Ranon, why don't you play for us?" Shira said.

Ranon glared at his lover. Before he could make some excuse or just refuse, Cassie said, "That would be nice."

*Trap set and sprung,* Gray thought, fighting to keep a straight face while looking at his friend's sour expression. Then Ranon called in the Shalador flute and began to play.

The notes meandered like a stream winding its way through a summer meadow. Soft. Easy. Gray wasn't sure if it was a song or just one note following another. Either way it was peaceful. Within minutes, both women were asleep.

The rustle of paper and the murmur of male voices twined with the flute, and Gray sensed the men relaxing. Their Queen was safe and she was content, so they could afford to let down their guard and rest.

★They're proud of her,★ Ranon said on a psychic spear thread. ★She scared the shit out of all of us when she drained herself like that, but there's a feeling of pride now. Even more than when she defended that landen family.★

★Why wouldn't they be proud to serve Cassie?★ Gray asked.

Ranon didn't answer for a minute, but the music became bittersweet. ★We've all seen too much, Gray. We've all done too much in defense of our people to trust without reservation. When she stood in front of us that first day, we knew we belonged to her, and that scared every one of us. We didn't know what kind of woman claimed our loyalty and honor. Now we've got a better measure of what kind of Queen we serve, and we're proud to be in her First Circle, almost to the last man.★

Almost.

Theran sat across from Powell, his face turned to the Coach's outer wall, shutting them all out, holding himself separate from the rest of them.

It was a shame that Cassie and Theran were back to strained tolerance with each other. The tentative peace that had begun between them after she found Lia's treasure broke under the strain of her draining her power into the land. They were all back to enduring Theran's undisguised unhappiness with the Queen he had brought from Kaeleer.

He was sorry that Theran was unhappy, but everyone else at Grayhaven— including the servants—was pleased to be serving Cassie, so Theran was the one who needed to accept the way she ruled. Hopefully once Theran saw how her understanding of the Queen's connection to the land would help all their people, he would be able to accept her as the Lady who could restore Dena Nehele.

"Do you play chess?" Cassidy asked Shira as they walked from the landing web up to the Grayhaven mansion.

"Yes, I do," Shira replied at the same time Ranon said, "No, she doesn't."

Cassidy laughed. "I was told chess is not a game that should be played between genders. Our style of playing is too different to be compatible."

"Style of playing?" Ranon muttered. "Being irrational is not a 'style.'"

"In the Dark Court, if a male couldn't behave himself when playing chess with a female, he was required to play a game of cradle with her as compensation."

"Cradle?" Shira asked.

"A card game Jaenelle played when she was young and then expanded on later. Well, she and the coven expanded on the basic game. The men loathed playing it because their thinking just wasn't flexible enough."

Gray snorted. Ranon growled.

Cassidy looked at Shira, who winked at her but otherwise kept a straight face.

She felt good. Rested. Ready for the next challenge. Tomorrow she would write a general letter to all the Queens in Dena Nehele, gently reminding them of the basic ritual for enriching the land with power. If they, like the Shalador Queens, no longer remembered that ritual, they would be welcome to come to Grayhaven where she would teach them.

She would ask Powell to help her smooth out the writing—or find someone who had skill with words. There had to be a wordsmith or two in a town this size.

As she pondered that, the door opened and Dryden, the butler, stared at her with a peculiar look of relief. For a moment, she thought he was going to lift her off her feet and hug her. Since she was almost as tall as he and had a bit more muscle, the intensity of his psychic scent and expression made her shift her weight and take a step back, bumping into Gray.

"Lady," Dryden said.

One word. Gray stiffened, but she felt the change in Ranon and knew the Shalador Warlord Prince was rising to the killing edge in response to Dryden's voice. She reached back and planted her hand against Ranon's chest, her touch a light chain that was the only thing holding him back.

The other men, who had been loitering to stretch their legs after the Coach ride, moved with purpose now, and the Warlord Princes among them were all rising to the killing edge. As Talon's second-in-command, if Ranon's temper snapped the leash, the others would go with him.

And she sensed *nothing* that would explain the reaction of any of the men—until she began to probe the mansion and picked up psychic scents that were familiar . . . and painful.

"You have visitors, Lady," Dryden said. "From Dharo. They arrived two days ago. I did inform the Lady that you were not at home, but she said she was a friend and insisted that you were expecting her. Her Consort and escorts confirmed the invitation."

There was a pleading look in Dryden's eyes, but it was a struggle just to breathe, and whatever he was trying to tell her was beyond her ability to comprehend.

"Cassie?"

The violence that vibrated in Gray's voice woke her up, snapped her out of her own bog of disbelief. If he, who was still learning to fit into the skin of an adult Warlord Prince, was that close to attacking her "visitors," Ranon must be a heartbeat away from slaughter.

And because a part of her wanted to step aside and give Ranon a target for his barely leashed temper, she said briskly, "Since they've been here this long, I won't keep my visitors waiting. Lady Shira, with me, please. Gentlemen, if you two will stand escort then the other men can settle in."

Having Gray and Ranon with her would be bad enough without the rest of them crowding into the room. Thank the Darkness Theran was still in the Coach. She didn't need *him* witnessing this meeting.

As Dryden stepped aside to let them enter, she felt the full weight of male temper at her back and realized that even a direct order now wouldn't stop any of her First Circle from coming in with her.

She walked into the large parlor and her heart clenched so hard she feared it would stop beating.

The woman who sprang up from one of the stuffed chairs looked as pretty and dainty as ever. The man standing beside her was as handsome as she remembered, but shouldn't Jhorma look more satisfied? After all, he was pleasuring the woman he'd lusted after. The other three men who had served in her previous court looked embarrassed.

As well they should.

"Lady Kermilla," Cassidy said with frigid courtesy.

"Oh, *la,* Cassidy," Kermilla said. "Is that any way to greet a friend?"

"We aren't friends."

Kermilla blinked and looked taken aback.

"Lady Cassidy, it's a pleasure to see you again," Jhorma said.

"Since you were never pleased to see me, a lie dipped in honey is still a lie," Cassidy snapped.

Hell's fire. Who was this bitch who had taken control of her tongue?

*Cassie? Cassie! Gray wants to know why we don't like this Queen.* Vae paused. *Ranon wants to know too.*

"Oh," Kermilla cooed. "Is that a Sceltie? Oh, I *so* envy you having one of the kindred."

Vae snarled, and the Craft-enhanced sound rumbled through the room.

The men tensed. Kermilla's smile wobbled.

The thought of locking Kermilla in a room with Vae for a few hours provided just enough humor to smooth out a few of the rough edges of Cassidy's temper. But not enough of those edges for her to hold on to civility.

"Come with me, Kermilla. I'll grant you a few minutes of my time, and you can say what you came to say. *Privately.*" Cassidy turned and looked at Ranon to make sure he got the message.

He didn't like it. *Hated* her being in a room alone with a stranger who might be an enemy. But he gave her a curt nod to indicate he would stand aside. Then he focused on the four men who had come with Kermilla, and Cassidy understood the danger. If *anything* went wrong, those four men were forfeit. The Warlord Princes in Dena Nehele had survived the twisted Queens who had ruled here, and they had survived two years of war against the landens. They wouldn't hesitate to tear her former court apart.

They might attack anyway if they realized those men *were* from her former court. Warlord Princes were possessive and territorial, and no one had been prepared for this visit.

"Kermilla, with me," Cassidy snapped as she turned and walked to the door.

"May I remind you that I outrank you?" Kermilla snapped back.

"May I remind *you* that you don't address *our* Queen in that tone of voice if you want to keep your tongue?" Ranon snarled. "And if rank is the pissing contest you want to have, then you may outrank her but *I* outrank *you.*"

*Ranon,* Cassidy said, putting as much steel in her voice as she could.

Those dark eyes blazed with fury. He wasn't backing down.

*I don't like her, so please let me hear her out and be done with this,* she told him.

*You don't need to waste another minute on her.*

*He'll kill her,* Cassidy thought, shocked by the truth. It was one thing to *think* about standing aside and letting him rip into these people; it was quite another to let him do it for no better reason than feeling bitchy and upset.

*No,* Cassidy said. *Prince Ranon, I'm asking you to step back from the killing edge. Let me deal with this, Queen to Queen.*

He struggled to pull back, struggled to obey. Finally, *Your will is my life.*

Words of surrender, of service.

Having gotten that much of a concession from him, she knew he would hold the other men back. But she didn't dare look at Gray because what she was picking up from his psychic scent wasn't good. She could only hope that he wouldn't do anything imprudent in the few minutes she needed to deal with Kermilla.

As she walked out of the room, she brushed past Theran, who looked pale and dazed. Until she dealt with whatever trouble Kermilla had brought to Dena Nehele, she didn't have the energy to wonder how much Theran had heard, or if it was her temper or Ranon's that had shocked him. Either way, he said nothing; just watched as she led Kermilla to the smaller parlor that had become the "Ladies' Room."


Theran stared at the beautiful young woman struggling to maintain her dignity as she followed Cassidy into the Ladies' Room. Dark curls framed a triangular face with dainty features and expressive blue eyes.

He felt a burn in his gut and a pull on his heart, and felt the breathless certainty that he had found the Queen he was meant to serve. Now he understood why Archerr, Shaddo, and some of the other Warlord Princes were so enamored with Cassidy. They'd been desperate to serve a Queen, *any* Queen, and had deluded themselves into believing they felt that burn for Cassidy because they'd had no opportunity to choose between her and another. But now he'd seen the Queen who should have come back with him, who could truly claim the loyalty of the men who formed the First Circle. *She* was the one he had hoped to find when he went to Kaeleer to beg Daemon Sadi for help. *She* was the Queen who should be ruling Dena Nehele.

She was the answer to his hopes and dreams.

A friend of Cassidy's come for a visit? A long visit, he hoped. A lifetime visit, if he could convince the Lady to stay.


"What are you doing here, Kermilla?" Cassidy demanded as soon as the other Queen shut the parlor door.

"I came to see you," Kermilla replied, her eyes wide and innocent—and on the verge of being filled with an expression of wounded dignity that was as false as everything else about the woman.

Cassidy wondered if Jhorma had figured out by now that there wasn't much substance once you got past the things that were directly related to Kermilla's pleasure and personal gratification.

Maybe that wasn't fair. After all, a flighty young Queen could mature into a solid ruler. But Cassidy wasn't much interested in being fair anymore where Kermilla was concerned.

"Why?" Cassidy asked.

Kermilla did her sexy pout, but the usual "aren't I being naughty?" twinkle wasn't in her blue eyes. "You didn't answer my letters, so what choice did I have but to interrupt my own duties and come here?"

"I didn't answer because I have nothing to say to you."

Kermilla stamped her foot. "Queen's gift, Cassidy. I need the money you owe me for taking over the court."

She hadn't known she could be this furious, hadn't known this much anger lived inside her. "I owe you nothing."

"You do! Queen's gift—"

"Is a *gift,* not an obligation. And you didn't take over a court from a re-tiring Queen, Kermilla. You *took* my court. There's a vast difference, and if you can't see that I suggest you have someone explain it to you." Someone with big, hard boots that could leave an impression where it might do the girl the most good. "The village treasury has the same amount of marks as when I came to Bhak. A little more, in fact."

"But that's the *village* treasury. Every copper spent from there has to be reported to the Province Queen. Those marks aren't Queen's income. I have expenses, Cassidy."

"So did I, and I had no more than you when I started. Merchants are willing to run an account for a Queen's personal expenses and court expenses. Those accounts are billed quarterly and deducted from that merchant's tithe."

"But they're sending *bills!*" Kermilla shouted.

Which meant the girl had already spent past the summer tithe owed by those merchants. Once the tithe was met, a Queen and her court were expected to pay for goods like everyone else in the village.

"Then I suggest you curtail your spending until the harvest tithe," Cassidy said.

"I'm not like you," Kermilla snapped. "I know what it takes to look like a Queen and dress like a Queen and *act* like a Queen. Those things take *money*."

"Then talk to your Steward. He'll tell you how much income you can expect after you settle your obligations to the Province Queen and village treasury, and pay your court."

"That's your answer?"

"That my answer. You rule Bhak and Woolskin. Your income comes from their tithes." *And may the Darkness have mercy on those people.* "I have work to do, and despite what you told Dryden, you are not a welcome guest. You've had your say. Now go. I don't want you in my Territory."

Kermilla looked stunned.

Cassidy strode to the door and reached for the handle.

"Cassidy . . . wait."

She couldn't wait. Her stomach burned and her bowels were turning to liquid. "Get out of my Territory," she said harshly. "And take your cocks with you."

Cassidy brushed past Theran, who was lingering in the hallway, and snapped at Ranon when he intercepted her on the way to her suite and tried to ask if she was all right.

She wasn't all right. Wouldn't be all right until Kermilla was back in Dharo and she could lock away all the painful memories. Again.

Kermilla dabbed her eyes with a lace-edged handkerchief.

Cassidy had been so *angry*. She had *never* seen Cassidy like that! And so unwilling to *listen*.

It had been a mistake bringing Jhorma with her. She had thought bringing her Master of the Guard might appear too much like a threat, and her Steward had to stay in Bhak to take care of all the *boring* details. That left

Jhorma to represent the Queen's Triangle—the males who were dominant in a court because they dealt with the Queen directly.

When she'd decided to come to Dena Nehele, she'd thought that reminding Cassidy that *she* was the Queen Jhorma had chosen to serve and pleasure would intimidate Cassidy a little. At least enough that Cassidy wouldn't keep ignoring the Queen's gift which *should* have been left as the seed money for Kermilla's personal expenses.

But Cassidy had seen Jhorma and gotten so *angry*. And that dark-eyed Warlord Prince was so *scary*! He looked like he wanted to rip out her throat with his *teeth*!

It wasn't fun being a ruling Queen. It should have been, but it wasn't. Being in Cassidy's court for her training had been great fun. She had danced and flirted and talked and attended the luncheons with the—well, they weren't aristos, but they were the most influential people you could find in a place like Bhak. Sure, she had to follow Cassidy around to "learn" how to be a Queen, as if she didn't *know* how to be a Queen, and she had made careful notes about what duties she would keep and what duties—the *boring* duties—she would require the Ladies in her First Circle to shoulder.

Then she found out she'd have to pay anyone who was officially in her First Circle, so she'd limited that Circle to the necessary twelve males. Which meant *she* had to take care of the boring duties, and since they *were* boring, she hadn't bothered with them half the time. And lately it seemed like her Steward was handing her a list of complaints every day. And her Master of the Guard . . . Well, he'd seemed so charming when he'd first begun to serve her, and he'd been a *darling* when she'd been training with Cassidy. Now she dreaded talking to him because he looked grim grim grim when he reminded her that she was the village's moral center and she *could not* allow rowdy young Blood males to use the landens for sport. There was already trouble because of a *little* mischief, but he'd wanted to publicly strap those boys because a landen had gotten hurt—and he hadn't looked at her with any kind of warmth after she forbade him to punish the boys. And that merchant! Whining over a broken window and wanting the Warlord's family to pay for the damages. Well, she couldn't order that, could she? The Warlord's sister was one of her closest friends. And then the merchant wanted to deduct the cost of the damages from the tithes and *her Steward let him.* Without asking her. Saying it was the only thing to do if she wasn't going to hold the Warlord responsible.

She didn't have a big enough court. That was the problem. There should be people taking care of these things so that she could be a *Queen.*

She'd spent some of the village treasury, which she shouldn't have done and wouldn't have needed to do if Cassidy hadn't been selfish. So now she had to have the Queen's gift in case the Province Queen's Steward asked her Steward for a financial report. She had to replace what she'd taken, or *she* would end up having to justify her expenses to Lady Darlena.

Even worse, because she was only twenty-one and this was her first court, Lady Sabrina, the Queen of Dharo, had given her Bhak to rule for one year. A proving ground, Sabrina had called it. If the villages, Bhak and landen Woolskin, prospered under her rule, she could keep them. If not, Sabrina would declare her court broken and arbitrarily reassign her males to other courts, and she would have to form a new court and find another village to rule since Bhak and Woolskin would be given to another Queen.

It was all *very* distressing.

"Are you all right?"

She gasped at the sound of a strange male voice, then turned to face him, dabbing at her eyes so she looked as woeful as she felt.

*Mine.*

The shock of it rocked her, that pull, that *demand* that she be the one to hold the emotional leash that would keep him balanced. She'd never felt anything like this. Was she *supposed* to feel anything like this?

"Yes, thank you, I'm fine," she said. "A little distressed is all. I seem to have come at a bad time and upset Cassidy."

He was so handsome with that dark hair and those dreamy green eyes and that golden brown skin. There was a hardness to him that said *warrior.* More than being a Warlord Prince who was ready to fight, this man had *fought,* had been on killing fields that *mattered.*

She was already a little in love with him, and she didn't even know his name.

"Who . . . ?"

"Theran Grayhaven."

"I am Kermilla." She offered her hand.

He raised her hand to his lips and *kissed* it. Not lips held a breath away from skin, but a real kiss.

"Why are you distressed?" he asked.

"Well, Cassidy and I had a little disagreement, and she ordered me to leave."

He stiffened. "Leave?"

Maybe she had an ally in this place after all. She gave him a wobbly smile. "As in, 'Get out of my house.' "

A weird, chilling heat filled his eyes. "It's not her house. She has no right to toss you out as if you were a landen."

"But . . . doesn't she live here?"

"This is my family home. I offered its use for the Queen's residence, but this is still *my* house, not hers. And if Lady Cassidy has forgotten her manners, I have not. I would be honored if you would be *my* guest for as long as you want to stay."

"Oh, that is most kind of you, Prince Grayhaven. Or may I be so bold as to call you Theran?"

His smile made her feel wonderful.

"I would be honored to be addressed as a friend."

She vanished the handkerchief, then slipped her arm through his. "In that case, perhaps you would indulge me by showing me around and telling me about the history of this place and your family." Men usually liked talking about such things.

He searched her face, but she had no idea what he searched for—or if he found it.

"Do you really want to know?" he finally asked.

No, but she could see it mattered to him. "Yes, I really want to know."

"It would be a pleasure, Lady."

He sounded like he meant it, and wasn't that the loveliest thing of all?

★    ★    ★

Gray yanked out weeds with controlled savagery. A few days gone at this time of year and the weeds crept in. Had to be vigilant. Always vigilant. Or the weeds crept in.

Snarling, he twisted around and threw the weeding claw as hard as he could.

Ranon shouted and swore as the claw hit the shield he threw around himself.

"Hell's fire, Gray! What's the matter with you?" Ranon roared. "No one shields on the home ground. You threw that damn thing hard enough to hook into someone's gut."

Gray rose to his feet and waited for Ranon to get within reach. "Maybe everyone better start shielding, home ground or not."

Ranon stopped. Stared. Looked at the mansion—and swore. "You feel it too."

"Wouldn't turn my back on her," Gray said.

"Yeah." Ranon stared at the flower bed. "Got no proof she's a bitch, except the snotty way she spoke to Cassidy. Got no proof she's done any harm to her people. But I wouldn't trust her with anyone I cared about. She's . . . off. Not twisted, not evil like the Queens who had ruled here before the witch storm swept them away. But something isn't right."

"Vae says Kermilla smells bad. Not her body, her psychic scent."

"Shit."

Gray looked toward the mansion—and went rigid. "What in the name of Hell is Theran doing? I thought she was supposed to leave."

But there was Kermilla, walking arm in arm with Theran, who had the balls to point to the place where the dead honey pear tree had stood for so long—until Cassie had started unlocking the spells that revealed the treasure hidden within Grayhaven.

A treasure that included thirteen honey pears that had survived centuries and were now the seedlings that would be the start of new orchards.

"Gray, don't," Ranon said softly. "Cassidy isn't feeling well. Too much upset."

"Only a fool would expect her to sit down at the same table with *that*."

And he had a sick feeling that Theran was going to expect exactly that—and be pissy about Cassie not coming to the table.

"She'll have dinner in her suite tonight with Shira," Ranon said.

Gray nodded.

"Let it go, Gray. Both of us need to let it go. Whatever business Kermilla had with Cassidy is done. Tomorrow she'll go back to where she came from, and we'll get on with our lives."

Gray nodded again.

"Are you going to sleep inside tonight?" Ranon asked.

He hesitated. Drought. Plague. Weeds creeping in and choking the good plants. That's what he felt when he looked at Kermilla. He didn't want to get anywhere near her, didn't want to be locked behind walls where she could reach him. The old fears gnawed at him, but something else, something new pushed at him harder.

"Do you think Cassie would mind if I slept on the sofa in her suite?" he asked.

"I think she would understand if you felt uncomfortable being in the family wing."

With no one but Theran nearby, and the "guest" too close for comfort.

"I am afraid to sleep alone tonight, but that's only part of it," Gray said.

"What's the other part?"

He looked at Ranon. "If I'm sleeping on the sofa, the only way someone can get to Cassie is by going through me."

Talon leaned against a tree, another dark shape in the night, and waited. Which one of the First Circle would come out to find him?

Hell's fire. He'd gone to sleep in a Coach full of men feeling hopeful and pleased, and woke to find the Grayhaven mansion inhabited by two armed camps that were barely obeying the command to keep the peace. Ranon and Theran looked ready to tear out each other's throats, and Gray . . . He wasn't sure what was going on inside Gray's head, and that was a worry—especially since Cassidy had retired to her suite before dinner, claiming to feel ill.

And all of this was because of the visitors from Dharo.

When he saw the man coming toward him, he was a little surprised that it was Powell instead of one of the Warlord Princes, but when he gave it a moment's thought, he realized it wouldn't have been anyone else. The Steward would be the one to approach the Master of the Guard to discuss how to direct the rest of the First Circle to best serve the Queen.

"Talon," Powell said.

A middle-aged man whose left hand had been badly broken by the last Queen he'd served, Powell's steadier temper was proving to be a good balance for the more volatile members of the court.

"Out to get some air?" Talon asked.

"Storm's coming."

"Might blow over." They weren't talking about the weather. Talon huffed out a breath. "What in the name of Hell happened? All I've heard from both sides is a lot of crap."

Powell tensed.

*Dangerous ground,* Talon thought. *Two Queens in the same house and all the men wary or edgy or just plain ready to kill.* "Put caste aside for a moment and tell me what you'd say if this was about social standing."

Powell relaxed. "Ah. Well. Plain girl. Comes from a simple family and expects to work for her keep. Earns the friendships she makes by being a friend. At a social gathering, she's never asked by a handsome man for any of the romantic dances unless he's an escort in training and is required to dance with the girls who wouldn't have a partner otherwise. Her heart's probably bruised because of that, but she's learned to accept it.

"Then there's the pretty girl. Spoiled and pampered. Her father's darling."

"Wait," Talon interrupted. "Father's darling would apply to both girls." Having met Lord Burle, it was clear he was more than proud of Cassidy, and not because she was now the Queen of a whole Territory. That pride was for his *girl,* who just happened to be a Queen.

"You're right," Powell agreed. "However, the pretty girl is used to getting her own way, is used to being preferred over the other girls, always has her dance card filled before she arrives at the dance, and if she snubs one partner in favor of someone more polished or aristo, she expects to be forgiven—and her actions defended—because she is an aristo darling.

"These two girls have competed in the same social arena."

"And when the plain girl did get a dance partner the pretty girl wanted, the pretty girl stole him just because she could," Talon said. "Yeah, it's clear enough there is some history between Kermilla and Cassidy."

"Theran made no effort to hide his preference. Cassidy told Kermilla to leave; Theran said she could stay. That had to hurt Cassidy's pride."

"And the pretty girl wins again." Talon sighed. *Sweet Darkness, please let it be that simple.* "Ranon and Gray have an intense dislike for her."

"Which has made the others edgy and politely hostile toward our guests." Powell paused, then added, "I have to say, Warlord Princes are the only caste of males who can act politely and still leave 'I want to kill you' hanging unspoken in a room. Ranon and Gray are the most attuned to Cassidy. Kermilla makes her unhappy, so they're going to dislike her, no matter what."

"And Theran? Is it a young man's cock lusting for a pretty girl, or is it a Warlord Prince feeling the pull of a Queen?"

"I don't know," Powell said.

"Shit." Until he'd met Cassidy and had felt that pull himself, he hadn't realized how powerful a chain that connection between Queen and Warlord Prince could be. If that was the reason Theran was reacting to Kermilla . . .

Talon scratched the back of his neck. "She came here for a reason. No matter what she says, Kermilla didn't come here to visit a friend, so she was expecting to get *something*."

"I agree, and I don't think she got what she came for. But she did win something by Theran inviting her to stay. The First Escort countermanding the Queen's order for his own pleasure? Can we allow that, Talon?"

"It's his house. He's right about that. And Kermilla being a Queen might not mean anything."

"It means something to Cassidy."

"Yeah, it does." But was the rivalry between Queens or women? If he took Kermilla back to the Keep tonight, which is what he should do to soothe his Queen, Theran would blame Cassidy for Kermilla's departure, and the tension between them could grow to an animosity that would cripple the court. If this was nothing more than a physical attraction between Theran and Kermilla, it could burn itself out in a few days anyway, and he would have widened the rift already present in the court for nothing.

"What should we do?" Powell asked.

"We wait—and we watch," Talon replied. *And hope I'm not hurting Cassidy too much by letting Theran take the lead on this and have the time to get to know the girl.*

# CHAPTER 9

## TERREILLE

Cassidy slowly made her way up to her suite. Her head ached and her stomach burned. Not an unusual combination these days. All it took was hearing "Oh, *la*" for the pain to start.

Shira had a tonic that could soothe the stomach and medicine that could ease the headache. But she couldn't go to the Healer. Not again. The first time, Shira had performed her duties without comment. The second evening it happened, those dark eyes held a sharp reminder that Shira was a Black Widow as well as a Healer, and poisoning a "guest" would be a simple thing to do.

She had to write her report to Prince Sadi, and she didn't know what to say. Didn't know what she *dared* to say.

It was happening again. She had failed. Again.

Kermilla shone. She dazzled. Just like the last time. She flattered and flirted, wore a different gown every evening that had the men's eyes popping out, and hinted that she was on the primary guest lists of the most influential aristos in Dharo.

Which may or may not be true, but there was no way to call Kermilla on it without sounding churlish.

Maybe she shouldn't have been surprised, but it had been a shock to have Theran come up to her suite that first day and inform her that Kermilla was now *his* guest, just as *she* was his guest, and he expected her to act her age instead of behaving like a pouting adolescent.

That statement coming from a man whose pants tented every time he was in the same room as Kermilla might have been funny in a dark, painful way if the rest of the court hadn't started acting just like her old court had done. They looked at Kermilla and then at her as if they were judging her and finding fault. Seeing her and Kermilla in the same room . . . The difference between a draft horse and a thoroughbred, Jhorma had once said when he had escorted her and Kermilla to a small party. He'd said it in a tone of voice that was supposed to mean he was joking, but everyone in the room had known he meant it. And everyone must have known that he resented riding the draft horse when he lusted for the thoroughbred.

Everyone but her.

Even when he said things like that—and justified saying things like that—she hadn't understood his enthusiasm in her bed had to do with getting his own relief and nothing to do with a commitment to take care of his Queen.

Did he enjoy taking care of Kermilla?

She couldn't think about that. She did her best to ignore the other Queen by spending time in the garden with Gray and working with Powell to send out messages to the surviving Queens in Dena Nehele.

At least one good thing had come from Kermilla's visit: Theran was too preoccupied with *her* to pay attention to the fact that Cassidy was reaching out to the other Queens in Dena Nehele.


Ranon stared at the special flower bed Gray had made for Cassidy—the plants were similar to ones found in Dharo but were native to Dena Nehele. The common ground, Gray called it.

He'd been coming out here every night since Theran had given *Lady* Kermilla an open-ended invitation to stay at Grayhaven. Shira was acting peculiar in a way that unnerved him. He loved the woman with everything in him, but he didn't forget he was sleeping with a Black Widow, and there was a reason why that caste of witch was feared.

"Thought I'd find you here," Talon said.

He half turned toward the voice, but didn't speak for a minute. "Something is draining the heart out of Cassidy."

"Oh, I think we've all figured out what that something is," Talon said. He kept walking, but he lifted his chin to indicate the stone storage shed where Gray used to live because he was too frightened to enter the house.

His heart pounding, Ranon glanced at the house before drifting toward the back of the shed. What did the Master of the Guard want to say to him that couldn't be said inside the house?

"What . . . ?" he began.

Talon raised his left hand. The two missing fingers were a reminder that this man had not lived a soft life—even after he became demon-dead.

A minute later, Archerr, Spere, and Shaddo slipped behind the shed. A minute after that, Bardric and Cayle joined them.

"Burne, Haele, and Radley are providing a presence in the parlor this evening," Talon said. "Archerr, you'll relay instructions to Burne and Haele. Cayle, you'll keep Radley informed."

*I'm your second-in-command,* Ranon said, using a tight spear thread to direct the words only to Talon.

*I know what you are,* Talon replied sharply. *You have the task of keeping Gray and the Black Widow leashed. And yourself.*

Shit. *You don't ask for much.*

*If you don't have the balls for it, tell me now.*

Stung by the verbal slap, Ranon didn't answer.

"What about Powell?" Archerr asked.

"I'll keep the Steward informed," Talon said.

*What did Powell say?* Ranon asked, wondering if anyone else had noticed a slight hesitation in Talon's reply.

*Later.* "Our Queen is distressed. The visitors are the reason. We need to find out why."

"How does Kermilla know Lady Cassidy?" Spere asked.

"I can't see that the two of them have anything in common except caste," Shaddo said.

"She reminds me of a carrion eater picking at the bones," Bardric said.

Shaddo nodded. "And Dena Nehele is the bones. We've seen bitches like her before."

"She's entertaining," Cayle said. "And she's false. You can see it in her eyes. What's she looking for here?"

Archerr snorted. "Control over the rest of us. What else?"

"If she did have that control?" Talon asked.

Ice swept through Ranon, but a steely look from Talon kept him silent.

The other men shifted their feet and looked uncomfortable. Finally Spere said, "Those escorts aren't fighters. Got some training—every escort does—but they're Warlords, not Warlord Princes."

Shaddo nodded. "Take them out fast and hard. Have someone coming in behind the others who is strong enough to take out the witch—burst heart and brain with a blast of power that will break her Jewels and finish the kill."

Ranon swallowed hard. He thought he'd been the only one thinking along those lines. Apparently not.

Talon nodded, as if they'd told him what he'd expected. "Not yet. She's a Queen from another Territory. Another Realm. We made the mistake of not looking for social connections to dark power when Cassidy first came here. Kermilla keeps hinting that she has powerful friends, so let's not make that mistake again. Cayle, Bardric, you two are least likely to be perceived as a threat, so I want you to spend time with the Warlords who came with Kermilla. Find out what you can about her court and about her connection to Cassidy. They're not friends, so let's find out exactly what they are to each other."

"We could force open the inner barriers of the lightest Jeweled Warlord and find out everything we want to know," Archerr said quietly.

"And become no better than what we fought against all those years?" Talon shook his head. "You don't do that to anyone but an enemy, and we don't know yet that these men are enemies."

"We know their presence is upsetting Cassidy," Ranon said.

"Yes, we know that," Talon agreed.

Ranon heard regret—and maybe a little guilt?—in Talon's voice.

"When we find out more, we'll decide what to do about it," Talon continued. "That's all. Any information you find out comes to me or Ranon."

"And we don't mention any of this to Theran?" Spere asked.

Even in the dark, Ranon saw the sadness in Talon's eyes.

"We don't mention this to Theran," Talon said. "I'm hoping it's just lust that's making him stupid, but if he feels the same pull for Kermilla that we feel for Cassidy, we can't trust him to stand for the Queen he promised to serve."

One by one, the men wrapped themselves in sight shields and slipped away until Ranon and Talon were alone.

"Powell," Ranon said quietly. "He said something. That's why you're giving these orders." He waited. "What did he say?"

"He said, 'It's starting to feel like old times, isn't it?' And may the Darkness have mercy on us, Ranon, I think he's right."

Talon walked away.

Ranon leaned against the shed, feeling sick.

It wouldn't come to that. It *wouldn't*. Not while Cassidy ruled Dena Nehele.

Theran sat in the parlor, happier than he had ever been.

Kermilla was wonderful, was everything he dreamed a Queen should be. The sound of her voice quenched a raging thirst inside him, and there was a spot on her neck that had a scent that aroused him and yet gave him peace.

She had been careful not to say anything outright, but she'd made it clear to him that, having come from an aristo family, the training that had honed her innate abilities as a Queen had been far more extensive than Cassidy's—the kind of training given to someone destined to be a Territory Queen.

Damn Ranon for stirring everything up so much that the other men were wary about getting to know her. But they would come around.

Sooner or later they would recognize the treasure that had come to Grayhaven.

# CHAPTER 10

## TERREILLE

She had to get out of here. Her hands shook, her stomach burned, and dinner was nothing but a foul smell in the toilet. She couldn't do this again, couldn't watch this happen again.

She couldn't stand to hurt this much again.

Go. Run. Get away from this place.

Because this time she might lose someone who truly mattered, and it was ripping her heart out.

This time, betrayal might truly kill her.

Ranon stood outside Cassidy's door, trying to leash his rage because he *had* to. There was no one else. Theran's verbal barbs had turned cruel enough to drive Cassidy out of the parlor in tears, so Talon had his hands full controlling Gray and making sure the two cousins didn't set eyes on each other before tempers had settled. Powell had walked out of the parlor and locked himself in his office. No one was sure what the man was doing in there, but they were all hoping the worst he was doing was getting stinking drunk. And Theran . . .

Couldn't the bastard see that Cassidy wasn't comfortable around Kermilla? But he kept insisting that Cassidy "do her duty" as a Queen and not leave the other Queen without company—especially since Cassidy was the lower-ranking Queen.

Damn Grayhaven to the bowels of Hell for slipping the verbal knife in every chance he got. Kermilla was pretty; Cassidy was not. Kermilla was vivacious—the kind of Queen who would appeal to the Blood; Cassidy was there because they hadn't been given a choice. Cassidy wore Rose; Kermilla wore Summer-sky, which made her dominant.

Dominant his ass. Sure it gave her a little more power since Summer-sky was one rank darker than Rose, but that was *all* it gave her. The little bitch was just good at playing people and presenting herself to advantage. At least they had gotten a couple of answers from tonight's little drama. The four men who had come with Kermilla had all served in Cassidy's court—and had abandoned a real Queen in order to serve pretty gilt.

Jhorma had been Cassidy's Consort. They all agreed they wouldn't mention *that* bit of information to Gray. Hell's fire! What had Cassidy been thinking? The woman couldn't have been *that* desperate for a lover to have settled for *him*.

*You're here to make sure she's all right. You can't do that from this side of the door.*

He knocked. No answer. He knocked harder, certain she was in her suite. "Cassidy?" He turned the door handle. The door wasn't locked, so he walked in—and caught her pulling back, as if she'd lunged for the door to lock it but didn't react in time.

No color in her face except the freckles standing out on milky ice and the dark shadows under her eyes. She stood there, frozen, so he looked around—and saw the trunks. The lids were open, and the trunks were full of her clothes and possessions.

"What's going on, Cassidy?" he asked, putting an Opal lock on the door as he closed it.

"I can't stay here," she whispered. "I'm sorry. I have to go."

"Where?"

She stared at him and didn't answer.

He thought about the past few days and what he had learned tonight. Her former First Circle had broken her court in order to serve another Queen. And now that same Queen had come to Dena Nehele and was making herself very comfortable in the Queen's residence—and Cassidy was breaking down under the hammer of Theran's words and his blatant preference for Kermilla.

Cassidy . . . running.

He grabbed her arms, and it was only the years of training that kept his savagery controlled.

"You're leaving us? Why?"

"I can't stay!" Cassidy wailed.

He shook her and roared, *"Why?"*

"Theran doesn't want me to stay. He wants Kermilla to be the Queen."

"Who gives a piss what Theran wants?" Ranon shouted. "Forget him! What about the rest of us, Cassie? What about the eleven other men who are loyal to you and want to serve? Are you going to walk away from us too? Are you going to walk away from Gray? Are you going to walk away from the people who are starting to hope again that a Queen will rule fairly? *Are you walking away from all of us because one man wants to hump a little bitch?*"

She stared at him, shocked, and finally whispered, "You're hurting me."

He eased his hold on her, certain her arms would be bruised black by morning, but he didn't let go.

Tears spilled down her pale, pale face. "Ranon, I can't watch Kermilla take over another court. And it will kill me when Gray starts falling in love with her."

Idiot woman. Couldn't she see that Gray *loathed* Kermilla?

He looked at her, really looked, and realized she couldn't see anything right now—not Gray's love, not his own loyalty. Nothing.

He gentled his hands, and forced himself to gentle his voice. "Cassie, do you trust me? As a friend, do you trust me?"

She hesitated, then nodded.

"Then listen. Please listen. I'm begging you not to walk away from Dena Nehele."

"I can't stay."

If she got to Dharo, they would never get her back. Hell's fire, if she got to the *Keep* in her present state, Sadi and Yaslana would never let her come back even if she was willing.

Then he remembered the last thing Lucivar had said to the First Circle before heading back to Kaeleer: "The Queen comes before anyone else. You take care of her, the rest usually falls into place."

Cassidy was focused on getting out, so he would take care of his Queen and get her out—and do his best to take care of Dena Nehele as well.

"All right," he said. "I understand. You need to get away from those people. I do understand. But you don't have to go too far away. I'll take you back to Eyota, back to the boardinghouse. You didn't mind staying there, did you? You're already packed. I'll take you tonight. Now. We'll slip out. No one else needs to know until you're ready for them to know."

"I don't—"

"You're the Queen, Cassie. *Our* Queen, and the Queen's residence is any place the Queen chooses to live. You don't want to stay here, you don't have to stay here."

"Gray will worry if I leave without saying anything," Cassidy said.

"I'll tell Shira enough so that she can reassure him. And I'll come back and talk to him as soon as you're settled at the boardinghouse. I promise."

"I don't know."

"You're upset, and rightly so." Ranon took a deep breath and let it out slowly. He couldn't force her to stay, but he was sure if he could get her to Eyota, he would buy enough time to convince her that there were people who didn't care if a face was pretty or not when the woman behind that face was special. "Come with me. Give yourself time to rest and breathe before making a decision. Please."

She called in a handkerchief and sniffled into it. "Should I leave a note? It's proper to inform the Steward and Master of the Guard."

She sounded so lost, so wounded.

He knew it was proper. As the Master's second-in-command, he should inform Talon at the very least. But if he involved anyone else in the court right now, most likely Cassidy would be talked into staying here—and the next time she decided to run, she wouldn't delay long enough to pack her things or leave a note. They'd find out about it when Yaslana landed on their doorstep demanding answers.

"No," he said. "No one needs to know where you are. Not yet."

He hadn't convinced her, and he didn't know what else to say. But he could think of one thing to do.

Using Craft, he closed the lids on her trunks—and vanished them.

Cassidy stared at the empty floor. "You took my trunks."

"I did." Getting his mouth to smile felt like he was trying to bend stone, but he did it. Or close enough. "I'll give them back when we reach the boardinghouse."

She studied him.

"What?" he asked.

She sniffled into the handkerchief once more, then vanished it. "For a moment there, you sounded like Lucivar."

He decided to take that as a compliment. "Let's get out of here."

"You'll talk to Gray?"

"I will. I hope you won't be upset if he decides to join you."

"Do you think he would?"

*Oh, Cassie. Are you hurting so much you can't remember that he loves you?* "I do, darling. I really do."

Ranon and Cassidy slipped out of the house, wrapped in an Opal sight shield to lessen the number of people who might be able to detect her. He trusted her to go down to the gate while he went to the stables to get a horse—praying to the Darkness that she didn't walk onto the landing web, catch the Rose Wind, and run to the Keep. Riding double to the Coaching station, they rented a small Coach, giving the driver who should have gone with them a generous tip to watch the horse—and not ask questions.

Riding the Opal Winds, switching from radial to tether lines whenever needed, they finally reached the landing web on the northern end of his home village.

And through the whole of the journey, Cassidy never said one word.

★   ★   ★

*Grandfather,* Ranon called as soon as he dropped the Coach from the Opal Web and skimmed over the landing web. He could handle a small Coach when riding the Winds, but using Craft and power to hold one steady as it skimmed above the road was an untested skill. *Grandfather!*

*Ranon?* Yairen sounded muddled. Then the voice on the psychic thread sharpened. *Ranon?*

*I need help.* He could picture his grandfather pushing himself up and swinging his legs over the side of the bed. After all, anyone in their right mind who wasn't demon-dead would be asleep at this hour. *I brought Cassidy. There's been some trouble.*

*Is she wounded?*

The genuine concern in Yairen's voice told Ranon that he'd made the right choice. *Not her body, but her heart is wounded.*

*Gray?*

*No. It's . . . complicated. She was going to leave us, Grandfather. I convinced her to come here instead.*

*Where?*

*The boardinghouse.*

*Go slowly, grandson. Give this old man a little time to prepare. I will meet you at the house. Janos will come too.*

*Thank you.*

Yairen broke the link. Ranon slowed the Coach to the pace of an ambling walk—and hoped Cassidy wouldn't ask him why the Coach was suddenly wobbling so much.

By the time he set the Coach down on the street in front of the boardinghouse, there were lamps shining in the windows of several rooms, and doors and windows were open to let in cool night air.

"We're here," he said, holding out a hand.

She slipped her hand in his, still saying nothing as she followed him out of the Coach and into the house.

His grandfather waited for them in the front parlor.

"The Rose has come back to us," Yairen said, smiling. "It grieves me to know you sorrow, but you are among friends here." He gestured to two chairs and a table. "Come and sit with an old man."

She sat, and she seemed so empty Ranon wondered if he'd brought more than a husk to Eyota.

Yairen waved a hand over the table. Two mugs and a carafe appeared. Using Craft, Yairen poured dark, steaming liquid from the carafe into the mugs.

"This is a special drink," Yairen said. "I usually make it when strong men need to speak of things that are troubling their hearts, but I think tonight your heart could use this."

"I don't think I can speak," Cassidy whispered.

Yairen smiled gently. "Even silence has a voice. Drink. Perhaps we will talk. Perhaps not. Perhaps I alone will talk and tell you more about the music of my people, even give you the first lesson in how to play a drum."

Cassidy took a sip of his grandfather's special brew of spiced whiskey and coffee. She took another sip. "I would like to hear more about your music."

"Good." Yairen looked at Ranon. "Are you still here, troublemaker?"

"Troublemaker?" Cassidy asked.

"Bah." Yairen waved one hand gently in front of his face. "The stories I could tell you about that one. Go on, now," he added, pointing at Ranon. "Leave us to talk without your bothersome presence."

Cassidy snorted and took another, larger sip of the brew.

*Tend to your business, grandson,* Yairen said. *The Rose will be safe here among us.*

*Don't tell her too many stories.* He looked at Cassidy. "I'll be back as soon as I can."

"You promised to give me back my trunks when we got here," Cassidy said.

"Oh. I did, didn't I?" This time his smile wasn't forced. He called in her trunks and set them at the other end of the parlor.

"See?" Yairen said, laughing. "Troublemaker."

★    ★    ★

An hour before sunrise, most of the First Circle gathered in a meeting room.

Ranon had figured he would face anger. He'd figured he would face temper.

What he faced was so much worse.

There was a chilling blankness in Gray's eyes, and Ranon couldn't shake the conviction that what was under that blankness was a violence that even the Blood would find shocking. There was a smoldering fury in Shira's eyes, and he hoped with everything in him that he wasn't the target.

He brushed lightly against the first of her inner barriers—and found nothing comforting.

*My first loyalty is to the Queen, remember?* he asked her.

She didn't respond, but he sensed a little less tension in her. He didn't blame her for being angry. All he'd told her was that he and Cassidy were leaving the mansion and she should inform Gray so he wouldn't be searching for her and alarm the First Circle. Of course, Shira and Gray had assumed Cassidy would be with him when he returned.

The other men looked a little pissed off at being summoned so early in the morning. Except Powell, who sat quietly, staring at his hands—especially at his left hand, which a Queen had broken because he cared more about people who needed food and clothes than about the Queen's purse.

Then Talon entered the room and put Sapphire shields around the room and a Sapphire lock on the door.

"All right, Ranon," Talon said. "You were very specific about who should attend this meeting—and who should not. We're here. Now talk."

He heard temper that was chained—but not for long. Not if he said the wrong thing. Talon outranked all of them, had centuries of fighting experience, and had locked them all in a room with the strongest predator in Dena Nehele.

Had locked *him* in a room with the strongest predator.

"I took Cassidy to Eyota, to the boardinghouse," Ranon said.

Gray snarled and took a step toward him.

Powell raised his head and stared at him.

He didn't want to turn his back on Talon, but Gray was the more volatile threat, so he faced the Warlord Prince who had been a friend—and might now be an enemy.

"She was going to leave us, Gray," he said quickly, wanting them to hear him, to know why he made this choice before someone's temper snapped the leash. "She was going to leave all of us. When I went up to her suite to check on her, her trunks were packed. She was going back to Dharo."

"She wouldn't leave without telling me," Gray said too softly as he took another step toward Ranon. "She wouldn't leave without me."

"I had to get her out of here, get her hidden so she would feel safe. I promised to come back and tell you, and I have, Gray. As soon as I got her settled at the boardinghouse, I came back. To talk to you. All of you."

"You should have talked to us first," Talon growled.

"Maybe I should have." Ranon turned enough to address Talon and still keep track of Gray. "But she was focused on getting out of this house. I did what the Queen needed, rather than what the court required." *Sweet Darkness, please let Talon understand the difference.*

"She's sick," Shira said, her voice oddly hollow. "She tried to hide it, but there's so much pain in her it's like a poison. She knew I could feel it. That's why she stopped coming to me for help. She didn't want anyone sensing that pain."

"As Steward, I must censure Prince Ranon for not informing the Master of the Guard that he was taking the Queen away from the protection of her escorts," Powell said quietly. "However, I also applaud the speed in which he acted on the Queen's behalf—and on the court's behalf. And I'm wondering if, despite the reason it came about, this might not be a good thing."

They all turned toward Powell.

"How so?" Talon asked.

Powell pulled on one earlobe. "From the day she formed her court, Cassidy has been hobbled by Theran's resistance to every attempt she has made to be a Queen to our people. He brought her here, so we have deferred to him, letting him dictate what she could and could not do. But I, for one, would like to see what Cassidy can do as our Queen without those hobbles."

*I'd like to see that too,* Ranon thought.

"So," Powell said. "Are we moving the Queen's residence to the board-inghouse? If that's the case, some work will need to be done to some of the rooms."

"Is that what we're talking about?" Archerr looked at Ranon. "A permanent move to a Shalador reserve?"

"I don't know," Ranon replied, feeling the need to tread carefully. "I just wanted to get her away from Kermilla and those Dharo bastards so Cassidy could rest without having that bitch in her face every time she turned around."

"Why haven't we booted Lady Kermilla out of Dena Nehele?" Shaddo asked.

"Or buried her," Spere said.

"Because she's a Queen from Kaeleer and a guest in this house," Talon said. "And despite the pain her presence causes Cassidy, Kermilla hasn't done anything to justify execution."

"However, Kermilla *was* involved in something that harmed Cassidy back in Dharo," Powell said. "Something that made her feel she was less of a Queen."

"The whip that drives Cassie," Gray said softly.

"Gray?" Ranon said just as softly. The blankness faded from Gray's eyes, replaced by a steely anger.

"When I went up to the Keep to talk to the High Lord, he said the whip that drives Cassie was shaped before she arrived in Dena Nehele—and left scars. That's why she drained herself too much and got hurt. She was trying to prove she could be a good Queen."

"I think we all have a good idea now whose hand held that whip," Talon said, his voice rumbling like icy gravel.

"All the more reason to keep Lady Cassidy away from this house while Theran's guest is in residence," Shira said.

Talon looked at Powell, who nodded.

"All right," Talon said. "We'll go to Eyota, and we'll go with the assumption we won't be coming back to Grayhaven, whether we stay in that village or not. And we have to move fast."

"Yes," Powell said. "It would be best if we depart before Theran realizes

Cassidy is gone. And it would be best not to leave any of the court's records behind."

A long beat of silence.

"What are you saying?" Ranon asked.

"That for a Queen who rules a small village in another Realm and is supposed to be a guest, Lady Kermilla is asking inappropriate questions about the tithes a Queen here could expect." Powell looked at Talon, whose mouth thinned to a grim line.

Watching the two men, Ranon wondered what else the Steward might be telling the Master of the Guard.

"We work the same way as if we needed to make a fast move from one camp to another," Talon said. "Grab your personal gear first. Make sure you take what you don't want to lose. That goes for all of you. Bardric, Cayle, and Radley, you're in charge of getting our horses and tack. Get them saddled and down to the gate. Use aural shields around their feet to keep the hooves silent."

"Done," Cayle said, looking at Bardric and Radley, who both nodded.

"Archerr. Spere. You'll give Shira a hand packing up the Healer's supplies." Talon looked at the Healer. "We can't take anything that belongs to this house, only what you've acquired on behalf of the court."

"Understood," Shira said, getting to her feet.

"Shaddo—"

"The honey pears," Gray said, breaking whatever Talon was about to say. "We aren't leaving the honey pears with *her*."

"We can't take them all, Gray," Ranon said.

A slashing look was Gray's only response.

"Shaddo, you give Gray a hand," Talon said. "The honey pear that was planted in the wish pot stays here. Gray, if you'd feel easier taking the other twelve, then bring them. Ranon, once you pack your gear, you'll give Powell a hand with the court papers."

"Yes, sir," Ranon said.

"Burne. Haele. You back up anyone who needs help. And keep watch. No reason to think the guests will be up this early, but I want the rest of you on your way before I inform Theran."

"You're going to tell him?" Powell asked.

"He's Cassidy's First Escort," Talon replied. "He needs to know where his Queen is residing. And there are a few other things Prince Grayhaven needs to know."

They all heard the threat under the words.

"Move," Talon said.

"A moment of your time, Talon," Powell said, rising.

"We'll talk while you start packing."

The men rose and slipped out of the room, warriors breaking camp.

Ranon waited, wanting a moment to talk to Shira, but she looked at Gray, who was lingering, and shook her head.

*Pack up my things along with yours,* she said.

*Is there anything private I shouldn't touch?* Ranon asked.

*Like personal supplies?*

She found it amusing that a warrior who didn't flinch when looking at the carnage of a battlefield got skittish around clean moontime supplies. He didn't find it amusing at all.

He winced. *I meant hourglass supplies.*

*No,* she replied, all amusement gone. *What is private I carry with me.*

He nodded as she left the room. Which left him alone with Gray.

"She was really leaving?" Gray asked, his eyes full of hurt bewilderment. "Without me?"

"She's confused, Gray." He couldn't think of any other way to say it, so he said it straight out. "She thought you were going to fall in love with Kermilla."

Gray's eyes widened. "Why would she think that? Did I do something?"

Ranon shook his head. "Theran's been making such an ass of himself, I guess Cassidy figured the rest of us were attracted to Kermilla too."

Gray shuddered. Ranon shared the feeling.

"Come on," Ranon said. "We've got to pack up and get out."

"Ranon?" Gray did a nervous shuffle from one foot to the other.

"What?"

"You didn't invite her to this meeting, so which one of us is going to tell Vae?"

"What's on your mind, Powell?" Talon asked as soon as they were alone in the Steward's office.

"Were you aware that Theran has been driving Kermilla all around town, introducing her to the aristo families here and . . ." Powell cleared his throat and suddenly got busy stacking account ledgers into neat piles before vanishing them.

"And . . . ?" Talon prodded. When Powell didn't answer, anger began to simmer under a reluctance to understand. "He's introduced *her* as the Queen?"

"Not directly," Powell said. "I believe he's introduced her as a Queen from Dharo and has not corrected people who made the wrong assumption."

"What kind of game is he playing?" *What kind of game did I allow him to play?* Cassidy's pain—and the fact that it ran so deep she'd been ready to run—was as much his fault as Theran's.

Powell sighed. Calling in some small slips of paper, he handed them to Talon. "Kermilla wanted to do some shopping. Theran ordered the merchants to open accounts for her since she hadn't brought sufficient marks with her to pay for extra expenses. So she said."

"Which means Theran will end up paying those bills from the treasure Lia hid for the family."

"No, Theran told the merchants all of Kermilla's expenses would be covered by the town's tithe to the Queen."

"*What?*"

"Kermilla spent more in a day than Cassidy spent in all the weeks she's been here." Powell paused. "The merchants wanted confirmation that they could deduct Kermilla's purchases from the tithe. I told them I would let them know as soon as I had a chance to discuss this with the Queen. The merchants who remained in Grayhaven are well aware of the dangers of dealing with a Queen. By not giving immediate confirmation, I've warned them to be wary of further transactions."

Talon prowled the room for several minutes while Powell packed up the maps he'd been gathering for Cassidy.

"We'll concede the town of Grayhaven," Talon said. "Theran can have fifty percent of the tithe to use as he pleases. The other half goes to the treasury to pay the guards' wages and maintain the town. I'll clear it with Cassidy, but I'll ask her to accept my decision and give up that much."

"In exchange for what?" Powell asked.

Talon shook his head. In exchange for nothing. At least, nothing he was willing to discuss with Powell.

He felt a respectful tap on his first inner barrier. "Ranon is on his way down. The boy cleared out his room fast."

"He wants to be gone." Powell rubbed his left hand. "So do I."

Talon sighed. "I raised Theran, taught him as best I could. Tried to hold on to the Old Ways even when I could feel them slipping away with each generation. I fought to keep him safe. I killed to keep him safe. You don't know how much it hurts to see him giving himself to Kermilla. I can't decide if protecting him from the twisted Queens all his life has made him blind to the kind of woman Kermilla is, or if he senses that something isn't right but is defending her because he can't admit he might be wrong about her. I can't decide—but tonight I'm wondering if men wasted their lives by defending the Grayhaven bloodline."

He shook his head and raised a hand, indicating he didn't want a response.

A moment later, Ranon walked into the room—and Talon walked out.

# CHAPTER 11

## TERREILLE

★Talon,★ Cayle said. ★We've got the horses loaded in the livestock Coach. Haele and Burne are at the station. Everyone else is gone.★

★Then go,★ Talon replied. ★I'm last man out.★

★See you in Eyota.★

★Yes, you will. May the Darkness embrace you.★

Standing outside the Grayhaven mansion, Talon watched the sun rise—and felt the light begin to drain the power from his demon-dead flesh. Smarter to stay here until sundown, but once he delivered his message, it would be best for all of them if he left. He'd need fresh human blood, not yarbarah, by the time he reached Eyota, but now he knew how to ask for it without feeling shame for what he was taking from the living.

He walked the hallways, delaying the moment when he would reach the family wing. Servants were already stirring. Dryden and Elle would be in the kitchen with Maydra, having a simple breakfast while the three reviewed the day's schedule. Birdie, who mostly looked after the rooms of the Queen, Steward, and Healer, gave him a sleepy smile as she passed him in a hallway. She was shy as a rabbit when she first came to work here a few weeks ago, but was getting braver because the Queen she served treated her with respect.

"Birdie," he called before she disappeared around a corner.

"Prince Talon?" She returned, looking uncertain since he'd never asked her for anything before.

He called in a half sheet of paper and the stub of a pencil, and wrote, "The Queen's residence has moved to Eyota, a village in the eastern Shalador reserve."

He folded the paper into quarters and handed it to her. "Give that to Dryden."

"Yes, sir." Birdie started to leave, then hesitated. "Sir? Do you think Maydra should make up a tray for Lady Cassidy? The Lady's stomach has been a mite tender, and maybe a peaceful breakfast would help."

A stab of guilt. The Warlords and Warlord Princes who had lived in the Tamanara Mountains had swept into villages to get supplies, visit friends and family, and hunt down the men who willingly served the Queens they viewed as enemies. Then they swept out again, back to their guarded camps in the mountains, leaving the villagers behind to endure the Queen's grace.

What would being at Kermilla's beck and call do to a girl like Birdie?

"Lady Cassidy won't need a tray this morning," he said. "Don't forget to give that to Dryden."

"No, sir. I'll do it right away."

He watched her go, a spring in her step. There was no spring in his. He needed to finish this task and get out.

When Theran answered the sharp rap on the bedroom door and blocked the view into his room, Talon wondered if there was someone with him—and who it might be.

"The Queen's court is no longer in residence," Talon said. "The Queen's court now resides in Eyota."

Theran's eyes remained sleepy and blank a moment too long. And that moment too long told Talon everything he needed to know about Theran's loyalty to Cassidy—and also confirmed another truth that had been hidden under his own strength and the Grayhaven name: Theran didn't have that subtle *something* that made a man a true leader.

Theran's face darkened with anger. "Why should we move there and inconvenience everyone?"

"Everyone being your guest?" Talon asked with a mildness that hid heartache and anger.

"Kermilla, yes, but the court as well. Why should we have to pack up just because Cassidy is acting like a spoiled child?"

Talon snarled. "Be careful what you say, boy. You're talking about the Queen."

"So you expect me to leave my family's home and go live in a Shalador reserve?" Theran snapped.

"You're not welcome there." He said the words because they were true.

Theran's eyes widened. He looked stunned, hurt.

"This is how it's going to be, Theran. Trust that I mean everything I say." No response but wariness. At least the boy had sense enough to be wary. "You will remain as First Escort so that the court remains intact. You promised to serve Cassidy for one year. That promise was witnessed by the most powerful men in all the Realms. But they aren't here. I am, and I will hold you to that promise. What you do the day after that contract is fulfilled is your own business, but you will do nothing to break this court. If you do, I will kill your whore."

"Kermilla is *not* a whore!"

"In exchange for keeping your oath of service, you will rule the town of Grayhaven on the Queen's behalf. All the tithes from the town will be your income to do with as you please. Half should go to the treasury, but no one is going to ask for an accounting of your expenses."

"Talon, you're making a mistake."

He heard a hint of panic in Theran's voice. Good. The boy was finally understanding that he no longer had the support that had always guarded his back.

"While she stands on Dena Nehele land, Kermilla will be confined to this town," Talon continued. "The Queen ordered Kermilla out of her Territory. You disregarded that command and made her your personal guest. The shame is on the rest of the First Circle, and especially me, that we let you do that. Because the fault is ours as well as yours, we will not raise a hand against Kermilla while she remains in Grayhaven. However, by sunrise tomorrow, every Warlord Prince in Dena Nehele will know she is considered an enemy of the Queen and tolerated only so long as she remains in the town under your rule. The moment she steps beyond that line, we will deal with her as we have dealt with every other enemy."

Theran looked shocked. "Kermilla is the Queen we should have had. She's the one who should have been here from the beginning, not Cassidy. I know you have to fulfill your contract with the court, and I respect that, but don't turn your back on the Queen you can serve next spring."

Sadness filled Talon. He'd faced this moment before with friends, but he had never felt this bitter. And now that he felt the bond that drove a Warlord Prince to serve a particular Queen, he finally understood why good men had served bad Queens—and had become twisted because of that service. He could only hope that the bond Theran felt broke before something in Theran did. "Kermilla is your Queen, isn't she? Something about her calls to you to cherish and protect."

"She's the right Queen for Dena Nehele. For all of us. If you'd just take the time to get to know her . . ."

"She's not my Queen, Theran," he said quietly. "She never will be. I look at her and see same kind of Queen I fought against for three centuries. Nothing is going to change that, boy. We're standing on opposite sides of a line now. I'm sorry for that, but that's the way it is."

"You'll regret this," Theran said urgently. "A year from now, Kermilla will be the Queen of Dena Nehele, and she may not forgive you for treating her this way."

"That may be. If she does take control of Dena Nehele . . ." Talon shrugged. "I've spent most of my life as a rogue in the Tamanara Mountains. If it comes to that, I'll finish my life the same way."

"You don't mean that. You *can't* mean that."

"I mean every word. Don't tell yourself otherwise."

They stood in a doorway, both feeling something break between them that would never truly mend.

"May the Darkness embrace you, Theran." He hesitated, then felt he had to say one last thing, try one last time. "I've taught you what I could about honor, about the Invisible Ring. The day may come when you have to make a choice, so I want you to remember this: it is better to break your own heart than to break your honor."

"When did you ever make that choice?" Theran asked bitterly.

*Right here. Right now.*

Talon walked away from one of the boys he loved, walked out of the mansion, and headed for the landing web beyond the gate. The sun's fist beat on him with every step until he caught the Sapphire Wind and rode it through the Darkness, heading for Eyota.

Part of him wanted Theran to come after him. Part of him hoped the boy would stay away until he was free of Kermilla.

And part of him had the sick feeling that Theran would use the Grayhaven name to justify breaking all of their trust.

Theran stood on the terrace, staring at the single remaining honey pear seedling. Gray had watered it, had given it that last bit of care before taking the other twelve.

Gray *left*. Even more than Talon, Gray's misguided loyalty to Cassidy hurt. Hell's fire, it hurt. Ranon? He didn't give a damn if he ever saw the man again, but if Ranon was gone that meant Shira was gone—and he needed to find someone else to act as Kermilla's personal Healer.

Probably for the best. He wasn't sure he would trust Kermilla's well-being to a Healer who was also a Black Widow.

"Oh, *la*. There you are." Kermilla slipped her arm through his and gave him a sunny smile. "Why the sour face?"

"Gray took the honey pears."

Her forehead wrinkled as she looked at the marks on the terrace where the other pots had been. "Just as well. That was such a hodgepodge of pots it was very unattractive."

"Those honey pears are a legacy, Kermilla. Their existence means a great deal to the Dena Nehele people."

"Oh," she said contritely. "I didn't realize."

Why didn't she realize? He had told her the story of how those pears were found after being buried for centuries. Of course, a guest would listen to the story as a *story*—entertaining, but not important. But a Queen preparing to rule a Territory with a past like Dena Nehele's needed to understand the significance of those seedlings.

Just because Cassidy probably would have understood the significance didn't make her a better Queen. She was older and liked to grub around in the dirt. Kermilla, being younger, just needed more guidance in some areas.

"Kermilla, would you have breakfast with me in private?" He'd tell her about the honey pears again—and about Cassidy's rude departure.

"Oh, *la*." She gave him a delighted smile. "You are being so *naughty*. My Consort will be jealous."

"It's not like that."

Her expression immediately turned woeful. "Oh. I thought . . ."

Was she hinting that she'd like to have him as her lover? He was willing. *More* than willing. Even if he had to dance around the damn Consort's presence.

"There are some things I need to tell you," he said. "And there are some possibilities we need to discuss."

No, he wouldn't break Cassidy's court and risk Talon going after Kermilla. But he would make the best use of the time to prepare the ground for the *right* Queen.

A wet swipe across her cheek. A slurp across her closed eyes.

"Aarhhh. Uuhhh."

*Cassie? Cassie! Gray says you must wake up so you can go to sleep.* A pause. *That is confusing, so it must be a human thing.*

"Wha . . . ?"

*Wake up!*

"Vae?" Cassidy grunted. Groaned. "Gray?"

"Here."

A warm hand covered hers.

She smacked her lips—and made a face. "Hell's fire. Did I swallow a cat? *Vae*." That because a Sceltie nose almost poked inside her mouth.

*I do not smell cat.*

"Why do you ask, Cassie?" Gray asked.

Bastard sounded like he was laughing at her. "My tongue feels fuzzy."

"How many cups of that brew did you give her?"

Ranon's voice.

"Enough to soothe a heart," Yairen said.

"How are you feeling?" Shira asked. "Do you want anything?"

Since no one else answered, Cassidy decided the questions had been directed at her. "Toast. Scrambled eggs. Bath." And something to scrape the fuzz off her tongue. "Who is here?" *And where is here?* Oh. Yes. Boardinghouse. She had meant to go to Dharo but had ended up here because Ranon took her trunks. The prick.

"Almost the whole First Circle," Gray answered, sounding tense.

"Oh," Cassidy said. Then her eyes popped open and she jackknifed to a sitting position. "The *court* is here?"

"Mostly," Gray said. "Talon hasn't arrived yet."

"Your bedroom is ready," Shira said. "What you need now is more sleep. After your bath, toast, and scrambled eggs."

"I can . . ." What? She was pretty sure she wasn't hungover, but she wasn't feeling smart either. "I can stay here."

*You are in the way,* Vae said. *But we are not supposed to tell you that because you are the Queen.*

"Come on, darling," Gray said, snorting in the effort not to laugh out loud. "Let's get you up to bed."

"I can—"

Gray hauled her to her feet. She felt a lot more tipsy now that she was standing up, so she didn't protest when Gray wrapped an arm around her waist and steered her toward the hallway and the stairs.

"Ranon, give me a hand," Gray said when they reached the stairs.

"If he puts his hands on my ass and pushes, I'll punch him," Cassidy said.

"That's not much of a threat when you can't keep your eyes open long enough to see him," Gray said.

"I can . . ."

"*Cassie.*"

*That* tone of voice coming from Gray woke her up.

Something in those green eyes. Something that warned her this was one of those times a smart woman yielded to male sensibilities.

"Are you going to swear at me?" she asked.

A slow smile, male and satisfied, because the question told him he had won. "I'm thinking about it."

So she had a bath. She had toast and scrambled eggs. And she asked one question.

"Is there anything I need to know about today?"

Shira pulled back the covers on the bed. "Not today."

She got into bed and let the world slip away for a few more hours.


"I took the liberty of composing a note on the Queen's behalf, and asked Spere to deliver it to the Keep," Powell said.

Ranon frowned. "Why alert them that there's trouble?"

"To avoid the potential for more trouble. And to prevent the messenger coming from Kaeleer from delivering Cassidy's correspondence at Grayhaven. They're going to know sooner or later. I thought it better to make the move sound matter-of-fact."

Ranon glanced at the clock on the mantel. Where in the name of Hell was Talon? Yes, he was the last man out, but riding the Sapphire Wind, he should have arrived right behind them.

Janos tapped on the door of the room Powell was using as a temporary office until they worked out the logistics of having a court take up long-term residence in a building that wasn't meant to hold a court.

"A messenger arrived with this," he said, holding out a wax-sealed note to Ranon. "It's for you."

He broke the seal. Simple message. " 'Gone to ground,' " he read. " 'Will join you this evening. Talon.' "

"A prudent decision," Powell said.

Ranon placed a hand on Powell's shoulder and smiled. "So was sending that message to the Keep."

They had a good court. They had a good Queen.

Now they needed to do whatever it took to keep both.

## EBON ASKAVI

"What do you make of this?" Daemon asked, handing the paper to his father.

Saetan called in the half-moon glasses and read the message. Twice.

"It's very carefully worded," Saetan said. "Too carefully worded."

He had the same impression. "First time we've received a message from Cassidy's Steward. Do you think there's trouble?"

"Almost certainly. And just as certainly, they don't want us asking questions right now about why the Queen has suddenly changed her residence from a mansion in Dena Nehele's capital to a boardinghouse in a small village located in a Shalador reserve."

Daemon frowned as he stared at the note. The report Cassidy had sent after her return from Eyota had been too brief for his liking, but he'd sensed nothing from her words that couldn't be explained by simple fatigue. Now . . .

"Has she gone back to Eyota to fix a problem, or has she left Grayhaven to get away from one?"

Handing the message back to Daemon, Saetan removed his glasses and vanished them. "Let's see what Cassidy says in her next report. What she doesn't say about this move will be as revealing as what she does say."

Daemon vanished the paper. "I'll ask my second-in-command to deliver the next batch of letters to Cassidy."

"Who?"

He smiled dryly. "Surreal. She's decided she's going to work for me."

"Doing what?"

"As far as I can figure out, whatever she damn well pleases. She hasn't told me exactly what I'm paying her for this privilege, only that I'm going to be outrageously generous. I can send her and Rainier to Eyota. Between them, they'll find out everything we need to know."

"Speaking of everything we need to know, I understand Jaenelle and Ladvarian went to Scelt to talk to Morghann and Khary. Do you have any idea why?"

"No," Daemon said, "and I'm not asking."

Saetan smiled. "My darling, you're not only becoming a wise man, you're becoming a smart husband."

# CHAPTER 12
## TERREILLE

The evening after their return to Eyota, Cassidy drank the restorative brew Shira had made for her and listened to the men argue, discuss, and sometimes snarl as they tried to figure out how to shoehorn a court into the boardinghouse. And that wouldn't do at all. It would be like having too many guests crammed into her mother's house at Winsol—fine for a few days when everyone was feeling cheerful and accommodating, but not something she would want to live with permanently.

Which meant drawing a line and refusing to let them shift it.

"Gentlemen," she said quietly.

Gray was the first to focus his attention on her; Ranon was a close second, followed by Talon and Powell, which forced the others to swallow their opinions so they could hear what she had to say.

"A court is formed when twelve males make the commitment to serve a Queen and offer her their strength, their skills, and their loyalty. There is nothing in any book of Protocol that says they have to live with her. In Kaeleer, most Queens who rule a District—which is anything from one to a handful of villages—don't live in a home large enough to accommodate the whole court." She smiled at them.

Twelve men frowned at her. So did Shira—and Reyhana, who had returned to Eyota to be of service to the Queen of Dena Nehele.

"Ranon, do the Shalador Queens live in houses large enough to accommodate their whole First Circle?" Cassidy asked, hoping he'd give her the answer that would help make her point.

"There are no official courts in the Shalador reserves," Ranon said. "The Queens merely help the elders keep the people under control so they will not offend the Province Queens or Territory Queen." Then he stopped, and his expression revealed a man torn between loyalties.

"What you mean is, in order to protect the Queens and the men who were loyal to them, the Shalador Queens have no official-*looking* courts that might have been viewed as a challenge," Cassidy said gently. "A Queen who can't form an official court has no more power than any other witch because the court is the instrument by which she rules."

Ranon said nothing. It was one thing for him to deny the truth about the Shalador courts once. That was an instinctive effort to protect his people, and probably something he'd been doing since he was a boy. But denying it twice would mean lying to her and that would be a break in trust.

"I have met the Shalador Queens, Ranon," Cassidy said, "and I'm sure their courts are *very* official. But not obvious to an outsider who expects a Queen to have a big house and lots of frills and ruffles."

*Which is Ranon?* Shira asked. *A frill or a ruffle?*

Cassidy couldn't hold back the quick burst of laughter that had all the men looking from her to Shira and back again.

Shira kept her head down and her hands folded in her lap. She would have looked demure if she could have stopped smiling.

"The point, gentlemen," Cassidy said, not daring to look at any of them yet, "is that this court's living accommodations should follow the arrangements that are typical for a Queen living in a small village."

"You don't rule a small village, Cassidy," Powell said respectfully. "You rule the Territory of Dena Nehele."

"Morghann is the Queen of Scelt—a Territory in Kaeleer. She lives in a small village not much bigger than this one. The only member of her First Circle who lives with her is Khardeen, the Warlord of Maghre. And the only reason he lives there is because he's her husband as well as her Consort. Their house is divided between family and court. There are offices for her and the Steward, a smaller office for the Master of the Guard, a large meeting room, and a room where the First Circle can gather to relax, plan, or do whatever is needed. There is a large dining room that can accommodate the whole First Circle for a meal—or be used for social functions. The rest of the house belongs to the Queen and her family."

"Then where does everyone else live?" Gray asked.

"In the village," Cassidy replied. "And that's what I'm proposing we do here."

"It's not safe." Half the Circle growled that opinion—including Ranon.

"This is what I had in mind." Cassidy raised her voice in order to be heard above the growls and mutters. "Talon and Powell will reside here with me. So will Gray, Shira, Ranon, and Reyhana since a young Queen training in a court requires a chaperon, and that is one of the duties of the First Circle. There are several cottages on this street and nearby streets that look abandoned, and they're all close enough to the stable we're using for the horses. If the village elders have no objections, the rest of the men can take up residence in those cottages."

"In Kaeleer, why don't those men want to stay close to their Queen?" Gray asked.

"Most of them have families," Cassidy replied. "For the First Circle, their work is the court. They're paid from the tithes. They have families. They have expenses. They have a life just like everyone else in the village." She looked around the table. "You've never seen this, have you?"

Talon didn't respond, but the rest of them shook their heads.

"Ranon, you must have seen this in the Shalador villages where the Queens lived."

"I can't say," he replied. "The Queens' safety depended on the rest of us not asking too many questions."

"A Queen is entitled to a private life too," Shira said.

Suddenly no one was looking at Cassidy—or Gray.

Powell cleared his throat. "Well, if such living accommodations are customary in Kaeleer, we can . . ."

"I have a wife," Shaddo said suddenly. He stared hard at the surface of the table. "I have two sons. There's no formal marriage contract. We couldn't risk it."

"Risk it?" Cassidy asked.

"The other Queens used to hold a wife or child hostage to try to force a Warlord Prince to surrender and subject himself to being controlled by a Ring of Obedience," Talon said grimly. "Half the time, if the man gave in, the woman or child was killed anyway."

"Mother Night," Cassidy whispered. No wonder these men had been so wary of her.

"My oldest son will have his Birthright Ceremony this autumn," Shaddo said. "Soli wasn't going to acknowledge the paternal bloodline."

"But your son would be considered a bastard," Gray said. "He'd have no social standing."

"But he'd be alive," Shaddo said.

"Where are they?" Talon asked.

"A village close to the western border. A little north of the western reserve, actually," Shaddo replied.

Cassidy swallowed tears, and her voice was huskier than usual because of them. "Shaddo, your wife should not be without her husband, and your sons should not be without their father. Unless the village elders have some objection, there is no reason why they can't be here with you."

Twelve men studied her, and she knew they heard the tears she couldn't quite hide.

"The elders won't object," Ranon said. "But this *is* one of the reserves. I doubt we can offer the kind of life they're used to."

"Any of those cottages is better than what they're living in now," Shaddo said.

"I have a sister," Archerr said. "She has three children, two boys and a girl. Their village was burned during the landen uprisings. They survived because they weren't home that day. They'd been out picking berries, and when they saw the smoke, they hid. She's doing the best she can, but she needs some help to make a new start for herself and the children."

*And neither of you mentioned these women and children in the weeks since the court was formed?* Cassidy wanted to rail at them for not speaking sooner. She couldn't because she knew exactly what Lucivar and her cousin Aaron would say: defend and protect. For Shaddo and Archerr, the best way to protect the people they loved was *not* to bring them to her attention.

Until now.

"Shaddo, if you want, take one of your Brothers in the court to help you get your family packed and moved here. While you're in the west, you can deliver messages to any of the Queens you can contact. Powell and I had sent messages about using the Queen's Gift to help the land. The Ladies should be told where they can find me if they need instructions. That goes for you, too, Archerr. Powell, you'll be responsible for converting the rooms the court needs for offices and gatherings."

Cassidy took a deep breath and let it out in a sigh. Now the fight began. "The rest of you will assist me."

"To do what?" Gray asked, narrowing his eyes.

He was getting too damn good at sensing when she was about to throw water on a bag of cats, as her father would say.

"This is the growing season," Cassidy said. "The land is in desperate need of help. The Queens need to do something to increase the harvest, and they need to do it *now*."

"No," Gray said.

"Gray—"

"*No!*"

His voice thundered in the room as he leaped to his feet, knocking the chair over.

Cassidy pushed away from the table and rose. Since he'd been sitting on her left, there was nothing but the corner of the table between them. So all they needed to do was lean forward a little to be nose to nose.

"Yes," she said.

"Doing that almost destroyed you, Cassie."

"I was careless. I won't make that mistake again. But it is *vital* to take care of the land and to do it now. Gray, you *know* it's vital. What the Queens can do will make a difference for everyone in Dena Nehele. And this is a ritual. This is part of the Old Ways you all said you wanted to learn."

"Not at the risk of you getting hurt again!" Gray snapped.

"I'm with Gray," Ranon said, starting to get to his feet.

"You sit down!" Cassidy pointed at him.

Ranon froze. Then he looked at Talon for instructions, which really pissed her off.

"Sit down, Ranon!" she yelled. "You too!" She gave Gray a push. It wasn't much of a push, but the look on his face had Ranon reaching across Shira to clamp a hand on Gray's arm.

"Hell's fire," said a voice full of biting laughter, "this sounds just like home."

The men whipped around to face the doorway. Shira had a look in her eyes that made Cassidy wonder if the woman was preparing to use some of the Black Widows' Craft. Reyhana looked fearful.

*Strap some steel to your spine.* Cassidy turned and stared at the black-haired woman who had delicately pointed ears and the handsome man who leaned on a cane.

Mother Night, what was Surreal doing here?

"Doesn't it sound like home, Rainier?" Surreal asked her companion.

"It does," he replied. "Although these two are clearly still novices. When Jaenelle and Lucivar used to go at it, they could make the glass in the windows shake—until their father had enough of listening to them and roared them into silence."

"Yes, Uncle Saetan is very impressive when he lets his temper slip the leash," Surreal said.

"Lady Surreal," Cassidy said, hoping no one had been foolish enough to stand in Surreal's way when she came through the house. "What brings you here?"

Surreal called in a stack of envelopes and held them up. "I'm delivering your letters. And I'm here to have a little chat."

"Why don't you and the Ladies go into the parlor for your chat while I stay here and answer the gentlemen's questions?" Rainier said.

"There aren't any questions," Gray snarled. "Cassie is *not* doing this."

"Not now, Gray," Cassidy said. Then to Surreal, "Thank you for bringing the letters, but there is nothing for us to chat about. This is Terreille, not Kaeleer, and I don't have to discuss anything with you."

"Trust me, sugar, you don't want to be summoned to the Keep to explain whatever this is to Sadi. Or Yaslana. Or the High Lord. Because I don't think they're going to be as flexible as I'm willing to be. Comes from them having cocks."

"I beg your pardon," Rainier said.

"You've got a cock too, so beg all you want," Surreal said. *Sugar, do this with grace because you don't have a choice. You either talk to me here or you talk to Sadi.*

Since Cassidy doubted Daemon Sadi would like what he heard, she also doubted he would stand aside after that "chat" and let her return to Dena Nehele.

Surreal was right. Talking to another witch was a much better choice.

"Ladies, let's adjourn to the parlor and leave the men to their own discussion," Cassidy said. She walked past Surreal and Rainier, then waited for Shira and Reyhana.

As Surreal closed the door, she heard Rainier say, "So what is it that Lady Cassidy isn't going to do?"

# CHAPTER 13
## KAELEER

Daemon settled in the chair behind the blackwood desk, crossed his legs, steepled his fingers, and tried to decide if his second and his secretary, who were *finally* coming to report, deserved a verbal ripping or if he should hold his tongue and his temper.

Surreal gave him a smile that dared him to say anything. Rainier gave him a panicky *don't expect me to control her* look.

"My darlings," he said with a mildness that would frighten any intelligent person—excluding females. "Breakfast is served here at the Hall every day. You didn't have to bypass the family seat last night and go all the way to Amdarh to get a meal this morning."

It wasn't that he minded them going on to Amdarh instead of coming to the Hall, even though that would have been more sensible since the Hall was closer to the Keep and its Gate. What pissed him off was that neither of them had sent a message last night to let him know they were safely back in Kaeleer. No, it was Helton who'd had sense enough to send a message to Beale early this morning.

"I wanted some time to think before coming here—and I chose to do my thinking in the family's town house in Amdarh," Surreal said with equal mildness.

She'd had plenty of time to think on the journey back from Dena Nehele, so she'd probably wanted a little more time to consider what she was—and wasn't—going to say.

Daemon raised one eyebrow and waited.

"Why don't you go first?" Surreal said to Rainier.

Rainier gave her a long look, then shrugged. "Our arrival interrupted a full-volume discussion between Cassidy and a Warlord Prince named Gray."

"So he's reached that stage, has he?" Daemon asked dryly.

"You were expecting this?" Rainier hesitated. "Gray is . . . different."

"He was held captive by a Queen and tortured for two years," Daemon said. "He was fifteen when he was taken."

Rainier nodded. "That explains the schism. I felt like I was listening to an adolescent who was still innocent enough to blurt out every thought and complaint, but it was a Warlord Prince around my own age who was absorbing the answers."

"That's about right."

Rainier shifted in his chair. "Anyway, there were twelve men around that table, and every one of them resented me asking questions about *their* Queen and *their* court."

"They resented me too," Surreal said.

"No," Rainier said, "they were afraid of *you*. Me they would have buried without hesitation if they thought they would survive the retaliation."

"Which they wouldn't," Surreal said.

"Something is going on, and no one wants to talk about what that something is," Rainier said. "However, Gray was more than willing to complain about Cassidy wanting to use the Queen's Gift of having a connection to the land to boost the potential harvest—and also teach the other Queens how to do the same thing. They all sat there with their mouths hanging open when I said Cassidy and the other Queens had left it a bit late since all the Queens in Kaeleer had done this in the spring. I told them how it's usually part of the spring planting festival most villages have and there's usually music and dancing in the evening—a bit of fun before people settled in to the summer work. And I mentioned that Queens habitually drain a little of their power into the land before their moontime because it makes

them more comfortable physically. They didn't know about that either—
and considering how many of those men blushed when I said the word
'moontime,' I have the feeling not many of them have had much experience
living with women for more than a few days."

"Most of Cassie's court are rogues as well as warriors," Daemon said.
"So you're probably right that this is all much newer ground than any of us
realized."

"They also didn't know about the tradition of fussing," Rainier said.
"So I took the liberty of explaining it—especially as it applies to a Queen
and her court."

Daemon laughed. Oh, Cassie was going to have some comments about
*that* in her next report. Then his humor faded as he looked at Surreal.

She shrugged. "Stone in a pond. Cassidy seems frustrated by how little
she's done in the weeks she's been in Dena Nehele. My sense is she's done
enough already to send ripples through the whole Territory—including
taking a young Shalador Queen into the court for training. I met the girl
the last time I was in Eyota. With the right hand to guide her, Reyhana will
be a strong, impressive ruler in a few years. She didn't say a word while
Cassidy and Shira talked, but she listened fiercely—and I had the impression she was hearing some of the same things that weren't being said that I
was. And didn't like them any better." She paused, then added, "Theran
Grayhaven wasn't in residence, by the way."

"Oh?" Daemon said, watching her carefully. Those gold-green eyes
held the ruthless chill of a first-rate assassin.

"Does the name Kermilla mean anything to you?" Surreal asked.

"No. Should it?"

Surreal shrugged. "This is what I was told. A Lady Kermilla arrived at
Grayhaven to have an audience with the Queen. Audience was granted,
and Kermilla's request was denied. Instead of leaving as she should have,
Kermilla has become Theran Grayhaven's 'personal guest,' over Cassidy's
objections. So Queen and court removed themselves from the Grayhaven
mansion and have taken up residence in Eyota, where Cassidy is determined to do some good for these people during her year in Dena
Nehele."

"I hope she's not set on leaving at the end of that year," Rainier said, "because *my* impression is that, however this started, her court is no longer thinking of her presence in Dena Nehele as temporary or as just a year to train someone else. They're starting to dig in, and they'll challenge anyone who tries to take her away from them. And that, Prince Sadi, includes you."

*Good,* Daemon thought. "So Cassidy relocated her court because of Theran's lover? I'm assuming 'personal guest' equals lover."

"I don't know that it does," Surreal replied. "But she must mean something if Theran chose her over the Queen he swore to serve." She leaned forward. "Kermilla is the key to this break between Cassidy and Theran because everyone was being very careful not to tell me where Kermilla came from or her caste. You don't know her. Maybe Jaenelle does. You should ask her."

*Why don't you?* He knew the answer to that. As strong as she was, as powerful as she was, and as fierce as she was, Surreal did not want to be the one who asked Jaenelle Angelline that question.

He waited until the midday meal. Surreal and Rainier had . . . fled, to be accurate, leaving him to ask what seemed a simple question.

"Do you know Lady Kermilla?" he asked as he cut into his beef.

"Why do you ask?"

Her voice—that midnight, sepulchral, lightning-filled voice—ripped icy claws down his spine.

And not just his spine, Daemon thought as he put down his knife and fork. There were ice crystals on his food, and the water in the glass was frozen solid. And when he looked up, the sapphire eyes staring at him were filled with cold rage.

Mother Night.

"I asked a simple question, Lady," he said, keeping his own voice quiet and respectful.

"She is someone who will never be a guest in this house if you want me to continue living here," Witch replied.

Had Surreal guessed this would be Jaenelle's reaction? A little more warning would have been appreciated.

"Hell's fire, Jaenelle, who *is* she?"

"She's the Queen who took Cassie's court."

"Then . . ." Oh, shit.

"Why are you asking about Kermilla, Prince?"

The look in her eyes and the lethal purr in her voice made him put a double Black shield around himself before he said, "She's in Dena Nehele, staying at the Grayhaven estate."

Daemon removed his shoes and socks. He checked one foot, then the other. He didn't respond to the knock on his study door, but the door opened anyway. Jaenelle walked in, carrying a large tray.

"What are you doing?" she asked, sounding contrite.

"Counting my toes."

A pause. "They're all there, aren't they?"

"Yes." Thank the Darkness.

She set the tray down on the low table in front of the sofa, then sat close to him. But not next to him.

"I'm sorry," she said. "I don't usually lose my temper like that."

No, she didn't. Her response was so fast and so fierce . . . Well, even a Black-Jeweled Warlord Prince can have the shit scared out of him— especially when one moment he was sitting at a large blackwood dining table and the next he was surrounded by a table, chairs, dishes, silverware, glasses, and food that had all been reduced to a pile of uniform pieces no bigger than grains of rice.

It wasn't the table exploding that upset him. It was the uniformity of the debris that was proof of the depth of her rage. And that rage, and whatever blend of power she had been channeling through Twilight's Dawn at that moment, had been strong enough to crack his outermost Black shield.

That was something he needed to talk to Lucivar about. *Soon.*

"You were wrapped in a double Black shield," Jaenelle said. "I didn't think you would get hurt."

"That's not the point." Now that he'd gotten over the shock of it, her slash of temper was starting to piss him off. But he leashed that because there had to be a reason for this. Jaenelle didn't explode like that as some kind of twisted entertainment. And the strength of her reaction got him thinking.

He rubbed his forehead to ease the headache building behind his eyes, then shifted and turned so he was close to her.

"Queens lose men or courts to rivals all the time. And even though Cassidy is a friend and losing her court did leave her bruised, that doesn't equal your rage. If Cassidy doesn't have enough spine to tell Kermilla to take a piss in the wind, then she'd better acquire some. From everything Surreal and Rainier told me, her court is becoming a solid team committed to their Queen."

"All of them?" Jaenelle asked softly.

"Except Theran Grayhaven." He brushed fingertips over her shoulder. "Jaenelle, what aren't you telling me?"

Those sapphire eyes studied him. "There is nothing you can do about this. Neither of us have any right to interfere in this. Is that understood?"

Oh, he didn't like the sound of that. "Maybe."

"I spun a tangled web after Cassidy discovered the treasure in the Grayhaven attics. I wasn't going to share what I saw with anyone, but I owe you that as an explanation for how I reacted."

Sweet Darkness. A tangled web. Dreams and visions.

"All right."

"Dena Nehele is going to fall."

He closed his eyes. Why now, when they had survived everything Dorothea SaDiablo had done to them? "Because Kermilla went there?"

"More because Kermilla is still there."

"I can bury the bitch," he said too softly, opening his eyes to stare into hers. "I'll go to Terreille, no matter the price, and bury the bitch if that's what you want. Or I'll let Surreal go. She'd be willing."

"No." Her fingers brushed through his hair, soothing. "It's up to them now. Their decisions. Their choices. Sorrow and joy, Daemon. There is sorrow and joy in what I saw."

*How can there be joy?* But he trusted her, and if she said there could be joy in Dena Nehele's fall, he would believe her.

"So there is nothing we can do for them," he said, making it a statement rather than a question.

"We can't interfere with another Queen's Territory. That would violate Blood law and our code of honor. But that doesn't mean there is nothing we can do. In fact, I've already helped make arrangements for a couple of things."

"How is that different from interfering?"

"In the first instance, I gave only the help requested by someone living in Dena Nehele. In the second, I'm simply making available something I think Cassie and her court will find useful. What they do with the material is up to them."

"That sounds intriguing." He looked at the food on the tray. "Why don't we eat the soup while it's hot, and you can tell me all about it?"

# CHAPTER 14

## TERREILLE

"Prince Theran," Dryden said. "There are some Ladies here to see the Queen."

Theran tried to relax his jaw. He'd spent the morning gritting his teeth as he waded through all the crap the Steward should be doing. He was going to have to hire someone to deal with the paperwork—and complaints—until he could get a new court established. Of course, hiring someone meant paying wages, and he still had to figure out how much income he would get from the tithe and what part of that was already committed to paying the guards who protected the town and its citizens. Now that Cassidy was no longer in residence, he also had to figure out if the servants could be paid out of the tithe or if he'd have to pay their wages out of the Grayhaven inheritance.

"What Ladies?" he growled. "Why are they here to see Kermilla?"

"They are Queens. They do not wish to offer their names or where they live, and as a courtesy to them, I did not press for that information. They said they received a letter from Lady Cassidy about some Craft the Queens can do to help increase the harvest. She offered to teach them."

Hell's fire. "Well, tell them . . ."

An opportunity. A chance for the other Queens to meet Kermilla—and a chance for Kermilla to show the Queens and, through them, the Warlord Princes that she had as much, if not more, to offer the people of Dena Nehele as Cassidy.

"Tell them Lady Kermilla and I will join them shortly." Theran pushed away from the desk and the nagging paperwork.

He found Kermilla in the parlor, playing cards with Jhorma and two of the escorts.

"Oh, la. You must be cheating, Jhorma," Kermilla said, throwing down her cards.

"I'm not cheating," Jhorma replied with tight courtesy.

"You must be! I haven't won anything in the last six hands!"

After playing cards with them a couple of times, Theran realized Jhorma cheated in order to ensure she *did* win a few hands. The man must not be in an accommodating mood today.

"Kermilla, I need your help for an hour or so," Theran said, glad he could offer an interruption. A display of bad temper was exactly what they didn't need with other Queens in the mansion.

"I might as well help you," Kermilla said, leaving the table. "Jhorma isn't being *any* fun."

*Good,* Theran thought. He wasn't sure how to approach a Queen to find out if she wanted to have sex, but if her Consort wasn't entertaining her sufficiently, Kermilla might be receptive to another man's interest.

She slipped her arm through his as he led her from the room. "Are we going to a party or one of those quaint outdoor concerts?" Her laugh tinkled through the hallway. "I don't mean to make fun but, *la,* the musicians aren't very good."

He tried not to wince. There wasn't much in the town that could entertain a vivacious young woman who was used to finer amusements. Since Cassidy had been so keen to attend one of the outdoor concerts, he'd figured Kermilla would enjoy going to one.

That evening only emphasized the differences between the two women. Kermilla might be younger, but she was far more aristo and sophisticated. Which made it difficult when the town, and the remaining aristo families, had so little to offer.

"No, this is something else," Theran said. "Some Queens have arrived to learn that Queen's Craft of using power to enrich the land."

Kermilla rolled her eyes. "Oh. *That.* Every Queen knows how to do that."

"No, they don't. The Queens here have forgotten. They need someone to lead them, to teach them."

She gave him a sexy pout that always made him wonder what her mouth would taste like, but there wasn't time for distractions.

"Cassidy offered to show them," Theran said.

"Then let Cassidy show them," Kermilla snapped. "She always liked digging in the dirt."

Theran hesitated. He couldn't make promises, couldn't give her assurances yet, but he *could* hint strongly enough that she wouldn't mistake his meaning. Not after the other hints he'd given her.

"A Territory Queen needs to be a strong leader, needs to teach the skills that will benefit the people." He stopped walking and looked at her intently so she would understand this was important. "When Cassidy's contract ends next spring, the Warlord Princes will need to select another Queen to rule Dena Nehele. They'll take the opinions and preferences of the Queens who are here today into account."

He waited.

Several seconds later, her eyes widened. "Oh. I *see*. Well then, since Cassidy isn't here to perform her duties, I will be happy to assist you, Theran. It would be a shame if my Sisters made a journey here for nothing."

He smiled, relieved. "Exactly."


*Surreal took his face between her hands and smiled. "You have a penis, and it makes you strange. Try not to be an ass on top of it."*

"I'm *not* an ass," Gray muttered as he watched Cassidy explain to another group of Queens the different ways of using their power to enhance the crops in a field.

"Are you still snarling about that?" Ranon asked, also keeping close watch.

"You'd be snarling too if she'd said it to you."

"Probably," Ranon replied, smiling. Then he sighed. Gray heard so much relief in that sound.

"Last one," Gray said. "Then we can go home."

They had fought it out for hours after Surreal and Rainier left. Powell had tried to keep things courteous, but it felt like yelling was the only way to bridge the gap between what Cassie wanted to do and what the court was willing to let her do.

In the end, neither side was happy, but the compromise was something they could all live with.

Thirty villages in five days, spread over the three Shalador reserves and the two southernmost Provinces. Fifteen Blood and fifteen landen. Cassie had insisted that the landens be included. *Every* man had been opposed to *that*—until Vae nipped Ranon in the ass. So Cassie, backed by Vae's teeth, had won that part of the argument.

Gray hadn't fought in the landen uprising. Hadn't seen the bodies in the burned villages. Hadn't found what was left of people he'd loved. But he understood why the other men had argued. It had been hard for the Warlord Princes especially to watch Cassie open a vein and fill that small offering cup to benefit landens.

But after the first landen village, they all understood why she had fought to do this. The landens were hostile and wary—and sure that a Queen's presence meant pain. Mother Night, the looks on their faces when they realized Cassie and the Queens who came with her were doing something that would benefit their village and increase their crops so they could pay the tithe and still feed their children through the coming winter.

"You can't erase generations of suffering and two years of war in a couple of hours," Ranon said quietly. "But, sweet Darkness, Gray, the people in this village won't look at the Blood the same way the next time we ride in."

Because of the Queen with hazel eyes and sunset hair.

The Queens walked the field, dipping into the barrels of water that floated behind them and sprinkling the ground with water enhanced with their blood and power. First and last plant in each row got a dipper full of water. Gray could already see a difference in the first rows that had been given the Queens' touch.

A gift. A part of what it meant to be a Queen. The ritual cup of blood made the water richer and nourished the land faster, but power alone could be released into the water or directly into the land. The results weren't as dramatic, but it was less physically demanding for the Queen and something they could do often without endangering themselves.

Learning about that option had almost started another quarrel between him and Cassie over her first careless release of power. Probably just as well that Surreal and Rainier had already gone home before he found out about it.

"I'm glad there's a way the Queens can use their gift without spilling their own blood," Gray said.

"Shira is pleased about that too," Ranon replied. "She wasn't happy about Cassidy opening a vein every time to siphon some power into the land. The men who serve can accept blood being given once a year in a ceremony when the rest of the time it's just the Ladies releasing a bit of power into the land or water." He paused. "Even using restraint and letting other Queens demonstrate, Cassidy has drained herself more than she should have."

"Well, she's going to go home and *rest* for a day," Gray said, feeling his temper sharpen at the thought of her collapsing again.

Ranon snorted. "Good luck getting her to do that."

Gray closed his eyes and began counting. "Her moontime is coming. She *has* to rest during those first three days. It's a *rule*."

He could feel Ranon watching him.

"And that fussing thing," he said, opening his eyes enough to keep track of Cassie. "That first time, Lucivar said something about being allowed to fuss during those days, but I wasn't paying attention."

He heard Ranon try to choke it back, but the laughter burst out.

"Hell's fire, Gray," Ranon said when he was able to speak again. "You're turning into a pain in the ass."

Something inside him shifted, settled. Felt solid—and right. He looked at his friend and said, "No, I'm turning into a Warlord Prince."

★   ★   ★

Kermilla lay back on her bed and smiled.

The Queen of Dena Nehele. She finally understood what all of Theran's circling had been about. He wanted to know if she was interested in ruling Dena Nehele after Cassidy's contract ran out. He didn't want Freckledy; he wanted *her*.

A Territory Queen. *La,* wasn't that wonderful? All right, it wasn't a rich, exciting Territory, and it *was* in Terreille, but the tithes had to be worth the responsibilities, so they would be *so much* better than that little sheep-shit village of Bhak or, worse, Woolskin. She'd try for a five-year contract. Theran would get it for her. And she wouldn't shirk her duties. Really, she wouldn't. But she'd make sure there was some *fun* too.

It had been satisfying to teach those other Queens about draining power into the land. Such a basic thing, and they didn't know it. *La!* They weren't much better than landens. Not that she'd *said* that. She supposed they were nice enough, but most of them were older than her and they looked so tatty and didn't talk about anything interesting. How could they expect anyone to take them seriously as Queens when they dressed like that and didn't know how to be interesting?

She would set an example, even set the fashion trends. Wouldn't that be fun? Of course, because Freckledy had gotten into a snit, she was stuck here in Grayhaven, which was supposed to be the capital of Dena Nehele and an Important Town. There wasn't anything here that *she* considered impressive. If this was the best they could do, maybe she didn't want to rule here after all.

No, of course she wanted to rule here. When would she get another opportunity to rule a whole Territory? Sabrina was going to be ruling Dharo for years and years, and there were too many other strong Queens to choose from when it came time for a successor. She could continue to rule Bhak and keep a connection with Dharo that way. A few days each season would be sufficient for whatever required her attention. Her Steward could run Bhak and landen Woolskin the rest of the time and just send her reports— and the all-important income from the tithes. Then, if she decided not to stay in Dena Nehele and nothing better turned up in Terreille, she could go home, a seasoned Queen who might not be offered a Province—yet—but should be given her pick of the larger cities that could offer more diversity in terms of society and entertainment—and shops.

If she was going to stay here, she would need more company. Not *too* much company, since Theran was more than a bit stingy and he would have to support any Ladies who were her companions. But that one young Queen who had come with the others—she and Correne had become friends within minutes, and the girl was enough like her to fit right in. At sixteen, Correne wasn't a baby, but she was still too young to be serious competition, despite being pretty. No Queen was serious competition until she had her Virgin Night and could offer some enticement to the males without risking her own power.

A knock on her door.

"Come in," she said gaily.

Jhorma slipped into the room and closed the door.

Kermilla watched him as he approached the bed. He was a handsome man and a skilled lover, but there wasn't the heat in his eyes for her that there had been while he was chained to Cassidy's bed. Oh, he came to her bed hungry to please—and to take his own relief as a reward—and he never made excuses to get out of performing the way he did with Freckledy toward the end of his contract. But he didn't look at her the way Theran did. She was getting the impression that Jhorma could swap her with any female body and be just as thorough and enthusiastic—as long as he got his own pleasure at the end. Theran looked at her as if she was the only one he wanted, the only one who could satisfy him.

Jhorma didn't remove his jacket before sitting beside her on the bed, didn't make any move to touch her.

"We need to talk," he said.

She ran a finger down his arm and smiled playfully. "Sex first, talk later."

He didn't smile back. "How much longer are we going to be stuck in this place?"

Her smile soured to a frown. "For as long as I say we stay."

"Cassidy isn't here, and it doesn't sound like she's coming back. When you decided to come here, you told Gallard we would be gone a couple of days. Three at the most. He assigned the escorts according to that information."

"So?"

"Aston and Ridley have families. They want to go home. They wouldn't have been given this assignment if the Steward had known we'd be away this long."

She sat up, stung that Jhorma was more interested in talking about Aston and Ridley than in having sex with her.

"Fine," she snapped. "Tell the whiny boys who are missing the nipple that they can go home."

Anger flashed in his eyes before he hid it.

He hadn't shown her anger since he'd signed a contract to serve as her Consort, but he hadn't hesitated to give her a verbal slap when she'd been training in Freckledy's court and had said something cutting about one of the other men.

But he'd always smiled indulgently when she'd referred to Cassidy as Freckledy. She'd just forgotten how testy the males could be when you made fun of one of *them*.

"I'm sorry," she said. "That was uncalled for. It's just . . . I don't feel like I have any support here."

"Then maybe we should all go back to Dharo."

*But I have a chance to rule a whole Territory.*

Not something she could say to him. *He* wouldn't be part of that court. She didn't pay attention when Theran began droning on and on about Dena Nehele, but she did understand that he and the other Warlord Princes here never would tolerate a ruling court made up of outsiders. Something about courts like that ruling here before and making a mess of things.

Maybe she could go back to Dharo and return here next spring when Cassidy's contract ended. No, she couldn't. She had to show these people she was the better Queen, and she couldn't do that unless she was here *showing* them she was the better Queen. Just like she'd done in Bhak when she'd won over Freckledy's court.

"There are reasons why I need to stay," she said. "If Aston and Ridley need to return to Dharo, they can go. But two others from the First Circle should take their place."

"I'll convey the message," Jhorma said. "Do you want sex now?"

"No, I do not want sex now." Especially when he might have been asking her if she wanted a cup of tea.

"As you please." Jhorma rose and walked out of the room.

She *had* wanted sex, but he'd spoiled her mood.

So maybe she'd take a walk in the moonlight with Theran this evening and see if he had any experience behind that enthusiasm.


Accepting Gray's assistance, Cassidy stepped out of the carriage and looked at the boardinghouse. Queen's Residence, she reminded herself. Somehow, while dealing with the snarls and grumbles that had been a constant background during this journey, she had agreed that the boardinghouse now be referred to as the Queen's Residence.

"It's good to be home," she said—and wondered if she would recognize the inside of the place. After all, she'd been gone five days and had told Powell he could do pretty much as he pleased.

"Those cottages across from the Residence weren't occupied when we left," Ranon said, studying the street while offering Shira a hand. "Shaddo and Archerr must be back."

The door of the Residence opened. Talon stepped out and strode over to them.

The way he looked her over—as if assessing a warrior he'd sent out on a difficult mission who had finally returned—she wondered how many reports, and complaints, the Master of the Guard and Steward had received in the past five days.

"Shaddo and Archerr are back?" she asked.

"They are," Talon replied. "Lady Shira, tomorrow will be soon enough, but I think a visit from the court Healer would be in order for both families. Those people have not had an easy time."

"Should I go over and welcome them?" Cassidy asked.

"No."

The finality of that statement shook her.

"Tomorrow afternoon is soon enough for them to have an audience with the Queen," Talon said.

"Surely we don't have to be so formal—" She swallowed the rest of her protest. It was clear Talon thought there was reason for that formality.

"Powell has worked out a schedule of afternoons when you are available to give audiences," Talon said.

"Afternoons?" Cassidy stammered. "Audiences? Hell's fire! I thought Powell was going to rearrange the furniture, not my life!"

"Did you?"

The amusement under the dry words made her take a step back. "Is tomorrow morning soon enough to go over my social calendar?"

"I think so," Talon replied.

"Good. Then there's enough time for a quick bite to eat before I meet Lord Yairen for my drumming lesson."

*"No."* Ranon backed away from her, his dark eyes filled with fear. "No, he can't do that."

Staggered by his distress, she said nothing as he strode down the street toward his grandfather's house. Then she turned to Shira.

"Yairen offered to teach you?" Shira asked, her voice breaking as tears filled her eyes.

"Yes. When Ranon brought me back here, Yairen stayed with me and we talked. He offered to teach me the drums. He said drums were a woman's instrument because they were the sound of the land's heartbeat. Shira, why is Ranon so upset? Is it against Shaladoran customs to teach an outsider?"

Tears spilled over. Shira shuddered with the effort to maintain some control. "We weren't forbidden music or stories or dances as long as they were from Dena Nehele—or Hayll. But anything that came from Shalador, that came from the hearts of *our* people was forbidden. Ranon's grandfather is a Tradition Keeper of Music. He taught people how to play drums and the flute. He wasn't as skilled with the fiddle and only taught the basics. But he defied the Queens who ruled here and taught the Shalador drum rhythms and the Shalador songs. So they broke his hands as punishment. And when his hands healed the first time, he continued to teach the music of our people. So they broke his hands again. The third time, the Queens' Healers made sure the fingers healed wrong so that Yairen could no longer play. Ranon was a small boy the last time Yairen's hands were broken. But, somehow, Yairen still taught Ranon to play the Shalador flute—and taught him the songs of our people."

Cassidy stood frozen while Shira dried her eyes and the men shifted uneasily.

How much trust had gone into what she'd thought was Yairen's friendly offer? How much fear had ridden alongside that trust?

"I want all the Tradition Keepers in this village here within the hour," Cassidy said quietly.

"Cassie . . ." Gray began.

She raised a hand, cutting him off. Then she looked at her Master of the Guard. "See that it's done, Prince Talon."

She walked into the Residence. Powell took one look at her face and swallowed whatever greeting or comment he intended to make.

She went up to her room, blind to whatever changes had been made in her absence. All she could see was the fear on Ranon's face before he walked away.

Cassidy stood in the street in front of the Queen's Residence. The Tradition Keepers stood before her in their shabby best clothes. Filling the streets around them were the people of the village.

"Lord Yairen." Cassidy used Craft to enhance her voice. She wanted everyone who had come to stand witness to hear her words.

Yairen stepped forward, standing tall. "How may I serve the Queen?"

"I have just learned today that your people have been forbidden to play the music that was born of Shalador, that you have been forbidden to perform the traditional dances, or teach the young the stories of your people. Is this true?"

"It is true, Lady," Yairen said. "All have been forbidden for many generations."

"But the Tradition Keepers have remembered these forbidden things?"

Yairen hesitated. How many times had one of the Keepers been cornered into answering a question that would condemn them?

She didn't have an actual psychic link to Ranon, but his psychic scent was filled with distress. Wouldn't know it to look at him, standing cold and arrogant with the rest of her First Circle, but the worry that he might have misjudged her was eating his heart out.

"Some things have been lost," Yairen finally said, "but those of us who are the memory of our people have held on to enough."

Cassidy nodded. "In that case, as of this hour, the music of the Shalador people will be taught and will be played openly. The dances of the Shalador people will be taught and performed openly. The stories of the Shalador people will be taught and told openly. The Queens in the Shalador reserves will be given a written decree so they will know these words are true. But it will be up to the Tradition Keepers to return Shalador's heart to its people. This is my will."

Silence.

Finally one of the Tradition Keepers raised his hand. "Does this mean we can perform the circle dances this autumn?"

"Yes," Cassidy replied.

Another silence.

Then Yairen pressed one of his crippled hands to his chest. "Our hearts are too full for words tonight."

Cassidy swallowed hard. "Then return to your homes. We will speak more of this tomorrow."

She took a step back, a clear signal this audience was over.

Ranon broke away from the rest of the First Circle. Hugging his grandfather, he put his head on the old man's shoulder and wept.

A hand linked with hers. Looking to her left, she saw Reyhana trembling with the effort not to cry—and felt the girl's hand tighten.

"The circle dances mean so much to my people," Reyhana said. "To *our* people." She choked, but went on. "Someone will write a song about how Shalador's Lady gave the heart back to the people, and all the children will learn it, and someday I will tell my grandchildren I was there and heard the words as they were spoken."

Mother Night.

A familiar touch on her shoulder. She looked at Gray, hoping for some help, but his eyes were too bright, too wet.

"I'd like to go inside now," she said.

It was Talon who nudged Reyhana aside and gripped Cassidy's arm to lead her into the house before she ended up weeping too.

"I told Ranon to spend the night with his grandfather," Talon said once he got her to the parlor. "He'll be better for it."

"Talon . . ."

"Don't say anything, witchling. Don't. I knew Jared. I've seen the circle dances. I know what the bitches took away from these people—and I know what you just gave back to them. I think it's best if you Ladies have a quiet evening for yourselves."

He kissed her cheek, then said, "Gray, let's see what can be put together for a meal."

Cassidy curled up on the sofa, stunned by the emotion that had swirled around her.

"You look like you got kicked in the head," Shira said when she and Reyhana came in a minute later.

"I thought the Tradition Keepers would be happy that they could teach openly again," Cassidy said.

"They are happy," Shira replied. "We're feeling too much right now to be just happy."

And her First Circle was going to want time to consider the ramifications of what she'd done tonight.

"Do you think the men would be upset if I went out and gardened for a little while?" Cassidy asked. "It's still light out." The sun had set, but they were still into the longest days of summer.

"Gray will have a fit if you pick up a weeding claw," Shira said. "And so will I."

Cassidy huffed. "There's too much feeling. I need to *do* something."

Shira eyed Reyhana, who looked confused about what she was supposed to do.

"Do you play drums?" Shira asked Reyhana.

The girl shook her head. "But I'm supposed to start learning. Shalador Queens all learn to drum."

"I'm not a Tradition Keeper," Shira said, "but I've been drumming since I was a girl. I can start teaching the basics to both of you."

"But we don't have drums," Cassidy said.

"We do have a wooden table," Shira replied, pointing at the table in front of the sofa. "And tonight, that's all we need."

## EBON ASKAVI

Saetan signed his name to the message, then waited for the ink to dry before folding the paper and sealing it.

Daemon had asked to be informed of anything to do with a Dharo witch named Kermilla. Having two of her escorts show up at the Keep, wanting assistance to go through the Gate and return home, certainly qualified as something of interest—especially since he *knew* those men hadn't gone through this particular Gate to get to Terreille. Granted, there were thirteen Gates that linked the three Realms, and those men could have used any of them—except this one and the one that was next to the Hall— without causing too much interest in their business. And granted, there weren't many Priestesses left in Terreille who knew how to open the Gates to let someone move from one Realm to another, so this was the best choice if someone wanted to get back to Kaeleer and not mistakenly end up in Hell.

But Daemon's interest in this witch sounded a warning inside Saetan because it carried the feel of a predator analyzing potential prey. And Daemon's refusal to say why he wanted information sounded a more ominous warning—because there was only one person who could muzzle Daemon Sadi.

What did Jaenelle know?

He couldn't ask—and didn't need to.

He folded the paper, melted the black wax, and added a touch of Black power as he pressed the SaDiablo seal into the wax. Black to Black ensured that this would be a private message, since Daemon was the only person who could open it.

His task completed, he placed the message in the basket with the rest of the mail that would be collected in the morning and taken to the message station.

Then he went to his suite and vanished everything from the surface of his desk. He placed a small wooden frame in the center of the desk and called in several spools of spider silk, different weights.

Since he could not ask Jaenelle or Daemon for answers about Kermilla, he would find his own answers. After all, he, too, was a Black Widow— one of only two males in the history of the Blood who belonged to that caste.

So during the silent, dark hours, Prince Saetan Daemon SaDiablo, High Priest of the Hourglass, spun his own tangled web of dreams and visions.

# CHAPTER 15

## TERREILLE

Ranon rode up to the Queen's Residence, dismounted, and gave his horse a pat.

Most mornings this past week, he'd loaded the horse and gear into the two-horse livestock Coach and headed out to one of the other Shalador reserves to ride through a village or two. He'd listened to the elders and Tradition Keepers, answered questions about things they had heard about the Rose Queen—and assured them that he, Shalador's only adult Warlord Prince, had heard Cassidy give Shalador's heart back to the people.

Today, he'd been assigned the ride through Eyota. It lifted his heart to see the people he'd grown up with smile and raise a hand in greeting when a member of a Queen's court rode by. That had never happened before in anyone's memory. He would never admit it, but every day he gave silent thanks to Theran Grayhaven for being enough of an ass to send Cassidy running so that she ended up here, among the people who needed her the most.

A quick psychic probe told him the only people in the house were Powell, Talon, and Vae, which meant Cassidy and Gray weren't back from their planned ride, and Shira wasn't back from her inspection of the nearby cottages. She wanted a Healer's House—a place where she could take care of people without intruding on Cassidy's privacy. There was only one other fully qualified Healer in Eyota, so even though Shira was supposed to be the court's Healer, she and Cassidy agreed to expand that to the court and their families.

He flicked an "I'm home" thought along a psychic thread aimed at Shira's sharp, loving—and sometimes dangerous—mind.

*Almost done myself,* Shira replied.

*Find anything?*

*Maybe.*

But she sounded more resigned than excited, so he didn't press her. Besides, the sound of another horse had him turning, his temper instinctively sharpening as Shaddo rode up to the Queen's Residence.

It was a Warlord Prince's nature to rise to the killing edge. Since coming to Eyota, all of them had discovered that their instincts were more keenly honed when they were around their Queen or her home. Even with each other, there was still a bristling moment when temper was poised between predatory instinct and conscious loyalty to the Queen and their Brothers in the court.

Watching Shaddo, who made no move, Ranon nodded to acknowledge that he had his temper leashed.

"Anything?" he asked. Shaddo had spent the day in the western Province where his wife and boys had lived, riding through a couple of villages to see who might want to talk to a member of Cassidy's First Circle.

"Lots of circling around questions no one was brave enough to ask," Shaddo replied, dismounting. "But everyone is interested in the special magic Queens can do to help the harvest. And I ran into a handful of Warlord Princes. I had the feeling they hadn't met up in that particular village by chance."

"Does that mean trouble for us?"

Shaddo shook his head. "I think . . . Hell's fire, Ranon, remember when Cassidy first talked about having the Warlord Princes step up and rule on behalf of the Territory Queen because there weren't many Queens left in Dena Nehele?"

"At least not many living in the open or having a visible court," Ranon said. In the past few days, Powell had received tentative messages from men in a dozen villages, all asking if they could see this special magic. Reading between the lines, there were Queens out there who wanted to learn but weren't willing to trust their lives and what little structure was left in Dena Nehele to a Queen who was still unknown. But men who served those Queens would come to watch and learn—and report back to their Ladies.

"Basically, they wanted to know how Cassidy would respond if they divided a Province based on who was available 'to rule on behalf of the Queen.'"

"I think she'd be relieved to have the Warlord Princes rule whatever the surviving Queens couldn't handle," Ranon said. Or didn't want to handle because it would call attention to themselves.

"I told them the Steward was trying to figure out how to divide the Provinces into Districts, but he was working blind because he didn't know how many of the Warlord Princes were willing to step up to the line and help their people."

Ranon winced. "Those words must have stung."

Shaddo shook his head. "They didn't, and that surprised me too since I'd meant them to sting. But word is spreading about what Cassidy did for the Shaladorans—and about her going into landen villages as well as Blood to do that special magic. Every man who had fought in the uprisings wanted to know how we could let her do something that dangerous."

"I hope you told them we don't *let* her do anything," Ranon grumbled.

Wasn't much of a grumble. Cassie might chafe at the boundaries the First Circle set for her protection, but the men were smart enough to keep expanding those boundaries as they settled down to a life here in Eyota. Besides, according to the Protocol Powell was studying every night, even the First Circle's right to protect the Queen had some limits.

"Papa! Papa!"

Ranon felt Shaddo's fierce joy as his two boys came running toward them, but he also saw the stern face and the hand quickly raised to stop them.

"What did I tell you about running toward horses?" Shaddo said.

"Don't do it." Eliot, the younger one, scuffed one shoe on the street.

"Can we walk the horses to the stables?" Eryk asked. "We'll be careful."

Saying nothing, Ranon handed his reins to Shaddo.

"You can walk them," Shaddo said. "And then we'll all take care of them."

"Yes, sir."

Hearing an odd whistle on the "s," Ranon studied Eliot. "Someone lost a tooth."

Eliot grinned, showing off the gap. "Mother is making a special tooth treat."

Eryk muttered something and looked sulky.

Eliot scowled. "She made special treats for *you* when you lost a tooth."

"I didn't knock one out to get a treat," Eryk said, just loud enough to assure the men heard him.

"I did *not* knock it out," Eliot said.

"Did to."

"Did not!"

"Did—"

*"Boys,"* Shaddo said.

They obeyed the tone instantly.

★I'm impressed,★ Ranon said, trying not to grin.

★Yeah, well, having me around all the time is still new to them,★ Shaddo replied. ★I figure the pissing contests will start soon enough.★

He watched Shaddo and the boys until they went into the stables. Then he smiled.

Tomorrow was a rest day, thank the Darkness. No work, no traveling, nothing but his woman and a sweet summer day. Maybe Cassidy and Gray would be interested in riding over to Mariel's Pond to swim and have a picnic. Or maybe he and Shira would go alone so they could have long talks and sweet kisses before coming back to their room for a different kind of talking and kisses that were hot instead of sweet.

With those thoughts in mind, he turned to go into the Residence to get a glass of ale and see if there was anything in the larder.

★Ranon, I'm at the northern landing web. We've got company, and they're heading for the Queen's Residence.★

Ranon tensed in response to the sharp edge in Archerr's voice. ★How many?★

An odd hesitation. *Depends on who you're counting.*

*What?* *Shaddo, someone's coming. Keep your boys out of sight.* As soon as Shaddo acknowledged the order, Ranon sent a command to Gray. *Keep Cassidy away from the Residence until you hear from me.*

He stepped out into the middle of the street, made a quick descent to the level of his Opal Jewel, and waited a heartbeat away from the killing edge for their "guests" to come into sight.

Then Vae raced out of the Residence, her joy sending out an almost staggering punch.

*They're here!* Vae shouted along a common psychic thread that could be heard by anyone within range—which was probably half the village. She raced down the street toward the northern landing web. *They're here!*

*Who's here?* Ranon wondered.

The answer to that question turned a corner and came down the street a few minutes later. One man, wearing a vest and jacket over a shirt—too many clothes for the season and the weather. A Sceltie trotted beside him on his right. A few paces ahead of him, Vae bounced and danced with so much excitement it made Ranon tired just to watch her. And behind the man . . .

Twelve of them, spread out in a V that covered the whole street—and gave every one of them a clear line of sight. Scelties. If men had been coming toward him in a fighting V, he'd know what to do. Faced with dogs, he wasn't sure how to respond—but a sudden memory of Vae pulling down a full-grown man in a fight had him creating a skintight shield around himself. Just in case.

Three of the Scelties spotted him and broke their position, dashing toward him. A barked order—literally—from the Sceltie trotting beside the man had them wheeling round, tails down in response to the reprimand, and returning to their position.

"Good afternoon to you," the man called.

Curly brown hair, handsome face, lean body. Not much of a fighter, since he was approaching a stranger with his hands in his trouser pockets as if he were taking a simple stroll in his home village. But the stew of power

Ranon was sensing from that group couldn't be dismissed, and there was something in the man's blue eyes that said this Warlord knew how to stop trouble—and how to make trouble.

"Good afternoon," Ranon replied.

★They're here!★ Vae bounced and danced, but the men ignored her.

"Would you be Gray?" the man asked.

"I'm Ranon, First Circle in Lady Cassidy's court and the Master's second-in-command."

"Ah. Well, since you were the second man I was asked to see, I think you'll do as well for both."

*Both what?*

"I'm Khardeen, Warlord of Maghre. And this is Lord Ladvarian." Khardeen held out a hand.

Ranon clasped the hand—and felt a quiver of fear when he saw the Sapphire ring on Khardeen's right hand. This man could rip through his Opal shields and tear him apart with a single thought.

Then he glanced down and got another shock. The dog staring up at him wore a gold chain around its neck. A Red Jewel shone against the white ruff.

The human wasn't the most dangerous Warlord to walk into their village.

Ladvarian looked at Vae.

★Ranon? Ladvarian wants to see the yard.★

"Uh . . . sure." Since she'd been bouncing a minute before, he was uneasy about Vae sounding so subdued—and cautious.

Khardeen took a step to the side as Vae came around to position herself on Ladvarian's left—the subordinate position. That done, fourteen Scelties trotted off and disappeared behind the Queen's Residence.

"They aren't going to dig, are they?" Ranon asked. "Gray will have a fit if they start digging in the gardens he's been restoring back there. So will Cassidy."

"No, they'll be all right," Khardeen replied. "Ladvarian was First Circle in the Dark Court. He knows about not digging in a Queen's garden. Of course, some of the youngsters will need to have it explained to them more than once, but they'll understand it sooner or later."

Khardeen's blue eyes twinkled. Ranon's stomach sank in response.

"I gather Vae didn't tell you about this?" Khardeen asked.

"About what?"

"Ah. Well, having been here long enough to assess the situation, Vae didn't think she could take care of all the humans who needed a Sceltie's help."

"Really?" Mother Night.

"She talked to Ladvarian about helping her find other Scelties to take care of the other humans while she took care of the court. Then those two talked to Morghann and Jaenelle, and there you are—twelve youngsters who wanted the challenge of taking care of humans who have no kindred of their own."

No. Oooh, no. "Who's Morghann?" He'd heard the name before, somewhere, but it was the only question Ranon could think to ask. The only safe question, anyway.

"Morghann is the Queen of Scelt."

Hell's fire, Mother Night, and may the Darkness be merciful. Now he remembered. Cassie had mentioned Morghann when she was explaining court living arrangements in Kaeleer. And she'd mentioned Morghann's husband, Khardeen.

The Queen of Scelt and the former Queen of Ebon Askavi had hand-picked these dogs to live here? How was he going to convince Khardeen to take them back? No matter what Vae thought, *she* was all the *humans* could handle.

"What are they supposed to do?" Ranon asked.

"Oh, they'll figure that out," Khardeen said with a breeziness that was a bit terrifying. "They're good at herding, and they'll herd anything—sheep, ducks, goats, cows, children . . . stubborn males."

"Can you take them back?"

"I can," Khardeen said. "But you'll be the one who will have to explain it to the Ladies, and any man who knows either of those Queens isn't going to get within a mile of you while you do it."

Shit.

A wave of fur came around the Residence and spread out, tails wagging while they busily sniffed their surroundings.

Then one of the Scelties raced up to him and began dancing on its hind legs.

*My human! This is my human!*

It was the homeliest little dog Ranon had ever seen. He—because Ranon had picked up the caste of Warlord—had the Sceltie face and the Sceltie body, but the fur looked like it had been taken from the leftovers of a dozen different dogs and patched together any which way. There was white, tan, brown, black, and three shades of gray. Hodgepodge dog.

*I will take good care of him. I am going to live with him!*

"No, you're not." The words were honest and out before Ranon thought about it.

The dog stared at him for a moment, those brown eyes full of heart-breaking woe. Then the whimpering started, turning to whines and keening and . . .

*My human doesn't want me!*

Ranon glanced at Khardeen. There was still some amusement and sympathy in those blue eyes, but underneath was the bite of anger.

*Can't you do something*? Ranon asked Khardeen.

*I'm not the one who hurt his feelings.*

That anger made him uneasy, although Khardeen made no overt threat. Then he discovered he had a lot more reasons to worry.

He hadn't seen them, hadn't sensed them coming toward him. One moment he had one whining Sceltie sitting in front of him; the next he was surrounded—and the thirteen pairs of brown eyes staring at him held more than a bite of anger.

*Of course he wants you,* Vae said. *But he is male and human, and sometimes he gets confused. Don't you?*

Ranon glanced at Khardeen.

*There is only one correct answer,* Khardeen said. *So take the kick in the balls, apologize to your little brother, and assure him that he can live with you.*

*Is there any other choice?*

*Not if you want to stay healthy. Darkmist is a year older than his little brother and isn't someone you want to tangle with,* Khardeen said.

Darkmist? Ranon scanned the Sceltie faces. The dogs were a variety of colors, but there were three that might fit the name—if the name was meant to fit. Two were a silver-gray and white, and the third . . .

Pewter and white with black speckles on the face. And an Opal Jewel.

*Warlord Prince.* Ranon stared at the dog who matched him, caste and rank. Then he swallowed hard and went down on one knee, aware he was putting his throat a lot closer to all those sets of teeth.

"What's your name?" he asked, tentatively extending a hand to the homely little dog.

Woeful brown eyes looked at him, but the tip of the tail gave a hopeful little wag. *Khollie.*

"Well, Khollie, Vae is right. I am confused. I've never seen so many Scelties, and I guess I didn't realize . . ." What? Then inspiration struck, and with a silent apology to his beloved, he added, "You can help me take care of my mate."

More tail wagging. Woeful began to lighten to happy as Khollie slipped his head under Ranon's hand for a pat.

*You have a mate? I will help you!*

Suddenly his arms were full of chin-licking, tail-wagging dog—and he really hoped Shira was going to forgive him for siccing a Sceltie on her.

"Vae, why don't you show Ladvarian and Khollie where Khollie will be staying," Khardeen said. The mild tone didn't make the words any less of a command.

Crisis over, the Scelties scattered to continue their sniffing exploration of the cottages and vegetation near the Queen's Residence, leaving the two humans alone.

Khardeen said nothing, giving Ranon time to regain some balance and think.

"It won't be that bad," Khardeen finally said. "A month from now, you won't remember what it was like to live in a village without Scelties."

What a terrifying thought. But it was remembering the look in Dark-mist's eyes and the *feel* of the dog that had Ranon watching the way they moved, spreading out from the Residence. Too orderly. More like a troop of warriors spreading out to get the most information about a place in the least amount of time. Which made him wonder about the twelve dogs that were going to be living among his people—and made him remember a comment that almost passed by his notice.

"You said Ladvarian was First Circle in the Dark Court?"

"Yes," Khardeen replied. "He was one of Lady Angelline's escorts."

Ranon looked Khardeen in the eyes. "He was trained to fight?"

"By Lucivar Yaslana, the Demon Prince, and the High Lord, among others," Khardeen said softly. "In turn, Ladvarian trained each of the youngsters who have come here. Don't underestimate Darkmist, Ranon. A Warlord Prince is a Warlord Prince, whether he stands on two legs or four, and Mist has received the best education when it comes to knowing what to do in a fight."

Mother Night.

"And they're all going to live . . . ?" Ranon looked at the Queen's Residence.

"Oh, they'll work that out. I suspect most of them will come back here for the first few days. Then they'll find their own place in the village—as well as their special humans."

Thank the Darkness.

He was not a coward. He knew that about himself. But the thought of living in the same house with more than two Scelties made his knees weak.

"About Khollie," Khardeen said. "Do you have any brothers?"

"One. Younger by ten years." Could he extend Khollie's "help" to Janos as well?

"Do you remember what it's like to talk to a four-year-old boy?"

Ranon nodded.

"Then you should have no trouble." Khardeen gave him a sharp smile. "Just think of Khollie as a bright four-year-old boy, and you're the older brother who needs to explain things to him so that his behavior doesn't cause trouble for him or the people around him."

Great. Just what he needed when there was already so much to do—a furry baby brother.

Khardeen called in a large metal trunk that immediately began to sweat in the heat, along with a large metal canister. "Here's a cold box of meat for them. And that's the oatmeal that is made into a gruel as part of their feed a couple of times a week."

"Vae doesn't eat that," Ranon said. Although, now that he thought about it, some mornings the porridge bowls left on the table looked a little too clean. Like someone had licked them clean.

"Well," Khardeen said, looking toward the house. "It's time we were heading back. I'm expected for dinner at the Keep."

Ladvarian, Vae, and Khollie came trotting out of the Residence—using Craft to pass through the door, Ranon noted. Which meant he wouldn't need to get up in the middle of the night if the dog wanted to pee.

Ladvarian gave the two youngsters a lick on their muzzles. Khardeen tipped his head, said good-bye, and the two Warlords headed back up the street to the landing web.

Then Khardeen stopped and turned to face Ranon.

*There was that second thing to tell you,* he said. *Lady Cassidy's report will go to the Keep three days from now?*

*Yes.*

*You're to be the messenger.*

*Why?*

*Because the Queen wants to see you.*

No doubt about *which* Queen was commanding his presence. No doubt at all. And no question that he would obey that command.

*I'll be there.* *And may the Darkness have mercy on me.*

He watched them until they were out of sight. Then he felt a flash of frustration and temper. He looked to his right and saw one of the Scelties—a witch by what he could sense—staring at empty air, gently wagging her tail.

A moment later, Archerr dropped the sight shield that should have kept him hidden and strode over to Ranon, quickly followed by Shaddo, who was trailed by his two boys.

"Hell's fire," Archerr said as the witch trotted away and a Warlord headed toward them. "What good is a sight shield if a dog is going to smell you and let everyone know you're there?"

"Not much," Ranon said. But damn useful if an enemy was trying to sight shield to get close enough to attack. With two Scelties living at the Residence, they were less likely to have any unwelcome company showing up to bother Cassidy.

*Boy puppies!* The black-and-white Warlord with a splash of white on his muzzle and tan markings on his face raced toward Shaddo's boys.

Shaddo swore mildly but didn't interfere with the meeting. Then he swore with more heat when his wife Soli stepped out of their cottage.

"Shaddo? What's going on? Is it all right for the boys to be out?"

The Sceltie turned toward the sound of her voice and froze. Dog and woman stared at each other.

Soli smiled. "Aren't you the sweetest boy?"

The human boys were abandoned in a heartbeat. The Sceltie launched himself into the air and ended up sitting in front of Soli, with one paw raised to shake—floating on air waist high.

"Hello, there," Soli said, holding the paw while she petted and cooed. "What's your name? Where did you come from?" She frowned a little. "You're Darcy from the Isle of Scelt?" She looked up at Shaddo, her eyes full of wonder. "He talks?"

*I talk,* Darcy said proudly. *But only to my special humans.*

"Hell's fire, Shaddo," Archerr said, choking back a laugh. "That sure looks like love at first sight to me. I think you just adopted a furry boy-child."

"Who is *not* going to be sleeping in our bed," Shaddo growled. But there was resigned humor in his eyes as he watched Soli introduce the dog to the boys. "He'll keep her company, so yeah, looks like I've got another boy."

"Who is already trained to fight," Ranon said quietly.

The humor drained out of the other two men.

He nodded in response to the unspoken question. "It's one step removed, but some of that training is courtesy of Lucivar Yaslana—and one of the Scelties is an Opal-Jeweled Warlord Prince."

"Mother Night," Archerr said softly.

"Once Talon rises, we all need to talk about this. For now, you two pass along the all clear, especially to Gray so he knows it's safe for Cassidy to come back to the Residence. I'll try to explain this to the village elders."

Shaddo said, "Who would send us a pack of warriors?"

Ranon felt a knot of tension ease as he answered the question. "The same person who understood why we needed Cassidy."

# CHAPTER 16
## TERREILLE

Gray led the newest member of the household out to the corner of the yard that sheltered the pots containing the twelve honey pear seedlings. Going down on one knee, he waited for the Sceltie to join him.

Compared to Vae, who had more self-assurance than a dozen people combined, Khollie seemed so . . . breakable. Or maybe the dog was still feeling bruised by Ranon's initial rejection and was afraid of being sent away.

"Come here, Khollie," Gray said gently.

Woeful eyes. Hopeful tail-tip wag.

"See these?" Gray pointed to the pots. "These are honey pears. They are very special trees. You do not pee on them."

*I did not pee on the little trees. Only the big trees.*

"I know you didn't pee on them"—*yet*—"but I want you to understand that we *never* pee on these trees."

*Humans too?*

"Yes, humans too. These trees are very, very special, and we all have to protect them."

The head came up, the ears came up, and the tail began wagging in earnest. *I will help you protect the little trees when I am not helping Ranon protect Shira.*

"Who's protecting what?" Ranon asked, carrying a mug of coffee in each hand.

*Ranon!* The shout went out on a common psychic thread. *Do not pee on the little trees or Gray will bite you.*

Oh, the look on Ranon's face.

Gray bit his lip to keep from laughing until Khollie trotted off to check the boundaries of his and Vae's personal territory, which was the land that belonged to the Residence.

"Do you think there is anyone in the surrounding cottages who didn't hear that?" Ranon asked in a strangled voice.

"No." Gray's voice broke with the effort not to laugh. "I think *everyone* on this street and the next two over knows not to pee on the little trees."

"Shit." Ranon handed him one of the mugs.

"He bruises easily," Gray said quietly. "His feelings, I mean."

"I figured that out, Gray. Not soon enough, but I did figure that out. It just takes a lot longer to fix the damage than to do the damage."

"Do you think they made a mistake with him? Maybe he's too young to be away from people who understand Scelties."

Ranon shrugged. "Doesn't matter now. He's here. Would you want to be sent home from your first assignment?"

Gray looked away, feeling his own heart ache a little.

Ranon swore. "I'm sorry. I didn't mean . . ."

"Never had a first assignment—or any assignment. My training stopped when I was fifteen."

"Do you want to resume that training?" Ranon asked.

Gray nodded. He'd spent a lot of time thinking while he'd worked in the gardens here. "I want to be able to protect and defend. That's what I was meant to do. I grew up being told I was Theran's blade, and I was educated to protect the Grayhaven line—until I was captured."

"You were Theran's blade, and now you want to be Cassie's blade. Is that it?"

"Yes, that's it."

They sipped their coffee and watched Khollie and Vae flush a rabbit out of the kitchen garden and herd it right into Darcy's jaws.

"Now what?" Ranon asked as the three Scelties snarled at one another for a minute before Darcy and Vae each grabbed a rabbit leg and the three dogs trotted away with their kill. "Khollie and Vae want the rabbit for us, and Darcy wants the rabbit for Soli."

"They'll take it to Cassidy, who will figure out a way for both households to have some of the meat so all three Scelties will be happy," Gray replied.

"The duties of a Queen." Ranon drained his mug. Then he sighed. "I came out here to ask a favor."

"Actually, there's something I wanted to ask you too."

"All right. Mine. Shira is supposed to take a last look at the cottages she was interested in. Something about this is making her unhappy, but she won't talk to me or Cassidy about it. I was hoping, if you attached yourself as her escort, she might talk to you. I'd go with her and try again to find out what's wrong, but I have to go to the Keep today. I'm just waiting for Cassidy to finish a letter to her mother before I head out."

"I can keep Shira company," Gray said.

"Thanks. What can I do for you?"

"I'd like to learn the Fire Dance." He saw Ranon's initial surprise change to thoughtful assessment.

"Have you and Cassidy . . . ?"

Gray shook his head.

"Because of Yaslana's rules about you having sex?"

He shook his head again. "When Cassie looks at me, she doesn't see a man. I don't know how to explain it. We kiss and we touch, and it's good. Mother Night, it's good. But there is something in me that is holding her back from letting me be her lover all the way. So I thought the Fire Dance . . ."

Ranon's hand felt warm on his shoulder.

"I'll teach you," Ranon said. "And this autumn, when that full moon rises, you'll dance with your Brothers."

They walked back to the house, left the mugs in the kitchen, and went their separate ways.

As Gray went to find Shira, it occurred to him that Ranon wouldn't have asked a man he thought was deficient in any way to stand escort to the woman who held his heart.

Kermilla looked through her mail again and sighed.

There were the usual reports from her Steward, saying the same things he said every time about the length of her visit to Dena Nehele—but hinting more strongly this time that it would be in all of their best interests if she returned to Bhak and took care of the villages she ruled. As if she were another Freckledy who really *wanted* to rule a sheep-shit village. Why did she need to be there? The men in her First Circle had been working that village for the five years they'd served Cassidy. They knew how to keep the landens in Woolskin leashed and how to discourage any complaints the Blood in Bhak might have about how the village was being ruled. If the person couldn't be discouraged from complaining, her males should make certain the complaint went no further than her own Steward. After all, their reputations and ambitions were as much at stake as hers, and were, in fact, dependent on hers.

But this time, along with all the dull reports, there were letters from a couple of aristo friends. Those letters talked about parties and picnics, moonlight rides and concerts—and hinted about a daring new gown being designed for the autumn season.

What could *she* write about? She was stuck in a town that thought outdoor concerts and having a dozen people for dinner at an aristo's house was outrageous and daring. And the clothes! Hell's fire, she was from Dharo, *the* Territory for weaving and fabric of the finest quality. Even the meanest cloth that was only fit for landens in Dharo was better than the best she could find in this dung-gray town.

And Theran was always *busy*. Doing what? Who could tell! Nothing interesting. Maybe she should summon Jhorma. Playing with her Consort would fill an hour or so. But they would need to be discreet. She'd invited Theran to her bed two nights ago, and now he seemed to think that gave him an exclusive claim. Maybe if he was bedding a merchant's daughter who wanted to climb the social ladder, but it would take a more lucrative offer than having him as a lover before she would consider giving him anything exclusive. Besides, enthusiasm couldn't replace skill, and a lover who brought his heart to the bed didn't provide the same pleasure as a man who had been trained to please a woman's body.

Despite the impression he gave of being in charge, Theran really didn't have much understanding about how courts worked, and the privileges that were hers simply because she was a Queen. But he really did care about her even if he was rather dull most of the time, and she did want to help him rule this land and make it wonderful again. For a few years, anyway.

But that was the exciting future when she would be the Queen of Dena Nehele, and this was the boring, boring, *boring* now.

A sigh made her look up at the only other person in the room.

"You really study this all the time?" Correne asked, closing the book of Protocol she'd been staring at for the past hour.

Kermilla nodded. "From the first year of schooling to the last. And anyone who actually serves in a court studies even more because court Protocol is more demanding."

"Well, when I set up my court, I'm going to forbid anyone from using all these tedious, stiff phrases."

Kermilla sat up, alarmed. "Oh, no, Correne. You *must* use Protocol, and *everyone* in your court needs to know it."

"Why?" Correne asked, pouting. "It's so *dull.*"

"Because if you know how to use them correctly, some of those phrases can stop a Warlord Prince from killing someone, or command him to step back from the killing edge before he attacks. Males are *controlled* by Protocol."

"What about the things males can demand from females because of Protocol?"

"Oh. Well. A smart woman can figure out how to get around *those.*" Kermilla smiled at the younger Queen. "Come on, let's go into the town and do some shopping."

Correne looked more unhappy. "Can't. I spent all the marks I was given, and my father won't send more until next month."

"Oh." Her smile turned sly. "I'll show you how to purchase a few things without having to pay a single copper for any of it."

Gray studied the two-story house and the neighboring one-story building, and said, "This is perfect." He glanced at Shira, who seemed painfully unhappy as she looked at the place that would be a wonderful residence for a Healer. "Let's take a look around."

She followed him with a noticeable lack of enthusiasm, but he led her around to the back. The small barn was big enough for a couple of horses, and its paddock bordered the pasture for the court's stables. The backyard had plenty of land for a kitchen garden, a Healer's garden, and the private garden a Black Widow would find useful, and still had enough space for children or dogs to romp. Best of all, this property backed the land belonging to the Queen's Residence, with only a low stone wall separating the two. And this place, unlike the others he had seen with Shira today, was inside what Ranon and Talon called the "Queen's square"—the perimeter of streets and houses that would be the most heavily shielded and defended if the village was attacked.

"Enough of this," Shira said. "Let's go back to the Residence."

Gray studied her, bewildered by the pain he saw in her dark eyes. "Why don't you like this place?"

"Because it's perfect," she snapped. "And it's nothing I can have."

"Why not?"

She turned on him, her hands clenched. He should have feared her. After all, she was a Black Widow, which meant she had that snake tooth under her right ring fingernail. His Jewels outranked hers—Purple Dusk against Summer-sky—so her venom wouldn't necessarily kill him, but it might cripple him even if he survived.

"I have no money, Gray."

"But . . ." He called in the paper the village elders had given to Powell. It was a list of land and buildings all around Eyota that the court could have for the asking—property that had no surviving family left to claim it. "This place is on the list. You don't need money."

"What about furniture? What about a worktable and storage cupboards for tonics and brews and dried herbs? What about tools? What about blankets and linens and healing supplies?"

"The Queen's gift . . ."

Shira shook her head fiercely. "No. I can justify what I have in the room at the Residence as a court expense, but I can't expect the court to supply a place like this. And Cassidy shouldn't pay for something beyond the court."

"But you like this place." He had an idea, but he needed to be sure of her first.

"Yes, I like this place."

"Okay." He looked around, then checked the list again. "I want to take a look at those two cottages. They're on the list too."

"Suit yourself." Shira sighed. "My apologies, Gray. I'm feeling sorry for myself, and I have no right to feel that way. The Shalador people have more now than we had dreamed possible a year ago, and I'm the court Healer to a Queen I like and admire. No Healer could ask for a better way to serve her people than to care for such a Queen." She gave him a wobbly smile. "We're almost home, so why don't I take the horse and pony cart back to the—"

"No."

She blinked at him.

"No," Gray said again. "I'm standing as your escort today. If you want to go back now, we'll go back. But you're not going alone."

"I can see the Residence from where I'm standing," Shira said when she finally found her voice. "I can see the stables' pastures from where I'm standing. Hell's fire, Vae and Archerr and Cassidy are standing in the yard right now watching us."

Lucivar had said, "*Strong women can get bitchy about Protocol when they think you're being bossy or overprotective or whatever damn thing they think you're being. Sometimes it's smart to give in, but if you know you're right, set your heels down, boyo, and be a polite, courteous wall.*"

He had the feeling Lucivar was still working on the polite and courteous part, but the man sure did know how to set his heels down.

"I could climb over the back wall and be home," Shira said.

"Fine," Gray said. "Then I'll assist you over the wall."

*And when you need help to do what should be done,* Lucivar had said, *"ask for it."*

★Vae?★ Gray called. ★I need you.★

Shira began sputtering at him that she didn't need help and didn't notice Vae heading toward them until the Sceltie jumped the wall.

★Shira? Shira! Why are you acting like a hissy cat?★

"You," Shira sputtered, glaring at him. *"You . . ."*

Whatever she was going to call him got lost in Khollie's joyous ★Shira!★ as he got over the wall and joined them.

"Shira wants to go home now, and I have something else I need to do, so would the two of you escort her home?"

★We will take care of Shira,★ Khollie said, his tail wagging as he looked up at Ranon's mate.

"Fine." Shira stomped off with two furry escorts who were more implacable than any Warlord Prince would dare to be.

*At least she's not unhappy anymore,* Gray thought. But he figured it would be prudent to stay out of her way until Ranon got home.

★Gray?★ Archerr asked. ★Is everything all right?★

★Shira is a hissy cat,★ he replied.

Archerr's snorted laugh had Shira stopping midstride to turn and stare at Gray.

Hell's fire.

His smile must have been sufficiently insolent because he could *see* her temper flare.

He felt a bit weak-kneed as he gave her a two-finger salute, then turned his back on her and walked to the front of the house.

It wasn't smart to piss off a Black Widow. On the other hand, she probably would be too angry to wonder about the "something" he needed to do.

He untied the horse and started walking down Wolf Creek Road to take a look at the two cottages that were also within the "Queen's square" and also available for the court's use. He hadn't reached the first cottage before the silver twins came running down the road, no doubt alerted by Vae.

*Are you going home now, Gray?* Kief asked, wagging his tail.

*We will take the horse back to the stable,* Lloyd said.

"Thanks, boys, but I still need the horse."

They stared at him, tails gently wagging.

Trying not to sigh, he held out the lead. "Hold him while I take a look at these buildings."

*I will watch the horse,* Lloyd said.

*I will go with Gray,* Kief said.

Now he did sigh, but he didn't argue. No point in arguing. It didn't take the humans long to figure that out. The Scelties seemed to know when they had to obey without question—and they knew when humans were acting like stubborn sheep and needed to be herded in the right direction.

The smart human yielded before getting nipped.

Not all of the Scelties had found their special place in the village, but some were settling in. The Warlord brothers Lloyd and Kief had taken up residence at the stables where the court kept their horses. The First Circle had dubbed them the silver twins because they were gray and white. Not really twins, but they were litter mates, and the only difference in their looks was that Lloyd had a wider blaze down his face. The men were still looking after their own mounts, but they felt easier about leaving the stable unattended now. After all, dogs who were smart enough to bring carrots out to the pasture to make friends with the horses were also smart enough to know when to fetch a human.

Prince Darkmist divided his time between Yairen and Akeelah, a witch who was a Tradition Keeper of Stories. It sure pissed off Ranon the first time he walked into his grandfather's house and was challenged by another Opal-Jeweled Warlord Prince. So Ranon and Mist were working out a few territorial issues. The fact that Ranon was Khollie's human and Khollie was Mist's little brother made things more . . . interesting.

As entertaining as that was—when you weren't the human involved—right now, he needed to take a good look at these cottages and see if his idea would work.

When he finished inspecting the second cottage, he stood out front, shaking his head and smiling. Lloyd had brought the horse and cart.

"Thanks, boys," he said as he climbed into the cart. They stood aside and waited until he'd given the horse the signal to walk on. Then they raced back to the stables, and he headed for a meeting with the village elders.

Kermilla slipped up to her room. She and Correne hadn't gotten around to shopping, but they'd still had a delightful afternoon once they'd met Garth and Brok, two Warlord brothers who weren't much older than Kermilla. They had gone to a dining house and talked and laughed for hours, while her two escorts sat at another table looking bored. Having older, experienced men serving in the court meant she didn't have to work as hard to rule her territory, but it was so much more work to hold their interest when she had to deal with them day after day. These young men hung on to every word she said—and they were *hers*. She'd felt that strange pull when she saw them—the same pull she'd felt when she first met Theran.

After making plans to meet up tomorrow to shop, she and Correne had returned to the mansion and the dull company waiting for her there. But she'd had so much fun with her new boys, she really would pay attention this evening when Theran droned on about what Dena Nehele needed. *He* officially ruled the town, but he seemed to think she should be doing as much as if she were already the Queen—without the compensation! Well, he did tell her she could put things on account against the tithes, but some of the merchants were getting that tight look in their eyes that meant these people didn't know how to show their loyalty to a Queen any more than the people in sheep-shit Bhak did. Which was fine for Freckledy—she had never had any style—but not for a Queen who wanted to be recognized in aristo social circles.

Kermilla opened her door and froze.

That dumb bitch Birdie, the "Queen's maid," was holding a bottle of scent Kermilla had acquired during her last shopping trip. Holding the bottle—and frowning.

"What in the name of Hell are you doing?" Kermilla demanded. She strode over to the dresser and yanked the bottle out of Birdie's hand.

"Cleaning the room, Lady, like I always do," Birdie stammered, taking a step back.

"I told you before I don't like my things smeared with someone else's psychic stink," Kermilla said, her voice cold and hard. "You use Craft to raise everything on the dresser and tables when you dust them. *Craft,* you useless bag."

"But I only wear the White, Lady," Birdie said. "I only use Craft to help with heavy lifting and the like, so I'm not drained when my work is done. Lady Cassidy—"

"I'm not Cassidy, and as long as you work in this house, you'll do things the way *I* want them done. And if you can't get *that* through your head, the only way you'll earn a living is by using what you've got between your legs! Is that clear enough?"

"But—"

One word. Kermilla heard it as a challenge—and no White-Jeweled *servant* could be allowed to challenge the Queen.

*You're still a guest here.*

Remembering that had her putting temper and not power behind the open-handed slap. The blow still knocked Birdie to the floor.

"Get out of my room," Kermilla said.

Whimpering, Birdie got to her feet and stumbled from the room.

Shaken, Kermilla looked at the bottle of scent. The girl probably didn't know what that small, paper-thin stone disk on the bottom of the bottle meant, but Kermilla was certain Theran would be furious if he discovered how she was stretching her income.

She didn't want Theran angry with her. For a little while she'd flirted with the possibility of falling in love with him, but those feelings had faded before they began. Still, she *did* like the man, and she didn't want him so upset that he would tell her to leave. After all, she needed his support to become Queen of Dena Nehele.

### EBON ASKAVI

The Keep. The Black Mountain. A place where a man was surrounded by stone and dark power.

But a strangely comfortable place, for all that. A place where a man could lower his guard and truly rest, knowing there was something else here that was watchful—and aware.

Ranon prowled around the sitting room where the Seneschal, that strange-looking female, had put him to wait. A human shape, but she wasn't human—not with that face or the sibilant way she spoke. He'd bet his life on it.

The door opened, and he turned.

The woman's exotic face, framed by golden hair, was a little too thin, but still beautiful in a way that tugged at his male interest—especially because she seemed unaware of the streak of dirt that accented one sharp cheekbone.

Then he looked into those sapphire eyes and felt his heart skip a beat. He was totally committed to serving Cassidy, and he loved Shira with everything that was in him. But if this woman asked it of him, he would crawl through fire or over knives—and never ask why she required it of him.

He needed no introduction to know he was looking at Jaenelle Angelline, the Queen who was Witch, the living myth.

Now he understood what kind of woman could hold the hearts of men like Lucivar Yaslana and Daemon Sadi.

*I belong to her in the same way I belong to Cassidy.* And if Jaenelle demanded it of him, he would turn away from everything else he held dear in order to serve her.

"Lady."

"Prince Ranon?"

"Yes." He'd been nervous about meeting her, but he hadn't expected to respond to her like *this*. As he continued to look into those sapphire eyes, he realized she felt that bond too.

"I'm the *former* Queen of Ebon Askavi, Prince Ranon." Her voice held both amusement and warning.

*Former?* A word said for the Queen's pleasure—and believed by no one except, perhaps, the Queen herself. But he understood that she neither wanted nor expected him to turn away from Cassidy and the loyalty he felt for Shalador's Lady.

"I brought the reports and letters." He called in the message sack and set it on a nearby chair. "Reports are probably a bit lean. Cassidy has been working hard. But not too hard. We've insisted she take rest days, but there's no point having a rest day if it's going to be spent writing reports, is there?"

Hell's fire, he was babbling.

"No point at all," she agreed with a smile that told him plainly enough she'd fought—and lost—that particular battle with her own court.

He only realized he was smiling back when her smile faded.

"Do you know the history of your people, Ranon?" she asked. "Do you know how your people came to be in Dena Nehele?"

"Yes, I know the stories."

"People looked beyond themselves and made room for you. Remember that, Prince."

"I'm not likely to forget it," Ranon replied, puzzled. Some other message there. Or a warning? "Lady, is there something I should know?"

"I've told you what you need to know. The rest is up to you."

"I don't—" He stopped. Felt the room do one slow spin as he looked at the strange Jewel around her neck—and the hourglass pendant she wore just above that Jewel.

Black Widow as well as Witch.

Mother Night.

"Now," Jaenelle said. "This is why I asked to see you."

Two trunks appeared in front of him. Glancing at her for permission, he went down on one knee and lifted a lid. Picking up one of the items on top, he stood and opened the thin cover.

Old. Delicate.

His hands began to tremble when he realized what he held.

"That trunk has journals that record the daily life of the Shalador people—and the decline of Dena Nehele after Lia's death. Two generations. No journals were sent after that. The other trunk's contents are more formal. When the Tradition Keepers saw the decline begin, they took it as a warning. So they wrote down the stories and the songs, wrote down the rituals of the Shalador people, and brought that writing to Ebon Askavi. They knew many of those things would be lost in the decaying years, but they also hoped the time would come when the forgotten things could be reclaimed. Based on the last couple of letters Cassidy sent to me, I thought it was time for these to come back to the Shalador people."

Ranon put the journal back in the trunk before a tear fell and damaged the ink. "Thank you."

"I have one other thing for you." Jaenelle called in another package and handed it to him. "This was left here at the Keep for Daemon, but he and I agree that it should go to you now."

He unwrapped the package. Another journal? He opened it to a random page and read for a minute. Then he looked at Jaenelle. "Jared? This came from *Jared*?"

She nodded. "This is his account of the journey he made with Lia."

"And with Blaed and Thera." *And Talon.*

"Yes."

"This should go to Theran. He's the last Grayhaven," Ranon said as his grip tightened on the journal.

"It's yours now to do with as you please. But I'll remind you that Jared was a Shalador Warlord, and he was proud of it."

Ranon pressed a hand against his chest. "My heart is too full for words."

"And I have said all the words I need to say." Jaenelle smiled. "I need to get back to Kaeleer. My father is here standing escort. In fact, he helped me locate the journals. But my husband gets snarly if I stay at the Keep in Terreille for too long."

"I thank you for your time, Lady. And for these." He pointed at the trunks. "They are a gift to my people."

"May the Darkness embrace you, Prince Ranon."

He bowed and waited until she left the room before sinking into a chair to regain his breath and his balance before he headed home.

### TERREILLE

"Lady?"

Cassidy looked at Powell, who was hurrying toward her.

"Told you they'd notice you were still working," Reyhana said quietly.

★Grf.★ That was Vae's grumpy opinion.

"Oh, hush up, both of you." Cassidy tossed the handful of weeds into the basket, brushed off her hands, and smiled at Powell. "I wasn't working. Really. I was just pulling a few weeds and keeping Reyhana company while she brushed Vae." Of course, if she wanted him to accept the "a few weeds" fib, she should have vanished at least half the weeds in the basket.

"Excellent," Powell said. "You don't rest as much as you should."

"Powell?" Cassidy asked sharply. The man was too distracted to notice the basket? Her Steward noticed everything.

"There are some people who need to see you."

Not want, *need.* She sent out a psychic probe to get a feel for Spere's and Archerr's tempers, since they were the escorts on duty this afternoon, and wished Ranon or Gray were back from their respective errands—or that it was closer to sundown and Talon could be with her.

Simmering anger, tightly leashed. That was all she was picking up from her men.

"Reyhana, stay here. Vae, you stay with her," Cassidy said.

"But . . ." Reyhana began.

*"Stay."* Until she knew what this was about, she was not putting Reyhana in a potentially explosive situation.

★We will stay,★ Vae said.

That much settled, Cassidy strode to the house, Powell puffing to keep up with her. When she reached the parlor that was the waiting room for anyone wishing to have an audience with the Queen . . .

"Dryden?" Cassidy looked at the Grayhaven butler. "What . . . ? *Birdie?*"

*There* was the reason for the anger—that dark bruise on the little maid's face.

★Shira,★ Cassidy called. ★I need you in the visitors' parlor.★

★Cassie, I really don't feel . . . ★

★The Healer's attendance is required.★

Shira didn't reply. Cassidy didn't expect her to. Shira the woman had been holed up in her room, riding a mood since she'd gone out to look at properties with Gray, but the Healer would arrive in the parlor ready to practice her Craft.

Putting an arm around the maid, Cassidy led Birdie to a sofa and sat down with her. "What happened?"

"I didn't do anything bad," Birdie whispered. "I swear by the Jewels, I didn't."

"If I may explain, Lady?" Dryden asked.

Cassidy looked past him to the other people in the room. Elle, the housekeeper; Maydra, the cook; and four of the young men who worked in the Grayhaven stable and had befriended Gray before he'd begun to heal from the emotional scars that had their roots in the torture he'd endured.

Shira burst into the room, took one look at Birdie, and said, "Hell's fire. Let me get some ice from the block in the freeze box."

"I'll do that," Spere said. He slipped out of the room.

"We did use a cold spell on a wet cloth to keep the swelling down," Elle said. Then she added bitterly, "Had enough experience dealing with this sort of thing before."

Cassidy rose and stepped aside, giving Shira room to work. Moving to the other end of the parlor, flanked by Archerr and Powell, she faced Dryden, who was flanked by Elle and Maydra. "Explain, Lord Dryden."

"Prince Grayhaven's guest hit Birdie," Dryden said.

A flash of rage, quickly chained. From Dryden.

"What guest?" Powell asked, but his tone said he already knew the answer.

"That . . . woman."

Oh, Hell's fire. This was bad. She'd only had this experience once, when an aristo witch who had been a guest had tried to coerce a footman into doing "bedroom work." Because of the social difference between an aristo and a servant, her butler had refused to say the woman's name when he'd come to her and reported the abuse.

Or maybe refusing to say the witch's name had been the measure of the man's contempt for her behavior.

"You mean Lady Kermilla?" Powell asked.

Dryden nodded.

Elle said, "Lady Bitch," under her breath, quietly enough that Cassidy pretended no one had heard the housekeeper's opinion of the other Dharo Queen.

"Why would she hit Birdie?" Cassidy asked. Her stomach felt like it was full of foaming milk. Hadn't she voiced concerns about Kermilla when the other Queen had been training with her? The court had adored the pretty, dark-haired girl; the servants had disliked her.

"Birdie was cleaning her room the way I told the girl she could clean—and the way you allowed her to do for you. But that other one didn't want her things touched, wanted Birdie to be using Craft all the time to lift or move every little thing."

"That makes no sense," Cassidy said.

"It does if the Lady doesn't want anyone picking up an object and noticing something unusual about it," Powell said, looking at Dryden.

The butler nodded. "Birdie picked up a bottle of scent from the dresser—a bottle that still had the theft disk on it."

Frowning, Cassidy looked at Powell for explanation.

"A spelled disk of paper-thin stone," Powell explained. "It was a common practice in the shops favored by the Queens and their aristo companions to put such a disk on small, expensive items that had a way of going missing. Since he didn't want to lose an eye or his tongue, the merchant couldn't acknowledge the theft, even if he saw the person do it. But a bottle of scent, for example, that left the boundaries of the shop with the disk still on the bottle would be spoiled."

"Spoiled?" Cassidy asked.

"Imagine a dozen rotten eggs breaking on the kitchen floor," Maydra said. "Of course, the way some of those spells worked, the scent smelled fine until it warmed on the skin for a little while. So the Lady was usually well into her social engagement before she, and everyone else, realized something was wrong."

"Oh." Cassidy clamped a hand over her nose in automatic response. Lowering her hand, she smiled sheepishly. Then she glanced at Birdie and found nothing to smile about. "So Birdie picked up a bottle of stolen scent and Kermilla hit her."

"Yes," Dryden said. "When I reported the abuse to Prince Grayhaven, Kermilla insisted that she caught Birdie trying to steal from her and that was why she struck the girl."

"Grayhaven believed that?" Archerr asked.

Dryden looked sad. "Sometimes a man only sees what he wants to see."

"Shit," Archerr said softly.

"Birdie was dismissed without references," Dryden said. "Elle, Maydra, and I talked it over, and handed in our resignations. We have worked for such witches before. We do not want to work for such a one again. As it turned out, four of the stable lads have no ties to the town, no family to hold them there, and they didn't want to stay either." He hesitated, then looked Cassidy in the eyes. "We came in the hope that you might have a place for us here."

She didn't know what to say. Powell, however, didn't have that problem.

"There are servants' quarters here, including a separate parlor off the kitchen. Didn't ask to have those rooms cleaned since we weren't using them."

Maydra frowned. "If you have no servants here, who's been cooking for you and your court?"

"Oh, well, I've been doing a bit of it, along with some of the women in the village." Cassidy's voice trailed away.

"You've been doing your own dusting too?" Birdie piped up, sounding shocked.

The Grayhaven servants stared at her.

*I wouldn't admit to running a dust rag over the furniture,* Powell said, sounding amused. *You've shocked them quite enough for one day.*

*As my father is fond of saying, I was born a daughter on the same day as I was born a Queen, and if I can get dirty weeding a garden, I can get dirty washing a floor.*

*Your father is a wise man, but I think it is time to relinquish some of your less-than-Queenly duties. Besides, they need the work, and we need the help. With your consent, I'll discuss duties and compensation with them.*

*All right.* She smiled at each of the servants and stable lads—and especially at Birdie. "Welcome to Eyota. There is plenty of work here for all of us. Prince Powell will discuss the details with you."

She walked out of the room, heading for the back door that would take her to the gardens. Then she changed direction and went up to her room. She wanted solitude. She needed privacy.

*Cassie?* Vae called softly. *Cassie!*

*There is no danger,* Cassidy said. *You can let Reyhana come in now.*

*She wants to talk to you.*

*No. I need to be alone for a little while.*

A hesitation. *We will wait for you.*

Cassidy lay down on her bed and stared at the ceiling. Theran probably would accuse her of telling tales, and Kermilla certainly would accuse her of acting out of jealousy and spite. But it was the bruised look in Birdie's eyes more than the bruise on her face that had to be the deciding factor. Besides, no matter how hard it was, she had a duty to report Kermilla's behavior. Since he ruled the town of Grayhaven, Theran should be the one who disciplined Kermilla—something he wouldn't do if he truly belonged to the other Dharo Queen.

Dharo Queen. That was the sticking point, wasn't it? Kermilla ruled a village in Dharo. Her conduct was the business of the Queen who ruled that Territory. So Cassidy had a responsibility to Sabrina, Territory Queen to Territory Queen, to inform the Queen of Dharo that the conduct of one of Dharo's District Queens needed careful review.

If Kermilla, as a guest, had struck a servant, what was she doing to the people in Bhak—people whose lives depended on their Queen's mercy?

*Get it done. This isn't about you and Kermilla, no matter what anyone else might think. This is about being a Queen.*

Sitting up, she called in the lap desk the High Lord had given her, selected a sheet of stationery with her initial on it, and began writing her letter to Sabrina.

"Ranon!"

Seeing Gray trotting toward him from the court's stables, Ranon stopped at the edge of the street and waited. He'd walked from the northern landing web, wanting the time to contact his grandfather, who would contact Akeelah. For now, two Tradition Keepers were enough to stand witness to what he'd brought home.

"Where's Shira?" Ranon asked when Gray reached him.

"She's been home for a while. I had another errand to run and just got back." Gray cocked a thumb over his shoulder toward the stables. "Four of the stable lads from Grayhaven are working at the stables here. Just started an hour ago. They're taking one of the cottages across from the stables as their living quarters. And some of the other servants from Grayhaven are working at the Residence. Did Cassie say anything to you about this? Or Talon?"

Ranon shook his head. "I just got back myself. Let's find out—" He stopped when Gray gripped his arm. "What?"

"I need to go away for a couple of days. Three at the most. I need you to come with me."

Ranon studied the other Warlord Prince. Something different. Of course, Gray seemed to be changing daily, but this blend of excitement, fear, and determination was new.

"Where are we going?" Ranon asked.

"To Dhemlan. In Kaeleer. To talk to Daemon Sadi."

A few months ago, Theran had been the one going in search of Daemon Sadi. Now it was Gray.

"There are things we need, for the court and for this village. I have an idea of how we can start to get them. But I need to talk to Daemon, and there are some decisions I can't make alone."

"Why me?"

"You're Shalador's Warlord Prince."

The words rocked him. Yes, he was the last adult Warlord Prince until youngsters like his brother Janos came of age, but Gray's phrasing gave a weight, a *duty*, to a truth he'd lived with for the past few years.

"If Cassie gives her consent to this journey, I'll go with you," Ranon said.

Gray huffed out a breath and smiled. "Good. So let's find out what everyone else was up to today."

*Plenty,* Ranon thought when Dryden opened the door and greeted them.

It looked like they were *all* going to have something to talk about that evening.

# CHAPTER 17

## TERREILLE

Kermilla frowned at the toast that was burnt around the edges. She tasted the eggs and made a face. As she pushed her plate away—and noticed Correne doing the same—Theran walked into the small breakfast room.

That was unusual. She and Correne, the "Ladies of the court," had breakfast alone, leaving the men to a working breakfast where they reviewed their assignments for the day and were allowed to be fools before they had to put on their manners.

It might be unusual to see him in the breakfast room, but his timing was perfect.

"Theran, what in the name of Hell is wrong with the cook today?" Kermilla complained. "The toast is burned, and these eggs are unacceptable. And the beef is . . . Well, I can hardly choke it down."

"I suggest you try," Theran said in an odd voice. "The woman who was the cook's assistant has a blind eye and a weak arm, courtesy of the last Queen she served. She's doing the best she can."

"Why is she doing it at all?" Correne asked, sounding pouty.

She was going to have to talk to the girl about when a good pout worked and when it caused nothing but trouble—and judging by the look in Theran's eyes, being anything but helpful today was going to cause trouble.

Ignoring Correne, Theran watched Kermilla. "The cook, the house-keeper, and the butler resigned yesterday."

She heard a hint of accusation in his voice. "Because I had to discipline Birdie?"

Theran's face tightened. "You call it discipline. You said it was necessary, and I'm sure you wouldn't have struck the girl without good reason. But Dryden called it abuse, said it was the same kind of treatment the purged Queens used to inflict on servants—and the kind of treatment I had promised him no one would endure in this house. So the senior servants resigned, along with four of the stable lads. It may take a while before I can replace them." He glanced at Correne. "Ladies."

Stunned, Kermilla watched him walk out of the room. That little bitch Birdie *had* to be disciplined. The other servants should have accepted that!

"What did he mean by the purged Queens?" Kermilla asked.

Correne pulled her plate back and began eating. "The Queens who were destroyed by that witch storm a couple of years ago." She shuddered. "I heard it swept through the whole Realm and consumed lots and lots of people."

"How many Queens?" Kermilla whispered.

"The Territory Queen and all the Province Queens. Lots of the District Queens too. That's why Cassidy had to come and rule here. There has been talk of letting Queens establish a court when they're eighteen, which is before the age of majority and before they're ready to make the Offering to the Darkness."

"Why would they do that?"

"The old Queens are too old to rule more than one village, so *someone* has to regain control of the Provinces." Correne leaned forward. "I got a letter from a friend yesterday. *She* said some of the Warlord Princes are claiming whole districts as their personal territory and ruling like they were *Queens*."

Having males rule on a Queen's behalf wasn't that unusual—at least, not in Kaeleer—but Correne sounded shocked. And with good reason. If the most aggressive and dangerous caste of male began taking control and ruling without a Queen's leash, the young Queens might end up being ruled by Warlord Princes instead of the other way around.

And the Queen who could stop *that* change would have the loyalty of every other Queen in this land.

"Look, look, look!" Powell danced into the breakfast room, waving a handful of papers over his head.

Momentarily frozen in the act of biting into a piece of toast—which Birdie *and* Maydra pointed out that she had *not* had to make for herself— Cassidy finished chewing while she, Shira, and Reyhana watched the gleeful Steward.

"What are we looking at?" Cassidy asked.

"The dominant Warlord Princes living in the two southernmost Provinces have sent in a proposed division of those Provinces into districts that would be ruled by a Warlord Prince if a Queen wasn't available."

"There aren't more than a hundred adult Warlord Princes left in Dena Nehele," Shira said. "Could so few actually rule effectively?"

Cassidy wiped her hands on a napkin and reached for the papers. "Let me see those." Her heart pounded and her hands trembled. No indication of which districts would be ruled by Queens. Not that she'd expected them to offer *that* much trust yet. She'd come to realize that the Queens who had met with her had been prepared to be sacrificed if the new Territory Queen turned out to be as twisted as the one who had ruled before. This was evidence that the Warlord Princes who had been disappointed when they had first seen her were now reconsidering what her knowledge might give their people.

"Maybe . . ." Reyhana began. She immediately hunched her shoulders and toyed with her scrambled eggs.

"Maybe . . . ?" Cassidy said.

"It's not my place to speak."

"Reyhana, I enjoy your company and I value you as a friend, but you're also here to learn how to be a Queen. I can't offer guidance if you don't tell me what you think."

The girl straightened up. "Are any of the Warlord Princes taking responsibility for a whole Province?"

"That would be a bit too aggressive," Powell said gently. "It's one thing to rule what the available Queens can't handle themselves; it's quite another to rule over a Queen."

"Although it is done," Cassidy said. "Daemon Sadi is the Warlord Prince of Dhemlan. He *rules* that Territory, and every Queen in Dhemlan answers to him. He is the exception, that is true, but Queens do sometimes rule within a Warlord Prince's Territory and not the other way around. Lucivar Yaslana is another example. He rules Ebon Rih, the territory that belongs to the Keep. The Queens who rule the villages there answer to him."

"I stand corrected," Powell said with a smile.

"Someone needs to rule each Province, isn't that true?" Reyhana said.

"Just getting the Warlord Princes to step up to the line and agree to rule a district is a victory," Shira said. "At least half of these men lived in the rogue camps in the Tamanara Mountains after they reached puberty. Actually living in a village with the families they left behind is a new experience for them."

"This is a good start, but it's just a start," Cassidy said.

"Why can't your First Circle act as Province liaisons between the districts and the court?" Reyhana asked. "The same way Prince Ranon does for the Shalador reserves?"

"The way Ranon does?" Cassidy asked, glancing at Shira—who was frowning thoughtfully.

"May I?" Powell asked, indicating an empty chair.

"Yes, of course," Cassidy replied. "Here, it's probably best if we look at these papers more carefully in your office."

Powell vanished the papers. Moments later, Birdie came in with a pot of fresh coffee, another cup and saucer, and more toast.

Cassidy wondered who had told Maydra that Powell was joining her for breakfast. Then she noticed Vae in the doorway. The Sceltie wagged her tail once and left, no doubt to herd a few more of her humans.

"Please explain about Ranon," Powell said.

"I don't think he ever visited all the villages," Reyhana said, "but Janos told me Ranon would visit all three of the reserves and meet with the elders at least once each season. So he always knew if there was trouble or when things were getting too hard. Even during the uprisings, when he was off fighting, he'd visit a reserve if he was close by."

"He's been doing that for as long as I've known him," Shira said. "Visiting the elders. I thought he was showing his respect. He never said otherwise."

*No, he wouldn't have said otherwise*, Cassidy thought. But that awareness of his people . . . Not so different from what the males in Jaenelle's court had done. Not so different at all.

"If a member of the First Circle visited a Province once or twice a month," Powell said thoughtfully, "and made it known he would carry back any concerns to the Queen, I think other men would approach him— especially if he's already known to those men. Not an official ruler, but a reminder that all others who rule in Dena Nehele do so on the Territory Queen's behalf. That is an excellent idea, Lady Reyhana."

Cassidy smiled at Reyhana and lifted her coffee cup as a salute. "Yes, it *is* an excellent idea."

Too bad Gray wasn't here to share this moment with her.


KAELEER


Ranon stood in Daemon Sadi's study, a stunned look on his face. "Mother Night, Gray. The man has a *butler* who wears a Red Jewel."

Gray looked around the richly furnished room. There had been a jelly-knee moment when the door to SaDiablo Hall opened and that large, formidable man had stared at them. But it was clear the High Lord had sent a message ahead of them and they were expected, because Beale had led them to this room and informed them that the Prince would be with them shortly.

Noticing the stuffed toy on the floor near the long sofa, he nudged Ranon. "He may have a Red-Jeweled butler, but he also has a Sceltie."

"Then may the Darkness have mercy on him," Ranon muttered.

The door opened. Ranon sucked in a breath. Gray turned.

Beautiful, deadly man. Had he felt that sexual punch the last time he'd seen Daemon, or was there a reason why that heat and power were sharper today?

"Gray, it's good to see you again."

*Is it?* Gray wondered, noticing Daemon's slightly glazed eyes. "Prince Sadi, may I introduce my friend Prince Ranon?"

Those gold eyes studied Ranon just a little too long.

"You're Shaladoran," Daemon said.

"I am," Ranon replied. "How did you know?"

"You have the look of your people. Why don't we sit down and you can tell me what brings you here."

Gray started to turn toward the informal side of the room. Daemon walked over to the blackwood desk and settled in the chair behind it, leaving him and Ranon no choice but to sit in the visitors' chairs.

He nodded to Ranon, who called in a package and set it carefully on the desk. "Lady Cassidy asked me to give this to you, along with this letter."

Daemon opened the letter and seemed to take a long time reading the single page. Then he opened the package that contained Jared's journal and brushed his fingertips gently over the cover.

"While I appreciate her efforts at economy, Cassidy's request, as written, is not the most practical," Daemon said.

"I'll convey the message," Ranon said. He reached for the package. It vanished before he touched it.

"Therefore," Daemon said, "I will take care of it as it should be done."

Ranon hesitated, and Gray understood why. Jared's story was one of the most precious gifts Jaenelle Angelline had sent back to the Shalador people.

Daemon steepled his fingers and rested the forefinger nails against his chin. "Is that why you asked to come to Dhemlan? I could have met you at the Keep."

"We need a loan." Gray hadn't meant to say it that bluntly. In fact, he'd spent a good part of the journey rehearsing what he would say. Too bad the words just plopped out of his mouth.

"*What?*" Ranon yelped.

"We need a loan," Gray said again, keeping his eyes on Daemon, who had done nothing more than raise an eyebrow.

"You are aware of the Queen's gift?" Daemon asked.

Ignoring the slight chill in the words—after all, he figured plenty of people would like to dip a hand into the SaDiablo wealth—Gray nodded. "But that's just for Cassie, for the things she needs that her people can't provide yet."

"All right, I'm listening."

*Gray, what are you doing?* Ranon asked.

Gray ignored his friend. "We need a loan to start building a life for the people again. For some simple things, like blankets and linens, and cloth so women can sew clothes for their children."

"*Gray,*" Ranon said, his voice a clear warning to stop.

"We need money to fix up a Healer's House. The village will give us the land and buildings, but Shira needs money to fix it up so that she can take care of the court and some of the villagers."

"Does she know about this?" Ranon asked.

"Not yet. She wants that place, and it's perfect. But I didn't want to tell her I'd gotten the deed made out for her until I talked to Daemon about a loan to fix it up."

Ranon looked ready to fall out of his chair. "Deed. You got an official deed?"

"Yes. I talked to the elders yesterday. They witnessed the deed. The property that backs the Queen's Residence now belongs to Shira." Gray paused. "To you, too, I guess, since you're living with her, but I asked to have it put in Shira's name since it will be a Healer's residence."

"*But you didn't tell her?*"

Why was Ranon getting so pissy? It was the best thing to do for the women and the court. "No. But I haven't told Cassie yet that the Queen's Residence belongs to her now. She'll feel better about fixing it up into the home she wants once she knows she holds the deed."

Daemon started coughing. "We'll . . . ah . . . have to talk about how to ease into these conversations so you don't stun the Ladies when you get home."

Gray looked at the Warlord Prince of Dhemlan. No chill in the voice now. No, Daemon seemed to be struggling with the effort not to laugh. "You think Cassie and Shira are going to go hissy cat about this?"

"Hissy cat?" Those gold eyes were starting to water.

"A Sceltie term for a riled human female."

Daemon's roar of laughter filled the room.

A couple of minutes later, Sadi finally regained some control. "So you want a loan to fix up the Healer's House. Anything else?"

"I don't know," Gray said, pressing his hands between his knees and leaning toward the desk. "But you have businesses in other Territories besides Dhemlan, don't you?"

Something pained and sad flickered in Daemon's eyes. "I used to have a few businesses in Dena Nehele. It helped some people defy Dorothea's bitches for a little while longer."

*But the land fell anyway. How many places did you help hold on a little while longer? No wonder Lucivar said you can't come to Dena Nehele the way he can. There's no place in Terreille you can go that doesn't hold bitter memories, is there?*

"We could use your help again," Gray said quietly. "In return for fixing up the buildings and providing the merchandise, since that's one of the things we don't have, the elders in Eyota have agreed to give you the buildings and the land they're on for a hundred years. That may not sound like a long time to you, but it's a long time for us."

Daemon looked away, and Gray got the impression that Sadi was trying to decide about something more important than a couple of buildings and some merchandise.

Then Daemon rose and came around the desk. "Let's go down the road and spend some time in Halaway. It's a small village and some of the shops there should give us all a reference point."

"Okay," Gray said as he and Ranon stood up and followed Daemon to the door.

A quick knock. The door opened.

Daemon froze midstep. His nostrils flared as Jaenelle walked into the room—and the gold eyes that now looked at Gray and Ranon held a barely controlled savagery.

"Daemon," Jaenelle said softly.

Daemon stared at the two men and snarled.

"*Prince.*"

Those gold eyes focused on her.

She, in turn, smiled at Gray and Ranon.

*Mother Night, Gray, I can smell moon's blood,* Ranon said. *We have to get out of this room before he kills us.*

*How?*

Ranon gave no answer, since moving toward the door meant moving toward Jaenelle, and that would be a lethal mistake.

Then two other males entered the room and stopped on either side of Jaenelle at the same time Daemon stepped closer to her.

Still smiling at Gray and Ranon, Jaenelle said, "I believe you know my little brother, Ladvarian."

Gray hadn't met the Red-Jeweled Sceltie Warlord when Ladvarian and Khardeen came to Eyota, but he nodded anyway.

She hooked an arm around her other companion's neck. "And this pretty kitty is Prince Kaelas."

The "pretty kitty" was a white, huge Warlord Prince who wore a Red Jewel—and wasn't half as terrifying as Daemon at that moment.

"You have some business to take care of this afternoon?" Jaenelle released Kaelas and turned toward Daemon.

"It can be postponed," he said in a croon that produced a chill down Gray's spine.

"There's no reason for that," Jaenelle replied. "At this moment, Beale and Holt are in my private garden, arranging a lounge chair in the shady spot, Mrs. Beale is making a pitcher of that fruit punch I enjoy drinking in warm weather, Ladvarian and Kaelas are going to keep me company, and . . ." She called in a book and held it up between them. "I have Fiona's new Tracker and Shadow novel to read."

Daemon studied his wife through narrowed eyes. "In other words, you have no use for me this afternoon."

"No use at all."

The words could have been cutting to a man in love, but not when they were accompanied by the look in Jaenelle's gorgeous eyes as she smiled at Daemon and gave his face a brief caress.

A code, Gray thought. Like the one he and Cassie had.

"You'll bring our guests back for dinner," Jaenelle said.

Daemon hesitated. "As my Lady wishes."

*He doesn't want us anywhere near her, but he won't hesitate to hurt us if we decline her invitation,* Ranon said.

*Did you read the section in the Protocol book that covers this situation?* Gray asked.

*Yes. Thank the Darkness.*

"Gentlemen," Jaenelle said before she left the room with Ladvarian and Kaelas.

"Shall we go?" Daemon asked.

He didn't wait for an answer, so they followed him out of the Hall.


Daemon stopped at the edge of Halaway and waited for his companions to catch up. Gray and Ranon had been trailing after him since he'd walked out of the Hall and headed for the village on foot. He had needed the movement, had needed to burn off some of the temper. When Saetan had contacted him to find out if he was willing to host Gray and Ranon, he'd warned his father that Jaenelle's moontime was close and he might not respond well to male visitors.

Jaenelle had decided that the visit shouldn't be postponed.

Daemon frowned. Gray and Ranon immediately stopped walking.

He sighed. "It's all right. I'm steady now and won't eviscerate you for being in the same room as my wife." But in the moment before Jaenelle had said "Prince" in a tone he recognized as a command, he had considered it.

Ah, well. At least he could tell Saetan that two of Cassidy's court had paid attention to the additional notes about how Warlord Princes reacted to the scent of moon's blood and how to avoid provoking an attack.

"You could have told us not to come," Gray said when he reached Daemon.

"My Lady decided otherwise," Daemon replied.

"So . . . no choice."

"None. But if it makes you feel any better, Ladvarian and Kaelas didn't object to your presence today. Since those two didn't see you as a threat to the Lady, I can keep my temper leashed."

"What kind of cat is Kaelas?" Ranon asked.

"Arcerian," Daemon replied. "In fact, he's the Warlord Prince of Arceria. All eight hundred pounds of him."

"Mother Night."

He liked these men, and while he wanted them to be careful during their stay at the Hall, he saw no reason to frighten them. So unless it became necessary, he wouldn't tell them what a Red-Jeweled Warlord Prince of Kaelas's size, speed, and strength could do to a human body when he got pissed off.

"Let's take a look at the village," Daemon said.

It was a small, healthy village, prosperous enough to take care of itself and the people within its boundaries.

Daemon noted the way that the males who were simply going about their business went on alert at the sight of strangers—and relaxed when they realized the strangers were with him. He noted how the village guards came trotting past to get a look at the strangers *despite* Gray and Ranon being with him.

"Does this village often see trouble?" Ranon asked when Gray stopped at a bookshop window and stared at the display, damn near vibrating with excitement.

"No," Daemon replied. "Considering its proximity to the Hall, if trouble starts here and the Queen's court can't handle it, I will."

"But all the males are ready to defend."

"It is our nature, Ranon."

The shop door opened and Sylvia walked out. She wore a sleeveless shirt tucked into a pair of knee-length trousers and sandals. Her short black hair looked deliberately mussed enough to be called sassy, and there wasn't a single thing besides her psychic scent that would give anyone a clue that she was the Queen of Halaway.

Daemon moved to join Gray, who had turned away from the window and given Sylvia a quick, assessing look before smiling brightly.

"Good afternoon, Lady," Gray said.

Sylvia narrowed her gold eyes. "You look familiar, but not."

"May I introduce Prince Jared Blaed Grayhaven and Prince Ranon," Daemon said. "They're here visiting from Dena Nehele. Gentlemen, this is Lady Sylvia."

Gray frowned at him. "You didn't introduce her as a Queen."

Proof enough that Gray was far more perceptive than his cousin when it came to recognizing caste.

He glanced at Sylvia, who gave him a tiny nod. "You're right. I didn't. Lady Sylvia rules Halaway and prefers to be informal in her home village unless formality is required."

Gray beamed at Sylvia. "That's the way Cassie wants things to be in Eyota. The Shaladorans are pretty comfortable with that because they're used to their Queens living among them, so I think she's happier living where we do now than she was when we were in Grayhaven."

Hell's fire, Daemon thought as he looked at Sylvia's slightly stunned expression and swallowed the urge to laugh. The earnest young Warlord Prince who had asked him for a loan had changed into a two-legged puppy.

"I met someone else named Grayhaven recently," Sylvia said.

"Jared Blaed and Theran are cousins," Daemon said.

Sylvia's smile had sharp edges. "And how is Theran getting along with Vae?"

"Oh, Vae lives with Cassie and me now," Gray said. "So does Khollie, but that's because Ranon and Shira live in the Queen's Residence with us."

"Well, that must make story time easier for all of you, since the humans can take turns."

"Story time?"

*Ah, no, Sylvia,* Daemon thought. But he wasn't going to stop her.

"You don't know about story time?" Sylvia asked, widening her eyes. When Gray shook his head, she opened the bookshop door and called to someone inside. "Do you have any copies of *Unicorn to the Rescue* or *Sceltie Saves the Day?*" She turned back to Gray. "How many Scelties live with you?"

"There are thirteen in our village," Gray said, looking back at Daemon.

*Finally figured out something is going on, haven't you, boyo?* Of course, it was much too late to *do* anything about it, but it was always good for a man to recognize when he was in trouble.

"What?" Sylvia leaned into the shop, then back out. "Oh, good. They also have a couple of copies of *Dragon and the Dangerous Deed.*"

"I don't think . . ." Ranon began.

"A gift," Sylvia said. "Enjoy your visit, gentlemen. Prince Sadi."

Daemon watched her hurry away and duck into a shop a couple of doors down from the bookshop. He huffed out a breath. "While we're in the shop, there are a few other books you might find entertaining." The Tracker and Shadow books were adventures or mysteries for most readers, but anyone who dealt with a Sceltie also found them instructional.

"She was laughing when she went into that other shop," Gray said as Daemon led the two men into the bookshop. "Why was she laughing?"

"Once you show those books to any Sceltie, you'll understand," Daemon replied dryly. *And may the Darkness have mercy on you.*

He let them look around while he selected a few books that he thought Cassidy would enjoy since Jaenelle or Marian had liked them. Ranon showed polite interest, but Gray loved books and stories, and kept delaying so that he could see "just one more thing." Daemon ended up selecting a few more books for them to take back to Eyota and then hauled Gray out of the shop so they could see more of the village.

Gray showed a boyish enthusiasm for everything he saw except, oddly, the bakery, which he glanced at and then bolted past. Ranon's emotions were more contained and more intense—especially when Daemon showed the Shaladoran the music shop. The place sold sheet music and instruments that spanned the Territories in Kaeleer, as well as the music crystals that had audio spells.

He didn't tell them Jaenelle owned this shop, which was the reason it had such an eclectic variety of music—and why it had an attached room with a small stage for performances. Twice a month, she joined the musicians and sang there—and on those nights, there was never an empty chair.

He mentioned the performances and pointed out the nearby tavern and coffee shop. Ranon appreciated the potential businesses. Gray was more dazzled by the small courtyards that were shady gathering places accented with flower beds.

By the time they settled at a table in one of those courtyards with glasses of ale and a plate of sandwiches, Daemon had a very good idea what kind of businesses would do well in Eyota.

"All right, gentlemen . . ." he began.

"It's the boy."

Daemon rose at the sound of that female voice and was pleased that Gray and Ranon responded just as quickly.

"Tersa," he said warmly as he kissed her cheek. Her long black hair was always as tangled as her mind, but it gave him comfort to know she could wander around this village and be safe. "Would you join us?"

"You are trying to feed me," she accused.

Of course he was. Even having a journeymaid Black Widow living with her, Tersa still didn't remember to eat when her mind traveled its own strange paths.

"Only a little," he said, giving her a boyish smile.

She gave his arm a light, dismissive smack as she glanced at Ranon. Then she looked at Gray, and Daemon felt the change in her—and saw Gray go absolutely still.

"This is the one," Tersa said softly. She called in a glass globe supported by a carved wooden base and set it in front of Gray. Then she touched the small amethyst in the base. "Watch."

Smoke filled the globe as the spell engaged.

*Changes,* Daemon thought. *Metamorphosis.* He watched as a dagger was cocooned, then emerged as a small boy who had no limbs. That image cocooned and emerged as a dead tree, which cocooned and emerged as a living tree that bore daggers as its fruit. That image cocooned and emerged as a dragon breathing fire—a powerful warrior.

All the color had drained out of Gray's face when he saw the first two images—and something Daemon couldn't name filled those green eyes when Gray saw the last image.

The sequence started again. When the image of the dagger tree co-cooned, the sequence stopped.

"This is where you are," Tersa said.

"How do I get to the last stage?" Gray asked, his eyes fixed on the shrouded image.

"When the time comes, accept the fire that lives within you."

*Tersa?* Daemon asked.

*Trust your wife—and trust your own heart.*

She kissed him and walked away.

Shaken, he sat down and drained the glass of ale. Gray and Ranon did the same, so he flicked a thought at the tavern owner, who hurried out a minute later with a cold pitcher of ale.

"Who is she?" Ranon asked after the second glass of ale.

"My mother," Daemon replied.

"She's . . . different," Gray said, clearly not wanting to offend, but just as clearly wanting an answer.

"She's a broken Black Widow," Daemon said. "She's been walking the roads of the Twisted Kingdom for a long time, but her mind completely shattered a few centuries ago when she made the choice to forfeit sanity in order to regain her Craft. In the past few years, she's been living closer to the border of sanity, which lets her have a life in the village."

"If she can't wear a Jewel, how does she . . . ?" Ranon asked.

"I don't know. Even my father doesn't know. But sane or not, Jewels or not, she has always been a formidable witch."

"Does Jaenelle know how Tersa regained power through madness?" Gray asked.

"Probably, since my Lady has walked roads even darker than the ones Tersa has traveled." But this was not something he wanted to think about right now, so he said, "Gentlemen. Let's talk about doing business."

## TERREILLE

*Thank the Darkness neither of us have to drive this Coach,* Ranon thought as he and Gray huddled in the comfortable back compartment of the SaDiablo Coach provided by Daemon. They'd had a delicious dinner. At least, he assumed it was delicious. He couldn't remember a single bite of it. Afterward, Sadi had opened the Gate next to the Hall and instructed one of the drivers who worked for the SaDiablo family to take his guests back to Dena Nehele. So they were heading home directly from the Hall, riding the Opal Winds.

"Mother Night, Gray," Ranon said, keeping his voice low even though they couldn't be heard through the closed door separating their compartment from the driver's. "Five million gold marks. Do you have any idea how much that is?"

Gray shook his head. "I don't think I've ever *seen* a gold mark. I got a ten silver mark once for my birthday, and I thought it was a fortune. Do you really think we could spend that many gold marks?"

Ranon took a deep breath and felt his body tremble as he breathed out. "Wouldn't be hard to do. We've had so little for so long, it wouldn't be hard to do. Paying it back is a different thing altogether."

"Shops and supplies," Gray said. "Forage for the animals if the harvest falls short this year."

"Food for us if the crops fall short this year," Ranon said. Although with so many Blood dead in the past two years, having people starve was less likely. Having the crops rot in the fields because there weren't enough hands to harvest them was a possibility, even if the Blood used Craft and drained their power every day to get the harvest in.

"We'll have to find the right kinds of buildings for the shops Daemon wants."

"We'll find them."

Ranon closed his eyes. A music shop like the one he'd seen in Halaway. A room where the Tradition Keepers like his grandfather could teach openly what had been forbidden for so many years. And Sadi's gift . . .

*"It's not the same,"* Daemon had said, *"but the music of Scelt has a complex simplicity that I think is similar to Shalador's music. At least as I remember it. You might enjoy it."*

The music crystals and the brass stand. Such a simple thing, really, and not so simple. Like Sadi casually pointing out some folk music from Dharo that could be played on a flute.

Sharing customs. Sharing hopes.

Kind of funny, actually. Now that the Shaladorans could honor their own traditions, it didn't sting to look beyond his own people and consider what other traditions might have to offer.


## KAELEER


A quick scan of the messages that had arrived that afternoon confirmed that nothing required his immediate attention, so Daemon went up to Jaenelle's sitting room. When she marked her place in her book and set it aside, he took that as an invitation. He picked her up, then sat down in the stuffed chair with her on his lap.

"Our guests are on their way home?" She ran her fingers through his hair, a soothing caress.

"They are." He called in Jared's journal and held it up for her to see.

"They didn't want it?" Disappointment filled her voice and eyes.

"They want to preserve the original and also be able to share the contents. Cassidy sent a note with the journal asking if the Queen's gift could be extended to having a couple of copies made so that people could read Jared's account of his journey with Lia."

She studied him. "That doesn't sound like an extravagant request."

"It's not. It's also not a practical request."

"Ah. And what would my darling Prince consider a practical request?"

He shrugged. "A thousand copies would be a good start."

She laughed. "What are you going to do with a thousand copies?"

"For one thing, sell them in the merchant's shop I'm opening in Eyota. They can buy the book there, then go over to the coffee shop I'm also opening and read while enjoying a cup or two of their favorite beverage."

She hooted. "How many shops did Gray and Ranon talk you into opening?"

He laughed with her. "Four. Plus a loan the court can use to help the people start rebuilding their lives and villages."

Then his laughter faded. He cuddled Jaenelle, needing that comfort.

"What's troubling you?" she asked.

"Did I do the right thing?"

"How big a loan did you give them?" she asked.

"Five million gold marks."

She laughed softly. "That explains why they both looked like they couldn't remember how to breathe when you brought them back from the village and couldn't string words together in a coherent sentence all through dinner."

"Jaenelle, did I do the right thing?"

"Why would you ask that?

"Because Dena Nehele is going to fall."

She rested a hand over his heart. "Daemon, pretend you never heard that. *Act* as if you'd never heard that. That's what I'm going to do."

"In that case, I'm going to talk to Lord Burle about doing a bit of work on my new properties in Eyota."

"You could also offer those properties as training ground if there were any youngsters in that village who wanted to learn the carpenter's trade and Lord Burle was willing to teach them."

"I could, could I?"

She gave him a kiss that was warm and sweet. Then she grinned. "Yes, my darling Prince, you could."

# CHAPTER 18

## TERREILLE

"Theran has hired the cook from the best dining house in Grayhaven to make the meal for this dinner party," Kermilla said as she, Correne, and her escorts, Lords Bardoc and Kenjim, drove to the place where they were meeting up with her two adorable Warlords, Garth and Brok. "Considering what a copper-pincher Theran is, these guests must be *very* important."

Correne rolled her eyes. "But not interesting. Warlord Princes?" She shuddered dramatically. "Why waste a good meal on them? It's not like they'll know the difference since they're always fighting or living in the rogue camps."

Glancing back at the unamused expressions of her men, Kermilla whispered. "Stop that. It's disrespectful."

"But it's *true*."

Hard to argue with that. Theran plowed through food she could barely swallow, and didn't care if a dish was bland or the potatoes were lumpy. In fact, as long as it didn't have dirt on it and was cooked enough that it wasn't still running, he didn't complain. Since he would be taking care of her residence when she became Queen, she was going to have to improve his palate. *Then* they would have the kind of dinner parties that would impress the aristos here in Dena Nehele.

"True or not, you don't say things like that when other men are around. If it gets back to the Warlord Princes, it will cause trouble."

Correne looked over her shoulder at Bardoc and Kenjim, then looked at Kermilla. "They belong to you, so *they* won't go telling tales about you. And I heard in the stables that this carriage driver had his tongue cut out so he *couldn't* tell tales."

Kermilla winced. No, her men wouldn't tell tales on her, but they didn't feel the same loyalty to Correne, which was something the girl couldn't get through her head. She acted like the men wouldn't *dare* say anything.

It might be useful to find out why the Queens here felt that way.

Then they were at the meeting place. Brok and Garth clambered into the seats behind the driver, all smiles and young-man juice.

"We're having a special dinner at the house tomorrow, so Correne and I need to do some shopping."

"Invite us to this dinner," Brok said. "We'll show you how to make it special."

It was tempting to have someone besides Correne to talk to, but Theran had emphasized several times that these Warlord Princes were coming to meet *her,* talk to *her,* so she couldn't have her own little party at one end of the table.

"Can't." Kermilla gave them a pretty pout. "But we'll do something fun together soon. Driver, take us to the marketplace in the landen part of town."

"No!" Garth sounded alarmed.

"Whyever not?" Kermilla asked. "Driver, move on."

"We *can't,*" Brok said, his voice full of bitter hatred. "Queen's orders. If we cross into *their* part of town, we'll be exiled from Dena Nehele."

Kermilla stared at them, too shocked to speak. "Why would Cassidy do that?"

"No reason," Garth muttered. "We were just having a little fun, and then she and that damn dog started raving."

"Dog?" Kermilla frowned. "Oh, the kindred Sceltie."

"Why don't you have one of those smart dogs?" Correne asked. "When I set up my court, I'm going to insist on having one of them. I think it would be quite amusing."

"They're more trouble than they're worth," Kermilla muttered. But there *was* a kind of status in having one of the kindred as a companion. Just not a bitch like that Vae. "Anyway, gentlemen, you needn't be concerned with any orders given by Lady Freckledy." She waited until Garth and Brok stopped guffawing, then tapped her Summer-sky ring. "I outrank her, which means I can countermand any order she gives. So I am formally re-questing your presence while Correne and I do some shopping in the lan-den marketplace." Since her escorts were behind her and couldn't see her face, she gave her boys a significant smile. "Maybe you could even point out a likely place for us to pick up a gift or two."

Brok smiled back. "Yes, Lady, we could."

"Poppi!" Ignoring the other two men who were standing with Gray and Ranon, Cassidy threw herself into her father's arms.

"There's my Kitten." Burle hugged her breathless, then took a step back to study her face. His eyes got misty. He sniffed and nodded sharply before turning to the men. "Prince Gray. Prince Ranon."

"It's a pleasure to see you again, sir," Gray said.

Burle frowned. "Sir? Huh."

Cassidy linked arms with her father. "Come inside and tell me all the gossip."

"Men do not gossip," Burle said. "We share news."

"Uh-huh. Well, come in and—"

"Time for that later. There's work to be done."

"You've got time for a little visit before you start," Cassidy protested. She wanted to have him to herself for a little while before he got involved in the whirlwind of work Prince Sadi's loan was about to create.

"I'll be here a whole month," Burle said.

She recognized the gleam in her father's eyes. She didn't know what kind of arrangement Daemon Sadi had made with Burle—and she was cer-tain neither man would tell her the exact terms of that arrangement—but Burle was excited by the possibilities.

"It's your decision, of course, Lord Burle," Rainier said with a smile, "but I've heard the High Lord say more than once that a daughter takes priority over any other kind of work."

"Over any other kind of *work*, huh?" Burle laughed.

Rainier indicated the man standing on his left. "Lady Cassidy, may I introduce Lord Marcus, Prince Sadi's man of business?"

"It's a pleasure to have you with us," Cassidy said.

"I suggest that Gray and Ranon show Marcus and me the buildings for the shops," Rainier said. "You can spend some time with your father, and then Lord Burle can look at what needs to be done in the Queen's Residence and the Healer's House. Prince Sadi did emphasize that those two places were to be done first."

"In that case, Cassie and I will have a little visit before we get down to work," Burle said.

She waited until the men climbed into the open carriage with Ranon in the driver's seat. Then she turned to her father. "I'm so glad you could come to help us."

"You're my girl. Of course I would help. Besides, training a few youngsters to have a trade, that's important too, and that's one of the reasons I'm here."

"Is Mother going to come for a visit?"

"She is. She had some things she wanted to look into first. Then she'll be along. And your brother's planning to come and help out for a few days too." Burle turned, looked at the Residence, and said wistfully, "Hate to waste good daylight."

Since she felt the same way about gardening as he did about building, she smiled. "In that case, let's get you settled into one of the guest rooms. We'll get a quick bite to eat so that we don't have to fib when we're asked if we took time for it, and then we can visit while I help you take measurements at the Healer's House."

"That's a deal, Kitten. That is a deal."

"Lady, I think it would be wiser to do your shopping in another part of the town."

"Oh, *la,* Kenjim," Kermilla said. "There's no need to be fussing about this." Besides, until Theran paid the bills at the few aristo shops she had found in this dung-heap town, the merchants weren't going to extend any more credit.

"Your companions have a questionable kind of honor," Kenjim said.

"How can you say that?" Kenjim served her, but Garth and Brok were *hers.* "How *dare* you say that?"

"I dare because I'm First Circle. Lady, we're not in Dharo. We aren't even in our own Realm. This isn't a friendly place, and those young studs could pull you into the kind of trouble that ends in bloodshed."

"That's ridiculous!"

"Is it?"

Lower lip trembling, she walked away from him. The fact that he stayed at the carriage instead of accompanying her to the tables of goods told her plainly enough that he wouldn't serve her one minute past his contract. And that made her angry as well as sad. Kenjim used to think she was a "delight to the senses." Now all he did was criticize.

They called this a craftsmen's courtyard? Kermilla looked at the half-empty tables and the sullen landen faces. They watched her with a look in their eyes that made her nervous. Maybe Kenjim was right. Maybe this wasn't a good part of town for her to be in. But giving in now would mean taking orders from a male who was supposed to serve her, and no Queen with any pride would do that.

She joined Correne, who had been studying a selection of leather belts.

"This one would be acceptable," Correne said. "The buckle is almost pretty."

The leather was lusciously soft and meant to accept the sweet curve of a woman's hips, and the pewter buckle was in the shape of an arbor and bench, a highly suggestive piece implying the pleasure that could be sampled in a garden—if a woman wore it in the right place.

"This is a fine piece, Lady," the landen said. "The price is thirty silver marks."

"Thirty!" Correne said. "You think I would pay a *landen* thirty silver marks for *anything*?"

Rage flashed in the landen's face, quickly masked but not quickly enough.

Brok and Garth stepped up to the table.

"You trying to give the Ladies trouble?" Brok snarled.

"Gentlemen," Kermilla said firmly. "There is no reason to be uncivil because of a simple misunderstanding." She looked at the landen and used the same tone that effectively cowed the landens in sheep-shit Woolskin. "I'm sure this man didn't realize a *Queen* was interested in the belt, and it is customary that when a *Queen* expresses interest in an item, it is given to her as a *gift*." She picked up the belt and handed it to Correne. "Therefore, haggling over the price isn't necessary. Is it?"

The landen looked at Brok and Garth. Then he shook his head. "No, it's not necessary. Please accept this belt as a gift, Lady."

"The guards are coming," Garth said. "Let's go."

Something in his voice had Kermilla walking back to their carriage. And something in Brok's voice when he looked at a weaver and said, "Tell your little bitch to keep an eye out for us," made her shiver.

Then the guards rode up and surrounded them—hard men with honed tempers.

"What is the meaning of this?" Kermilla demanded.

"These two Warlords were forbidden to come into the landen part of town," a guard said. "The penalty for disobeying the Queen's command is exile. Or death."

"No!" Kermilla's heart pounded. How could this man be such a brute? He had no business threatening her boys. None! "You can't do that."

"The Queen's command—"

"I outrank Cassidy, and *I say* these men are free to come and go as they please!"

The guard looked at her, and there was no indication he was going to yield.

"Your Jewels may outrank Lady Cassidy's, but *she* rules Dena Nehele."

"For now," Kermilla snapped. "Come spring, *I* will be the law here, and I won't forget who caused trouble for me and mine."

A humming, terrible silence.

"Warlord," Kenjim said politely as he stepped up to stand at her left. "The Ladies were not aware of this command when they asked these two Warlords to stand as additional escorts."

"Garth and Brok were aware of it," the guard said. "They almost blinded a young girl. That's why they were banned from this part of town."

"If Lord Bardoc and I had been aware of this, we would have opposed those Warlords coming with us," Kenjim said.

Kenjim's anger was a scalding heat against her skin. Kermilla took a half step away from him.

"We'll escort you all back to the line," the guard said. "And we'll take Garth and Brok back to their father's house. This will be reported to the Master of the Guard. If he feels that more needs to be done, he'll take care of it."

If more needs to be done? Kermilla frowned. What did that mean?

"Fair enough," Kenjim said.

"Fair enough?" Kermilla stared at Kenjim in disbelief. Then she glared at the guard. "You won't report to anyone. Grayhaven is *Theran's* town."

"Last I heard, it was still part of Dena Nehele. Prince Grayhaven may rule here, but he still has to answer to the Queen and her court. And that includes Talon, the Master of the Guard."

Theran would be *furious* if Talon came here and started chewing on him over this.

She offered no other protests as Kenjim and Bardoc helped her and Correne into the carriage.

*I vanished the belt before the guards arrived,* Correne said once they were all seated.

*As if that was the least bit important right now,* Kermilla thought.

Two of the guards escorted them all the way back to the spot where she had met up with Brok and Garth. Then they rode off with her two boys, leaving her with Bardoc's discomfort and Kenjim's simmering anger.

As soon as they returned to the mansion, Correne scurried to her room and Bardoc made some excuse about needing to talk to Jhorma. Which left her alone with Kenjim, who followed her right into her room.

"What in the name of Hell are you doing, associating with bastards who would try to blind a child?" Kenjim growled.

"Garth and Brok are mine." Kermilla thumped a fist against her chest. "Mine!"

"They tried to blind a child!"

"A stupid landen!" Kermilla shouted. "Who cares about landens?"

He stared at her before saying quietly, "A Queen with honor."

The insult silenced her. She studied his eyes, felt the sharp heat of his temper. She tried a delicate psychic probe to find out what was under the moment's temper—and found disgust, disappointment, and contempt.

"If Garth and Brok belong to you, then I don't." Kenjim's voice was dangerously quiet. "I don't know what kind of game you're playing, claiming that you're going to be Queen here—"

"I *am* going to be Queen! Theran promised me!"

Kenjim let out a huffing laugh that held no humor. "Then he's as much of a fool as we were."

Kermilla walked over to the window and stared at nothing. Bardoc was unhappy about this misunderstanding with those stupid guards who were protecting landens, but she could talk him around. Kenjim, however, was now a danger to her. He wouldn't be able to turn Theran against her, but his anger could sour the opinion of the Warlord Princes who were coming to meet her. He might even try to ruin her chance of becoming the Queen of Dena Nehele.

She turned back to face him. "Pack your things. You're returning to Bhak immediately. I'll have Gallard assign another in the First Circle to stand escort here."

"As the Lady wishes." Kenjim's smile held a sharp, terrible edge. "Before you, I served an honest—and honorable—Queen for five years. But that doesn't mean I don't understand the value of negotiating."

"What does that mean?"

"If you try to smear my reputation by distorting what happened today or by misrepresenting this conversation, I will go to Lady Darlena and counter your report with a charge of mistreatment."

"You wouldn't dare!"

"Wouldn't I?"

Kermilla paled. As a District Queen, she ruled under the hand of a Province Queen who, in turn, ruled her piece of Dharo under the hand of the Territory Queen. If Kenjim went to Darlena with a charge of mistreatment, more than the Province Queen would be taking a look at her court. And that wouldn't do at all. Not when spring was so many months away. If Darlena—or even worse, Sabrina—took Kenjim's side in this and released him from his contract right now, it would break her court, and she wouldn't have the income from Bhak and Woolskin to support her, as insufficient as it was.

If she asked Theran to kill Kenjim, would he do it without asking questions?

No. Not without questions. Even if Theran would do that for her, Jhorma and Bardoc would insist on some justification—and would insist on her leaving Dena Nehele, which would ruin everything.

*Kenjim has already considered that. He knows the knife he's holding against my throat is sharper than any I can hold against his. I can't strike against him without hurting myself more.*

"Very well," she said coldly. "We'll just say that you've completed your rotation as escort and are returning to Bhak to take up other duties on behalf of your Queen. Is that satisfactory?"

"Quite satisfactory."

"In that case, *get out*."

He reached for the door but didn't open it. When he looked at her, she thought she saw regret, maybe even sorrow, in his eyes.

"Do yourself a favor, Kermilla. Cut the acquaintance with those two young Warlords. Stop playing these games. Go back to Bhak and start taking care of what is already yours. If you don't, I won't be the only man who walks away from your court." He opened the door and walked out.

She didn't go down to dinner that night, claiming a sick headache. And that wasn't far from the truth, since she had blurred the afternoon with many generous glasses of brandy.

Tonight she would brood and sulk and get gloriously drunk. Tomorrow, when those Warlord Princes came to dinner, she needed to shine.

# CHAPTER 19

## KAELEER

*Bastard?*

**B**astard?*

Daemon opened his eyes, not sure if the call that had broken his sleep had been real or part of a dream.

*Bastard?*

Ebon-gray psychic thread. No doubt now that the call was real. *Prick?* He waited. Didn't get a response. Just a sense of pain running through that psychic thread. *Lucivar?*

*I need help.*

Daemon flung the sheet aside and rolled out of bed, startling Jaenelle. *Where are you?*

*Home.*

*Are you hurt?*

*No. Marian . . .* Pain. Grief.

Mother Night. *I'll be there as soon as I can.*

He rushed into the adjoining bedroom to dress. Jaenelle rushed in right behind him.

"What's wrong?" she asked.

"I don't know." He pulled on trousers and a shirt that he didn't bother to button. He grabbed a jacket, shoes, and socks, then vanished them. "Something about Marian."

"May the Darkness have mercy." Jaenelle ran back to her bedroom, hollering as she went, "Get one of the Coaches. I'm going with you."

He hesitated, even considered arguing with her. She was still in the days of her moontime when she couldn't use more than basic Craft without causing herself excruciating pain. But she was a Healer, the best Healer in the whole damn Realm, and she was Lucivar's sister and Queen. If Marian needed more help than the Eyrien Healer could provide, Jaenelle would step in, no matter the cost.

And this time, as long as her own life wasn't at risk, he wouldn't try to stop her.

"I'll wait for you downstairs." He was out of the room and running through the Hall to reach the outer door closest to the stables and the building that housed the carriages and Coaches.

The footmen who were on night duty didn't call to him, but word must have passed as they figured out his direction because Beale was waiting at the outer door for him.

"Because of your haste and the late hour, I assumed the small Coach would be sufficient," Beale said. "It's being brought around to the landing web since that would be more convenient for the Lady."

Still panting from the run, Daemon nodded. It seemed Beale was thinking a lot more clearly than he was. "Guess I should have contacted you to begin with."

"You have other things on your mind."

He hurried through the corridors, buttoning his shirt as he went, and reached the great hall at the same time Jaenelle came running down the stairs. They raced out the open front door to the Coach on the landing web.

Holt waited beside the Coach, dressed in nothing but a pair of short trousers. As Jaenelle entered the Coach, a basket suddenly appeared beside the footman. He grabbed it and shoved it into Daemon's hands.

"The best Mrs. Beale could do in the time," Holt said.

Daemon handed the basket to Jaenelle and took the driver's seat while Holt closed the door and moved away from the landing web.

Jaenelle took the seat beside Daemon, still holding the basket. "Did Lucivar say anything?"

"He's scared, he's grieving, and he's in pain."

She didn't ask anything else.

He raised the Coach off the landing web, caught the Black Wind, and raced to Ebon Rih as fast as the Black could take them.

"Wait until I set this thing down," Daemon snapped as Jaenelle started to rise from her seat. "If you fall off the damn mountain, you won't help any of us."

She gave him a look that normally produced a cold sweat. He ignored the look, just as he ignored the odd way his hands trembled when he remembered the way Lucivar sounded.

Couldn't think about that. One of them needed to be the warrior who could draw the line and defend it. It didn't sound like Lucivar was in any shape to defend anything, including himself.

Especially himself.

Daemon opened the Coach door, and they both rocked back from the emotions flooding from the eyrie above them.

"Can you deal with him?" Jaenelle asked.

"I'll deal."

She left the Coach and raced up the stairs. He stayed a couple of steps behind her so he wouldn't trip her. She ran past Lucivar, who was standing in the flagstone courtyard in front of the eyrie—standing so perfectly still, as if even a deep breath might shatter him.

Daemon approached his brother slowly, cautiously. "Lucivar."

Lucivar continued to stare straight ahead, but one tear slipped down his face.

Daemon did a fast psychic probe of the eyrie and surrounding land. Marian and Nurian, the Eyrien Healer, were inside with Jaenelle. But the other two people he'd expected to find were missing. *Father?* he called on a Black spear thread.

*Daemonar is with me at the Keep,* Saetan said. *Take care of Lucivar.*

*Done.* Knowing the boy was safe, he focused once again on his brother. "Lucivar?"

"Miscarriage." Lucivar's voice broke. "We lost the baby."

*Mother Night.* "I'm sorry."

Daemon brushed a finger over Lucivar's shoulder, an offer of contact with no expectations. A moment later, he was holding on to a sobbing man.

"Is it my fault, Daemon?" Lucivar asked. "Is it my fault?"

"How could it be?" Daemon stroked Lucivar's hair and added another layer to the soothing spells he was wrapping around his brother.

"Sh-she got pregnant during the rut. You know what we're like during that time. *You know.* Maybe I damaged her inside. Maybe . . ."

"Shh." Daemon rocked him gently. Rocked and soothed. He had a feeling Saetan was doing much the same thing with a frightened little boy. "Shh."

He wouldn't let Lucivar say it, wouldn't let Lucivar keep thinking that. But it was possible, and they both knew it. That was part of the pain. Until Nurian—or more to the point, Jaenelle—said otherwise, it was a possibility.

The tears finally eased, but Lucivar still clung to him. Since he was facing the eyrie, he saw Jaenelle first.

"Prick," he whispered.

Lucivar straightened up, wiped his eyes, and turned toward her.

Jaenelle studied Lucivar. "If you've been out here grieving, that's fine. If you've been out here blaming yourself, you're going to piss off your wife as well as your sister."

"Cat . . . ?" Lucivar looked so vulnerable.

"There was nothing you had done before—or could have done now—to change this," Jaenelle said gently. "The babe didn't form right. It couldn't survive, so Marian's body released it. A simple and natural thing, despite how much the heart hurts because of it."

"Marian?" Daemon asked.

"She'll be fine in every way," Jaenelle said, still looking at Lucivar. "She needs to rest for a few days—and she needs to grieve without feeling that you see her grief as a kind of blame. Marian lost a baby tonight. So did you." She turned her head toward the eyrie. "Nurian has everything cleaned up. Go be with your wife, Lucivar. She needs you."

Lucivar hesitated. Then he gently touched Jaenelle's cheek and went into the eyrie.

Daemon slipped an arm around her waist. "Did you tell him the truth?"

She gave him a puzzled look. "Why would I tell him anything else?"

"To spare him if he was responsible for the miscarriage."

The air around them chilled. "A smart man wouldn't call a Healer a liar," she said too softly.

"A smart man also knows that Healers sometimes lie." He looked in her eyes and waited.

"Healers sometimes lie," Jaenelle acknowledged. "But not this time. Blaming himself for something that wasn't his fault and wasn't anything he could have changed is an indulgence his wife and son can't afford. Neither can he. If you can't help him see that, his father will."

Interesting. Especially since she sounded absolutely sure of that.

Nurian walked out of the eyrie, looking tired. "I have a healing brew simmering on the stove. Needs another ten minutes."

"I can finish it," Jaenelle said.

"I took the linens," Nurian said, lowering her voice. "Marian asked if I could get them cleansed, but . . ."

Jaenelle shook her head. "A Black Widow might be able to cleanse the psychic residue out of the cloth enough to be acceptable to Marian, but no one is going to be able to cleanse those linens enough for Lucivar to tolerate. We'll get them replaced."

"I thought that would be the way of it." Nurian paused. "Should I wake Jillian and send her to the Keep to watch Daemonar?"

"Let her sleep. It would be better to have her help later in the morning when the High Lord needs to rest. You get some rest too. We'll be here to look after them."

"All right. I'll be back in the morning."

Spreading her wings, Nurian flew to the eyrie she shared with her younger sister.

"I'd better keep an eye on that brew." Jaenelle gave Daemon a quick kiss and walked into the eyrie.

He was still standing outside an hour later when Surreal showed up.

"I heard, more or less," she said as she climbed the last stair and joined him in the courtyard. "So who needs to be babied and who needs to be bullied?"

"What did you hear?"

"Something is wrong with Marian. Lucivar is distraught. Daemonar is staying with Uncle Saetan." Surreal hooked her hair behind one ear. "And you're in trouble, by the way. Mostly forgiven because it was clear you had left your brains somewhere between the bedroom and the landing web and couldn't be relied on right now."

He stiffened. "I beg your pardon?"

"Apparently there are rules when there is a family crisis. You broke the rules."

"I wasn't aware of any," he said coldly.

"Uh-huh. Uncle Saetan is, and after you arrived here, he contacted Beale, and Beale then informed Mrs. Beale of where you were and why. Rainier is on his way, but he has to wait for the first round of food Mrs. Beale has prepared. Chaosti is also on his way, but he'll stop at the Hall for whatever wasn't ready when Rainier headed out."

Hell's fire. Was any of that supposed to make sense? "Surreal."

"Don't snarl at me. You're the one who pissed off your cook by not telling her there was a family emergency and asking her to prepare food so none of us needed to think about that."

"Marian lost the baby. No one gives a damn about food right now."

"Shit." She looked out over the mountain. "Shit."

He didn't like being jabbed about it, but there were going to be a lot of people coming and going over the next few days to give whatever help they could, and they would need to be fed.

Surreal drew in a breath and huffed it out. "All right, then. You and Uncle Saetan can baby Marian until she starts snarling at you, and Jaenelle and I will bully Lucivar."

He bristled. "Don't you think Lucivar deserves a little pampering too?"

She gave him an odd look. "Sugar, to an Eyrien male, being bullied *is* a kind of pampering. Don't ask me why, but sometimes nothing says 'I love you' to a male better than getting a whack upside the head."

She walked into the eyrie, leaving him out there to ponder the perversity of his own gender and the mystery of hers.

# CHAPTER 20

## TERREILLE

After renting a horse at Grayhaven's Coaching station, Ranon headed for the parts of the town where he'd spent some time. He didn't want to be here, didn't want to be wasting a day pursuing something Shira couldn't explain. But she'd gone all hissy cat on him last night and insisted that he come to Grayhaven *today*.

*That wasn't fair,* Ranon scolded himself as he rode through the streets and felt a grim uneasiness settling over him. Saying she had been a "hissy cat" diminished the power of the feelings Shira had last night. And remembering the tightness in her face, the worry in her eyes . . . Something was pushing her to push at him, but this time her tangled web only gave her a sense of *when* something was coming and not *what* was coming.

Now that he was here, he wished he'd asked Archerr or Shaddo to come with him.

This town didn't feel right anymore. Or more to the point, it was starting to feel the way the towns and villages had felt for the past several generations: discouraged, resigned, wary. Angry. He rode through the shopping district and had the odd sense that shopkeepers were letting their windows stay dirty and weren't bothering to sweep the walks as a deliberate way to discourage the interest of some customers.

Like aristos. Or Queens.

*You don't have to go up to the mansion,* Shira had said. *Just go to the places in town where we'd shopped or visited. Then listen to your heart.*

He could have used something less cryptic. Then again, maybe the messages were here. The women who sold them plants when Gray was working on the gardens at the mansion asked him if the Rose Queen was coming back to Grayhaven. Some of the shopkeepers came out of their stores to ask if the court was returning. He heard the hope in their voices when they asked, and he saw the dull acceptance in their eyes when he told them Cassidy and her court were remaining in Eyota.

He stopped at a tavern for a short glass of ale. It was late morning, too early for a drink as far as he was concerned, but he'd gone in because you could usually get a feel for what the men were thinking—and there were too many men there for the time of day. That in itself was not a good sign.

Why wasn't Theran seeing any of this? The man was supposed to be ruling this town. Why wasn't he heeding warnings that were so clear? Grayhaven was the capital of Dena Nehele. When Cassidy left a few weeks ago, there were signs of people shaking off the years of war and the decades of abuse at the hands of twisted Queens. Now shops that had been open were closed, empty. Now people hurried along the walks with the same hunched wariness that had been typical of the people everywhere in Dena Nehele.

What was Theran doing that people were reacting this way? Ranon didn't like him, but that was a clash of personalities. It didn't mean Theran wasn't a good man or a good Warlord Prince. So why wasn't he *doing* something to fix whatever this was?

Ranon continued riding through the streets, becoming more and more edgy. Enemy camp. Enemy ground. His instincts shouldn't be telling him those things, but he could feel himself preparing for a fight.

When he reached the guardhouse that marked the line that separated the landen part of town from the Blood, he hesitated for a long moment before he urged his horse forward and continued down the street.

There was an ugly feeling here. As he rode toward the craftsmen's courtyard, he created a skintight Opal shield around himself. Where were the craftsmen? Where was the merchandise?

He looked over at the area that had been occupied by the weaver family and saw James Weaver step toward him, looking grim, angry, and battle-hard.

"Prince," James said, "I would speak to you." He caught himself, as if just realizing he'd issued a kind of challenge. Then he added, "If you will permit it."

Ranon stared at the man, assessing the temper he saw in those eyes. He and Shira had come here often while Shira was healing JuliDee's face and checking the eye that had almost been lost because of two Warlord pricks. Those sessions, and his and Shira's presence among these people, had become cordial enough that Shira would have a cup of tea with the wife and daughter while James shared a glass of ale with him.

So what would put *that* look in a man's eyes? Why would there be so much tension just because one of the Blood rode by?

The answer came to him. He was off his horse and grabbing James's arms so fast the other man didn't have time to react.

"Is something wrong with your family? Is that why they aren't with you? Your wife? Has something happened to your daughter, your son?"

James relaxed. "They're all well, Prince. I thank you for asking." Then he looked uneasy, so when he stepped back, Ranon let him go. "The Rose Queen stood up for us landens, and your Lady healed my little girl. You helped me and mine, so I thought . . . fair warning, like."

"Fair warning about what?" Ranon felt a chill settle in his gut.

"When Prince Grayhaven's bitch takes control of Dena Nehele, there's going to be another uprising. And this time it won't end until all of us are dead—or all of you."

Ranon stared at James, shocked speechless. Then he shook his head. "Cassidy's court stands. She rules everything but this town, which is under Prince Grayhaven's control. Kermilla isn't going to rule Dena Nehele."

"She says she is."

*No.* It wasn't just that he wanted Cassie to rule; the thought of Kermilla ruling filled him with dread.

"Thing is," James said, "I'm tired of destroying, tired of fighting and killing. But if it has to be done again, I'd rather fight *for* something than against something."

A plea in those eyes. Messages under the spoken words.

And suddenly Ranon remembered what Jaenelle had said to him: *People looked beyond themselves and made room for you. Remember that, Prince.*

Before he could work out what he wanted to ask James, a handful of guards rode up.

Ranon turned and put up an Opal shield behind him, protecting the landen since the hostility in the guards' psychic scents was sufficient warning that he'd walked into some kind of trouble.

The senior guard, Lord Rogir, stared at him for a moment—and the Warlord's aggression faded with recognition. "Prince Ranon?"

Ranon nodded, noting the way the other guards had fanned out. Two were keeping an eye on the landens; the others were watching him.

"Prince, if I could have a few minutes of your time?" Rogir asked.

Taking a careful measure of the tempers around him, Ranon dropped the Opal shield behind him and turned to James. "I'll be back." Then he strode far enough away to be out of earshot.

Lord Rogir dismounted and followed him.

"Is the Rose Queen coming back to Grayhaven?" Rogir asked.

"No," Ranon replied. "She's settled in Eyota. So is the court."

"Is Lady Cassidy leaving in the spring? Is it true the other Dharo Queen is going to rule Dena Nehele?"

"You all seem to know something more than Cassidy's court knows," Ranon said. "Lady Kermilla can fart words all she wants. Doesn't change who is ruling Dena Nehele now—or who is going to continue to rule. The court stands. If the Queen is challenged, we'll fight." It wasn't really his place to make such a statement without more of the First Circle present, but he was sure of the truth of it.

Rogir glanced at James Weaver. "Can you do anything for them? This town isn't safe for that family anymore."

"What are you talking about?"

"Whether she rules officially or not, Theran Grayhaven has given this town over to the other Queen. She says she outranks the Rose Queen and can countermand any orders we've been given." Fury swept over Rogir's face. "She brought those two Warlords, Garth and Brok, into this part of town a few days ago—and she made the kind of warning threats we've all heard before about what will happen to anyone who opposes her now. Since then, my men and I have kept a close watch on this courtyard. Those Warlords came back this morning, and they were looking for Weaver's little girl. They blame her for the punishment they damn well deserved. If they get their hands on her this time, they'll do a lot worse than throw horse shit and stones."

Ranon felt sick, cold.

"I've got a wife and a daughter about the same age as his." Rogir tipped his head toward James. "I've kept an eye on these folks because of that. Gotten to know them. Blood and landen . . . We may be from the same race, but we're not the same. We'll never be the same, so we don't fit together easy. But a father is a father, and I think about the fear that would be eating my gut if two Warlords had *that* look in their eyes when they asked about *my* little girl."

Easy enough to guess where this conversation was heading, but the words had to be said. So Ranon waited.

Rogir cleared his throat. "Those landens need to get out of Grayhaven. And I want my family out of here. The guards who have been riding with me to protect the landens and have followed the Queen's command? They want to get out too. Especially the one who is newly married and hoped for a better life than he or his wife had known before."

*People looked beyond themselves and made room for you. Remember that, Prince.*

"I can't make any promises before discussing this with the Queen," Ranon said.

"Understood."

*Listen to your heart.* "I'll meet you back here after dark, and one way or another, we'll figure out how to get your family out of this town. The other guards as well." He glanced at James Weaver. "And them."

"I've got a sister . . ." Rogir trailed off.

"Have a list ready for me." Ranon hesitated, but it had to be said because it could make a difference between someone choosing to go or stay. "You'll probably end up living in the same village as the court. That means living in a Shalador reserve."

"I'll let the others know, but if the court is there and your people are willing to have us, I don't think anyone who wants to leave is going to care about those kinds of boundaries."

Ranon nodded and returned to James. "How many of you want to get out?"

James looked at him as if not quite daring to believe the question. A glance at the other craftsmen, who nodded. "Several families. All have skilled craftsmen who aren't afraid to work hard."

*That would please Burle,* Ranon thought. Cassie's father wasn't afraid of working hard either and required the same commitment from anyone who was going to work for him.

"My brother has sheep." James sounded cautiously hopeful. "They give a fine wool that my wife spins for our weaving. And Tanner's cousin has cattle for meat and leather. I know a dairyman too. Maybe . . . maybe a dozen families in all." He looked sad. "Too many here think the past will be our future. They've given up hope. They'll stay here to fight or die. Some of us would like more for our families."

Ranon signaled for Rogir to join them. Looking at Rogir, he tipped his head toward James. "Can your family shelter his tonight?"

"We can," Rogir replied without hesitation.

"I don't know where you will end up, and I don't know what I can offer beyond the promise that I'll help you get out of this town," Ranon said.

"I'll talk to the men I know want to get out," Rogir said. "Tell them to pack up what they don't want to leave behind."

James made a gesture that took in himself and the other craftsmen who were watching them so intently. "We were relocated here after the uprisings. We were allowed only what could fit in one wagon. Everything we have can still fit in that wagon."

Ranon looked at the two men. They had stood on opposite sides during the uprisings. Now they stood together as fathers and husbands—and men who, if they had to fight again, wanted to fight *for* something instead of against something.

"Start packing," he said. "We'll meet back here during the aristo dinner hour." Less chance of running into Theran or Kermilla at that time. "I'll give you the Queen's decision then."

Mounting his horse, he rode back through town and found himself passing one of the shops that held the kind of merchandise only an aristo could afford. He stopped, dismounted, and went in, not sure what he was doing there.

Hell's fire. He *knew* what he was doing there: looking for something to sweeten the half-promises he'd made on his Queen's behalf.

"May I assist you?" the merchant asked.

Sweets. Cassie had dipped into the loan Sadi had given the court and given her First Circle half what was due them from the coming tithe, so he had a few marks he could spend.

"Chocolates," he said. "A small treat for the Ladies." He emphasized small because the stuff was wickedly expensive.

The merchant studied him. "You serve Lady Cassidy."

Ranon felt his body tighten, but he wasn't sure why since the man had made no hostile move. "I do."

"I heard she is now living in a village in the eastern Shalador reserve?"

"She is."

"Is she intending to stay there?"

"She is."

A hesitation. "Would there be room in that village for another shop?"

Ranon blinked. *Another one looking to run?* He looked around the shop. "The Shalador people couldn't afford your fine merchandise."

"I can adapt and sell what people need."

There weren't any shops like this one in Eyota, but there were going to be the shops owned by Sadi. "The Warlord Prince of Dhemlan now owns a few shops in the village. His man of business is talking to anyone interested in managing those shops. Lord Marcus will be in Eyota for a couple more days."

"Thank you for the information."

As the merchant went behind the counter, Ranon spotted the small boxes of chocolates. He winced at the price, but he chose the box that held a dozen pieces—three each for Cassidy, her mother Devra, Shira, and Reyhana.

He set the box on the counter. The merchant looked at the box, then reached under the counter, set a box twice that size beside the one Ranon chose, and vanished the smaller box.

"The one you chose is stale," he said. "I'll give you this one for the same price."

Ranon frowned. "Why would you leave out stale sweets?"

The merchant smiled wearily. "It doesn't sting as much when they are stolen."

"Have you reported this theft?" Ranon asked. "Who has been stealing from you?"

The man's silence was the answer.

Ranon paid for the chocolates, then vanished the box and headed for the door. He wanted to get away from here. He wanted to be *home*.

But he hesitated at the door and turned to look at the merchant. "If you come to Eyota, tell Lord Marcus I suggested he talk to you."

"Thank you, Prince."

As he rode back to the Coaching station to return the horse, he kept his eyes on the street, aware of how many people noticed him and half raised a hand to catch his attention. He'd had enough for one day—too much for one day—so he pretended he didn't see them.

But he couldn't ignore the four Warlord Princes who walked out of the Coaching station just as he rode up.

He hadn't ridden with any of them during the uprisings, and didn't know any of them as friends. But when there were only a hundred of your caste left to defend your land, you knew the names and faces—and reputations—of those men.

"Ranon," Ferall said, sounding cordial—and surprised. Since Ferall's Opal Jewel outranked the other three, he stood as their leader while they were together.

"Ferall," Ranon said. Then he nodded to the other men. "Gentlemen."

"You were up to the mansion?" Ferall asked.

He shook his head. "Had some personal business in the town. I offered to pick up a couple of things for the Ladies that weren't available in Eyota."

"We have some personal business here ourselves," Ferall said.

*Like a meeting with Theran?* But it wasn't a question to ask, because silence was being offered. They wouldn't mention his presence in the town to Theran and he wouldn't mention them to the court by name.

He nodded and led the horse to the stables. Then he caught the Opal Wind and headed back to Eyota.

*He's dancing on the knife's edge,* Cassidy thought as she listened to Ranon's too carefully thought-out report. He was skilled enough at offering this kind of information that she couldn't tell what he was withholding, only that he wasn't telling her everything.

She glanced at her Master of the Guard. Whatever reason Ranon had for tempering his words now, he was going to tell Talon everything.

Easy enough to guess though. He'd been in Grayhaven. If he'd had a meeting with Theran—or Kermilla—he wouldn't want her to know. Then again, Shira had said that *she* had sent Ranon to Grayhaven because of a vision.

Did the reason really matter? Cassidy wondered. Did whatever Ranon was hiding matter? There were people who wanted to leave Grayhaven and begin a new life, and had asked a member of her First Circle for help. She had the uneasy feeling that some of those people might not have *any* life if she didn't support the tentative offers Ranon had made on behalf of Queen and court.

And in truth, he had acted as a Warlord Prince in Kaeleer would have acted. He had acted because he believed in her and the Old Ways her presence was bringing back to the Blood in Dena Nehele.

When Ranon finished his report, a heavy silence filled the room as all the First Circle who had returned from their duties in time for this meeting waited for her response.

She stood up and walked over to Ranon, who tensed but showed no other sign of nerves.

"Since the day I met you, you have championed the Shalador people, argued so their concerns wouldn't be ignored. Today you are standing for a people who are not your own but needed someone to speak for them. By doing so, you honor the justice I want for all the people of Dena Nehele. I'm so proud of you and—" Her throat suddenly closed. Tears filled her eyes and spilled over. She swallowed hard, put a hand on her chest, and said, "My heart is too full for words."

Suddenly she was in his arms, being hugged breathless. Then he released her and stepped back.

Wiping tears off her cheeks, Cassidy looked at Gray and Powell. "We need to consider land and buildings. Any suggestions?"

"If the merchant is willing to be a manager rather than own a shop, I think he'll be a good choice for one of Prince Sadi's shops," Powell said. "However, I suggest that a condition of his managing a shop in this village is that he hire one or two Shaladorans who want to learn the merchant trade and teach them the skills needed to run their own shops one day."

Cassidy's smile widened until her muscles ached. "That's an excellent idea."

"The guards who have families may want to look at the available cottages within the Queen's square," Archerr said. "From a tactical point of view, having more trained fighters within that ground is better for all of us."

"Agreed," Talon said.

"So we should pick a couple of cottages?" Powell asked.

"You will not," Cassidy and Shira said.

Powell blinked.

"The women will choose their own homes," Cassidy said firmly.

Powell blinked again, apparently not sure if there was any safe ground at the moment. "Very well. We will charge rent?"

Cassidy started to deny it, but Ranon said, "That's fair. The village is giving the land and buildings to the court to do with as you please. That doesn't mean letting anyone beyond the First Circle live here free. Cassie, if you don't want to keep the rent as income for yourself or the court, it could go back into the village treasury. Or you can offer the cottages as part of the wages the guards receive from the village treasury or the tithes."

Cassidy chewed on her lower lip. Too much to think about.

"Why don't we work out those kinds of details later?" Powell suggested.

Gray looked up from a rough sketch of the village and the available buildings. "Ranon, what's this place beyond the village?"

Ranon braced his hands on the table and leaned to see the sketch better. "Used to be a kind of tradesman's school. I think. My grandfather might remember when it was last inhabited."

"Would it work for craftsmen?" Gray asked. "It looks like a walled community that has a considerable bit of open land attached to it. And it's a couple of miles beyond the rest of the village."

Ranon nodded. "It was far enough out to be vulnerable to attack. I think that's why it was abandoned."

"We don't have to worry about attacks now," Gray said. "How about offering this place to the landens?"

Cassidy saw something flicker in Ranon's eyes when Gray said they didn't have to worry about attacks. "You think the landens would be at risk if they lived so close to us?"

"No," Ranon said quickly. "In fact, this might be a fair compromise. They'll have a place that is their own, but it's close enough for them to come into the village for market day and other supplies. There's enough land attached to the place for them to graze their livestock as well as grow some crops beyond kitchen gardens. Only one big barn, but it was built to hold all the animals in the community, so it might do for them for this year at least."

"So we're agreed on what we can offer?" Cassidy asked, looking at her First Circle and waiting for their nods of agreement. "In that case, Ranon, go back and talk to them."

"I'll draft letters of passage," Powell said. "That way if the landens are stopped along the way, the Blood will know they're traveling at the Queen's command."

"Good idea," Talon said. "Ranon, see if the guards who don't have families to settle would be willing to ride escort for the landens."

"I'll ask," Ranon said.

"Gray, get a couple of horses saddled," Talon said. "I want to take a look at these places, and I want you to come with me since you've been looking at these buildings more than the rest of us."

"Yes, sir." Gray vanished the sketch, gave Cassidy a smile, and left the room.

"I think that will be all, gentlemen," Powell said. "If you would come to my office, we'll discuss tomorrow's duties."

Powell had a knack for being a Steward, Cassidy thought as the men except Ranon and Talon left the room.

"Cassidy, Reyhana, and I have drum practice tonight, so I think Maydra prepared a stew for dinner," Shira said, looking at Ranon. "I'll see if it's ready so you can have a quick meal before you head back out."

"Before you go," Ranon said. He called in a box, set it on the table, and nudged it toward Cassidy. "I picked up some chocolates for you Ladies."

Cassidy stared at the box, then let out a whoop of laughter. "You really *were* nervous about this report, weren't you?"

Looking completely baffled, Ranon said, "Huh?"

"The last time I saw a box of chocolates this size was when my father had done something to piss off my mother and was trying to work his way back to the sweeter side of her temper." Cassidy looked at Ranon more closely. Hell's fire. The man was *blushing*.

★You hit the target dead center that time,★ Shira said on a distaff thread. She hurried out of the room.

Ranon was strong, brave, as arrogant as any other Warlord Prince, and wouldn't back down from a fight. But he had shy spots when it came to living with women, and he wasn't always sure of how he should behave.

Then again, maybe he did understand how some things balanced other things.

She picked up the box, thanked him, and left the room.

Shira was waiting for her.

"Do you think this is in proportion?" Cassidy asked, lifting the box.

Shira frowned at the box. "In proportion to what?"

"To whatever Ranon thought would hurt so much that I would need this much consolation."

★    ★    ★

Talon used Craft to close the door. Then he put an aural shield around the room and a Sapphire lock on the door. The last wasn't to keep Ranon in as much as to keep everyone else out.

He studied the Shaladoran's back. Stiff. Tense. Waiting for the Master of the Guard to make the first move.

"Tell me what you wouldn't tell her," Talon said.

Ranon turned around.

Hell's fire. How had the man managed to hide *that* much anger?

"Theran has given his . . . *Lady* . . . free run of the town. The Warlord brothers who hurt the landen girl? *She* brought them with her to the landen part of town—and then threatened the guards when they stood by our Queen's command. I gather she's been stealing from some of the merchants. And she has the expectation that, come spring, Cassidy is going to be gone and *she* is going to be the Queen of Dena Nehele." Ranon's hands curled into fists. "And since *that* expectation was the reason Cassie ran in the first place, I was *not* going to tell her about the rumors."

Talon frowned. Landens, guards, and merchants were all looking to leave the town? To him that added up to more than rumors. "What else?"

"I met four Warlord Princes who were just coming into town as I was leaving. I think all four of them come from the Heartsblood River Province."

Recruiting, Talon thought bitterly. Trying to woo enough Warlord Princes to support Kermilla and form a court in the spring that would be strong enough to challenge Cassidy's—and break Cassidy's court in the process.

But he'd known when they left Grayhaven that Theran wanted Kermilla to rule and Cassidy's court would break when Cassidy's First Escort, the man who had brought her to this land in the first place, walked away. And the reason he said nothing then was the same reason he would say nothing now: Gray.

The man Gray was becoming might be able to serve in a court, or at least fill an empty space and keep *this* court intact. He wanted to give the boy as much time to season as possible before that decision had to be faced.

"You hear anything else, I want to know," Talon said. "I'll make sure the Steward is aware that we may be looking at a fight come spring. But it doesn't go further than the three of us. You understand me?"

"Yes, sir, I do," Ranon replied.

"Get some food and head out," Talon said. "Take Burne and Haele with you. And take the biggest Coach you can handle from the Coaching station here."

Ranon paled. "You're talking about a fast retreat. Take the most vulnerable and run. Leave the stronger to pack up what can be saved before the enemy takes notice. You can't believe Theran would attack women and children, landen or otherwise. You *can't* believe that."

He didn't believe it possible of the boy he'd raised, but he wasn't so sure of the man anymore. With Kermilla holding the leash, he wasn't sure what Theran would do.

"How many times have you seen someone poised to run who didn't survive long enough to find safe ground?" Talon asked. Ranon paled even more, which told him the man had seen firsthand what had happened to some of those people. "I don't care if you stuff them into a Coach and move them on the Winds or have them on the road in wagons, but you get those people out of Grayhaven tonight."

Talon released the Sapphire lock and dropped the aural shield.

Looking dazed, Ranon walked out of the room.

Talon sank in a chair and rubbed his maimed left hand over his face.

So Theran was recruiting. And either Kermilla was making an ambitious assumption because she was living in Theran's house—and sharing his bed?—or he had told her he was going to try to make her the Queen of Dena Nehele.

Damn young fool. With Cassidy, they had a real chance to bring Dena Nehele back to what it had been. If Theran let a pretty face dazzle him stupid, he could ruin this for all of them.

Before that happened, he, Talon, who had been Jared and Lia's friend, would spill whatever blood needed to be spilled. Even if he had to tear his own heart out in the process.

*I still think he's a good man, but he's not a good leader. He's proving that every time he doesn't stand against Kermilla and defend his people. So I promise you this, Lia. I won't let your bloodline destroy your people, no matter the price.*

Having made that promise, he rose and went out to the stables to join Gray.

Theran leaned back to let the servant he'd hired for a thief's wage remove his plate.

The dinner wasn't going well. That wasn't Kermilla's fault. She was doing her best to entertain these men, but he should have realized Warlord Princes who had spent most of their lives being both predator and prey in the ongoing fight to protect what they could of Dena Nehele wouldn't have much interest in the conversation of a twenty-one-year-old woman they couldn't bed.

They were polite. He couldn't fault them for their manners. They even extended the courtesy of showing interest they clearly didn't feel. At least, it was clear to him.

They were also getting pissed off at Correne's catty remarks. The girl wasn't liked in her own village. In fact, she was one of the young Queens the Warlord Princes were vehemently opposed to seeing rule even the smallest village. That she seemed to be trying to compete with Kermilla for the men's attention—and the fact that Kermilla was taking the bait and blatantly flirting—wasn't lost on these men.

"Kermilla has been helping the Queens in the northern Provinces relearn the aspect of their power that nourishes the land and benefits the harvest," Theran said, laying his hand lightly on Kermilla's wrist.

She gave him an arch look, and for a moment he thought she might say something imprudent. Then she slipped her wrist out from under his hand and smiled at Ferall.

"Yes," she said. "I was shocked to learn that my Sisters had forgotten such a basic part of what makes a Queen a Queen."

The skin around Ferall's eyes tightened.

Kermilla added hastily, "So I was, naturally, pleased to be of some small service to them."

"You haven't set up a court yet?" Ferall asked.

"Silly man, of course I have a court." Kermilla gave Ferall a dazzling smile. "I rule a Blood village and a landen village in Dharo."

"So who has been taking care of the Queen's duties there while you've been visiting Theran here?"

Anger flashed through Theran. Had Kermilla heard the criticism in that question?

Kermilla put aside the flirtatious playfulness as easily as she might put aside a shawl. She gave Ferall a look at the Queen beneath the young-woman banter. "Dharo is an old Territory with a strong web of Queens. The village I rule can be run very well by my Steward and Master of the Guard for the time being. I am kept apprised of what is happening there and would return home in an instant if I was urgently needed." She placed her hand on Theran's arm. "I am not negligent in my duties, Prince Ferall, which is what you are implying. But a village that is well established requires little supervision from its Queen, so I offered to stay and give Theran whatever assistance I can in repairing the damage that has been done to his people."

Her speech warmed Theran's heart, but Ferall seemed less impressed. He gave Theran a hard look and said, "I thought that's why Lady Cassidy came here. I thought that's why we all agreed to have her as the Queen. And she didn't leave the people she'd promised to rule in order to 'give assistance.'"

Where was that anger coming from? Theran wondered. Nothing Kermilla said should have offended Ferall that much. Unless he wanted to be offended for some reason?

Kermilla, however, felt the punch in Ferall's words. "No, she didn't leave her people," she snapped. "She didn't have any. She wasn't Queen enough to hold on to her court!"

"Kermilla," Theran said in soft warning, touching her wrist again.

Kermilla pulled away from him. "And where is Cassidy now? Here in the capital city? No. She's in some cow-dung village that belongs to a people the rest of you would rather pretend don't exist."

"Hold your tongue, girl," Ferall snarled. "You don't know us. Any of us. Especially the Shaladorans."

"I know Cassidy is a country girl from a trademan's family who can't talk about anything except livestock and crops and wouldn't know how to sit at a table with a true aristo if all your lives depended on it."

Theran's heart jumped in his throat. Thank the Darkness these men didn't know about Cassidy's connection to Sadi and his wife. Those two were as aristo as you could get.

"Her manners are as rough as her face, and neither is fit for polite company," Kermilla finished, her chest rising and falling impressively as she sucked in air.

Correne snickered. "Back in her old village, they called Freckledy the 'spotted draft horse of Queens.'"

A tense silence shrouded the table for a long, long moment.

Then Ferall looked Theran in the eyes and pushed back his chair. "We're done here. There's nothing more to say."

Ferall walked out of the room, followed by the other three Warlord Princes.

Stunned, Theran didn't move for several heartbeats. Then he ran after them and caught them at the front door.

"Ferall, wait." He grabbed the other man's arm.

"There's nothing more to say." Ferall pulled out of Theran's grasp.

"She's young and high-spirited."

"Too young," Ferall said. "She should have slapped that little bitch down for insulting the Queen like that. And if people in her old village *did* say that about Cassidy, who told Correne about it so that it could be slung around here?"

"Probably one of Kermilla's escorts," Theran snapped. "They're here too, and they come from Dharo."

"A court takes its temper from its Queen," Ferall said. "And what was at that table tonight is not something I want ruling my village. Good night, Theran."

He let them walk away. There was nothing else he could do.

No, he thought as he closed the door, there *was* something he could do. But he would wait until Kermilla retired for the evening. Maybe he'd even wait until tomorrow when things settled down a little more.

*   *   *

Hell's fire, Ranon thought when he led the horse out of the Coaching station stables and ran into Ferall and the other three Warlord Princes. Could his timing be any worse today?

"Ferall," he said, then nodded to the other men.

"More personal business?" Ferall asked.

Ranon shook his head. "Queen's business in the town." Meaning, it wasn't the business of anyone who lived in the mansion.

Ferall hesitated. Actually looked uncomfortable. "Does the Queen have any objections to visitors in her home village?"

What an odd question. "No objections at all," Ranon said.

"Would it be all right if the four of us came by a week from today to take a look around?"

Something was going on. Too bad he didn't know what it was—and couldn't afford to care. Not tonight. "I can't promise Lady Cassidy will be available, but I'll make sure I'm there. Why don't you come by in the morning?"

"We'll do that. Good evening to you, Ranon."

The other Warlord Princes followed Ferall into the Coaching station. Wasn't any reason for them to hire a Coach to ride the Winds back to their homes—unless they wanted that time to talk among themselves before going their separate ways.

"That's a worry for another day," Ranon muttered as he mounted the horse. Good thing they hadn't seen him leaving the Coach he'd brought. There would have been questions about that—and about Burne and Haele being with him if they'd been spotted by the other men.

He kept the horse at a walk, waiting for his Brothers in the court to catch up. When they did, the first thing Haele said was, "What was Ferall doing in town?"

"Not our business," Ranon replied.

"You know better," Burne said. "Ferall is a savage fighter, even beyond what you'd expect from the Opal. And it's said he's the eyes and ears of a half dozen Queens in the Province where he lives."

*Like me*, Ranon thought. The Shalador Queens hadn't left the reserves for a few generations. That had kept at least some of them safe from the twisted Queens. But that didn't mean they hadn't been aware of what was happening in the rest of Dena Nehele, because there had always been men who reported back to them.

And some of those men had paid for being a Queen's eyes and ears by losing their eyes and ears—and tongue.

Ranon said, "Maybe we'll have a better idea of what Ferall was doing here today when he comes to visit us in a week."

Haele swore softly. They respected Ferall as a man, but he *was* a savage fighter. The thought of Ferall being in their village for any reason that wasn't peaceful was a reason to sweat.

*Don't borrow trouble*, Ranon thought. *We've already got plenty.*

They didn't speak again until they reached the craftsmen's courtyard and found it empty.

"Are we ahead of time?" Burne asked as he scanned the surrounding buildings and the street.

"No," Ranon replied. "And if we were late, someone would have waited."

"Unless they decided not to come," Haele said.

Not likely.

Lord Rogir rode up a minute later.

"Those Warlord pricks found out where Weaver's family lived. They tried to force their way in. My wife and daughter were there. I figured if we worked in teams and used some Craft we could get the households packed up faster."

"Is everyone all right?" Ranon asked.

Rogir nodded. "My wife threw shields around the room where the females were and held on long enough for me and two other guards to arrive. We forced Garth and Brok to leave, but they'll be back."

"Won't matter," Ranon said. "Where is everyone?"

"Weaver's wife and daughter are with mine at our house. Weaver and his son took off with their wagon, heading on the south road. They'll reach his brother's place by morning. I sent one of my men with them. Tanner almost has his family and tools packed up. His wife is also with mine. He and his sons are taking the wagon and heading out to his cousin's place. Potter and two other families are still packing up. They've agreed to go to the Dairyman's place."

"That's it?"

The guard nodded. "Don't think the other landens around here believed any good would come of it, so they're not leaving."

Ranon called in the letters of passage. "You'll need to get one of these to Weaver and make sure the other two parties have one, as well as a guard riding as escort."

"Done," Rogir said.

"I'll need you to come with us to represent your men."

Some nerves now, but Rogir nodded.

"We've got a Coach at the station. We'll take the women and children and as much of the household goods as we can pack into the thing."

"Appreciate it. We've all used Craft to vanish things and store them, but that takes power, and we're all holding more than is comfortable."

And compromising their ability to fight by draining the reserves in the Jewels that way.

"The men at the Coaching station said they have a Coach and driver we can use if we're relocating folks," Haele said. "I did tell them some of those people would be landens, and he said as a courtesy to the Queen, he'd charge the same price for each passenger."

Another message, Ranon thought. Landens weren't forbidden from buying passage on the Coaches that could ride the Winds, but they were usually charged double—sometimes triple—what any of the Blood would pay, so most couldn't afford the luxury of speed.

A feeling crawled just under his skin, scratching at him. He used to feel like this when he was trying to finish an assignment and get out before a Queen's guards arrived.

"Let's do this and get out of here," he growled.

Maybe he wasn't the only one who had that feeling because they all settled into their tasks with grim efficiency, and by the quiet hours of deep night, they were all out of Grayhaven and traveling, by one means or another, to Eyota.

# CHAPTER 21

## TERREILLE

Two days after that disastrous dinner party, Theran went into the Steward's office, sat behind the desk, and pressed his hands against his forehead. The damn headache had teeth, and it wasn't going to let him have the hour of peace he needed before he had to face the rest of a miserable day.

Then he noticed the neat stack of papers placed in the center of the desk and swore as he read the first merchant's bill. The swearing, and the headache, increased in intensity as he looked through the rest of the stack and realized what they were.

"How in the name of Hell could she spend this much?" he muttered. Yes, he'd offered to pay for the expenses Kermilla would have because she was staying here, but obviously he hadn't been explicit enough about how much she could spend.

Feeling sick, he added up the bills three times, hoping he'd find some mistake that would reduce the total.

No mistake. He vanished all the bills and pushed away from the desk. He had to talk to the merchants *now*. And he'd have to pay the price of Kermilla's misunderstanding.

And that would make this day a whole lot worse.

★ ★ ★

Kermilla lifted her chin to indicate the tavern two doors down from where she had arranged to meet Garth and Brok. She hadn't heard from her boys since they'd been taken away by those nasty guards the other day, so it was a good thing they'd set up this meeting before they separated. "Trae, go inside and see if they're still in there."

Trae hesitated. "I'm the only escort you brought today. I can't leave you unattended, Lady."

"You can if I say you can." She tapped her foot to indicate she was annoyed. He used to smile and give in when she did that. Now he looked uneasy. "Fine," she said. "I'll walk down with you and stand outside. It isn't suitable for me to go into a tavern."

"You went into the tavern back home," Trae said.

Kermilla stiffened. "I never did. That was an aristo establishment for fine wines and conversation."

"As the Lady pleases," Trae replied.

As good as calling her a liar without saying anything that could justify discipline.

They walked to the tavern, and Trae stepped inside the doorway. Moments later he stepped out with a young Warlord. "This is a friend of Garth's."

"Please tell Lords Garth and Brok that I'm waiting." Kermilla put a little chill in her voice.

"Can't," the Warlord replied. "They're gone."

She frowned. "Gone? Gone where?"

The Warlord shifted his weight from one foot to the other and looked at Trae instead of her. "They weren't supposed to go into the landen part of town. Queen's command."

Kermilla rolled her eyes. "Oh, *la*. I countermanded that order."

"Well, you should have told that to the Master of the Guard," the Warlord said hotly. "Talon came for them last night, and now *they're gone*."

She forgot how to breathe. That fierce, maimed old Warlord Prince had come for her boys? "He exiled them?"

"Don't know. The courtesy fingers weren't on their father's doorstep this morning, so maybe they were just sent away."

"Courtesy fingers?" Trae asked.

The Warlord shook his head and backed away. "I've said enough. You want to know anything more, you ask Prince Grayhaven."

"I will," Kermilla huffed as the Warlord hurried away. "I certainly will."

"Lady," Trae said quietly. "I think it would be better if Jhorma and I asked about the fingers. I don't think you're going to like the answer."

"Let's go back to the mansion," Kermilla said. "That's not the only answer I want from Prince Grayhaven."

The biggest one being where he had gone so early this morning. And why Correne had gone with him.


When he got back from his discussions with all the merchants, Theran found another package on his desk: a small, plain wooden box.

He knew what that box meant. Anyone who lived in Dena Nehele knew what it meant.

Using a psychic thread, he summoned Julien, his new butler. He picked up the folded and wax-sealed paper that had been on top of the box, but he didn't break the seal or open the paper.

"Prince Grayhaven?" Julien took one step into the room and came no farther until he looked around and confirmed there were no females present. Then he approached the desk.

Julien was a Warlord who had a handsome face and a cold temper. Like Gray, his body had been tortured—and scarred. When he applied for the butler's position, he'd told Theran straight out that he would gut any woman who tried to ride him, but as long as Theran kept the *Ladies* away from him, he'd be pleased to have the job.

After seeing Julien sharpen the cook's knives one afternoon, Theran made sure the man was never alone with Kermilla or Correne.

"When did this arrive?" Theran asked.

"I found it early this morning on the table where visitors' calling cards are left," Julien replied. "You were already gone, so I put it in the butler's pantry to avoid upsetting the other servants. I meant to give it to you when you returned this morning, but you left so soon after . . ."

So Talon had been here last night. Had he still been home, or had he been riding the Winds to return one problem to her home village?

If he'd been home, if Talon had slipped in and out of here without even trying to talk to him . . . that was as much a warning as the box.

"Is Lady Kermilla in?" Theran asked.

"She's in her room. She seemed distressed when she returned from the village. She wants to speak with you, but Lords Trae and Jhorma have requested an audience before you talk to the Lady."

"Send them in."

He waited until Julien was out of the room before breaking the seal and opening the paper. Simple words with nothing wasted—and an unflinching and unforgiving judgment.

> Garth and Brok disobeyed the Queen and went into the landen
> part of town. For that alone, they would have been exiled, as the
> Queen commanded. But they went to the weaver's home intending
> to rape the wife and little girl. This I know as fact.
> They are forfeit.

No signature. There never was a signature on a note like this, but he recognized Talon's writing.

A quick knock on the door. Then Jhorma and Trae walked into the room.

"Lady Kermilla had a disturbing experience today," Jhorma said. "A Warlord mentioned something about 'courtesy fingers,' but wouldn't explain further."

Theran pointed at the box. "You can open it."

Leaving the box on the desk, Trae raised the lid. Then he stumbled back, swearing.

"When a man was hunted down and executed by a Warlord Prince, his ring finger and his ring, drained of power, were sent back to his family." Usually the hunt was done because the bastard's offense had been "forgiven" by a twisted Queen. But one way or another, the people of Dena

Nehele got justice—and the fingers were an assurance that no one needed to worry about the bastard coming back to hurt them again.

He wasn't going to share that part with the men who served Kermilla. That would tell them too clearly what Talon thought of her, and they might try to convince her to go back to Dharo and her safe little village.

"Mother Night," Jhorma said softly. "I didn't meet them. I gathered from Bardoc that those two were little pricks, but surely escorting a Queen traveling in a questionable part of town shouldn't warrant execution."

"It didn't. This did." Theran handed the paper to Jhorma—and watched the man pale.

"Can you verify they tried to do this?" Jhorma asked.

"Talon wouldn't have executed them if he wasn't sure of their intentions." And he would have been sure after he ripped open Garth and Brok's inner barriers and got the truth from their own minds.

No, Talon would have been certain even before he took that action. The confirmation from their own minds before the execution was only a formality.

"They were hers." Trae looked sick and confused. "She'd gone to meet them and found out Talon had taken them away. On the ride back here, she kept saying he had no right to touch a male who belonged to her."

*They couldn't belong to her.* Theran's stomach rolled. *Not the same way I do. She couldn't mean that. How could I belong to a Queen who would claim men capable of raping a child? Trae's mistaken. Or he's lying. He has to be.*

"Are we talking about Prince Talon, Lady Cassidy's Master of the Guard?" Jhorma sounded wary.

"Yes." Theran's stomach rolled again. He knew exactly why Talon had left the fingers here instead of on their father's doorstep—because he, as the ruler of this town, should have exiled Garth and Brok for breaking the Queen's command.

"Do you have anyone who could deliver this to the Warlords' family?" Trae asked.

Theran shook his head.

"Then I'll do it for you."

Theran looked at Trae with grudging respect. He'd thought of Kermilla's escorts as useless appendages, unwanted chaperons who restricted what he could say to his lover—and to the woman who should rule his people. But these men were First Circle. If they'd been home, they would be taking care of the business of the court, just like Cassidy's First Circle did.

Offering to take the box to the Warlords' father was a kindness he hadn't expected from Kermilla's present court.

"Take Laska with you," Jhorma said. "There has been enough death over a foolish decision, and I don't imagine anyone reacts well when they receive one of those boxes—unless they're truly relieved to receive it."

"Thank you." Theran nodded at the paper Jhorma still held. "You can give him that too. He should know why his sons were forfeit."

As soon as Jhorma and Trae left, Theran called in a bottle of brandy. He had downed his first large glass before Kermilla stomped daintily into the room.

"Did Trae tell you about the dreadful thing that happened in town today?" Kermilla put her hands on her hips and looked stern. "You should tell Talon he has no business interfering with this town. *You* rule here."

"Garth and Brok are forfeit, Kermilla. There is nothing anyone can do about that."

"You have to do something! They're mine, Theran. They're—"

*"Dead."* Hell's fire. He hadn't meant to be that blunt.

She paled. Pouring more brandy in the glass, he guided her to a chair. "Drink this." He waited until she chugged the brandy. "I'm sorry, Kermilla, but Garth and Brok are dead. They were executed."

She gasped for air, then wailed, "Why?"

He pulled up a footstool and sat in front of her. "They went to a landen's house with the intention of raping the wife and daughter. That's unforgivable, even here where we've forgotten so much of the Old Ways of the Blood."

"They wouldn't do that," Kermilla protested.

She didn't believe them capable of that obscenity. She hadn't realized what kind of men they were when she'd claimed them. Thank the Darkness for that. "They did."

Calling in a small, lace-edged handkerchief, she looked at him with big blue eyes and sniffled, turning an ordinary body sound into something feminine and delicate.

"What about Correne?" Kermilla asked. "I know she went off with you this morning, which is very naughty of you, Theran. She hasn't had her Virgin Night yet. She shouldn't go anywhere with a man without a chaperon."

"I took her home," Theran said quietly. "She's back in her home village now."

"*Why?* She was my only friend here. My only female friend," she added hastily when he stiffened.

He took the glass from her and set it on the table next to the chair. Then he took her hands. "She wasn't a friend to you, although she hid her intentions well."

She jerked her hands out of his. "Whatever are you talking about? Of course she's my friend."

The headache was still there, gnawing inside his skull. So he spoke without softening the blow. "Because of her, you made enemies at dinner the other night." He pulled back. He should have asked this question before. He *had* asked this question before. But not so bluntly that he would have to have an answer. "Maybe I've presumed too much from your staying here after Cassidy moved her court to Eyota. If I have, I apologize. I thought you were willing to become the Queen here next spring. I thought you had stayed to learn what the people here need from their Queen. I've been bringing influential people here to meet you so that they would support your intention to rule."

"What influential people?" Kermilla snapped. "There are only a handful of aristo families in this town and I'm not allowed to go anywhere else."

"Influential doesn't always mean aristo," Theran said, tightening the leash on his temper. "Ferall is an example. He's a savage fighter, and he's respected by other Warlord Princes and the surviving Queens because of it."

"He wasn't very nice at dinner."

Kermilla stuck out her lower lip. The pout usually made him think of carnal things he'd like to do with her. Today, with his head pounding unmercifully, it just made her mouth look puffy and unattractive.

"You should have slapped Correne down when she made that remark about Cassidy."

"Well, she *was* called Lady Freckledy."

"That doesn't matter. She wasn't the Queen of a Territory then. Ferall didn't join Cassidy's court and he may not serve her directly, but he *was* insulted on her behalf. When you did nothing, you lost his support—and the support of the other three Warlord Princes who came with him. That means you lost the support of any of the Queens who pay attention to how Ferall reacts to people who might have great influence in our land."

"Why should he be insulted? You just said he wasn't hers."

"You don't know what it's like to live under a bad Queen. I believe you would be a better Queen for Dena Nehele, but Cassidy has been making an effort to help the people, and the Queens and Warlord Princes are paying attention. They aren't interested in parties and concerts, Kermilla. They're interested in a harvest that will feed everyone through the winter."

"You just don't want to have any fun."

"Fun is a luxury we can't afford yet." He took her hands again. "And there are some other things the people can't afford yet. I got the bills from the merchants today."

"Oh, Theran. You're not going to grumble about that too."

He released her hands and moved away from her, needing some distance. "I told the merchants I would pay what was on these bills and nothing more."

She stared at him, clearly hurt and insulted.

"I'm sorry, Kermilla, but the shops you've been patronizing have fulfilled their tithes until next spring. *All the tithes.* Not just what would have come to me as income, but also what should have gone into the town's treasury to pay the guards and maintain the basic necessities of the town itself."

"Can't you pay it?" she asked in a small voice.

"With what?" Thank the Darkness she didn't know about the treasure

Cassidy had found in the attics here. "I have enough money from my family to pay for the servants and start doing some repairs here."

"But you live *in a mansion*."

"This spring was the first time I set foot in this house. My family hasn't lived here for generations. Couldn't live here because the Territory Queen had claimed it for herself."

She looked around the room, as if casting about for something she could understand.

For a moment, he thought she was going to ask him to sell off some of the furnishings in order to pay for another damn dress. But she looked at him with a tiny frown. "Can't you raise the tithes?"

"And give more people a reason to leave?" He raked his hand through his hair. "Have you paid any attention when we went driving around the town? Have you noticed all the empty houses and empty shops?"

"Yes." Her frowned deepened. "Grayhaven is the *important* town. Why aren't there more people living here?"

*"Because they're dead."*

Her eyes filled with tears. Her lower lip quivered.

He closed his eyes for a moment to regain control.

*She's young, inexperienced. She's lived in a safe little village her whole life. Sweet Darkness, please let her understand this time.*

"Half the Blood in Dena Nehele were destroyed by that witch storm that ripped through the Realms a couple of years ago. Then the landens rose up against us, and half of the survivors died. Do you understand, Kermilla? For every four Blood who were alive three years ago, *only one of us is left*."

She stared at him, her face wiped clean of all expression.

Returning to the footstool, he sat and faced her again. "I can't give you what I don't have. I think you can be a good Queen, but you've let a few questionable companions persuade you into making bad decisions. You've lost the respect of some powerful men because of it."

"Theran, I'm truly sorry. I didn't know how bad it's been for all of you."

*Why not?* he wondered. *I've been telling you since the first time we took a drive around the town.*

"I guess I didn't understand that things would be so different here. That ruling would be so different here."

Theran's heart pounded. She sounded regretful, almost apologetic.

"I'll do better," Kermilla said in a subdued voice. "I promise."

He kissed the back of her hand, then said with all the conviction he could put in his voice, "We can have a good life, Kermilla. It's just going to take time and work."

Nodding, she pulled away from him gently and left the room. She didn't join them for dinner that night, which he didn't think odd, but he did regret that her door remained locked to him when he tapped on it later that night.

And he tried not to think about the sounds he'd heard a moment before he knocked. Sounds an aural shield could have politely hidden if she hadn't wanted anyone to hear.

Sounds that indicated she'd found consolation with someone else that night.

# CHAPTER 22

## TERREILLE

Standing in the doorway of the dining room, Dryden announced, "Princes Ferall, Rikoma, Elendill, and Hikaeda have arrived. I have put them in the visitors' parlor."

Ranon almost spit a mouthful of coffee across the table. "They're here *already*?" When he'd suggested they come in the morning, he hadn't expected the four men to arrive *this* early.

Wiping his mouth with a napkin, he pushed away from the table. "Thank you, Dryden. I'll be there in a minute."

"It will be fine, Ranon," Powell said. He was the only other person left at the table.

"Will it?" Not knowing if Ferall now served Kermilla and was here as her eyes and ears made Ranon edgy. That uncertainty had gnawed at him ever since he'd agreed to this visit.

"They'll see what they want to see. Show them the village. Show them the people. That's all you can do. I'll inform Maydra that we will have four guests for the midday meal."

"Where is Cassie?" Ranon asked.

"I believe she went upstairs to change clothes."

Ranon hurried to the visitors' parlor. The four men hadn't taken a seat. When he walked in they were doing a slow prowl around the room, looking a little baffled.

"Good morning," he said.

Ferall nodded, as did Rikoma and Elendill. Hikaeda smiled and said, "Have we come to the right place, Ranon? When we arrived at the landing web and asked for the Queen's residence, we were directed here."

"Used to be a boardinghouse, so it has a big dining room and kitchen, several parlors, and sufficient bedrooms and bathrooms for the Queen and some of her court, as well as rooms for special guests. Also has enough land for a big kitchen garden, herb garden, and flower gardens, plus some ground Gray says will suit the honey pears." Ranon shrugged. "It's not a typical building for a Queen's residence, but it pleases Lady Cassidy."

As they took another look around the room, Ranon felt his shoulders tighten, even though feeling defensive was foolish. The furniture was old but clean and polished. The room had the scent of a place that was cared for. And the fact that the Queen wasn't buying new furniture to impress visitors while the people were still struggling to have enough clothes and a decent pair of shoes was something her court would not apologize for. To anyone.

Footsteps. Female voices.

Cassidy suddenly appeared in the doorway wearing shortened trousers and a shirt that looked like she'd rescued it from the rag bag. Probably the same rag bag where she got the cloths that were stuffed into the bucket she was holding.

"Ranon, Dryden said . . ." She looked at the other four men in the room and her hazel eyes widened. "Oh, Hell's fire. Is that *today*?"

"It appears we have come at an inconvenient time," Ferall said stiffly.

"No, you haven't," Cassidy said, stepping farther into the room. "No. My apologies, gentlemen. We've had several families come to the village, and we've been working to get them settled into their new homes. Between that and the work in the shops and trying to get the Healing House and Shira's residence set up, I lost track of the days."

"Cassie, if we're going to get the last rooms in the Healing House cleaned out properly so Shira can start working there, we're going to need— Oh."

Another tall, big-boned woman with a long, plain face, freckles, and red hair stepped into the room.

"Gentlemen, this is my mother, Devra."

Four Warlord Princes tipped their heads in a respectful bow.

"We are honored by the introduction," Ferall said.

"Cassie, give me the bucket." Devra wrapped her hand around the handle. "You're needed here. Besides, you've been working too hard lately."

"I have not." Cassidy tightened her own grip on the bucket.

"Yes, you have. Even your father thinks so."

"Haven't been working any harder than the rest of you."

Devra narrowed her eyes. "Daughter, you fell asleep in the middle of drum practice last night. That should tell you something."

"We promised to work only half a day today," Cassidy protested.

Devra gave him a stern look. "Ranon."

He raised his hands in surrender. "No. With all respect, Devra, I am *not* getting in the middle of this."

"When we made this appointment with Ranon, he did tell us that the Queen may not be available," Hikaeda said.

"See?" Cassidy said, trying to tug the bucket out of Devra's hand. A futile effort.

Ranon sent out a psychic call for help. He'd already learned that when Cassidy and Devra squared off to argue about something, there was only one person in the house who was willing to step in and deal with two stubborn women.

*Cassie? Cassie!*

Vae appeared in the doorway and looked up at Cassidy's back. Or more likely, at Cassidy's ass since that was Vae's preferred spot to nip.

*Ranon will talk to the other males and show them male things.*

Cassidy pressed her lips together, and her face turned bright red. Devra just looked interested. All five Warlord Princes squirmed.

*You will work with Shira and Devra. Then you will eat. Then you will not work. It is time to work now. Shira is waiting for you.*

Vae trotted off, no doubt to wait at the back door.

"If you will excuse us," Devra said tightly, "it is time to work now. The Sceltie said so." She walked out of the room.

"It was a pleasure to see you, gentlemen," Cassidy said. She hurried to catch up to Devra.

No one said anything for several moments.

"You called the Sceltie to deal with the Queen?" Elendill asked.

"Oh, yeah," Ranon replied. "Some days I think if we'd had Vae planning tactics, we could have defended our people even better than we did."

Ferall laughed softly. "Well, let's get on with these male things we're supposed to do."

"What would you like to see?" Ranon asked.

All the humor in their faces faded away. Ferall said, "Whatever you choose to show us."

A careful phrasing, but Ranon knew that what wasn't shown would be as important as what *was* shown. In Ferall's place, he would have paid attention to both. "Are you all comfortable with doing some walking?"

Ferall nodded.

"Then let me show you what the Queen's presence has done for Eyota."

He began with the Queen's square, introducing them to Shaddo's wife, who was standing outside the family's cottage with a look of grim amusement on her face.

"Shaddo already left to do a circuit around the village," Soli said. "Do you need him?"

"No," Ranon replied. Since she looked like she was edging toward a hissy cat mood, he added, "Anything I can do for you?"

"Thanks, but it's been taken care of."

Since he knew what *that* meant, he led a retreat that didn't look hasty for all its speed.

"Problem?" Ferall sounded amused.

"Not for us," Ranon replied.

"Then who?" Rikoma asked.

The answer came trotting up the street.

"For Eryk and Eliot, Shaddo's sons," Ranon said.

The boys were moving smartly, with Darcy trotting right behind them.

"Ranon!" Eryk rushed up to the men. "Tell Darcy we weren't doing anything wrong! We were just playing at the pond in the park!"

Darcy growled and lunged at Eliot's heels, giving the boy good reason to scramble past his older brother. *Soli wants you home. *Now.**

"Did your father give you permission to go to the pond—or the park?" Ranon asked, already knowing the answer.

"He didn't say we couldn't," Eryk said.

"Your mother wants you home," Ranon said. He owed it to Shaddo to keep his expression stern and his voice firm, but damn, he wanted to laugh.

*Home!* Darcy said.

Eryk glared at Darcy. "Just wait until I have my Birthright Ceremony. You won't be so bossy then!"

*I will still have sharper teeth.*

*Hard to argue with that,* Ranon thought. But he would have to mention that comment to Shaddo tonight. He wasn't sure Eryk's Birthright Jewel would end up outranking Darcy's, but the boy couldn't be allowed to use power to hurt someone in his family—even if that family member had four legs and fur . . . and sharper teeth.

He and the other men continued down Autumn Road, passing the house where Lord Rogir and his family were settling in. Several girls were in the front yard, jumping rope. Or more precisely, two of the girls were swinging the rope and Keely was jumping over it.

He didn't stop. The girls were still uneasy around strangers, and Keely, despite looking like a live furry toy at the moment, had appointed herself the Protector of Young Females living in the Queen's square and wouldn't hesitate to attack if proper introductions weren't made. And he really didn't want to take time for the kind of proper introductions—with thorough sniffing—that Scelties deemed necessary before letting an unknown get close to their humans.

"That was another Sceltie?" Hikaeda asked. "How many are there?"

"Feels like hundreds some days, but there are twelve of them, plus Vae," Ranon replied. And in a village that only held a few hundred people, the odds were *not* in the humans' favor.

He took the men down a few other streets. The occupied houses were carefully tended. Not many people visible, but there was still a sense of energy and purpose, of work being done with good heart.

His people had always had heart. Now there was also joy.

"You lost people," Ferall said quietly, tipping his head to indicate the empty houses.

"Here in Eyota, most of the families who are gone were lost before the purge and the uprisings," Ranon replied. Meaning most had been slaughtered by the twisted Queens who had been encouraged to eliminate the Shalador people.

"I'm sorry," Ferall said.

"We survived, and now we have hope."

Ferall gave him an odd look, but they turned onto the main street, and his guests stopped. Just stopped.

Anyone who farmed was with his animals or in his fields, getting ready for the harvest that would begin in a few more weeks. And many craftsmen of all kinds were in their own shops working. But the first impression for someone who hadn't been watching this carefully planned frenzy grow on a daily basis was that every male who was old enough and strong enough to lift and carry, and every person who had some skill with tools—or wanted to learn to have skills, regardless of gender—was on the main street, scurrying in and out of buildings.

"Mother Night," Elendill said.

Calling in the watch his grandfather had given him for his twentieth birthday, Ranon opened the cover and checked the time. Then he vanished the watch. "This will quiet down right about . . . now."

Sure enough, Burle stepped out of one of the buildings. In a Craft-enhanced voice, he hollered, "Break!"

All the pounding, sawing, clattering noises stopped. People came out of various buildings and headed up the street.

"Elders' Park is being used as a rest station," Ranon said. "There is food and water there, and one or two of the elders are there each day to listen to the people or answer questions."

"Hell's fire, Ranon," Hikaeda said. "How are your people able to do this?"

Ranon took a deep breath and let it out slowly. He heard the envy in Hikaeda's voice—and worried about Ferall's silence. But they needed to know why this prosperity was starting here.

"This is the Queen's home village, and it is because of her that we have been able to make certain business connections that will be able to benefit all of Dena Nehele in time." He paused. "Gray has become friends with Daemon Sadi and made a deal with him: in exchange for Prince Sadi owning a few businesses here in Eyota, the court was given a loan for supplies the people in Dena Nehele will need, especially this coming winter."

A shocked gasp from all four men—and a hint of fear. Just hearing Sadi's name had that effect on most men.

"*Gray* has become friends with *Sadi*?" Elendill asked.

"Yes." Not a surprising question considering the shape Gray had been in for the past ten years. "We'll be able to purchase things like blankets, clothes, and shoes—things that are in short supply here," Ranon continued. "A weavers guild in the southern Province was burned out during the up-risings. By borrowing from the loan, they will be able to purchase looms and wool, fix up a couple of empty houses as a new workplace, and begin to make a living again."

"How does a village ask for such help?" Rikoma asked with extreme courtesy.

"Whoever rules the village submits a request to Lady Cassidy, telling her what is needed—and the cost." Ranon sighed. "Our land was destroyed over generations. It will take more than one season to fix all the wrongs. But we have the means now of buying feed for livestock and food for our people if the harvest falls short this year. We have connections we wouldn't have dreamed possible a year ago."

"If you're worried about envy, don't be," Ferall said. "It's right and fitting that the Queen's home village receive the first benefit of her efforts. And like her court, it should be an example of what is possible."

Before he could think of what to say, a voice called his name.

Rainier pulled up next to them.

What had Ferall said about no envy? Hell's fire! *He* felt envy. That pony cart Rainier was driving practically screamed *aristo*. Not because it was fancy, but because of the quality and craftsmanship that had gone into the making of it. And the bay gelding pulling the cart was a gorgeous piece of horseflesh.

"Glad I found you since no one seems to know where Gray is working today," Rainier said.

"He'll be at the Queen's Residence for the midday meal," Ranon replied.

"Can't stay. I swung by to see if Marcus needed anything, and then put this lad through his paces to make sure there wouldn't be any problems. Now I'm heading back to Kaeleer. Prince Yaslana's wife is indisposed, so I'm going to stay in Ebon Rih for a while and help out with administrative tasks. Lucivar is too short-tempered right now to deal with paperwork—or the people who bring it."

Rainier smiled when he said it, but Ranon saw the concern in the other man's eyes. "Is there anything we can do to help?"

"No, but he'll appreciate the offer."

Rainier continued to smile as he looked at the other men, but Ranon had the feeling the Kaeleer Warlord Prince had just completed a very quick—and thorough—assessment of his guests.

"Well," Rainier said, "I'll get this boy to the stables and be on my way."

"Stables?"

Rainier made a gesture that included the horse and cart. "Ladies Morghann and Jaenelle sent this to Ladies Shira and Cassidy. Queens and Healers in Scelt like this cart's design because there are storage compartments under the benches in the back, and it's small enough to be comfortable for a Lady to drive. Lord Khardeen raised the horse up from a foal and trained him personally, so the lad is solid and dependable. He's not kindred— Khardeen figured you had enough adjustments to make without that particular bit of fun—but the horse is used to being around Scelties, so he'll settle in just fine with Kief and Lloyd to look after him."

"Rainier, it's very generous, but we can't afford this," Ranon said.

Rainier gave him an odd look, and his smile sharpened. "Ranon, darling, I'll bet when you took a piss this morning you noticed you have a cock and balls. That means you have no say in this. Cassidy's friends want her to have the horse and cart. They figured she'll share it with Shira since Shira is the court's Healer. If you want to argue about this with the Queen of Scelt and . . . Prince Sadi's wife, you go right ahead. I'm not about to." He gathered the reins and clicked to the horse, turning back the way he'd come.

Ranon had heard the hesitation and conscious choice of how to identify Jaenelle—and knew that Rainier might work for Daemon Sadi, but the man still served the Queen of Ebon Askavi.

He watched the pony cart turn a corner.

*What in the name of Hell just happened here?* Ranon asked Rainier on an Opal thread.

Rainier's laughter came through the thread. *I didn't tell your friends all of Cassidy's connections. And whether you tell them why Cassidy knows so many Territory Queens in Kaeleer or why they're all paying so much attention to what happens in Dena Nehele is up to you.*

*Are they paying attention?* Ranon's heart started to pound hard.

*Ranon,* Rainier said gently, *the rulers of Scelt, Glacia, Dharo, Nharkhava, Dhemlan, and Ebon Rih all have a connection to your Queen or her court. Not to mention the High Lord of Hell. Of course they're paying attention. And it doesn't hurt if the Queens and Warlord Princes in Dena Nehele know a little more about your Lady's credentials.*

Being so busy day after day, focusing on repairs and crops and the things the people would need to get through the winter, it was easy to forget how much power could arrow down on their land.

But being so busy day after day never quite smothered the knowledge that Theran's actions might be setting up Dena Nehele for another violent storm.

He turned to the other men. "Shall we continue?"

Rikoma, Elendill, and Hikaeda looked at Ferall.

"Is there any place we could get a drink and sit for a bit?" Ferall asked.

"There is. It's down this way."

They'd had enough. Whatever they had come here to see, whatever questions they had wanted answered, they had gotten more than they'd expected.

So he took them to Elders' Park and got them coffee and food, and gave them silence as they watched the workers return to their assignments. And knew with absolute certainty that something had changed.

They arrived back at the Queen's Residence earlier than anticipated, so Ranon took the other men around to the back of the house. He didn't think any of them knew any more about gardens than he did, but they looked around politely as he pointed out the Healing House and the cottage Gray wanted to convert into a loaning library.

"Gray is working with Lord Marcus, Prince Sadi's man of business, to figure out costs and what will be needed," Ranon said. "Since many people can't afford books right now, he wants to have this library and obtain a wide variety of books to educate and entertain. The villagers would pay a couple of coppers to take a book for a month, then return it. We want to keep the fee small enough that people can afford it, but it also has to pay for the books themselves, the librarian's wages, and the repairs and upkeep of the cottage."

"Gray thought of this?" Hikaeda asked.

"Gray is a bundle of ideas," Ranon said dryly.

Powell had given Gray his own little space in the Steward's office to stash all his notes about possibilities for Eyota in particular and Dena Nehele in general. Only the knowledge that every available person was going to be helping with the harvest this year, and the need to get the shops finished up and stocked with merchandise, kept Gray from trying to add one more thing to the list of projects to be accomplished before winter set in.

They moved away from the wall and ended up standing near the table and chairs under the big tree.

*Ranon!*

The joyful shout was the only warning he had before he turned and ended up with his arms full of Sceltie. Coughing from the dust that rose up as Khollie smacked into his chest, he said, "What have you been doing?"

★The females were cleaning Shira's den. I helped.★

The tail banging against him with enthusiasm raised more dust.

"You used your tail as a dust rag, didn't you?"

★Yes! Shira says you need to wash my tail before I'm allowed in the house.★ Khollie squirmed as he tried to lick Ranon's ear.

The tail wasn't the only thing that needed to get washed.

Ranon's face heated as the other men watched with amused interest. He hated himself for feeling the tiniest bit of shame, but that didn't change the truth. Khollie was different. There was a sweetness to him that wasn't about his being younger than the other Scelties, or just a trait of personality. He'd seen children who had a similar kind of sweetness. They weren't the same as other children. Weren't quite right.

Not that Khollie wasn't a bright boy. He was. He needed things explained carefully, but only one time. And he did wear a Tiger Eye Jewel.

But if Ranon had to be a Sceltie's human, why couldn't it have been someone like Keely or Darcy or, Hell's fire, even Darkmist? Catching sight of the Opal-Jeweled Sceltie Warlord Prince had made Ferall stop and stare.

Darkmist made hardened warriors sit up and take notice. Khollie, the homely little patchwork dog, just amused them.

Elendill shifted to the left, giving Ranon a clear view of his brother Janos—who was bent over double with his arms wrapped around himself. Laughing.

But the boy straightened up quickly enough and headed over to them.

"Come on, Khollie," Janos said. "Ranon has to stay with the other humans, so I'll help you wash up."

★I owe you,★ Ranon said as Khollie jumped out of his arms and whapped him in the face with a dusty tail.

★You do,★ Janos agreed.

*Not a youth anymore, despite being eighteen,* Ranon thought as he watched Janos and Khollie walk to the house. *And much changed even from last summer.*

One of the reasons for those changes walked out of the house. Reyhana wore a long, simple summer dress and sandals.

Ranon heard Janos's sharp command that stopped Khollie from a joyful leap. He watched the way his brother went down on one knee to be closer to the cowering dog's height and pointed to Reyhana, who nodded as if agreeing with Janos's words. He watched Khollie straighten up, no longer afraid once he understood that Janos's sharpness had been intended to protect him from doing something wrong—like jumping into Reyhana's freshly bathed arms.

And he saw the way Janos looked at Reyhana, saw the brush of fingers against her hand when Janos rose to take Khollie to the laundry room for a bath.

A hard choice for a young man who burned for more than a few kisses and petting. Reyhana was the Shalador Queen with the most potential in her generation, and it would be a couple of years or more before she would have her Virgin Night. It would cost Janos his life if an imprudent coupling damaged the girl in any way.

But he knew what it was like to be young and have a woman hold your heart. After all, Shira had been sixteen when he'd fallen in love with her.

Reyhana walked toward them, and Ranon watched for the moment when the other men picked up her psychic scent and realized she was a Queen. And he wondered why the men tensed, especially Hikaeda and Ferall.

"Gentlemen," Reyhana said, tipping her head in a small bow.

Ranon made the introductions.

"Lady Reyhana," Ferall replied as the men gave her a matching vow.

"We have about half an hour before the meal," Reyhana said. "Would you like to sit out here and have a glass of ale while you wait? It's a lovely spot when there's a breeze like there is today."

"That would be welcome," Ferall said.

Reyhana turned her head, her eyes having the distant look the Blood sometimes had when they communicated on a psychic thread.

"Are you staying here?" Rikoma asked her.

"Yes. I have the privilege of working as part of Lady Cassidy's court to learn Protocol and the Old Ways of the Blood, as well as the rights and duties of a Queen and court. It's very exciting to be a part of this new beginning for all our people."

Elendill looked past her shoulder. "You have many servants here?"

Reyhana laughed softly. "The Queen's court acts as a training ground. We have a butler, a housekeeper and her assistant, and a cook. The footmen and maids are all young people from the village who want training in domestic service. They get training; we get extra help."

"There aren't many aristo houses anymore that need servants," Hikaeda said.

"No, but there are boardinghouses and inns," Reyhana said. "And there are people like Prince Spere and Prince Haele who share a cottage in the Queen's square rather than having the whole court living here. Being members of the First Circle, their residence is cared for by the servants here, but there are others who would be willing to pay to have some cooking and cleaning done. Aristo houses are not the only places that need such skills."

Reyhana's face, like her voice, shone with enthusiasm. Hearing a sound, she looked behind her, then looked at the men. Her green eyes twinkled with good humor. "Please step aside to leave a clear path to the table. The girls are still getting used to being around Warlord Princes, and they get nervous. But they're getting better and drop fewer things. We've only had one broken glass this week."

Birdie, who was now assistant housekeeper and assistant trainer of maids, carried the pitcher of ale. Copper, a village girl in training, carried the tray of glasses.

Watching Copper's hands shake as she glanced at the men and crept after Birdie, Ranon held his breath. Then pitcher and tray were on the table and both girls were retreating back to the house.

"You'll notice there is a shield around the edge of the tray," Reyhana said. "It won't help anything if the tray is dropped, but it does prevent a wobble from tipping a glass off the tray."

"Did you think of that?" Rikoma asked.

"No, Vae did."

The men laughed, and Ranon guessed that had been Reyhana's intention. Warlord Princes were lethal predators, and they were used to being feared. Being given an opportunity to laugh with a woman was a moment both appreciated and prized.

Reyhana went back into the house. Hikaeda poured the ale and passed the glasses. For a few minutes, the men looked at the gardens and spoke little.

Then Cassidy walked out of the house. Like Reyhana, she wore a long, light summer dress, but her hair had been put up in a simple knot at the back of her head.

She had just reached Ranon when . . .

"Cassie!"

*Cassie? Cassie!*

Cassidy crossed her eyes and made a face as Gray and Vae caught up with her.

*Hat, Cassie!*

"No," Cassidy said. "If I put a hat on now, the hair will fall down, and it's too hot today to have it down."

*Gray, tell her!*

Coming up on Cassidy's left side, Gray nodded to the men. He wore a plain white shirt and black trousers—and his Purple Dusk pendant and ring.

There was nothing challenging about a man wearing his Jewels, and there was nothing special about the clothes, but Ranon felt a curious tension in the other men.

Gray gave the men a conspiratorial smile as he looked each of them in the eyes. That smile included a mischievous wink when his eyes moved to Hikaeda. Then he called in a parasol, opened it, and held it over Cassidy.

When she did nothing but look up at it, Gray said politely, "Are you going to take the parasol, or should I hold it for you?"

"You're spending too much time with somebody," Cassidy muttered as she took the parasol. "You're getting too good at this."

"Do you want to hit me?" Gray asked.

"I'm thinking about it."

Cassidy and Gray smiled at each other—and those smiles had enough heat to take everyone by surprise. Including Ranon.

"Gentlemen," Gray said, "if you would join us, the meal is ready."

He raised his right hand, an escort's gesture. Cassidy placed her left hand over his in automatic response—like a Queen would respond to her First Escort or Consort . . . or her husband.

Cassidy and Gray walked back to the house. Ranon started to follow, then realized the others weren't coming with him.

Hikaeda stared at nothing. "We were friends," he said softly. "Before he was taken and hurt so badly, we were friends. I never thought . . . It's good to see him again. It's good to see Jared Blaed."

Hikaeda headed for the house, followed by Rikoma and Elendill. But Ferall still lingered.

"Something wrong?" Ranon asked.

Ferall shook his head. "I want this for my own village, for my own Province."

"Then come inside," Ranon said. "There are people around the table who can help."

"Yes," Ferall said softly, "I think maybe there are."

# CHAPTER 23

## TERREILLE

Ranon gave his horse its head and caught up to Burle before the man reached the landen community.

Something had surprised Lord Rogir when he stopped at the community to see how the cleanup and repairs were coming along, and anything that would surprise a senior guard was something Ranon wanted to check out for himself—especially when Cassidy's father was about to ride into that community.

Ranon rode through the arched gateway ahead of Burle, then reined in, understanding Rogir's surprise.

Lilly Weaver and JuliDee had been staying with Rogir's family since the flight from Grayhaven. Lilly and Rogir's wife had worked together to clean up the senior guard's household. Other women in the village had also pitched in to give two other cottages a good scrubbing. One cottage went to Lord Brandon and his wife, and the other was to be a general residence for the unmarried guards. After that, the women had been driving out to the community to start cleaning up the attached row houses.

Now there were several wagons parked close to the houses and many unfamiliar faces—and there was James Weaver, hugging his wife.

Rogir stood off to one side with a couple of his men, watching the reunion. Deciding that was the best choice for an explanation, Ranon guided his horse over to the men and dismounted. James, spotting him, gave Lilly one more hug and joined them.

"You made good time," Ranon said. "I don't think all the houses are ready to be occupied."

"Lilly says they have three that are clean and in good order," James said. "Mostly good order. Lilly wanted to know about—"

*Puppies!*

Ranon stiffened. So did Rogir. Burle just climbed off the wagon and headed over to them as Wynne, a Sceltie with a pure white head, and black-faced Duffy jumped out of the wagon.

Burle looked at Ranon and shrugged. "They wanted to come."

*Puppies!* Wynne wagged her tail at the smaller landen children.

Then Duffy froze for a moment before shooting straight up into the air to hover well above the buildings. His tail began wagging so hard the motion knocked him sideways as he shouted, *Sheep!*

*Oh, shit,* Ranon thought.

"You outrank the rest of us," Rogir said.

The man didn't have to sound so damned cheerful—and relieved—about it. Of course, Keely had taken up residence with Rogir's family. Having enough experience now trying to deal with just one, the man could be somewhat forgiven for not wanting to deal with a pair of Scelties.

"Duffy, come down now," Ranon said.

*They have *sheep!**

*And may the Darkness have mercy on them.* "Duffy," he said firmly.

Duffy dropped out of the air so fast, Ranon was sure the dog would hit the ground. But he came to a stop an arm's length from the ground and gently floated down the rest of the way.

"What did your lady want to know?" Burle asked.

Looking a little apprehensive, James pulled his attention away from the Scelties. "There isn't an ice chest that she could find in the kitchen area." He sounded apologetic. "It would help our food last longer if we could purchase some ice."

Burle frowned. "There are cold boxes, and each of them have a small freezer inside the main box. I checked them out, and they're all in good working order. Need a good scrubbing, of course, but if that's been done, they're ready for a cold spell."

Seeing James's discomfort, Ranon said, "I think that's the problem, Burle. The cold boxes don't work without Craft, and landens can't do Craft."

"There aren't any youths in your village who are interested in earning some pocket money?" Burle asked. Then he huffed. "Look. I know things have been hard here. You just need to look around to see it. And I know there have been bad troubles here between the Blood and landens. But the fighting is over, and from what I understand there wasn't any of that kind of fighting in Eyota. These people are here because you all decided you were willing to work together to build a new life. Isn't that so?"

"Yes," Ranon said.

"So." Burle looked at James. "Cold box is more dependable than ice. The spell needs to be renewed on a weekly basis." Now he looked at Ranon and Rogir. "Around Weavers Field, where I come from, a couple of enterprising young Warlords go to the neighboring landen village where some of the people have bought cold boxes. They charge a fee for maintaining the spell on each cold box. Now I know things are tight here and no one has much coin to spare, but these houses also have a tank for hot water that needs Craft too. So it seems to me that charging three coppers a week for both spells would be fair. At least for this first little while."

"I can ask around the village and see if anyone is interested," Ranon said.

*We could do those spells,* Wynne said.

*We know our Craft,* Duffy said.

The men looked at one another. No one had noticed the Scelties joining them.

"Well," Burle finally said. "You come with me. I'll show you the spells, and you can give them a try. Then we'll see."

*What happens if they do it wrong?* Ranon asked Burle.

*Then I guess I'll be buying that landen family another cold box or ice chest,* Burle replied as he and the Scelties went into one of the houses.

"We didn't expect you for a few more days," Rogir said.

"That was my decision, sir," Jaego said.

"Mine too," Ristoff said. "Moore is about a day behind us with the rest of the landen families and livestock."

"You must have driven the animals awfully hard," Rogir said.

"No, sir. We had help." James shook his head and sounded like he still didn't quite believe what had happened.

Jaego nodded, then looked at the other guard. "Ristoff and I took the liberty to make some decisions on the Queen's behalf."

Ranon stiffened, then forced himself to relax. Hadn't he also taken the liberty to make some promises in Cassidy's name? If these men were going to serve as guards in her court, he had to show some confidence in their decisions—at least until those decisions proved unworthy of that trust. "Explain."

"People are still feeling plenty uneasy, and we were concerned about the landen families traveling so far," Jaego said. "Especially since some of the raiding parties had traveled the same way during the uprisings. Some animals, and a couple of women with a lot more men."

"Two days out, we stopped at a Coaching station on the outskirts of a village," Ristoff said. "Showed the Coachmen the letters of passage from the Queen's Steward, and told them that she wanted these craftsmen and the other families settled near her home village as part of her plans to restore Dena Nehele. They had heard of some of the things Lady Cassidy has done already to help restore our land, so they offered their livestock Coach and a passenger Coach. Since it required several trips, and we had to load the wagons into the livestock Coach after the animals, we agreed on a spot south of the Heartsblood River as a place to disembark."

Jaego called in some papers and handed them to Ranon. "We didn't have enough marks to cover the usual fares, but the Coachmen didn't name a price. Those papers indicate the number of trips they made, the number of wagons and livestock taken. They said they'll accept whatever fee the Queen deems fair."

"They did ask that we mention their names," Ristoff said. "They wanted Lady Cassidy to know there are others beyond her court who are willing to serve in their own way."

*The ripples from one heart can change so much,* Ranon thought. *Cassidy has changed so much.*

"Well done," he said, his voice warm with approval. "Well done."

Then he noticed Burle coming out of the house. The man kept scratching the back of his neck, but Ranon didn't think the itch was on Burle's skin.

"Problem?" he asked.

"No," Burle replied. "Not exactly. Those two youngsters are right. They do know their Craft. They learned both those spells after being shown once, and they can do them better than a good many young humans I've known."

"Then what's the problem?" Why did he ask the question when he didn't really want to be given the answer?

Burle wasn't looking any of them in the eye, and that made Ranon nervous.

"It's like this," Burle finally said. "Wynne and Duffy want to try out this payment-for-work idea humans seem so fond of."

*Ah, shit.*

"So they'll maintain the spells on the cold boxes and water tanks for three coppers a week for each household." Burle looked at James Weaver.

"That sounds fair," James said.

"They also want three coppers a day to guard and herd livestock."

"I thought they liked herding sheep," Rogir said.

"A man who likes his work still wants to be paid for it," Burle said.

"Anything else?" Ranon asked.

Burle nodded. "Since they'll be helping guard the community, they'll live in the guardhouse with whoever is stationed here. They want their own big chair so the humans can't snarl about them being on the furniture."

Ranon found himself nodding in time with Rogir.

"One of them is free each week to go to story time in the village," Burle continued. He glanced at James. "Do you have a teacher for your children?"

James nodded. "Potter's wife has been teaching some of our children."

"Well, Wynne and Duffy want a little time with the teacher each day to continue learning to read and do their sums."

Ranon's jaw dropped. "They read? *They can read?* Then why do *I* have to read *Sceltie Saves the Day* every damn night?"

Rogir and James looked at him.

"You don't have children yet, do you?" James asked.

The Rock of Foreboding sank in the pond of Ranon's belly.

*Hell's fire.* He had read that damn book too many times.

"Think of this as practice," Rogir said.

"Next thing you know they'll be writing their own stories," Ranon muttered.

Burle shook his head. "No, I don't think so. Writing requires special Craft for a Sceltie, and it's hard to learn. Someone named Ladvarian can write a whole letter, but he got special training from the living myth. Of the Scelties here, only Vae can write a little."

Vae could write? Hell's fire, Mother Night, and may the Darkness be merciful.

"Anything else?" he asked. Damn it! He was a Warlord Prince. Running away was *not* an option.

Running away sounded like a very good idea, though.

"That was all of it," Burle said. "If James here is willing to represent his people and we have a bargain, I'll tell the youngsters and we'll finish the deal."

James looked back at the other landens. The men nodded, so it was obvious they had chosen him to be their spokesman and interact with the Blood. "We have a deal."

Burle waved a hand.

Wynne and Duffy trotted up to them.

"You have a bargain," Burle told them. "A handshake before witnesses is considered a fair agreement."

The Scelties popped up to hover on air about waist high. They sat and offered their right front paws to James, who seemed to have a sudden understanding of just what he was getting himself and his people into. But he shook with Wynne and Duffy, sealing the bargain.

The Scelties, along with the guards, went off to the guardhouse to see what would be needed. Burle waved at the landens and headed for his wagon. Ranon mounted his horse and rode out too.

As he rode back to Eyota, he wondered if Jaenelle Angelline and Morghann, the Queen of Scelt, had known exactly what they were doing when they let these particular Scelties loose on an unsuspecting people.

And he knew he would take perverse pleasure in watching the faces of the rest of the court when he told them about this day's adventure.

# CHAPTER 24

## TERREILLE

Kermilla crumpled the letter from Correne, tossed it into the fireplace, and blasted it with witchfire, turning it to ash in seconds.

She paced her bedroom, feeling more misused with every circuit she made. She'd wasted the whole summer, when she should have been enjoying picnics and parties instead of being criticized for not working in the damn garden. And despite her pointed hints, Theran remained oblivious to what she'd given up to stay here and wait until he could make her the Queen of Dena Nehele.

There was nothing to do in this dung-heap town. *Nothing!* She could visit a couple of aristo girls she'd become acquainted with, but they had no *interesting* conversation, so there wasn't much point. Besides, about the only things they could do during these visits were walk around the village or drive around the village. And if they did that, the girls wanted to browse in the shops, and what was the point of going into shops if you couldn't buy anything? She'd written *three* letters to her Steward, Lord Gallard, telling him to double the forthcoming autumn tithes because she needed the income, and also *commanding him* to send her some marks from the village treasury to hold her over.

His single answer had been vague about the autumn tithes and totally lacking in the required marks.

She could summon her Consort, but there had been a change over the summer in Jhorma's attitude that made her feel like she was alone in bed even when he was pumping inside her.

She could *work*. That would make Theran happy. But she saw no reason to exert herself when her efforts would benefit someone else's purse instead of her own.

So there was nothing, nothing, *nothing* to do around here until spring when she would rule the whole of Dena Nehele and not be stuck in this town.

And she didn't have the status symbol that had captured the fancy of the Blood in this land.

She didn't have a Sceltie.

She'd written to Morghann, the Queen of Scelt, indicating she would be amenable to having one of the dogs as a companion, but Morghann had shown a distinct lack of manners and had not replied.

And now Correne's letter this morning.

> *I've heard Freckledy has a whole pack of Scelties entertaining visitors with their tricks, and even Warlord Princes are impressed enough with the dogs to overlook her flaws. Have you gotten a Sceltie yet? I think all the prominent Queens are going to have one as a companion.*

Why did old Freckledy need a whole pack of them? The bitch was just trying to secure her position. She *knew* she couldn't retain the title of Territory Queen after the year's contract was done unless she did *something* to catch the Blood's interest.

Theran had explained about the contract that gave Cassidy and the people of Dena Nehele one year to decide if Cassidy would become the fully acknowledged Queen of Dena Nehele.

She didn't have access to Cassidy's court here, so she couldn't use her skills to coax the men into believing she was the better choice. That meant she didn't have an already formed court to claim, and that meant she was going to have to entice twelve males here to serve in her First Circle, and *that* meant she couldn't be seen as lacking in any way.

Which meant getting a Sceltie.

*Laska, please attend.*

He hadn't been with her when she first arrived in Grayhaven. Cassidy's First Circle wouldn't recognize him, so Cassidy would be the only person he'd have to avoid. He'd be able to slip in and out of that stupid Shalador village, fetching her a special little friend in exchange for being allowed to go home, which was the *only* thing her First Circle seemed to want to do anymore.

And once she had a Sceltie to help her entertain the men Theran brought here to meet her, *no one* would remember old Freckledy's name.

Wrapping himself in a sight shield, Laska dropped from the Summer-sky Wind to the northern landing web in Eyota. A handful of men were outside the small Coach station near the web, talking and playing cards. Probably a couple of Coach drivers along with the men who took care of the horses for hire and drove the carriages that served as conveyances for visitors.

One of the men looked toward the landing web as Laska arrived. After a moment's study of the area, the man returned his attention to the card game, and Laska snuck away, feeling more confident that he would remain undetected long enough to complete his assignment and return to Grayhaven.

As he slipped along the village streets, looking for the required prize, he wondered why he couldn't approach one of Cassidy's First Circle and just ask for a dog. Why had Kermilla emphasized the need for stealth? Had she already asked Cassidy and the request had been refused? Or was Kermilla using this as a pissing contest to prove her court was better than the court Cassidy now ruled? That a member of *her* court, a Summer-sky Warlord, could slip in and out of a village that several Warlord Princes regarded as their personal territory?

He didn't care anymore what Kermilla wanted. Her appeal had soured at a devastating speed once she had control of a court, and despite having months left in his contract, he was already counting the days until he wasn't hers to command.

A dog barked. Laska hurried toward the sound. Then he turned a corner, stopped, and swore under his breath.

There were Scelties here all right, the first ones he'd seen. But he was on the main street of the damn village, and there were an awful lot of people out and about.

Maybe that would work to his advantage. With so many people milling about, who would notice him in a crowd? And he wouldn't have to go all the way back to the landing web. Courtesy and formality dictated that landing webs be used when arriving or leaving a village, but people could catch or drop from the Winds anywhere along the way. He didn't even need to catch the Summer-sky Wind. Any of the lighter Webs would do. There wasn't a thread of any Wind he could access running over the main street, but he'd be able to find *something* between here and the landing web.

He could grab a Sceltie and be gone from this village before anyone realized the dog was missing. And once Kermilla had a special little friend, he would be allowed to go home.

With that in mind, Laska retreated and circled round to approach the main street from the other direction.

Breathing in that first scent of autumn, Ranon stopped at Elders' Park and looked at the main street of Eyota, his heart aching with pride.

They had done so much. The businesses owned by Daemon Sadi were in operation. The Lady's Pleasure—named, he'd been told, for Lady Angelline's enjoyment of the beverage—served coffee imported from Kaeleer, which was much smoother than the rough drink he'd always known as coffee. They also served small cups of thick hot chocolate—frightfully expensive, but a drink a young man bought a lady he wanted to impress. Small sandwiches and pastries were also served.

The coffee shop provided a playroom and a fenced outdoor play area for young children so that mothers could have a quiet moment to visit with friends. The shop had hired two young witches to watch the children, as well as Kharr and Bryant, two Warlord Scelties with a no-nonsense attitude when it came to herding *anything*.

The shop had been open a week, and it already was an important gathering place, as was Whistler's Tavern. The tavern also served food—mostly sandwiches in the warm weather, but it would serve soups, stews, and meat pies once the season turned colder.

Merchants, the variety shop managed by Lord Careth, had received its first shipment of practical goods from Kaeleer, along with a crate of books that would have made Gray whimper in lust if four crates of books for the loaning library hadn't arrived at the same time. Gray had spent an evening helping the newly hired librarian sort the books just so he could look at them.

And then there was Heartbeat, the music shop, where Ranon was meeting his grandfather to look over the instruments. Yairen wanted to hear the Scelt whistle, an instrument similar enough to the Shalador flute. Being made of metal instead of wood, the Scelt whistles were less expensive, and Yairen wanted to consider if they could be used as a beginning instrument for youngsters here.

"I'm going up the street to see Yairen," Ranon told Khollie. "You're going to stay here for story time?"

*Yes.* Khollie wagged his tail. *Wynne is here, and Vae and Darcy are here, and Mist is coming soon.*

"All right. If I'm not at the music shop when story time is done, I'll be nearby."

Shaking his head in amusement, Ranon continued up the street. Next month, when the weather turned colder, the weekly afternoon story time would move to the room in Heartbeat where performances and lessons would be held. Indoors or outdoors, hearing Shalador stories told in public was a strange experience for the whole village.

Having Scelties in the audience who wouldn't tolerate children misbehaving and interrupting the storyteller was also a strange experience. Not that there was much misbehavior but, somehow, it was more shaming to be nipped by a Sceltie than cuffed by an adult.

Hurt more, too.

He entered the shop and nodded to the Shaladoran couple who had been hired to run the shop and teach music. Laithan taught Shalador flute and the fiddle. He had been one of Yairen's students—one of the last to learn from the Tradition Keeper before the old man's hands were broken for good. Jade had a lovely voice and ran two classes to teach the traditional Shalador songs. Mostly, though, Jade ran the business end of the shop.

And Lizzie, the Sceltie who had claimed the music shop as *her* place, ran everyone.

"There you are, grandson," Yairen said. "Laithan has given me some of his time to hear the drum that came from the Isle of Scelt. Now it is your turn so I can hear the metal flute."

"I don't think our traditional songs sound right on the Scelt whistle," Laithan said, "but Dena Nehele folk songs suit the instrument's range. Jade has sorted out most of the music that arrived. I'll see if there is anything that was written specifically for these whistles."

Ranon picked up a whistle. It was shorter and half the circumference of a Shalador flute, but the finger holes were the same. Setting his fingers, he blew a note.

A different sound than the wooden flute. A sharper sound. But pleasing all the same. He tried a piece of a traditional Shalador song and then a folk song from Dena Nehele. Laithan was right; the folk songs sounded better than the music of Shalador.

"Here," Laithan said, returning with several sheets of music. "Try one of these."

Ranon looked over the music. Folk songs, he guessed. One had a lively pace; the other was slower. He chose the slower piece—and he understood why the Shalador people might find common ground with the music of Scelt.

Bright and yet bittersweet. A sound that slipped past the mind and spoke to the heart.

"It's good," he said a few minutes later, setting the whistle on the counter.

"A gift," Laithan said, "along with this music."

"Laithan . . ."

"In exchange for you coming to play here once or twice a month." Laithan laughed. "Don't make such a face, Ranon. You won't have to perform alone. I've kept one of these whistles for myself because I want to become acquainted with this music too. One night of Shalador music and one night of Scelt to teach and entertain our people through the winter months." He held out his hand. "Deal?"

Ranon shook hands. "Deal." Then he vanished whistle and music and looked at his grandfather. "Would you like to—"

*Ranon!*

The dog sounded panicked. *Khollie? What's wrong?* By the time Ranon turned away from the counter and took the first step, Lizzie had passed through the door and charged down the street.

*Ranon!*

More than panic now. All he heard was terror.

Ranon burst out of Heartbeat and headed down the street, not quite running as he shaped a tight, double layer of Opal shields around himself— the kind of shielding a Warlord Prince used on a killing field.

Not quite running toward the commotion near Elders' Park, but aware of everything around him. Aware of confused feelings edging toward anger that created a psychic buzz so thick and harsh it was almost a sound. Aware of Wynne and Kharr herding the children who had come for story time into a tight flock that could be defended. Aware of Vae, Darcy, and Lizzie snapping and snarling as they circled around something that kept trying to move away from Elders' Park and all the people.

*Ranon?* Archerr called. *What in the name of Hell is going on?*

*I don't know.* Ranon slowed down as he scanned the street. *The Scelties are all acting strange. Maybe a piglet or chicken got loose and they're making a game of herding it.* But he'd see or hear an animal if it was caught between the three dogs. And that didn't explain Wynne and Kharr's behavior—or why he couldn't spot Khollie.

Then Vae charged the empty space within the Sceltie triangle and hit *something* with a blast of Purple Dusk power.

A sight shield broke, revealing an unknown Warlord.

Ranon froze for just a moment as he remembered the day the Scelties arrived in Eyota and how one of them had located Archerr by scent, despite the Warlord Prince being sight shielded.

*They had known he was there. He'd slipped past us, but they had . . .*

That was when he saw the rest, and a cold rage burned through him as he strode down the street.

The bastard had a hand around Khollie's neck, holding the dog off the ground that way. Not by the scruff, *by the neck.*

The Scelties looked at him and hesitated a moment, then resumed their attack, hitting the defensive shields the stranger threw around himself.

At first Ranon wondered why Vae and the others were throwing themselves against the stranger's shields. That tactic was draining the Scelties' power as well as the Warlord's, and Ranon thought it a waste of their strength until he realized the brilliance of their fight. The dumb, two-legged sheep was caught in a snapping triangle, unable to run away—and too harried to notice the enraged Warlord Princes closing in on him.

As he moved toward the fight, Ranon's eyes flicked from one side of the street to the other. Kharr and Wynne had the children and elders well shielded. Shaddo and Archerr were coming up the street to flank the bastard. Vae, Darcy, and Lizzie continued their relentless attack, wearing down the Warlord's power and shields.

And Khollie . . .

Khollie hung limp and unmoving in the bastard's grasp.

Ranon called in his fighting knife and used Craft to create a flash of light on the blade, deliberately forcing the Warlord's attention on himself now.

"Let him go," Ranon snarled.

The Warlord shifted his arm to use Khollie's hanging body as a shield. "You've got plenty of them." He sounding desperate. "We only want one. We'll take this one. He's already damaged."

"How dare you?" Ranon's voice sounded barely human. "*Let my little brother go!*"

No way for the man to catch the Winds from this part of the street. No way for the Warlord to get away, not with the three Scelties keeping him pinned. No chance of the bastard winning a fight, not with three Warlord Princes standing on this killing field ready to rip him apart.

Then Darkmist charged up the street, heading straight for the Warlord.

Perfect. If Darkmist hit the Warlord in the back, that would be the distraction Ranon needed to strike without endangering Khollie.

*Vae,* Ranon said. *As soon as I break that bastard's shields, you grab Khollie and run.*

*We will catch Khollie,* she replied, continuing to keep the Warlord in position for the best strike.

He kept his eyes on the stranger, but he could *feel* Darkmist and knew the moment he needed to unleash a punch of Opal power and break the man's shields so the dog could strike.

A second after the shields broke, Darkmist leaped . . . and *missed.* The man's open coat flapped as the dog sailed past.

An odd look flashed over the Warlord's face as he staggered a step and dropped Khollie. At the same time, Vae leaped, grabbed one of Khollie's front legs, and kept going, running on air and pulling Khollie with her as Darcy and Lizzie scattered.

Then Ranon noticed the blood on Darkmist's muzzle. Saw the thing in Darkmist's jaws beat once, twice. And once more before those jaws closed on a still-beating heart.

Darkmist whirled to face the Warlord. Ranon felt the punch of furious Opal power—and saw the man's head puff for a moment before he fell to the ground.

The dog hadn't missed. Hell's fire, Mother Night, and may the Darkness be merciful. The dog hadn't missed. He'd *passed through the man's body* and snatched the heart right out of the man's chest.

The thought of the skill and training it took to do something like that knocked Ranon back from the killing edge.

Vanishing the knife, he rushed over to the spot where Vae guarded Khollie. He dropped to his knees and reached for the little dog—and snatched his hand back in time to keep from losing a finger as Mist, still riding the killing edge, dropped the heart and snapped at him.

"Let me help him, Mist," Ranon said. "He's your brother, but he's my friend. Step back now. *Step back.*"

There were sounds all around him now, people all around now, but the only thing that mattered was the other Opal-Jeweled Warlord Prince.

Mist took a step back. His eyes were still glazed and he still growled. Probably wasn't even aware of it.

Watching Mist, Ranon placed a hand on Khollie. "Khollie?" He felt the dog's heart beat, felt the lungs rise and fall with each breath. "Khollie?" He began a careful exploration, hesitating when he got to the neck. Was it damaged?

The dark eyes, usually filled with joy, were closed.

"Hell's fire, Ranon," Shaddo said, approaching carefully since there were two Opal Warlord Princes whose tempers were unpredictable right now. "Is he all right?"

"I don't know." Ranon stripped off his shirt and wrapped Khollie in it before he stood up and looked around. "I need to get him to Shira, but I . . . we . . . walked over."

"Prince Ranon, here." Guard Jaego hurried up with his horse.

Ranon took a step, then looked at Shaddo and Archerr.

"We'll find a place to store the carrion until Talon rises and can get a look at the bastard," Archerr said.

"Go on," Shaddo said. "We'll take care of things here."

Freed of any duties beyond the dog in his arms, Ranon mounted Jaego's horse and galloped back to the Queen's Residence with Darkmist racing after him.

One of the Scelties must have alerted the silver twins because Lloyd was waiting for him when he reached the Residence. He dismounted and tossed a rein to the Sceltie, who led the horse to the stables.

"*Shira!*" Ranon roared as he entered the house. Sweet Darkness, let her be here. He took Khollie into the parlor the court used and laid the dog on the sofa.

"Hell's fire, Ranon," Shira said, rushing into the room. "What are you—" Seeing Khollie, she shoved him aside so hard she knocked him on his ass.

He snarled at her, still too furious and too close to the killing edge to tolerate the shove, even from her.

"Prince Ranon, attend."

Cassidy's voice. Strong. Demanding. A leash that held his fury.

Breathing hard, he rose and walked out of the parlor.

"Report," Cassidy said, then held up a hand and led him to the meeting room.

Powell came into the room, followed by Spere, Burne, and Cayle. A moment later, Gray, dirt-streaked and panting, rushed into the room.

"Report, Ranon," Cassidy said.

He told them everything from the moment he had left Khollie at Elders' Park for story time to the moment he had wrapped the Sceltie in his shirt and ridden back to the Residence to get help.

Almost everything. Watching Cassidy's increasingly pale face, he couldn't tell her how Darkmist had killed the bastard, couldn't tell her about seeing the still-beating heart in the dog's jaws.

"Hell's fire," Spere said when Ranon stopped talking. "I'm not going to wonder why the fool thought he could get away with it, but why did he do it in the first place?"

*He belongs to the other Queen.* Vae stood in the doorway. Ranon couldn't tell if she quivered with anger or fear. *I remember her smells. She is on his clothes.*

Cassidy swayed. Gray wrapped an arm around her waist.

"Kermilla did this?" Cassidy asked.

*Her smells are on him.* Vae left the room.

"Did you recognize him, Ranon?" Burne asked.

Ranon shook his head.

Cassidy swallowed hard. "If he belongs to her First Circle, I could identify—"

"*No,*" Ranon said. After Darkmist unleashed that punch of Opal power, the man's head had looked *wrong.* Until he figured out why it looked wrong, he wasn't letting Cassidy near the body. Wasn't letting Shira near it either.

"Archerr and Shaddo are going to find a place to store the body until Talon rises," Ranon said. "As Master of the Guard, this falls to him now, Lady."

"Ranon is correct," Powell said. "And as Talon's second-in-command, the decisions of what to do with the enemy are Ranon's to make, Lady, not yours."

Maybe she would have argued, but just then Shira appeared in the doorway, hugging herself.

"I don't know," Shira said, coming into the room. "He's alive. His heart is beating and he's breathing. His neck may be bruised, but I have no sense of anything broken. But he's not there. I can't wake him up, not with healing Craft or the Hourglass's Craft. Vae says . . ." Her voice broke, and Ranon watched her pull on all the strength inside her to continue. "Vae says sometimes humans try to force kindred to live with them. It's almost impossible to control the cats once they start growing up because they're wild and so big. The wolves, like the cats, are too wild, and the horses, unicorns, and dragons are big. But Scelties are small, so sometimes humans try to take them. And s–sometimes a Sceltie goes away to a place deep inside himself, where humans can't find him. Where humans can't follow."

"What happens then?" Cassidy asked.

Tears filled Shira's eyes. "He either comes back . . . or he dies."

"What can we do?" Ranon's voice was rough. "Shira, what can we do?"

She shook her head. "We wait. Vae and Darkmist said to leave him wrapped in your shirt because it has your smells. They think that's a good thing for him right now."

She walked out of the room.

*Ranon?* Archerr called softly.

*Yeah?*

*We didn't know where else to put it, so we brought the body to the Healing House.* Archerr hesitated. *Keep Shira away from here. Shaddo and I have had a closer look at what Darkmist did to this bastard and . . . Keep Shira away from here. Cassidy too.*

*Can you put a shield around the Healing House to keep everyone out?*

*I can. I have, in fact. I'd rather not be inside with . . . that . . . more than I have to.*

"Why would Kermilla do that?" Cassidy asked. "Why?"

"Come on, Cassie," Gray said gently. "Come away now."

Ranon watched Gray lead Cassie out of the room.

*Ranon?* Janos called.

Mother Night. *Where are you? Are you okay?*

*We're fine. Reyhana and I got back from a ride and . . . Could you tell Kief to let us go? He's got us trapped in a stall, and he says we can't leave until you say it's safe.*

On another day, that would have been funny. *We've had some trouble, Prince Janos. Khollie's been hurt.*

*How bad?*

*Don't know yet. Here are my orders for you and Kief: Both of you escort Reyhana back to the Residence. I want all three of you shielded, you hear me?*

*Yes, sir. I hear you.*

And *he* heard the Warlord Prince in his brother's voice.

"I'll be in my office if you need me." Powell touched his arm—a gesture full of understanding—before following Cassidy and Gray out of the room.

"Burne and I will head over to Main Street and see what needs to be done," Spere said.

Ranon nodded. "Jaego was on the street and probably already alerted Rogir, but pull in everyone you can to ride circuits. Make sure the landen community is put on alert, too. I don't know what kind of game that bitch was trying to play, but we're not giving her a second chance at it."

"I'll do that," Cayle said.

"And you, Ranon?" Spere asked.

"Shaddo, Archerr, and I will hold the Queen's square. Once Talon rises . . ."

Hours yet. It would be hours yet. And all any of them could do was wait.


Talon pressed two fingers against the deceased Warlord's head, then took a step back, shuddering.

Felt like pebbles in a bag of mush. It would have been less disturbing if the head had exploded from the blast of power. They'd all done that on a killing field at one time or other. But having the ability to explode bone and brains and still leave the skin intact indicated a frightening level of skill in the use of Craft and power.

More than frightening since that level of skill belonged to a dog who wore Birthright Opal and was still growing into his full strength.

"Have you seen anything like this, Talon?" Archerr asked.

The First Circle—and Gray—had gathered at the Healing House to look at this corpse. Talon scanned their faces. Wasn't one of them who wasn't sickly pale. Not that he blamed them for that. He was demon-dead, and even he was finding it hard to be in this room.

"No, I haven't," Talon replied. "Passing flesh through flesh is dangerous to the point of stupidity. Healers do it, sinking their hands into a person to heal injuries inside the body, but that's a controlled, steady movement, and they spend years training to do it so they don't lose parts of themselves within the other flesh."

"This was fast," Ranon said, his voice oddly hushed. "So damn fast. I thought he missed. Until I saw the blood on Darkmist's muzzle and the heart, I thought he missed the bastard."

"Shaddo and I were behind this one," Archerr said, tipping his head to indicate the corpse. "Damned queer feeling, seeing the dog disappear like that. We weren't even sure what we'd seen."

"No hesitation," Shaddo said. "The Scelties. Before we had time to figure out something was wrong, they'd decided who among them was fighting and who was defending. Fast. Hell's fire, they were fast."

"Wasn't just the Scelties on the street either," Spere said. "Duffy knew. He told Moore there was an attack in the village, then left Moore to defend the people working in the landen community while he went out for the shepherds and livestock. And Keely herded every child in the Queen's square who was playing outside into the nearest house."

Talon listened to them all. Strong men. Good men. And every one of them, himself included, hadn't really understood what lived inside those small furry bodies. Despite being around Vae, they really hadn't understood that these dogs were Blood who had been given exceptional training in Craft—and in fighting.

Once things calmed down, he was going to find out exactly what the Scelties could do.

"They weren't waiting for me," Ranon said quietly. "Vae could have taken that bastard. She wears Purple Dusk. He wore Summer-sky. She and Lizzie and Darcy were holding him in place, keeping him pinned, but she could have broken his defensive shields and attacked. I thought she was waiting for me to reach the fight." He shook his head. "They were waiting for Darkmist."

*That bruises you, doesn't it?* Talon thought. *It hurts your heart some to realize they weren't sure they could count on you to defend one of them. Now you all know the answer.*

Powell cleared his throat. "How did this man manage to get his hands on Khollie in the first place?"

"Snatched him," Shaddo said. "According to Darcy, the three of them heard a man's voice calling to them. Vae didn't like something about the voice and stayed put, but it sounded friendly, and Khollie had no reason to think anyone in the village would hurt him, so he moved toward it. So did Darcy, but from another direction. That's why he picked up the scent and realized the voice was coming from someone who was sight shielded. That made him wary, and he stopped. But Khollie was already close enough to grab. The moment he disappeared, Darcy and Vae warned the other Scelties and launched their attack. You know the rest."

Talon didn't know nearly enough, but he knew what had to be done next. "Archerr, Spere, and Haele are coming with me. Ranon—"

"I'm going with you."

Talon shook his head. Ranon's eyes were too bright, and he couldn't tell if the Shaladoran's temper was leaning toward hot or cold. Which meant Ranon was too unpredictable for this assignment.

"I'll hold my tongue and my temper," Ranon said. "You have my word on it. But if you're taking this back to the mansion, I want to stand as witness. For Khollie's sake."

"I'm coming too," Gray said.

"No, you're not." He'd give in for Ranon, but not for Gray. "You're needed here, Gray. Cassie's parents are home in Dharo. Even if we sent a message now, they couldn't get back to Eyota until tomorrow. That means Cassie needs you to be here with her. Your duty is to your Queen, Prince."

He watched Gray absorb the words—and felt relieved when Gray nodded.

"The rest of you split up. I want the landing webs, north and east, guarded at all times. Anyone can drop from the Winds anywhere along the thread, but from now on, we consider anyone a potential enemy who doesn't arrive in the village at the landing webs or refuses to tell the guard on duty his business in our village." Talon flipped the blanket over the corpse, glad to hide that head. "Let's get this done."

*And may the Darkness have mercy on me if Theran knew about this.*

Gray found Cassidy in the garden, leaning against one of the big trees.

"Cassie." He drew her against him, back to chest, and wrapped his arms around her.

"What am I supposed to tell Jaenelle?" Cassidy asked, her voice breaking. "She trusted me to look after the kindred. She wouldn't have allowed them to come here otherwise. What am I supposed to tell her?"

He pressed his lips against her temple. "Nothing. Tonight, there is nothing to say. We'll know more in the morning."

She turned in his arms and held on to him while she wept.

He held on too and hoped with everything in him that Khollie would wake up because, better than Cassie ever could, he understood the seductive lure of going away from fear and pain and never coming back. Even if that meant dying.

Julien opened the parlor door and said, "Prince Grayhaven, Prince Talon needs to speak with you. It is urgent."

Theran glanced at Kermilla as he set aside his book and rose. She'd become more and more agitated throughout the afternoon, although she'd refused to tell him why. Even Jhorma couldn't get an answer from her. Now, hearing Talon's name, she looked frightened.

"Bardoc, stay with the Lady," Jhorma said as he pushed away from the card table and approached Theran.

Jhorma had no business assuming he could be part of this meeting, but Theran wasn't going to argue. Jhorma was a rival for Kermilla's affections—and her bed—but lately he'd shown himself to be a sensible man who had a fair amount of court polish. And right now, Theran wasn't going to turn away anyone's help. "Julien, tell Prince Talon—"

Talon walked into the room, brushing Julien aside. Ranon, Archerr, Spere, and Haele followed him, carrying a stretcher that held a blanket-wrapped bundle.

"Theran," Talon said. "Lord Jhorma." He looked at Kermilla, who was still sitting at the card table, and said nothing—a deliberate social cut.

"I think this belongs to your Lady," Talon said, turning his attention back to Theran. Using Craft he pulled aside the blanket far enough to reveal the head.

"Mother Night," Jhorma whispered. "That's Laska."

"Laska?" Kermilla squeaked.

"What happened to him?" Theran asked.

The look in Talon's eyes. Hard. Unforgiving.

"This afternoon, this man came to the village of Eyota and tried to abduct a young Warlord," Talon said. "The youngster's brother, a Warlord Prince, eliminated the enemy. Afterwards, a member of the court identified the man as one of *hers*. So we have returned him."

"It took a lot of rage to do that," Jhorma said, staring at Laska.

"There was a reason for the rage," Talon replied, his eyes never leaving Theran.

Theran's heart banged against his chest. "Is the youngster all right?"

"The Healer has done all she can. We don't know if it will be enough," Talon said.

Hard eyes. Unforgiving eyes. Accusing eyes.

*Hell's fire, Talon, how bad is it?* Theran asked. *Why would Laska do it?*

*As for why, ask your Lady,* Talon replied. *As for how bad . . . We won't know that until we know if the youngster will live.*

Theran looked at Ranon. Cold, black fury in *those* eyes. And pain. Mother Night.

"I appreciate you returning the body to us," Jhorma said. "I recognize the courtesy you have extended to us in doing so. I will take the body back to Dharo. Shame will shroud his family's grief because there was no honor in how Laska died, but his family will still grieve."

*Talon, I am so sorry,* Theran said.

*Laska's family isn't the only one who has a reason to feel shame because of this.* Talon walked out of the room.

After lowering the stretcher to the floor, Ranon and the other men followed Talon. Julien hurried out after them.

"I'll leave as soon as I'm packed." Jhorma vanished the body and stretcher.

"Let Bardoc give you a hand with the packing."

Jhorma gave Theran a long look, then signaled Bardoc, who joined them with too much haste.

"I think Bardoc should accompany me to Dharo," Jhorma said. "He and Laska came from the same village. He knows the family."

Theran nodded. He didn't care what Jhorma did, not when all his hopes for Dena Nehele were breaking around him.

He closed the door behind Jhorma and Bardoc—and put a Green lock on it. Then he turned to face Kermilla, who had left the card table and was now standing in the middle of the room, looking pale and scared.

"What was Laska doing in Eyota?" He moved toward her while his temper strained the leash. "He had no reason to be there. He had *no business* being there."

"I don't know," Kermilla said.

"*Don't lie to me.*" He stopped, not willing to tempt his control by getting too close to her. "He's a member of your court. You have to know."

"I don't know!" Some anger in her voice and eyes now that he was challenging her.

"Hell's fire, Kermilla. Do you know what this has done to your reputation? One of your First Circle tried to abduct a young Warlord. I can tell you two reasons the Warlord Princes are going to think of when they hear about this: torture and rape."

"Laska wasn't like that," Kermilla snapped. "Laska wouldn't *do* that. I would *never* have anyone in my court who would do that!"

*You would have brought Garth and Brok into your court. If you could overlook one kind of rapist, why not another?*

He pushed that thought away and buried it deep.

"Then what was he doing in that village, and what was he doing with that boy that would piss off a brother enough to kill Laska *that* way?" Theran shouted.

"He wasn't getting a boy!" she screamed. "He went there to get me a Sceltie!"

Theran took a step back, staggered by the foolishness that cost a man his life—and probably cost the rest of them in other ways.

"A Sceltie." He raked his fingers through his hair. "Hell's fire, woman, have you lost your mind?"

"The Warlord Princes are all so impressed that Cassidy has some, and they're not going to take me seriously until I have one too." Tears filled her eyes and her lower lip trembled. "They wouldn't have missed one in that stupid village. Besides, you sent Correne away, and that awful Talon killed Garth and Brok, and I wanted company. *You're* always too busy to pay attention to me even though you *say* you love me."

"So this is *my* fault because I'm working in every way I can to get this town through the coming winter?" He paced, circled, wanted to tear up the room and smash the furniture. But he couldn't afford to replace whatever he destroyed, so he held his temper and circled. And paced.

"Even if Laska had managed to snatch one without being detected, how would you have held on to it?" he asked. "They're *kindred*, Kermilla. *Blood.* Didn't you notice anything while Vae was here? She's a *witch*. She wears a Purple Dusk Jewel. Mother Night, woman, *she outranks you.*"

"How dare you!"

He stopped in front of her. "That's fact, Kermilla. Vae's Jewels outrank yours. So what were you going to do with this Warlord if he didn't want to stay here? Chain him? Cage him? Beat him and torture him until he was too broken down in body and spirit to run?"

"He wouldn't be of any use if he was like that." She stamped her foot. "But he *would* have wanted to stay with me. Once he got here, he would have."

"Doesn't matter now." Theran sank into the nearest chair, leaned back and closed his eyes.

Kermilla wasn't like the Queen who had tortured Gray. She *wasn't*. But she'd made an error in judgment that would not be fixed easily. If he could fix it at all.

"Theran?" Kermilla climbed into his lap and pressed against him. "Theran, I'm sorry about this little trouble."

"One of your men died. That's not a little trouble," he said wearily. "Talon, the most respected man in this land, is against you. That's not a little trouble. The fact that Talon isn't making a distinction between kindred and human Blood in this instance . . ." He sighed. "In a couple of days, every Warlord Prince is going to know that you sent a man to Eyota to abduct a young Warlord, and no one is going to care if you intended to take a boy or a dog."

She snuggled down and put her head on his shoulder. "What does that mean?"

"I don't know." He put his arms around her, unable to deny her whatever comfort he could give. "I really don't know."


Ranon stood in the parlor doorway, unable to take that last step into the room. Vae looked up from her spot on the sofa and gave him one tail-tip wag. Darkmist, who was on the floor in front of the sofa, gave him no greeting but also didn't challenge his presence.

A hesitant touch of a hand on his back. He turned and followed Shira to the healing room in the Residence. As soon as she closed the door, he pulled her into his arms and held on.

"I was ashamed that the least of them had chosen me," he whispered into her hair. "I felt embarrassed when Ferall and the others saw him that day. And now . . ."

"Hush, Ranon, hush," she said as she stroked his back.

"Is he coming back to us, Shira?"

"I don't know, but I'm hopeful."

He eased back enough to rest his forehead against hers. "Where is everyone?"

"Gray took Cassie upstairs. She's distraught. Powell has been in his office since you left. The rest of the First Circle and the guards have been patrolling the village in shifts. I sent Reyhana and Janos to your grandfather for the night. They spent hours in the parlor this evening, taking turns reading *Sceltie Saves the Day,* and they both needed to be away for a while. Vae and Darkmist have been here all the time. The other Scelties come for an hour, then go out with one of the men to patrol."

"Shira . . ."

"He's hiding under your shirt." She said the words quickly, as if she needed to silence any questions she couldn't answer. "Vae thinks that's a good sign because he's been making tiny movements to get himself completely covered. You can't see anything but the tip of his nose now."

"I'm so tired, love. I was in a fight once that lasted a whole day. It was a relentless battle on a killing field, so we were all committed to winning or dying. Barely had time for a sip of water or a mouthful of food in the rare spaces between one enemy and the next. When I finally walked off that field, I didn't feel this tired."

"Come to bed," Shira said, caressing his face. "We'll take Khollie up with us. Maybe we'll both get a little rest that way."

He followed her back into the parlor and very carefully lifted the bundle hidden in his shirt. They went up to their room, and he tucked Khollie on the bed between them.

The last thing he remembered after stretching out on the bed was linking fingers with Shira.

*Ranon?*

A scared little whisper of a voice, but enough to have his eyes opening to stare at the bedroom ceiling.

*Ranon?*

Ranon turned his head to look at the bundle on the bed. *Khollie?*

Pinching a little of the shirt, he eased it back until he could see the dog's head—and the dark eyes staring at him.

*Hey, little brother. We were worried about you.*

Khollie peered at his surroundings. *I am on the bed. I am not supposed to be on the bed. It is a Shira rule.*

*I know. But she said you were allowed this one time.*

*Ranon? I need a tree.*

*You want some food too?*

*Yes.*

*Come on, then. We'll see what we can find.*

He helped Khollie untangle himself from the shirt, then eased out of bed.

Shira immediately woke up. "Ranon?"

"It's all right," he said quietly. "Khollie and I are going to get something to eat."

She rolled over to look at Khollie, who gave her a quick lick on the chin before jumping off the bed.

"Oh," she said. "All right."

As Ranon let them out of the room, he heard her muffled sob.

He closed the door as quietly as he could, but he'd barely taken a step before Cassie's door opened and Gray stood there.

He knew about Yaslana's rules concerning Gray and Cassie's physical relationship. Hell's fire, *everyone* knew about Lucivar's rules. But he wasn't going to ask where Gray was sleeping tonight.

Gray looked down and smiled. "Hey, Khollie."

Khollie wagged his tail and whined softly.

"We're going downstairs," Ranon said.

Gray nodded and closed the door.

When they reached the back door, Khollie stood in the doorway, trembling.

*Khollie?* Vae joined them. *Are you going outside? I have to go too. We will go together. Ranon will guard us.*

"Yes, I will." He put an Opal shield around the backyard. Nothing would get in—or out—without him knowing about it.

He stood in the doorway, watching, and didn't turn when Gray came up behind him.

"I told Cassie that Khollie woke up," Gray said. "She wants to cry by herself for a little while."

"Shira is crying too." Maybe it wasn't fair to ask, but there was no one else he could ask. "Will Khollie be all right, Gray?"

Those green eyes held too much knowledge. Then Gray said, "We'll help him be all right."

# CHAPTER 25

## EBON ASKAVI

Saetan sat on the wide arm of a stuffed chair and watched a storm gather in one of the Keep's sitting rooms.

The first warning of trouble had been the two Warlords who arrived at the Keep a couple days ago. They wanted passage through the Gate in order to return to Dharo—and they brought the body of another man.

The second warning had come in a note from Daemon yesterday, requesting his presence at a meeting. Official, careful wording. Not a message from son to father but from Consort to Steward.

When Jaenelle was pissed off about something, she didn't seem to remember that she no longer had an official court.

And no one was ballsy enough to remind her. Including him.

The third warning was Daemon's note to Draca, asking the Keep's Seneschal to accommodate several overnight guests.

Saetan wanted to believe the meeting was being held at the Keep to accommodate Lucivar, who still felt uneasy about leaving Marian on her own for too long. But when the others began to arrive, he knew why Jaenelle had chosen the Keep: It was the Sanctuary—and lair—of Witch.

Jaenelle and Daemon arrived first. She wore a cobwebby, spidersilk dress known as Widow's weeds, and her Jewel was mostly Gray with streaks of Red and Sapphire—and a single thread of Black. Daemon wore a face that revealed nothing of his thoughts or feelings. He wasn't there as Jaenelle's husband or Consort or as the Warlord Prince of Dhemlan. He was in that room as the Queen's weapon.

Lucivar walked in. "Cat, what's this—" He looked at Daemon's face and didn't finish the question.

Sabrina came in next, tense and nervous, followed by Aaron, Morghann, and Khardeen.

*Four of Jaenelle's childhood friends,* Saetan thought as he watched Sabrina greet the others. *Four people who had served in Witch's First Circle. Will they still be friends when this discussion is over?*

Jaenelle sat on a half sofa across from several chairs. Daemon sat beside her, his right arm stretched out over the sofa's back, looking calm and lazy.

Saetan watched the way Lucivar prowled the room without ever turning his back to Daemon and felt a shiver of fear.

The women sat. Aaron and Khardeen remained on their feet, tense and alert.

Then Karla walked into the room.

"Kiss kiss. Sorry I'm late." She made her way to the chair closest to Saetan's. "I was trying to undo an . . . incident . . . that turned a large white cat into a bright pink and blue cat."

A flash of warm humor from Jaenelle flowed through the room. "Did you fix it?"

"When I left, KaeAskavi was an evenly tinted mauve cat—and he was *not* happy."

That produced a few chuckles, but the humor quickly faded as all their attention focused on Jaenelle.

"I received a letter from Cassidy yesterday," she said. "I felt you should all know what happened and that we should come to an agreement about what will—and will not—be done."

She called in the letter and handed it to Daemon. Lucivar immediately came around to the back of the sofa to read over his brother's shoulder.

Daemon read the letter and handed it to Khardeen. That beautiful face revealed nothing, and there was nothing Saetan could detect on a psychic thread, even at the level of the Black. Daemon had his emotions tightly leashed.

But the room grew cold.

Lucivar, on the other hand, began swearing softly, viciously in Eyrien as he resumed his prowling.

Hot anger. Cold fury. The room filled with temper as, one by one, the friends who had been First Circle in the Dark Court at Ebon Askavi read Cassidy's letter. Finally Karla read it and passed it to him as he called in his half-moon glasses.

How many times did Cassidy write that letter before she achieved sentences that were so carefully honest? She didn't accuse anyone of anything. She didn't offer opinions or feelings. She didn't report anything that hadn't been witnessed. She didn't *say* Kermilla had given the order, but there wasn't a single person in the room who couldn't read between the lines. The only break from that control was Cassidy's excessive assurances that Khollie was still a little frightened because of the incident but they were confident that he would recover completely.

Which meant there had been some doubt that Khollie would recover at all.

"What in the name of Hell is going on there?" Khary said.

"This wasn't Cassie's fault," Aaron snapped, instantly ready to defend his cousin.

"I didn't say it was," Khary snapped back. "But something should be done."

"Nothing will be done," Jaenelle said quietly. "At least, not by us."

Daemon stiffened. Nothing anyone else would notice, but Saetan had been keeping a wary eye on him and saw the change.

*He knows something. Or suspects something. But his tongue, like his temper, is held by the Queen's will, and he'll tell us nothing.*

"What is Kermilla still doing in Dena Nehele anyway?" Sabrina snarled.

"You were aware she had gone to visit Cassidy?" Jaenelle asked.

"And aware of her mistreatment of a servant while she was a guest there. Believe me, that will weigh heavily in my decision about whether she's going to continue ruling *anything* in my Territory." Sabrina paced back and forth behind the chairs. "But that happened in early summer. We're into the autumn harvest now. What's she still doing there?"

"Causing more trouble?" Khary suggested.

"Khary," Morghann said in quiet warning.

"Don't hush him, Morghann, he's right," Sabrina said. "Kermilla has no business being there, and it's past time to go to Dena Nehele and haul the bitch's ass home."

"No," Saetan said. "You can't take action outside of your own Territory, Sabrina. That line was drawn thousands of years ago, and it does not—*cannot*—change." *Because that was the line Dorothea and Hekatah crossed in their efforts to take control of the whole Realm of Terreille. As much as I love all of you, for the good of the Realms and the Blood, I will kill any one of you who tries to cross that line.*

He glanced at Jaenelle and saw the way Witch looked at him. Looked through him.

*And if it came to that, she would expect me to do nothing less.* "Besides," he continued. "Kermilla is, and has been, Theran Grayhaven's guest these past few weeks, not Cassidy's. If the Queen of Dena Nehele wants Kermilla out of her Territory, it's up to her to take care of it—and her First Circle has the strength to do it without help."

"Cassidy's too polite," Sabrina snapped at him, then turned to Jaenelle. "They have a history. You know that."

Jaenelle's sapphire eyes held Sabrina. A moment passed. Two.

Saetan wished fiercely that he was privy to that psychic thread and knew what passed between the two women. Because *something* had surprised Sabrina enough to drain the Dharo Queen's temper.

"Are you asking me to be blind to what's happening?" Sabrina asked.

"Outside of your own borders, yes," Jaenelle replied. Then her lips curved in a sharp, chilly smile. "Would I ask you to be blind to what's happening within your own borders? Never." She considered. "Almost never."

Four Queens who began ruling at a young age—as soon as they had made the Offering to the Darkness, in fact. Each one was capable of great compassion—and of being totally ruthless. Saetan watched them, certain that in these few seconds of silence they had reached an agreement of how they would work together to achieve a desired result *without* crossing that unforgivable line.

As curious as he was about what had passed between Sabrina and Jaenelle, he was equally certain that he *didn't* want to know what the four Queens had decided to do. And maybe, if he was lucky, he wouldn't have to know. After all, he was supposed to be retired from the living Realms.

And the sun might shine in Hell tomorrow.

★Coward,★ Daemon said softly on a Black spear thread.

A hint of humor, of relaxation. The Queen's weapon would not be needed tonight.

"The Warlord who acted on Kermilla's orders came from Dharo?" Sabrina asked thoughtfully.

"That's the assumption, since he didn't come from Dena Nehele," Jaenelle replied.

"And the body was brought back to Kaeleer," Saetan said. When they all stared at him, he lifted an eyebrow. "Draca opened the Gate for them. If you think anyone is more qualified to decide who may use the Gate here at the Keep, then you can take it up with her."

Jaenelle was the only person who might be able to challenge Draca's decision and overrule the Seneschal about who could or couldn't use the Gate. Since she seemed to have no objection, the rest of them backed away from any criticism they might have had.

"How many men are in Kermilla's First Circle?" Karla asked.

"Twelve." Sabrina stared at Karla. "She had the same twelve men who had been Cassidy's First Circle."

Karla's lips curved in a wicked smile. "Then Kermilla's court is broken, isn't it?"

"Technically, yes," Saetan said. "But no court that's sound breaks because of a death, even when there aren't more than twelve males in the First Circle. The court continues for a few days, sometimes even weeks, while the Queen considers the men in the Second Circle and decides who will be invited to fill the opening in the First Circle."

"I don't think she has a Second Circle, Uncle Saetan," Sabrina said. "The First and Second Circles are paid with the Queen's tithes. Cassidy didn't need more than her First Circle to work exclusively on the court's behalf, so she didn't have anyone in her Second Circle except youngsters who were with her for training and court polish. I know she paid them because Darlena, the Province Queen who rules that part of Dharo, had been impressed by Cassidy's generosity as well as by the number of requests she received from youngsters of all castes who were willing to serve in a small village court because of that generosity. Darlena also noticed how many of those youngsters retracted their requests when they learned that Kermilla now ruled Bhak instead of Cassidy. So I don't think the current Queen of Bhak has anyone who can fill the vacant place in her court."

"Which means the court is broken," Aaron said.

"Not yet," Jaenelle said quietly, looking at Sabrina.

Sabrina tipped her head. "If her court doesn't tell me, I can pretend not to know."

Aaron swore but did nothing else because he, like the rest of them, knew there was a reason Jaenelle wanted some things to be ignored.

Even if she chose not to tell any of them the reason.

"There was an interesting miscalculation when the summer tithes for Bhak and Woolskin were sent to Darlena's Steward," Sabrina continued. "It was swiftly corrected, but Gallard had never made that kind of miscalculation when he served Cassidy."

"Tried to short the Province Queen of her rightful share of the tithes?" Khary asked.

Sabrina's smile was sufficient answer. "I think my Steward and Darlena's should personally collect the autumn tithes from a few of the District Queens and review their court accounts." She looked at Jaenelle. "Don't you think? That would be a fair warning to a Queen who had been granted a provisional year to prove herself—especially if she truly wanted to retain those villages as her territory."

"Who gives a piss about being fair?" Lucivar growled.

Saetan felt his temper rise, but before he could respond, Daemon said mildly, "We all give a piss about being fair when it buys needed time."

Lucivar stopped prowling and stared at Daemon. "Oh. *That* kind of being fair. All right, fine. But someone should still go to Dena Nehele and explain to that bitch that a young Warlord can't be snatched off the street just because he has four legs and fur."

"That's been taken care of," Jaenelle said.

"By who?" Lucivar demanded.

"By someone who can explain things even better than you." Jaenelle smiled at Lucivar.

Lucivar took a step back and resumed his prowling.

After a few moments of uneasy silence, Khary said, "There might not be much we can do about Kermilla right now, but I can go to Eyota tomorrow and bring Khollie home."

"I don't think you can take Khollie anywhere without a fight," Jaenelle said.

Khary gave Jaenelle, then Morghann, a hard stare. "He's delicate. You both *know* that. And Ranon didn't want him in the first place."

"What was true then isn't true now. Ranon needed some time to gain clarity in his feelings."

Khary made a rude noise. "He's—"

"One of us," Jaenelle said quietly.

Silence as the men took a long moment to assess the implications of that statement.

*One of us,* Saetan thought. Those three words told him a great deal about Ranon—and explained even more why Jaenelle had avoided telling him any details about her meeting with the Shalador Warlord Prince. Damned hard to insist that you were a "former" ruler when a newly met Warlord Prince recognized a bond with you that could hold him.

When Gray had recognized her as *the* Queen, Jaenelle had slid around facing the truth that she wasn't a former anything by arguing that Gray was confused by his developing sense of being a Warlord Prince. But there was nothing wrong with Ranon that she could use as an excuse.

Which made this particular meeting even more interesting.

"What Circle?" Khary finally asked.

"Second," Jaenelle replied.

Meaning, if the Dark Court still officially existed, Ranon would have been accepted into the Second Circle. Not as intimate a companion as someone in the First Circle, but those who served in the Second were still close enough—and trusted enough—for confidential assignments and direct service to the Queen.

"And Gray?" Daemon asked.

"Second Circle," she said.

Anger still smeared the room, but it no longer had heat or teeth.

"So that's it then," Aaron said.

"Not quite. I received this letter from Cassidy a couple of days ago, before the attempted abduction," Jaenelle said. She called in another letter and handed it to Khary.

By the time Khary got halfway through the first page, his mouth was hanging open. "Payment for work? *They're getting paid to herd sheep?*"

"Three coppers a day," Jaenelle said cheerfully. "Wynne and Duffy are also maintaining the spells on the cold boxes and hot water tanks for the landen community and get three coppers a week for each household."

Since Khary seemed frozen, Aaron snagged the second page. "Oh, Mother Night. Two of them are working in a children's play area."

Sabrina snorted, then had to call in a handkerchief to blow her nose.

Morghann twisted in her chair so she could read the other side of the page. "They call Lloyd and Kief the silver twins. And the boys are working in the stables. That's good. They like horses."

"I guess I understand the Scelties wanting to learn about being paid for work, but what are they going to do with the money?" Daemon said. "Save up their coppers to buy their own little steading and a small flock of sheep?"

Morghann and Jaenelle looked at Daemon. Just looked at him. And then they smiled.

Lucivar caught Khary before he landed on the floor, and Saetan watched Daemon—his brilliant, lethal son—turn pale. Probably at the thought of someday having to negotiate a business deal with a Sceltie.

*Coward,* Saetan said on a Black spear thread.

Daemon gave him a sideways look.

"It's not that bizarre," Jaenelle said. "Ladvarian and I own the little cottage and acreage where he trains other Scelties."

"What?" Khary yelped.

"What?" Daemon whispered.

Jaenelle looked at Khary. "I thought you knew that. Morghann, didn't you know that?"

"I did, yes," Morghann replied. "But it seemed best not to mention that bit of paperwork."

Jaenelle patted Daemon's thigh. "Ladvarian and I have owned that property since before you and I got married, so I never thought to mention it. Besides, having that place is so much better than having a dozen Scelties living with us whenever we're in Maghre."

"Yes, that's so much better." Daemon looked a little woozy.

"The relationship between Scelties and humans is too well established in Scelt," Morghann said. "And not all Scelties want to change the relationship they already have with humans. But in a new land, there would be opportunities the Scelties couldn't explore as easily here."

Everyone looked around the room without quite looking at one another.

"Are we done?" Karla asked Jaenelle. "Because if we're done, I'd like some help in figuring out how to turn a mauve cat back into a white cat."

"Draca is serving a late supper in about an hour," Saetan said.

"That should be enough time," Jaenelle said.

*For what?* Saetan wondered. But it wasn't a question he would ask because his darling girls might tell him.

The Ladies left the room, leaving the men to collapse into chairs, not sure if they should be scared or pissed off, or should laugh like fools.

The room held nothing but a blissful, and exhausted, silence for several minutes.

"Can you stay for supper?" Daemon asked Lucivar.

"No choice," Lucivar growled. "Marian said if I want to stay married, I'm going to stay out for the whole evening."

"You have been a bit too possessive lately."

"Maybe. She says she's fine."

"What does the Healer say?"

"Nurian also says Marian is fine, so she's fine. Everyone is supposed to be fine. Well, I'm *not* fine. She scared the shit out of me with that miscarriage." Lucivar snarled. "Next thing she'll be wanting sex again."

"They do that," Aaron said sympathetically while Khary nodded. "They do."

"Well, then . . ." Saetan began.

*Bang!*

They all straightened up and looked toward the door.

"What was that?" Daemon asked.

"Sounded like something blew up," Lucivar replied. "What kind of spell were the girls trying to fix?"

They all looked at him.

"No," Saetan said firmly. "If you want to find out, you go ahead. I am not leaving this room."

The other four men looked at one another.

Daemon held out his hand. "We've got some time before supper. Let me see that letter again."

### TERREILLE

Having exhausted his patience for card playing, Theran left Kermilla sulking over a hand of solitaire and noticed the Sceltie standing perfectly still near the parlor door.

He moved toward the dog. "Vae?"

No, not Vae. Same coloring but different markings, and a sense of maturity—and power.

He saw the Red Jewel at the same time Kermilla spotted the dog and hurried toward him, clapping her hands in delight.

"Oh, *Theran*. You got me a Sceltie."

She took another step. The dog bared his teeth and snarled.

Kermilla shook her finger. "Bad dog!"

Something more than the Sceltie snarled, and the sound filled the room.

*I am Lord Ladvarian,* the Sceltie said, staring at Kermilla. *This is Prince Jaal.*

A large brown cat with black stripes suddenly appeared on Ladvarian's right, dwarfing the Sceltie. If the cat had the strength that body implied, it could pull down a full-grown horse or cow without any trouble.

He didn't want to think about what it could do to a man.

Then he noticed the Green Jewel around the cat's neck and acknowledged the title his mind wanted to deny. *Prince* Jaal. A Warlord Prince who wore a Jewel equal to his own and had a body he couldn't match for strength or speed.

*And this is Prince Kaelas,* Ladvarian said.

Theran's bowels turned to water. The white cat now standing on Ladvarian's left was *huge.* Even the striped cat looked small in comparison.

Worse, Kaelas wore a Red Jewel.

The Sceltie was focused on Kermilla. The cats were focused on *him,* and he knew, with absolute certainty, that if anything went wrong now, he had no chance of surviving.

*You hurt Khollie,* Ladvarian told Kermilla.

"No, I just—"

*When you hunt one kindred, you hunt all kindred. Remember that, because the next time you send a male to hunt down one of us, we will come hunting for you.* Ladvarian paused. *This is what Kaelas does to enemies of kindred.*

Theran felt a surge of power and realized a moment too late that Ladvarian had forced at least one of Kermilla's inner barriers open, no doubt to show her exactly what that huge white cat could do.

She whimpered and her eyes widened. Then she bent over and vomited.

The dog, damn its heart, put up a shield to keep the kindred from getting splashed as Kermilla heaved, then heaved again.

Ladvarian looked at him. *You are not a friend.*

Beads of sweat popped out on his forehead. He'd stood on killing fields. He'd seen slaughter. But he was certain he had never seen anything that could equal what that white cat would do to a man.

And he was grateful he'd been spared seeing whatever memory had been forced upon Kermilla.

Ladvarian turned and trotted through the closed parlor door. Jaal followed him. When they were gone, that walking white death stared at him a moment longer—and disappeared.

Theran froze. Was Kaelas gone? Or was the cat standing there, sight shielded, waiting for him to move, to become prey?

No sound. Not even breathing. Nothing he could detect. *Nothing.*

Then the door began to open. Julien peeked into the room. "Prince Grayhaven?"

"How am I going to get it out?" Kermilla whimpered. "How am I going to stop *seeing* that?"

Theran didn't move.

Julien pushed the door open and stepped into the room, a distasteful look on his face when he spotted the mess on the carpet. "Prince, I saw—" He gasped and leaped away from the door. "Something just brushed past me."

*It's gone.* Theran closed his eyes. *Thank the Darkness, it's gone.*

"I don't believe our guests will be back," he said, and almost laughed at how calm he sounded. "I'll escort the Lady to her room. Can you . . . ?"

Julien looked at the carpet and nodded. "If I can't get it cleaned sufficiently, I'll burn the damn thing."

He put an arm around Kermilla and led her out of the room.

On another day, he would have voiced an opinion about a butler deciding whether or not to destroy a carpet he couldn't afford to replace. Tonight he didn't have enough balls left to argue with anyone.

He'd gotten the only warning he would ever get. If those three ever had a reason to come looking for him again, the only sounds he would hear were his own screams.


## EBON ASKAVI

Daemon lay on his side, facing away from the rest of the bed. When he felt Jaenelle slip under the covers, he pressed his face into the pillow and began chanting silently, *Don't laugh, don't laugh, don't laugh.*

If he started laughing again, she would kick his ass out of bed.

But, damn, it was hard not to laugh when his darling wife looked like a brightly colored, demented sheep. Not that he would say *that*. He knew better. Lucivar didn't, but he knew better.

Lucivar was sent home with a note from his father explaining to Marian why Lucivar *had* to go home before his sister, and Karla, killed him flatter than dead. Whatever that meant.

Jaenelle poked his back with a finger. "I'll fix it."

*Don't laugh, don't laugh, don't laugh.* "I know you will."

"Tomorrow Karla and I will figure out what went wrong, and we'll fix it."

"Uh-huh." He tried to resist and couldn't. Damn his curiosity, it was going to get him into trouble. But he rolled onto his back so he could look at her—and had to clench his teeth until he gained *some* control. "I was wondering . . ."

Her sapphire eyes narrowed.

He made a twirling motion with one finger. "How did your hair . . . ?"

It wasn't the splotches of bright pink, blue, and mauve in her golden hair that broke his control. It wasn't even the streaks of green, which made no sense since they weren't part of the original spell Karla was trying to fix. It was the fact that the colored hair had also corkscrewed and . . . *sproinged* . . . out from her head.

Hence Lucivar's comment about demented sheep.

Laughter bubbled up. Threatened to spill out.

Jaenelle huffed and said something in the Old Tongue that was, no doubt, *very* rude. "Go to sleep. You're not going to be good for anything else."

He blinked. Blinked again. The laughter vanished. He looked at the silly little sheep sitting so foolishly close to him and another kind of amusement swelled inside him. And swelled a particular part of him.

"Was that a challenge?" he purred.

Her eyes widened. She shifted her hips away from him. "No."

He sat up. "I think it was. I think—"

He pounced. Her squeak of surprise as he pinned her to the bed did all kinds of delightful things to the predatory side of his nature. Even better was the way her breath caught after he vanished her nightgown and used his teeth and tongue to give her breasts some lavish attention.

He closed his teeth over his favorite spot on her neck, followed by soft kisses.

"Don't you know that laughter can be an aphrodisiac?" he whispered in her ear.

She shook her head. Brightly colored, corkscrew curls bounced against his nose.

Smiling he raised his head and looked at her. Nerves in those beautiful eyes. Nerves . . . and hot desire.

*Mine.*

"Then let me expand your education a little," he purred.

She said nothing, so he sheathed himself inside her.

He expanded her education a whole lot more than a little, but by the time he was done, they were both too exhausted—and too satisfied—to care.

# CHAPTER 26

## TERREILLE

Gray brushed one fingertip over the globe Tersa had given him.

*This is where you are,* she'd said.

Not whole. Not fully formed. Not who he could have been.

The fire dance celebrated the Shalador males' sexual and emotional maturity—and acknowledged their willingness to accept adult responsibilities as well as adult pleasures. Would this dance really make a difference in the way Cassie saw him?

Would it make a difference in the way he saw himself?

*When the time comes, accept the fire that lives within you.*

Brushing a finger over the globe again, he thought, *It's time. Win or lose, it's time.*

He'd been twenty-two when he'd made the Offering to the Darkness. Something inside him had swelled and pushed at him, demanding release, demanding that he open himself to his mature potential. But he'd been too emotionally damaged to endure that grueling test of Self, and instead of embracing the dark glory that could have been his, he'd fled from it—and had ended up with a Purple Dusk Jewel that was a little darker than his Birthright Purple Dusk.

The Offering could be made only once, and what he might have been had been severed by his own fear and refusal to accept it.

He couldn't reclaim the power that was lost forever, but maybe, with the fire dance, he could finally meet and embrace the man he should be.

Gray opened the door to his room and found Ranon leaning against the hallway wall, waiting for him.

"You ready?" Ranon asked.

He looked at the other Warlord Prince, a man who had become a closer, stronger friend than any he'd ever had. Tonight there was heat in Ranon's dark eyes. Heat and a glitter that wasn't temper but wasn't far removed.

"I'm ready." May the Darkness have mercy on him if he wasn't ready. If he failed this time, too many of his dreams would fail with him.

They walked out of the Queen's Residence together, then stopped when they reached the street. Currents of feminine power drifted through the village, along the streets, stropping against Gray's inner barriers.

Ranon closed his eyes and breathed deep. Gray had the sense that his friend was breathing in more than air.

"Do you hear it?" Ranon whispered.

He didn't hear anything, but he felt it in his blood.

The drums were calling the men to the dance.

Ranon took in another breath, then let it out in a sigh as he opened his eyes. "Come on, Gray. It's time to dance."

Cassie was there tonight among the drummers, was there among the women who had come to watch the fire contained in a vessel of male flesh.

*Cassie.*

"Yes," Gray said as he began walking toward the sound of the drums. "It's time."

Cassidy looked around as she set up her drum and stool between Shira's and Reyhana's. This park, named The Dance, had been a tangle of weeds and overgrown bushes with a pile of stones in the center of the almost impenetrable mess. Gray had been frustrated that the elders wouldn't let him clean up this park when they let him work on the others in Eyota. He'd grumbled and fussed about it so much the elders finally told him politely but firmly to keep his hands off the place.

Now there was a large circle of fine sand that had been carefully raked. The tumble of stones in the center was a large fire pit piled with wood that was ready for a flame's kiss. Freshly mown grass filled the rest of the space, and bushes defined the boundaries and provided some privacy. Eight archways created entranceways to The Dance.

"This wasn't cleaned up in the past couple of days," Cassidy said quietly. Or as quietly as she could over the sound of the two women who had begun drumming.

Shira smiled and looked a little embarrassed. "We've had to be careful for so long . . ." She shrugged. "Illusion spells. Lots of them, woven in and around one another. The Dance is always tended, even though most years it wasn't safe to use such a place."

"So you didn't do these special dances?" Cassidy asked.

"We did. But not like this." Shira smiled fiercely, but her eyes were tear bright. "It was too risky to do the whole celebration together, so it would be spread out over the weeks between the Autumn Moon and the next full moon. This is the first time in a very long time my people will come together on one night for these dances."

It hurt that they hadn't trusted her enough to release the illusion spells and reveal The Dance for what it was, but it also told her how deep the fear ran in the Shalador people. She didn't ask Shira what the penalty had been for those who had been caught doing these dances. She didn't want to know.

And yet, despite that fear, they had invited her to participate in this celebration, to be "part of its heart."

"Drummers and the other musicians will be going in and out as the dances change, so if you lose the rhythm, just drop out until you can pick it up again," Shira said.

"Janos is dancing tonight," Reyhana said.

Cassidy looked at Shira, who looked at Reyhana and smiled, but then said, "Remember, you go nowhere tonight without a chaperon."

"But . . ."

"No."

"Is there a problem?" Cassidy asked.

Reyhana looked away. Shira sighed and said, "Heated blood can eliminate good sense, and sometimes young people do things they regret the next day—or make mistakes they can't live with."

Reyhana's face blazed with color, but she held her head up. "I know my duty to my people."

"And to yourself," Cassidy added softly.

Reyhana met her eyes and nodded. "And to myself. That's why Janos asked Darkmist to act as our chaperon tonight."

"Oh." Shira pressed a hand against her mouth to stifle a laugh. "In that case, I apologize for treading where I had no reason to tread."

"As the court's Healer, you had a right to express concern," Cassidy said.

*In that case,* Shira said, *I'll ask if you've been drinking the contraceptive brew since your last moontime.*

Cassidy felt the heat rising in her face. *Yes, I have.*

*Good.* Shira sat on her stool and placed her smaller drum between her knees. "Ah, the Priestess is giving the signal. The rest of us will join the drumming in a minute."

Cassidy took her place and got her own drum in position. They had practiced for these dances over the past few weeks. Yairen had declared her ready to join the drumming for all but the Fire Dance.

The Shalador women were gathering. Many stopped at a small stone altar and opened a vein over a large silver chalice—the blood the Priestess would use to cast the circle for the dance.

Two more drums joined the first two drummers. Then two more, and two more. A simple rhythm that would split into something more demanding. Cassidy had been assigned the simpler beat, and Shira and Reyhana had chosen to stay with her instead of doing the more complex beat. She appreciated that when her turn came to join the drummers. There was plenty to think about, and when the drums were suddenly enhanced with Craft and the sound flowed out of The Dance, she felt the seduction and the power of this tradition.

As the last drummer took up the beat, the Priestess's voice rose in wordless song, calling the men to the dance. Another voice joined hers. Then another. And another.

The first men arrived. Some were fathers with sons who were old enough for the Boys' Dance. Most were older men, including Ranon's grandfather Yairen, who would begin the celebration with the Wisdom Dance.

The Priestess cast the circle with blood and Craft as the women's voices quieted until it was only her voice and the drums calling, calling, calling.

Cassidy drummed, grateful for the simple beat she could maintain and still observe the people.

The Priestess extended her hand and brought Yairen across the circle. Then they both extended their hands to bring two more men into the dance. As she took the hand of the last elder who was participating in the dance, she stepped out of the circle.

All the drummers except the lead drummer stopped and shook out their hands as the lead drummer made the transition to the new beat. Then the rest of the drummers joined in again, along with the musicians playing fiddles and flutes.

A blur of images and sounds. Cassidy focused on the drumming, catching glimpses of the men as they danced the same formal steps their ancestors had performed centuries ago.

She lost her rhythm through part of the Boys' Dance because the younger ones—those who had recently gone through their Birthright Ceremony—turned into brainless puppies, forgetting most of what they had learned so they ended up bouncing along with the older boys. And more than a few of them stopped dancing altogether to wave at their mothers, which caused tangles as the boys still dancing tried to move around unplanned obstacles.

Despite Shira's earlier assurance that drummers dropped out of the music, Cassidy felt embarrassed that she'd lost the rhythm after so many weeks of practice. Then the Boys' Dance gave way to the Youths' Dance, and Reyhana lost all ability to drum because she was laughing so hard at Janos's antics. Hearing other bursts of laughter followed by a stumble in the beat, Cassidy suddenly understood that perfection wasn't expected during this joyous celebration. So she watched Janos and laughed with Reyhana.

He performed the steps exactly as he should, but Cassidy learned a great deal about attitude. Most of the young men who were within a year or two of making the Offering and being considered adults were fiercely serious as they performed the dance. Janos gave the steps a lightheartedness, making fun of himself and the others who were on the cusp of manhood.

Cassidy felt more than heard Shira's sigh of relief and understood the feeling even while she laughed. Janos knew there were lines he couldn't cross, and he'd done what he could to keep himself—and Reyhana—from temptation.

The Youths stepped out of the circle as they brought over the last group of dancers. The adult men walked in a quiet circle as all but the lead drummer once again went silent.

"Well done, Janos," Cassidy said. Then she noticed Reyhana vanishing her drum and stool. "Aren't you staying to see the last dance?"

The two youngsters gave her startled looks.

"No, Lady," Janos finally said. "We're meeting some friends at The Lady's Pleasure. Then we'll go back to my grandfather's house for the night."

*Don't ask,* Shira said as she vanished her smaller drum and called in the large drum, settling it between her thighs.

One by one the drummers joined the lead drummer, and The Dance once more filled with sound.

Noticing how many people were leaving, Cassidy leaned toward Shira. "Why aren't they staying?"

"The Fire Dance isn't for children." Shira began drumming.


Gray circled with the rest of the men, letting their bodies shield him from Cassie's view.

His life, his dreams . . . everything came down to this dance.

Ranon was on his left, but on his right, the side closest to the fire . . . a shadow. Primal. Lethal. Seductive.

*You ran from me once*, something whispered. *I can't give you now what was lost then. But I can give you the rest if you're ready to accept it. Will you run from me again? Or will you embrace the fire?*

*Who are you?*

*You know.*

A brush of heat against his right arm. A shivery awareness of what he still could claim for himself.

The man. The Warlord Prince.

*Yes, I know who you are,* Gray thought. *You are Jared Blaed.*

*Will you run from me again?*

Gray caught a glimpse of Cassie's fiery hair and felt a hunger for more than sex—and knew how to get everything he wanted.

*No, I won't run from you again. This time, I'll take everything you can give me.*


Cassidy didn't catch the signal, but moments after the last child left the park, the dance began.

Clothes vanished with the first thumped step, and looking at a circle of men who wore nothing but their Jewels and their pride, she understood why the Fire Dance wasn't witnessed by children.

Hell's fire, Mother Night, and may the Darkness be merciful!

Shadows and fire. Hard bodies glistening with sweat as they performed that hot, grinding dance.

She caught sight of Ranon and almost slid off her stool. Then she glanced at Shira and saw the same fierce glitter in *those* dark eyes. The Black Widow no longer played the drum as music. The beat, the *sound*, became a challenge, female to male, and every move and thrust of the dance was Ranon's answer to that challenge.

Then she looked at the man dancing next to Ranon, looked into a familiar face that held the glittering green eyes of a stranger.

A dangerous stranger.

"Gray," she whispered.

★ ★ ★

As he performed each turn and thrust of the dance, the shadow clung like a second skin—primal, lethal, seductive. Then it became his skin, filling him with a wild heat.

And then, as he looked into Cassie's eyes, it became him.

Ranon and Gray moved on with the other dancers, stomping, thrusting, whirling. The scars on Gray's back silvered in the firelight, and Cassidy had the feeling those scars would no longer be a source of shame; they would be a testimony of courage.

Round and round. She couldn't take her eyes off him, following his progression around the circle even when the fire hid him from sight.

Round and round until the drums were a thrumming in her blood.

The drums stopped without warning, and the silence was a painful scraping over her senses, over her skin.

"Cassie." A voice roughened by lust, by need, by something more than both.

Her legs trembled, but she forced herself to stand and look Gray in the eyes.

"Cassie." His hands cupped her face. The slight tremble in his fingers helped settle her own nerves.

Until he kissed her.

Heat. Drums. A hot, grinding dance. A firestorm of feelings as his tongue swept into her mouth, asking and demanding.

"Gray." Ranon's voice sounded just as rough. "Put some pants on and let's go home."

*How am I supposed to keep my hands off him long enough to get home?* Cassidy wondered as she watched Gray call in a pair of trousers and put them on.

The air was cool at this time of year, but Gray didn't bother with a shirt or shoes. He just grabbed her hand and headed for one of the archways, followed by Ranon and Shira.

She didn't know who, if any of them, had contacted the silver twins to bring the horse and pony cart, but Lloyd and Kief were waiting for them. They piled in, Ranon and Shira on the driver's seat while she and Gray shared the back bench seats with the Scelties.

They piled out again in front of the Queen's Residence. The silver twins headed back to the stables with the horse. Ranon and Shira headed around the back of the house while Gray grabbed Cassidy's hand again and headed into the house.

Ranon and Shira hadn't moved into their own place yet, but it seemed they were going to spend the night there. Probably just as well, considering the way Gray hustled her up the stairs and into her room.

He took her in his arms and pressed a soft kiss on her temple—a kiss that trembled with tenderness as well as the violence inherent in a Warlord Prince.

"Cassie," he whispered. "Let me love you. Let me be your partner in this dance."

She shifted enough to look at his face, to look into his eyes. The Fire Dance had burned out what was left of the scarred boy he had been. A man stood before her, waiting for her answer.

"What about Lucivar's rules?" Not that she gave a damn about Lucivar's rules right now, but she had to ask while she could still think.

"A useful leash that kept us both safe. But a man doesn't need someone else to hold the leash. This has nothing to do with Lucivar. Not anymore. Just you and me, Cassie. Now it's just you and me."

"Yes," she said. "I'll take you as my partner, as my lover."

"Cassie." That was all he said. All he needed to say.

Soft. Sweet. Hot. Hard. They touched and tasted, learning each other's bodies as sweat-slicked skin slid across skin. He surrounded her—and she surrounded him—a claiming that went beyond the body. When he brought her up and over the crest a final time and poured himself into her, she knew everything had changed.

Gray woke instantly, his arm tightening over Cassie as he listened for whatever had snapped him out of a sound sleep.

Nothing. And yet, *something* kept scratching at his senses, demanding acknowledgment.

He slipped out of bed and pulled on a robe. Whatever he was sensing wasn't in this room.

He reached for the door that opened onto the hallway. The scratchy, demanding feeling faded. When he stepped back from the door, the feeling returned.

He probed the room again—and felt his temper sharpen, felt himself rising to the killing edge as a natural response to a potential threat to his Queen.

That *something* wasn't in Cassie's room and it wasn't beyond her room either. That left . . .

He slipped into the adjoining bedroom. His room.

A glint of light near the dresser caught his attention. Despite the scratchy feeling, he sensed nothing dangerous, so he walked over to the dresser, then used Craft to form a small ball of witchlight.

He stared for a long time as his temper eased back from the killing edge. Then he extinguished the witchlight and went back to Cassie's room.

"You okay?" Cassie murmured when he slipped back into bed.

"I'm fine." He wrapped an arm around her and kissed the sweet spot on her neck. "Go back to sleep, love. It's early yet."

She dropped back into sleep instantly, but he didn't. He waited until there was enough daylight; then he went back to his room and stared at the globe Tersa had given him.

The dragon, the symbol of himself as a whole man, stared back at him.

# CHAPTER 27

## TERREILLE

Julien stood in the breakfast room doorway. "There is a man digging in the garden. He says he's your cousin."

Theran set his coffee cup down, wiped his mouth with a napkin, and pushed away from the table. "Gray's here?"

Gray. Digging in the garden. Not coming near the house.

Mother Night.

He glanced at Kermilla and suppressed a sigh. This morning she wasn't pleased with anyone who had a cock. Jhorma hadn't returned. Neither had Bardoc. And the escorts who should have arrived for their rotation of service were still in Dharo.

She'd accused him of not sending her letters to her court, claiming he was jealous of her men. That was true, up to a point. He craved her in a way he'd never craved anything else. She was a fever in his blood, and even when she did things that made him uneasy or they argued about money, he *knew* the problems were simply because she was a young, inexperienced Queen—and because she came from a family who had wealth he couldn't imagine—and he still wanted to shape things to meet her wishes and will as much as he could.

So, yes, he was jealous. But he was practical enough to recognize that having a couple of her First Circle here to help entertain her would have worked to his advantage.

All in all, this wasn't a good day to ask her to talk to Gray.

"I'd better go out and see him," he said.

"Your cousin is the gardener, isn't he?" Kermilla spread jam over her toast in a fussy manner and didn't look at him. "It's good he's come back. The flower beds have been looking very weedy and unkempt lately. It gives visitors a bad impression."

Theran saw Julien's face tighten. The butler worked in the garden as a way to relax and was doing what he could to keep things tidy. But the grounds weren't part of Julien's duties, and Kermilla preferred to enjoy the results of someone else's labor—and complained when the results didn't meet her expectations.

"Julien, bring another pot of coffee," Kermilla said, not looking at either man as she continued to spread the jam on the toast. "And tell the cook to pay attention to what she's doing this time. This last pot tasted like wash water."

Julien turned and walked away. Theran followed him.

"Julien?" Kermilla yelled. "Did you hear me?"

Julien stopped and turned to Theran. There was a queer look in the butler's eyes. "I'm not going back in that room. I have other duties."

"What are you doing this morning?" Theran asked.

Julien's mouth curved in an unnerving smile. "I'm sharpening the cook's knives."

Theran hurried out to the garden. He hadn't heard from Gray since Cassidy ran away to Eyota. Talon had written to him a couple of times early on, Master of the Guard to First Escort, and news filtered through from some of the Warlord Princes he knew, but he hadn't heard from Gray.

A large woven basket sat at the edge of the Queen's flower bed. The bottom of it was filled with bulbs.

"Gray?"

Gray looked over and smiled at him. "Morning." He brushed the dirt off two more bulbs and put them in the basket. Then he pushed the spade's head into the soil to keep the handle upright. "This bed could use some water. So could the rest of them. I guess you haven't had rain up here for the past few days."

"No, we haven't." Theran's heart lightened. "I'm glad to have you back—and not just for the gardens."

Gray gave him a puzzled look and shook his head, still smiling. "I'm not staying. I just came by to pick up some of the bulbs I got for Cassie. Figured I'd divide them. That will leave this bed looking a little sparse next spring, but it will fill in."

"You came back to Grayhaven for *bulbs*?"

Gray shrugged. "I planted them for Cassie, and I paid a hefty sum for a few of them. Besides . . ." He looked around the garden. "I didn't think you would care."

"That's not the point."

"What is the point?" Gray looked past Theran's shoulder, and a dark, feral look came into his green eyes.

Before Theran could ask what was wrong, Gray pulled the spade out of the soil. Except it was no longer a spade. It was a pitchfork, and Gray held it more like a weapon than a tool.

For a moment, Theran just stared. It took a lot of skill in using Craft to vanish one object and call in another so smoothly a person couldn't see the transition. Where had Gray learned to do that?

Then he remembered that *something* had sparked his cousin's temper and looked behind him.

Kermilla pranced over the lawn toward them, her expression one of sharp delight. That expression usually meant she was going to delight in using the sharp side of her tongue.

"It's Gray, isn't it?" Kermilla said. "The gardener? Have you finally re-membered your duties and come back to be useful?"

What Theran saw in Gray's eyes made the queer look in Julien's seem warm and comforting in comparison.

"I don't work for you, bitch," Gray snarled. "I never will."

"*Gray*," Theran said, shocked.

Kermilla's face went white with anger. "You should be careful about saying 'never,' gardener. Things change."

"Some things change," Gray agreed. "Some things don't."

Kermilla took a step closer. Gray raised the pitchfork, and there was no doubt of how he would use it if she came any closer.

"I'm a Queen," Kermilla hissed.

"You don't outrank me, and I don't serve you, so that means nothing," Gray snarled. "And nothing like you is ever going to lay a hand on me again."

A moment of choice.

Theran put himself between Kermilla and Gray. "That's enough, Gray. Kermilla, please go back inside."

"I want—"

"*Kermilla.*" He'd pay for giving her an order in front of someone, but Gray would try to hurt her, maybe even try to kill her, if she didn't get out of sight.

He waited until Kermilla was safely inside the house; then he focused his anger on his cousin.

"What in the name of Hell do you think you're doing?"

Gray stared at him. "Do you actually serve that bitch? Sleep with that bitch?"

"Stop calling her that!"

"I'll call her what she is."

"You don't even know her."

"I may not know *her*, but I knew one just like her. I have the scars to prove it."

"She's not like that! She's *nothing* like that! And you better mind your tongue, boy. When Kermilla becomes the Queen of Dena Nehele, she is *not* going to forget your insults."

"Then it's fortunate she's not going to become the Queen." Gray drove the pitchfork deep into the soil. "Cassie is the Queen of Dena Nehele."

"Only until spring. When her contract runs out, Kermilla will rule."

"No," Gray said. "*Cassie* is the Queen."

"One-year contract, Gray. Then she's gone."

"No. She's settled in. She's chosen to rule."

"I'm not serving a minute beyond my contract, and when I leave, Cassidy's court will break and re-form around Kermilla as the new Queen."

Gray laughed. "You really think men like Archerr and Shaddo are going to serve Kermilla? You think *Ranon* is going to serve someone like her?"

"They'll serve if I say they'll serve. Or have you immersed yourself so much in that shitty little Shalador slum that you've forgotten who I am?"

He regretted saying the words the moment he gave them voice—and regretted them even more when Gray's eyes filled with something frigid and bitter.

"How could I forget who you are?" Gray said. "You're Grayhaven. You're the last of the line, the one who needed to be protected and defended at any cost. For what, Theran? So you can play the pony now for *her*? If that's what you wanted, you should have come down from the mountains years ago and given yourself to the Queens who were here. They were no different than her, and they would have used you just fine. If you don't believe me, I'll take off my shirt and show you my back. I guess you've forgotten what it looks like." He paused. "I paid a high price to protect you."

"And now you regret it?"

"Yes, I do. Today, I do. Today, I wish I'd told you to get your own damn box of sweets if you wanted them that much. But you wanted the box of sweets from the bakery and the sweets between that girl's thighs—and you got them both. What did I get? Two years of pain and fear and nightmares about things you will never know, and ten years beyond that of being frozen in a shroud of boyhood. And for what, Theran? For what?"

Theran took a step back.

"Because of you, I'm less than what I could have been, and I have to live with that. Every day, I have to live with that."

The air between them crackled.

"You're not thinking this through, Gray. You're not seeing this clearly."

"Oh, but I am, Prince Grayhaven. I am seeing things quite clearly. You're the one who wants to ignore what you've done and pretend someone else is to blame."

"And what have I done?"

"You drew the line, and now you don't want to admit that we're standing on opposite sides. If you make Kermilla the Queen, I will fight her with everything I am—because I would rather die than live one day under her hand." Gray flung out his right hand, aiming for the flower bed. All the plants and bulbs exploded out of the ground and hung in the air for a moment. The bulbs vanished; the plants fell back into the flower bed.

A moment later, the basket vanished too.

"I changed my mind," Gray said. "I'm taking all the bulbs I planted for Cassie. If your bitch wants a spring garden, she can plant one herself." He walked away, heading around the house to reach the landing web beyond the gates.

"Gray!" Theran yelled.

Gray stopped and turned. "My name is Jared Blaed."


## EBON ASKAVI

Saetan opened the Gate and stepped through to the Keep in Terreille.

He was going to have to talk to Gray about the timing of these unscheduled visits. The boy had a knack for catching him at the end of his waking hours.

He opened the door of the sitting room, then stayed in the doorway, assessing the changes in the man who furiously paced the length of the room.

"Prince," he said as he stepped into the room and closed the door.

Gray rushed toward him, those green eyes filled with a fury that must have been building every minute of the journey here.

"You have to teach me how to be a Consort," Gray said.

"Boyo, I don't have to teach you anything," Saetan replied mildly.

"Theran's going to break the court," Gray snapped. "He's planning to push Cassie out come spring and put that bitch Kermilla in her place."

"Gray . . ."

"It's not fair! After all the work Cassie has done, all the good she's done, and he thinks he can snap his fingers and everyone will drop to their knees and lick Kermilla's ass."

"Gray . . ."

"Well, I'm not licking anyone's ass, not again, and he is *not* going to break Cassie's court. So you—"

*"Gray!"*

Gray drew in one deep breath after another, as if he'd been running hard. His hands were clenched, and there was a wild look in his eyes. "My name is Jared Blaed."

"And my name is Saetan. I suggest you remember that."

A month ago, he would have been more lenient with the boy. But Jaenelle's remark that Gray could have been Second Circle changed things. A Warlord Prince who had the personality and strength to stand in the Second Circle of the Dark Court at Ebon Askavi was a dangerous man. Not just because of the Jewels he wore but because of the *kind* of man he was inside. So Gray was going to be held to some very strict standards from now on.

"If I become Cassie's Consort when Theran leaves, then her court won't break," Gray said.

Two Queens. Two courts in a fight for the same Territory.

If the fight remained between the courts, a few good men would die—and possibly the vanquished Queen as well. If the fight escalated beyond the courts . . . it would be war.

"This is what is going to happen today," Saetan said. "You're coming back with me to the Keep in Kaeleer. I'll ask Daemon and Lucivar to join us. Then we'll discuss your concerns and your request for training."

Gray opened his mouth, and if he said what the look in his eyes indicated, Saetan wouldn't hesitate to toss him out of the Keep with the firm understanding that he wouldn't be allowed back in until he'd learned some manners.

Apparently Gray had already learned some manners because he reined in his temper and said, "Thank you, sir. That would be appreciated."

"Fine. Since I was about to retire and get some rest, I'm going to do that until Daemon and Lucivar arrive. And what will you be doing?"

A long pause while Gray eyed him warily. "I'm going to be making mulch?"

Saetan's smile had a razor's edge. "I'm delighted we understand one another."

"Yes, sir. I'm delighted too."

*Hardly,* Saetan thought as he led Gray to the Gate and opened it to the Keep in Kaeleer.

After leaving Gray in a courtyard with an empty barrel and enough wood to keep the boy occupied for the rest of the day if need be, he sent a thought on a Black psychic spear thread. *Daemon.*

*Father?* Instant concern.

*Gray is here. I need you and Lucivar at the Keep as soon as you can get here.*

*Is Gray all right?*

Saetan snorted softly. *Prince Jared Blaed is pissed off and doing just fine.*

A thoughtful assessment he could feel through the psychic thread.

*Are you going to get some rest before we arrive?* Daemon asked.

*Yes.*

Amusement filled the thread. *So what do you have him doing with his time? Chopping wood or making mulch?*

*Since Lucivar has been working through a lot of temper lately by chopping wood, there's already enough stacked to supply his eyrie, the Keep, and The Tavern for the next year or so.*

*Ah. So Gray is making mulch.*

*Or sawdust.*

Saetan broke the link and went up to his suite. If the discussion turned out to be as lively as he expected, he was going to need all the rest he could get.

Tired, sore, and dressed in clean clothes after taking a long, hot shower, Gray mopped up the stew in the bottom of the bowl with the last bite of bread. Full, he sat back and noticed the books that filled one shelf in the wall.

He'd just made his selection when Daemon walked into the room.

"So you decided to stir things up today, did you?" Daemon said, smiling.

Gray put the book back on the shelf. "Did Uncle Saetan tell you why I'm here?"

"No, he just said Lucivar and I were needed."

"I didn't think he told you. You wouldn't be smiling if he had."

"Be careful, puppy," Daemon said softly. "I consider you a friend, but that doesn't mean you shouldn't be careful."

Daemon walked out of the room. Gray followed to the sitting room where Saetan and Lucivar waited. Daemon took a seat. Gray didn't.

"Now," Saetan said, "say what you need to say, and we'll listen. And then *you* will listen."

The anger, and the feeling of betrayal, that had been building since his fight with Theran that morning overflowed, and he told them everything. He told them about all the things Cassie had done for the Shalador people and for Dena Nehele. He told them about the village and how it felt to be part of that community. He told them about the landen community and the people who lived there. And then he told them about going to Grayhaven early that morning to retrieve some of the special bulbs he'd planted for Cassie and learning that Theran intended to replace Cassie with Kermilla, just tossing Cassie aside after all the work she'd done for their people.

And he felt jagged ice fill his gut when he realized the three of them didn't seem the least bit surprised to hear about Theran's plans for Kermilla.

"That's why I want to train to be a Consort," he finished. "So I can take Theran's place and keep the court intact."

Silence. Then Daemon said, "First Escort, not Consort."

"Cassie and I are lovers. I should be her Consort."

"When did this happen?" Lucivar asked. "I don't recall discussing it—or giving my permission."

The mildly curious tone made Gray nervous. Then he remembered the fire dance and the primal power that he'd finally welcomed without reservation. He was no longer just Gray, the man. Now he was also Jared Blaed, the Warlord Prince. "With all respect, Prince Yaslana, the rules you set in the spring protected me as well as Cassie because I wasn't emotionally ready to be a lover. Now I am, and we don't need those rules anymore—and frankly, what she and I do together is none of your business."

Lucivar smiled. "You can look me in the eyes and say that, so you're right. It's none of my business anymore."

*Thank the Darkness for that.*

"First Escort, Gray, not Consort," Daemon said.

"You were Jaenelle's Consort," Gray said.

"And make no mistake, I still am. But the Queen's Triangle is about the court, and while the Consort provides a very intimate kind of service, his position and his status are still about the court. In terms of the court, a First Escort performs the same function except for the sex. Your relationship with Cassie is personal. You want to keep it that way. She was hurt by the last man who served as her Consort. You don't ever want her to wonder if you're in her bed because you want to wear the Consort's ring and have the status and reputation that goes with it."

Gray sat down. "I hadn't thought of it like that."

"You're into the last of the harvest now, aren't you?" Saetan asked.

"Yes, sir. Except for the autumn squashes that we'll harvest next month, the rest has been brought in."

"All right," Saetan said. "You'll come here once a week, late afternoon. Plan to stay over until the following morning. You'll be studying Protocol with an eye to how it applies to a First Escort."

"What should I tell Cassie?" Gray asked. "I don't want her to know about this. Not until she has to. It will break her heart."

"Tell her I've decided you require more training, and I'm going to personally provide that training. If she has any problem with you spending time at the Keep, she may discuss it with me."

"Do you think she will discuss it with you?"

"No."

*Didn't think so.*

"You'll also work with Daemon and Lucivar."

"We'll let him practice with Jaenelle," Lucivar said. "When he can keep up with her—and keep track of her—for half a day, he'll be able to make the run with any other Queen."

"That's settled then," Saetan said.

"What happens when Theran breaks Cassidy's court?" Gray asked.

"If Theran has the same misunderstanding about courts that you do, he's in for a rude awakening," Saetan said. "Except when a court is first formed, not everyone joins at the same time. People come in, people move on."

"And sometimes timing can be a delightful knife rammed up someone's ass," Daemon purred. "The moment Theran announces his intentions to make Kermilla the Queen, Cassidy can demote him to a regular escort in her First Circle and you can sign a contract to serve as First Escort. That gives her thirteen males in the First Circle. If Cassie chooses not to dismiss him, Theran has to fulfill his contract to the last minute. Next spring, she already has a court that stands, and he's left trying to build one around a Queen of questionable morals."

Gray looked at Daemon. "Did you know he would do this when you let Cassie come to Dena Nehele?"

Daemon stared at him for a long time. "If I'd known, I would have buried him in a grave that could never be found. But that's done now, and we have to let this play out as it will."

*Why?*

He looked at the three men who watched him with such predatory patience and knew the answer.

Jaenelle.

If Jaenelle thought Cassie could win against Kermilla without direct help from these men, then she could win. Would win.

In the next few months, he was going to learn everything he could from these men to make sure of it.

"When do we start?" he asked.

"Since we're all here, now would be a good time," Saetan replied.

## TERREILLE

Cassidy glanced out the window again. Gray had left very early that morning, and no one had seen him since—or knew exactly where he'd gone.

"He had to have told someone where he'd gone," she said to Talon. "Could he have told one of the Scelties? Someone we didn't think to ask?"

"Ranon received a message from Gray around midday saying that he had an appointment and would be back late this evening," Talon replied. "Cassidy . . ."

"But he didn't say *where* he would be! That's not like him, Talon. You know that."

"I'll send word through the rogue camps. Maybe he's up in the mountains somewhere."

*Why?*

After a couple of nights in her bed, was he already looking for a way to leave?

"Cassidy . . ."

She finally heard it. She'd been so preoccupied about Gray, she'd ignored the obvious. Talon had something to tell her, and he wasn't comfortable saying it.

"I made a promise a long time ago," Talon said, "and twice a year I keep that promise. It means I'll be gone for a day. Maybe two."

"Where?"

"I can't tell you. Saying more would break a long-standing trust."

If she ordered him to, he would tell her—and that would break the trust building between them.

"Can you promise me that what you do will not harm Dena Nehele or any of its people?" she asked.

He relaxed. He even smiled. "That I can promise with everything in me."

"Then we'll look forward to your return."

"Thank you, Lady."

After Talon left the room, Cassidy curled up in a window seat.

It wasn't fair to compare Gray and Jhorma, to compare a man who said he loved her with one who had wanted to list being her Consort on his credentials. It wasn't fair, but Gray's unexplained absence made her wonder if he would continue to want her now that he was emotionally healed. Being his first lover didn't mean he wanted her to be his last.

If that was the case, she would find the strength to let him go with grace. But after he was gone, would she be able to hide the heartache well enough to escape the pity of her own court?

# CHAPTER 28

## TERREILLE

Dena Nehele Queens rode the trails through the Tamanara Mountains in secret and in silence. Some had made this journey many times over many years. For others, it was the first time they had dared to give anyone this much trust.

Each of them had the list of trails to follow. Their escorts knew the exact time they had to pass the checkpoints on the trails. Miss the time, and you had a choice: turn back or die. There was no leniency or mercy in the spells that protected the mountain trails—and in this time and place, there was no mercy in the Sapphire-Jeweled Warlord Prince who created those spells year after year, generation after generation. He was the assurance that the Queens who had gathered twice a year to talk with each other were safe from the ones who had ruled.

When they reached the meeting place, they left horses and escorts behind and entered the clearing alone. Many embraced, relieved to see familiar faces again. But no one asked for a name. They never asked for a name. Even if they lived in neighboring villages and knew each other, they did not acknowledge such things, or ask about children, lovers, or parents.

Too many had been tortured to death over the years for them to leave all caution behind.

When the last Queen who chose to make the journey entered the clearing, the Sapphire shields went up around them—protective shields, sight shields, aural shields.

Witchlight and warming spells made them comfortable. They called in stools, benches, or chairs. Then, safe within the Sapphire shields that would hide them until dawn, they shared their knowledge of their land and their people.

"It was a good harvest. The best we have had in many years. There will be enough food this year for everyone. The Craft the Rose Queen called the Queen's Gift made the difference."

"Harvests were not so good in the north. The Other Queen was not as generous with her time. She wears a stronger Jewel than the Rose, but I do not think she is as skilled in her Craft—or as caring of the people."

"There was trouble in Grayhaven. Some people moved away because of the Other Queen's presence."

"I heard the Rose Queen allowed a community of landens to settle close to her home village. They are courteous and hardworking. They come to the Blood village for supplies and for social events. They show great respect for the Rose."

"Warlord Princes who have gone to the Rose's village have been impressed by the work being done, and by the feel of the village. Fear no longer creeps through the streets. Even Ferall was impressed."

"Jared Blaed has healed."

A stunned silence.

"I have heard that too. And that he is the Rose Queen's lover—by choice. He is becoming a strong leader, and it is said that he knows some very powerful men in Kaeleer."

"There is a rumor in the north that the Rose Queen will leave when the spring flowers bloom and the Other Queen will take her place and rule Dena Nehele."

"That one wants much and offers little."

"The south has not heard these rumors. There is no sign that the Rose intends to leave. Her court is strong and gathers strength around itself."

"I have heard the rumor too. Theran Grayhaven wants the Other to rule and will give her our land."

"There was some . . . strangeness . . . about the way the Rose departed from Grayhaven and ended up with the Shaladorans. It is speculated that it had something to do with the Other Queen."

"The Rose has brought a young Shaladoran Queen into her court for training. The girl is learning the Old Ways and Protocol. She is respectful and performs her duties well. And there is real affection between the girl and the Rose."

"The Other also had a young Queen as a companion for a while. Many of the Warlord Princes had strong reservations about the girl's behavior and her ability to be a good Queen. After seeing her with the Other in Grayhaven, they are of one voice—they will not tolerate her setting up a court in Dena Nehele, not even in the smallest village. They say the girl embraces too much of what was hated in the Queens who were purged by the witch storm."

"The Other chose such an undesirable Queen for a companion and yet Theran Grayhaven wants her to rule the rest of us?"

"In the Rose, Ranon has found a Queen for his people. If the Other tries to take Dena Nehele, he will fight such a change."

"Will Jared Blaed?"

Another silence.

Throughout the night they talked—and sometimes they cried. At the first whisper of dawn, the Sapphire spells began to fade, so they vanished their stools, benches, and chairs. They drew the power that had fueled the witchlight and the warming spells back into themselves and prepared for the journey out of the mountains.

As they made their way back home, they thought about the things that had been said, and they all knew one thing: the Black Widows had been right. Come spring, Dena Nehele would either embrace a hopeful beginning—or face a terrible end.

# CHAPTER 29

## KAELEER

"Gray?"

A warm hand rubbed his leg just above the knee.

"What . . . ?" Gray opened his eyes. They must have been closed because now he could see Daemon crouching in front of the chair he'd collapsed into when he walked into Daemon's study.

"Drink this," Daemon said. "It's a warm tonic. It will help put some bone back in your legs."

"Where did the old bone go?"

A pause.

Gray tried to focus on the blurry mug floating in front of him. Too much effort. He let his head fall back against the chair and stared at the ceiling. It wasn't doing anything. He liked that. A lot.

He was so damn tired. He had never ever, in the whole of his life, been this tired.

How did these men *do* this every day?

"Gray, did you remember any part of the Protocol that dealt with the First Escort arranging rest periods for the Queen and her escorts?"

"Huh?"

"Obviously not."

The dry humor in Daemon's voice told Gray he'd missed something.

"How's he doing?" Lucivar's voice. He sounded amused too. "Looking at him, I guess it's good Jaenelle doesn't have as much energy as she used to."

Gray had spent one whole morning and afternoon acting as First Escort to Jaenelle Angelline. He whimpered at the thought of her having more energy.

"It's all right." Daemon gave him a soothing pat.

"Dinner is almost ready," Lucivar said. "Apparently Mrs. Beale figured a few people would want to turn in early tonight, so dinner is being served early too."

"A good decision on her part," Daemon said. "Come on, Gray. Maybe some food will help."

Help what? He'd have to chew it, wouldn't he? What help was that?

"Gray?"

"In a minute," he murmured. "Just give me another minute."

Gray pushed himself to a sitting position, catching the blanket as it slid off his legs. He still felt tired, but he was much better for taking that minute to rest before dinner.

"Good evening." Daemon closed the book he was reading and set it on the table next to his chair.

"Guess I'm still a little groggy." Gray tried to tidy his hair by running his fingers through it. "I didn't see you there. Is it time for dinner?" He looked to one side, then the other. "Wasn't I sitting in a chair before? How did I end up on the sofa?"

"Boyo, it's closing in on midnight, and the rest of us had dinner hours ago. You're on the sofa because Lucivar and I couldn't keep you awake long enough to get you any farther. We figured you'd sleep just as well there as anyplace else we could carry you."

Gray braced his head in his hands. Weeks of studying, working, traveling to the Keep and to SaDiablo Hall for training. "I failed, didn't I?"

"You didn't remember the part about the First Escort being able to insist on rest breaks, but I figure you'll learn that Protocol fast enough for self-preservation if for nothing else. As for the rest, Lucivar and I agree that the only thing you're lacking is the finesse that comes from experience. And that you will learn by working beside your Queen."

Gray raised his head. "Really?"

Daemon smiled. "Really. In fact, I have this for you." He called in a sheet of paper and used Craft to float it over to Gray. "The High Lord wrote it out, so you can be sure the Protocol is exact for retiring a man from a dominant position in a court and giving that title—and the duties that go with it—to someone else."

He stared at the words but didn't try to read them. "When do you think Theran will tell Cassie?"

"The first day of Winsol is a week from now. Unless he's a complete bastard, he'll wait until the celebration is over and people are settling into the routine of winter days. He can't wait much longer than that to start gathering the men who will form a First Circle, but the moment he does more than try to feel out who might be interested in serving Kermilla, every Queen and Warlord Prince is going to know about it—and Cassie will hear about it. That's when *she* should make her declaration of whether she's going to stay or leave. After that, a lot depends on which Queen the other Queens and Warlord Princes are willing to have rule over their lives." Daemon stood up. "Come on. We'll warm up the food Mrs. Beale set aside for you. Then you can get a bit more sleep and be on your way in the morning." He paused. "My advice is to forget about all of this and enjoy the days of Winsol."

Gray's stomach rumbled. He got to his feet, feeling awake enough to be enthusiastic about food.

"There is one other piece of advice I could use," he said.

Daemon raised an eyebrow. "And what is that?"

"What do you buy a Sceltie for Winsol?"

# CHAPTER 30
## TERREILLE

Theran fanned out the gold marks. Twenty ten-marks. He'd rarely seen gold marks. The silver marks were easier to come by when the rogues sold game to folks who couldn't afford to buy meat from the butcher's shop. Easier to come by and not as noticeable when spent. Usually only aristos— or the twisted Queens and their First Circles—had enough income to use gold marks.

Talon had given him twenty ten-marks for his twentieth birthday—the first and only time he'd held that much spending money. It still felt like a fortune.

After deducting the expenses for the town treasury and the Grayhaven estate, he figured he would have four hundred gold marks as an annual personal income from the town's tithes. He'd need a few new clothes in the coming months and there would be the expense for the occasional evening's entertainment, but he knew how to live lean. Hell's fire, he'd been doing it his whole life. That's why he had decided to give his Lady half of that income as a special surprise.

Kermilla walked into the sitting room. "The bastard butler said you wanted to see me."

"He's not a bastard, Kermilla," Theran said. "You know it's unkind to insult a man by saying he has no father."

She rolled her eyes. "Then let's say it describes his temper and attitude if you don't want to besmirch whatever bloodlines he can claim." Then she saw the gold marks and her breath caught.

He almost reconsidered what he was going to do, but maybe her recent bitchiness was a sign of frustration. There was little society in the town and less public entertainment that she felt was worthy of her notice. And she seemed to find his efforts at lovemaking less and less enjoyable—so much so, he'd stopped asking for sex and decided to wait for her invitation.

"What's that?" she asked, eyeing the gold marks.

He held them out. "This is for you."

She took the fanned marks and counted them twice. "Two hundred gold marks? Theran, where did you get this?"

He shrugged and smiled, warmly pleased by the light in her eyes. "I know there hasn't been much money and the income hasn't arrived from your village's tithes. Winsol starts in three days, and I thought you'd enjoy doing a bit of shopping."

She'd been hinting hard enough that the failure of her Steward to send the income owed to her was making it impossible for her to buy any gifts for her family or to select the expected gifts for her Steward, Master of the Guard, and Consort—or to buy anything for him.

The gift itself wasn't important. It was the fact that Kermilla wanted to give him one. He hadn't had a gift from a woman since he'd left his mother when he was seven years old.

"Oh, Theran!"

Kermilla threw her arms around him and kissed him with enough heat to fire his blood. Before he could get another good taste of her, she backed away, wagging a finger at him while she smiled playfully.

"That's for later," she said. "Now I have to see what's left in the shops."

"Don't spend it all in one place," he said, trying to keep his voice light but hoping she heard the warning to spend carefully.

"Silly man," she said as she danced out of the parlor.

A few minutes later, he looked out a window and saw her heading down the drive in the pony cart with one of the stable lads as her driver. He also saw a man in a messenger's livery walking up the drive. Not a messenger from the town. One of them would have come on horseback. This man must have ridden the Winds and arrived at the landing web just beyond Grayhaven's gates.

He started to go to his study, then turned and headed for the front door. Any message coming here was most likely for him anyway. No point having Julien track him down when he could be on hand.

He timed it so it looked like he was passing through the entranceway on his way to the stairs when Julien opened the door and took the message.

The messenger's tone sounded courteous, but there was clearly something on the man's mind. Theran saw hot anger in the eyes that stared at him before Julien shut the door and handed him the wax-sealed heavy paper.

Theran broke the seal and opened the message—and wished he'd waited until he'd reached the privacy of his study.

"Trouble?" Julien asked.

He shook his head. "Already taken care of."

"I know what that phrase means—a bitch got buried. Will anyone weep?"

The coldness of Julien's words stung him.

He went into his study and locked the door. Just a physical lock, just an indication he wanted no company and no one disturbing him.

He read the words again and again. As he sat there through the morning, staring at letters and reports and seeing nothing, he was glad he'd given Kermilla the gold marks—glad she would find some sweetness in what would be a bitter day.


Kermilla rode back through the Grayhaven gates, her color high with the pleasure of a long morning in the shops. She glanced at the basket of packages in the back of the pony cart and felt a prick of guilt, which was easily dismissed. It wasn't her fault. She hadn't had anything new in weeks, months, *forever*. So she'd gotten a bit extravagant buying things for herself—like that gorgeous red dress that cost ninety gold marks.

Of the two hundred gold marks Theran had given her that morning, she had ten left. She'd meant to be careful, she really had, but it felt so *good* to have money again that she couldn't stop herself from buying all the things she'd been denied.

She'd regained some control at the end when she realized she had to come back with some packages that were gifts for other people—things she could let Theran see. He didn't have to know that she'd grabbed a few things off the shelves of a shop an aristo wouldn't normally enter and had put those gifts into the boxes of the things she'd bought for herself in the only aristo merchant shop left in the whole dung-heap town. If he noticed that the quality of the goods didn't match the implied quality of the box, he would blame the merchant.

She'd known he was being stingy and had been holding back on giving her any money. But she'd worn him down until he finally acknowledged that she deserved a Queen's due—and a Queen's income.

Theran was like her father in that way. *He'd* grumped and grumbled about her spending, had asked her—almost begged her sometimes—to be less extravagant, but he always ended up giving her the marks she needed to pay for the clothes or the entertainments that were vital to bringing herself to the notice of the men who had enough reputation and potential to form a court around her and provide her with a place to rule that would, in turn, provide her with the income she deserved.

Theran wouldn't be happy that she'd spent all the marks he'd given her, but she'd wiggle more out of him.

"Good afternoon, Julien." She kept her tone frigidly polite.

"I trust you had a pleasant outing," he replied.

No matter how cold she made her voice, the damn butler would match it—and then add just a little more ice.

"Prince Theran is in his study," Julian said. "He asked that you join him there when you returned."

She handed him the basket of packages. "Take these up to my room, if that won't interfere too much with your other duties."

He tipped his head in a bow that was less than he should have given her.

She knocked on the door and felt a quiver of uneasiness when she heard the *click* of the lock turning before the door opened.

Theran stood halfway between his desk and the door, as if he couldn't decide where he was supposed to be.

"You enjoyed yourself?" he asked.

She rushed up to him and gave him an enthusiastic hug. "I did. And I was pleased to see so many people doing a little something to make the town look festive for Winsol." She played with a button on his shirt, looked up at him through her lashes, and gave him the smile that always made men sigh indulgently before doing what she wanted. "But I was a *little* bit careless because everything looked so wonderful." She caught her lower lip between her teeth. "So I'm going to need more money in order to finish my shopping for Winsol."

She saw it in his eyes, felt it in the way he seemed to step away from her without actually moving. A bad miscalculation on her part. She should have remembered that he wasn't used to aristo measurements of spending. A trifling expense to her was an almost unthinkable extravagance to him.

"I'm sorry, Kermilla." Now he did step back. "I gave you everything that could be spared from the tithes and the estate. I'm sorry it wasn't enough."

"Oh, Theran." She grasped his hands. "I'm the one who's sorry. I see this grand house, and I forget that . . ." No, that wasn't the right way to regain the ground she'd just lost.

"It doesn't matter."

*Why not?* That he gave up without anger or arguing troubled her.

"I need to talk to you about something else." He led her over to the stuffed chair and footstool that were tucked on one side of the room. Once she was settled in the chair, he sat on the footstool.

"What is it? What's wrong?" Something bad. She could tell that much.

"It's about your friend Correne."

"Theran, I haven't even written to her lately, so if she's making remarks about Cassidy—"

"She's dead, Kermilla. She enraged a Warlord Prince who was visiting friends for Winsol and he killed her, right on the main street in full view of half the village."

She couldn't think, couldn't breathe. "Why?"

Theran took her hands. The warmth of his hands showed her how cold she'd become, chilled to the bone by his words.

"She wasn't liked or trusted by the Warlord Princes who lived near her village," Theran said. "Whatever leash had kept some of her behavior under control disappeared after her visit here. She'd been shopping and stole some items. Didn't even try to be subtle about it. A boy who was in the shop with his older brothers saw her and told the merchant, who then reported her to the village guards. She claimed that the merchant should give her those things as 'gifts' because she was a Queen." He snorted softly. "Which just proved she'd been tainted by the bitches who had ruled here before."

She didn't realize she'd been whimpering until he made soothing noises.

"I'm sorry, Kermilla, but it's important that you know what this girl was like. You have to understand that befriending her and being influenced by her the way you were is going to make it harder for the Warlord Princes and Queens to trust you. They aren't going to tolerate having that kind of Queen rule in Dena Nehele. Not again."

She didn't speak. Couldn't speak.

"She had to reveal everything she had taken. Because of her age, the humiliation was deemed sufficient punishment. But the next day, she attacked the boy when he was out with friends . . ." Theran closed his eyes. When he opened them, they were filled with grief. "The village council didn't give me the details. I can find out if you need to know. But they called in Healers from neighboring villages to help the village Healer. Even with that much skill, not all of what she did to the boy can be healed. He acted with honor—and he'll never be the same because of what she did."

*What kind of people are they to kill a Queen over some stupid boy?*

"The Warlord Prince who was in the village hunted Correne down and executed her on the main street."

She swallowed against the sickness clogging her throat. "What did they do to him? What did they do to the bastard who killed a Queen?"

He gave her a queer look. "Nothing. He did the same thing he'd been doing his whole life—eliminating an enemy who had no honor."

She pulled her hands out of his. "I don't feel well. I'm going up to my room to rest."

"Of course." He stood up and held out a hand.

She didn't want to touch him. Wasn't sure she could stand to touch him.

She'd known the males here could be brutal. After all, *every* Warlord Prince was brutal. Maybe she hadn't wanted to see that Theran wasn't any different from the rest of them.

She looked into his eyes and saw grief for the boy, who was still alive, and no regret—none at all—for Correne's death. Did she really want to live among these people? Could she survive among these people?

She stood up, avoiding his hand. Somehow, that didn't surprise him.

He opened the door for her. She walked out of the study.

Theran's dismissal of Correne's death troubled her, even scared her— but it didn't scare her half as much as seeing the dark pleasure in Julien's eyes and knowing that pleasure was there because he'd heard the news.

# CHAPTER 31

## TERREILLE

Cassidy hurried into the meeting room. Gray was finally home, and she wasn't sure if she was relieved or angry. A hasty message saying he'd been delayed but would be home before Winsol hadn't soothed her, not when he'd been so vague about these required meetings with the High Lord—and not when Jaenelle's response to her inquiries was a gently worded message that still translated to "It's none of your business, Cassie."

"Gray, are you all right—"

He grabbed her, twirled her, hugged her breathless—then kissed her in a way that made her dizzy and more than a little self-conscious since her whole First Circle was watching them.

"Sorry I've been gone so long." Gray's green eyes blazed with happy excitement, and he didn't look sorry at all. "I asked Daemon for a favor, and then he wanted me to wait and bring along a special delivery for you. I couldn't say no."

"Gray, stop bouncing," Ranon said.

"Sorry." Gray grinned. "I'm just glad to be home. The SaDiablos are wonderful people, but they're exhausting to be around for any length of time."

"Try spending four months with them," Cassidy muttered.

Gray hooted.

"When my boys get like this, I take them to the park and make them run around until they're almost too tired to walk home," Shaddo said. "Think that would work with him?"

"No." Gray looked around the room—and then looked under the table. "Where are Vae and Khollie?"

"Outside," Shira said.

He shrugged out of his coat. "Good. Ranon, would you put an Opal shield around the room and a lock on the door?"

Cassidy felt tension ripple through the room. "Is there a reason for this, Gray?"

"I don't want Vae and Khollie joining us right now," he replied.

At least he was starting to settle down, Cassidy thought as everyone gathered around the table.

"I did some shopping while I was in Kaeleer," Gray said.

Cassidy frowned. "I thought we agreed that we would buy our gifts from local shops, and anything we bought that came from Kaeleer we would purchase at Merchants."

"We did agree, but there were some things we wouldn't be able to make in time. Not this year, anyway." Gray ran a hand down her arm, silently asking her to understand. "I asked Daemon to take me to Scelt. We spent a day in Maghre. I met Lady Fiona and Shadow, the Sceltie Warlord who is her inspiration for the Tracker and Shadow books. I know he's the inspiration because he told me. Several times. We also spent some of the afternoon with Lord Khardeen. And I bought some things."

An odd assortment of toys and other things appeared on the table.

"I got these brushes for Lizzie, Wynne, and Keely. See? Their names are etched into the wood. And these," Gray brushed a finger over the top of several small containers, "have nail paint that can be used safely on Sceltie nails as well as girl nails."

"Why would dogs want painted nails?" Archerr asked.

"They don't," Gray replied. "But apparently Scelties who live with young girls end up with painted nails, and this is the only nail paint that should be used."

Shira muffled a snort and said on a distaff thread, *I guess that means Wynne and Keely will have pretty toenails.*

Cassidy pressed her lips together and didn't answer.

"These braided ropes are good for playing tug or toss or chase—with or without humans," Gray continued. "And these rawhide strips are for chewing. We'll be able to figure out how to make these here, but for now I bought plenty for everyone."

Archerr tapped one of the bright-colored balls on the table. "These things are as big as the dogs."

"But lightweight," Gray said. "These are the kinds of toys folks in Scelt buy for the Scelties."

"And this?" Shaddo picked up a stuffed baby bunny.

"I thought you might like to give that to Darcy for Winsol," Gray said. "That way he'll have a pet Soli will let him keep."

Shaddo laughed. "Yeah, they had this 'discussion' two or three times a week over the summer. He'd bring home a bunny or some other small thing, wanting to keep it as a cuddly, and she couldn't find a way to explain that the bunny he wanted to keep as a pet would grow up into the rabbit he'd catch for dinner. This just might satisfy both of them. Thanks, Gray."

"That's why I bought a variety of things," Gray said. "Everyone living with a Sceltie will have a gift that's appropriate so they won't feel left out of the celebrations. We choose what we want, and the rest goes to Merchants as stock for future gifts or treats."

"Well done, Gray," Powell said, looking bemused.

Gray called in a stuffed toy and held it out to Ranon. "I thought Khollie would like this."

A lamb about half the size of the Sceltie. Big enough to cuddle with but small enough that Khollie could carry it around with him.

Khollie, who was still afraid to be alone. Who had been so terrified to go outside one day that he ended up peeing on the floor and then hid in a corner and whined all day until Ranon came home.

Gray shifted, still holding the toy that Ranon hadn't taken. "Lambie is stuffed with rags, so he can have a bath whenever he needs one. Might need some Craft to help the insides dry, but . . ."

Cassidy saw Ranon's throat work, saw his dark eyes fill with tears. A moment later, he was holding on to Gray, his eyes squeezed tight.

She glanced at Shira. A mistake. They both looked away, trying not to blubber. Didn't help to see Powell knuckling away a tear.

"Thank you," Ranon said hoarsely, finally stepping back. Gently holding the toy, he turned and offered it to Shira, who took it and vanished it.

"Why don't you vanish those toys and things, Gray," Talon said. "You and Shaddo should talk to the other folks so they can pick out what they'd like."

"All right." Gray vanished the Sceltie gifts, then rubbed his hands. "That was my shopping. I do have some crates to deliver to Merchants. But these are to be opened by Cassie, and she is to do with the contents as she pleases."

He called in several crates and set them near the wall. He pointed to the crate on the right. "That one first."

"Let me give you a hand with that, Cassie," Archerr said. He opened the crate and set the lid aside.

Cassidy lifted the first item. They were individually wrapped in heavy brown paper but not sealed. She set it on the table and opened the brown paper.

A book with a fine leather cover. The kind of expensive book that was meant for a family library. The kind that was meant to be handled and read by generations.

She opened it to the title page and gasped. "It's Jared's account of the journey he made with Lia. I asked Prince Sadi to have a couple of copies made so the story could be shared without risking the original. I never expected him to do *this*."

"It's beautifully made," Powell said.

Gray poked around in the crate. "Cassie, there must be a dozen of these leather-bound volumes in here. Maybe more."

Enough for the Grayhaven family and her First Circle. And one for her. She was certain of it.

Ignoring their stunned protests, which lasted only until each man held a book, she passed out the leather-bound volumes. She put two in front of Talon. *Would you see that one of these is delivered to Prince Grayhaven?*

Talon studied her for a moment. *I will.*

After giving Ranon his copy, there were two left—one for her and one for Gray.

Wondering if there were more surprises, she watched Gray and Archerr open the next crate.

More copies of Jared's account, but these had an ordinary binding.

Gray opened the wax-sealed note resting on the books in the last crate. "Daemon says these books are a gift to be distributed to whomever Cassie wishes or to be used in the loaning libraries. More copies of Jared's account were printed, but those will be sold through Merchants, along with other copies of these books." He frowned as he vanished the note and picked up two of the books. "He didn't mention any of this."

"What are those?" Cassidy asked, peering over Gray's shoulder.

"More books, but . . ."

Powell yelped and grabbed a book. Then grabbed another. "How did he find these?"

"What?" several men asked.

"I've heard of these authors, but their work was destroyed when the tainted Queens first took control of Dena Nehele," Powell said. "There might be a few copies of their books hidden in family libraries, but no one has read their stories in a couple of centuries at least."

"Maybe someone sent copies of those books to the Keep so they wouldn't be completely destroyed or forgotten," Cassidy said.

A dozen copies of a dozen books—including two novels by Shalador authors Ranon had never heard of. Gray insisted that she have a full set of the books for the Residence's library and that the loaning library in Eyota be given a full set. Everyone agreed that Gray and Powell could decide what to do with the rest of the copies later.

*Cassidy?* Reyhana's call was followed by tapping on the door a moment later. *Maydra says dinner is almost ready, and Dryden said to remind you that we have drumming tonight.*

*We'll be out in a few minutes,* Cassidy replied. She wanted a few minutes alone to regain her balance. Her parents and brother were joining her for Winsol here in Eyota. She still had some shopping to do, as well as some social events to attend as the Queen before she could be a daughter for a few days.

"Is there anything more?" she asked.

"Nothing that needs your attention," Gray replied.

She considered the phrasing and was fairly certain she'd just been asked to leave.

"Come on, Shira," she said. "We have drumming tonight, so Maydra is going to serve dinner in a few minutes."

"I should—" Shaddo jerked, then gave Gray a sharp look.

"This won't take long," Gray said, smiling at Cassidy.

Ranon released the Opal lock on the door, and Cassidy and Shira left the room.

"That man has been spending too much time with Jaenelle's First Circle," Cassidy muttered. "He's starting to sound like them."

"Is that bad?" Shira asked as they walked up to their rooms.

"You couldn't budge those men with a sledgehammer once they'd set their minds to something."

Shira laughed. *Foolish woman.*

Going into her room, Cassidy sat on the bed and brushed a finger over the leather cover of the book. *Jared and Lia when they were young.* Before their world had turned dark and terrible and bloody. She had never found any journals at Grayhaven from Lia's younger years. Maybe the woman hadn't started keeping a journal until she was a little older.

And maybe this would give her a glimpse of the young Queen who, in the last months of her life, had left behind the clues that led to the treasure Cassidy had found.

She opened the book, then closed it and put it on the bedside table. There was always a quiet afternoon or two during Winsol. That was family tradition. She would save the book for one of those days.

Gray waited until Ranon restored the Opal lock on the room. Then he faced the men who formed the First Circle. "A few months ago, Theran told me straight out he intended to break the court and set up Kermilla as the Queen of Dena Nehele."

"When the sun shines in Hell," Archerr snarled. "I've already had my fill of *that* bitch."

"Since then, I've been going up to the Keep once a week to study with the High Lord, and sometimes Daemon and Lucivar as well. They gave me the training needed to stand as a Queen's First Escort. This was the last time. By their standards, I'm qualified to serve in a court."

Silence. Then Talon snorted. "If you meet their standards, no one here is going to dispute your credentials."

The rest of the men nodded.

"I was also given this." He called in the paper and set in on the table in front of Powell and Talon.

"Mother Night," Powell said after reading it through twice. "I didn't know anyone could write something so devastatingly courteous."

"Who did write this?" Talon asked.

"The High Lord. Daemon said Saetan was very exact about the Protocol used to demote a member of the court for failure to fulfill his duties."

"This holds Theran to his contract with the court, but it also strips him of the title of First Escort and ends his status as part of the Queen's Triangle." Powell looked at Gray. "The moment you sign a contract with Cassie, the court stands, with or without Theran."

"Without Theran," Gray said quietly. "No matter what else happens, the court will stand without Theran."

He'd had plenty of time to think about that on the way home. He still loved his cousin, still cared about the man. But he wouldn't want a Warlord Prince who couldn't be loyal anywhere near his Queen.

"It pains me to say it, but I agree," Talon said.

"What now?" Ranon asked.

"I was told we should put this aside and enjoy Winsol," Gray said. "I think that's what we should do."

"Any of you who want to visit family, we'll work out a way to give you a few days' leave," Talon said.

Yes, they would put it aside and enjoy Winsol, Gray thought as he went upstairs to wash up for dinner. Men like Shaddo would savor the days with their children. Others would spend a few days with brothers or sisters or parents—the people they had seen only during hurried, secret visits for so many years.

They would visit them now, openly—perhaps for the last time.

That was the truth behind Talon's words—the acknowledgment that, come spring, not all of them would walk away from the killing fields.

# CHAPTER 32

## TERREILLE

Theran waited in the front hall for Kermilla. It would have looked, and felt, less clumsy if he'd waited in his study, but he wasn't sure she would seek him out, and he didn't want to miss this chance to see her one last time.

He'd known this was coming, had seen it in her eyes after he'd told her about Correne's death. The males in Dena Nehele weren't sufficiently civilized for a vivacious young woman like Kermilla, and Correne's savage execution made her realize she wasn't as safe here as she'd thought. Being a Queen had never saved any witch from a Warlord Prince's knife if her actions snapped the leash that held back a formidable temper. Without the security of a court or the presence of more than one man she could trust with her life, leaving was the prudent thing for her to do.

But, Hell's fire, it hurt that she was leaving the day before Winsol began. Thirteen days of celebration that honored the Darkness; honored Witch, the living myth; celebrated the longest night of the year; and marked the last days of the old year.

Every aristo family still living in the town had invited him and Kermilla to parties or dinners or outings of one kind or another. Nothing overly sophisticated about any of those activities, he supposed, but he'd been looking forward to all of it—and would still have to attend out of duty, if not for pleasure.

Kermilla came down the stairs, hesitating on the last step when she saw him. He walked up to her, almost eye to eye with her since the step gave her a few added inches.

"You're ready to go?" he asked, taking her hands in his.

"Yes." She tried, but she couldn't manage her usual flirtatious smile. "I should have told you sooner that I was needed back in Dharo. I thought . . ." Her voice trailed off.

*I guess being with me isn't enticement enough for you to stay.* The thought saddened him. "I have something for you." It was tempting to add "It's not much," but he was afraid she would agree with him, despite how much he'd paid for the gift.

He called in the box and gave it to her.

The excited light in her eyes when she took the box faded when she opened it.

He'd been right. Kermilla didn't think much of his gift. There was only one good jeweler left in Grayhaven. He'd been honest with the man about how many gold marks he could spend, and he'd thought the delicate silver bracelet was as fine a piece as any he'd seen in Lia's jewelry box—the old box Cassidy had found that had contained the gifts Lia had received from her husband and children.

"Thank you." Kermilla closed the box and vanished it.

Not even good enough to put on so he could see her wearing it before she left. Not even good enough for that.

The front door opened. Julien stood in the doorway, letting fresh cold air fill the entrance.

"The carriage is out front, if Lady Kermilla is ready to go to the Coach station," Julien said. When Theran didn't move, he came in and closed the door.

"It was a lovely visit," Kermilla said. She couldn't quite make the words sound sincere.

"I'm glad you were here," Theran said. "I'll miss you."

He waited, still blocking the steps.

She gave him a look that was polite but a trifle annoyed. "I have to get to the station. It's a long journey, and there will be a lot to do when I get home."

He hesitated a moment longer, then stepped aside. He escorted her out to the carriage and watched until she passed through the gates of the estate.

"Would you like some coffee brought to your study?" Julien asked.

"Yes, thank you." He could occupy himself with paperwork. There was always plenty of paperwork.

Once he was inside the room, he looked around carefully.

Nothing out of place. Nothing added.

He had hoped, but it appeared that had been foolish.

Despite what she'd hinted, despite what she'd told him, apparently none of the gold marks she'd spent had been on a gift for him.

## KAELEER

Kermilla huddled in the back of the horse-drawn cab. Damn driver hadn't even offered her a lap rug to ease the chill inside the cab, let alone the spell-warmed lap rug he *should* have offered the Queen who ruled his village. He hadn't put a warming spell on the inside of the cab, either, which he also should have done. She could create the warming spell herself, but that wasn't the point. A Queen shouldn't have to do menial spells when there were others around to tend to her needs.

And that was a lesson this particular driver was going to learn very soon.

Having made that decision, she stared out the cab's window.

Snow. Big, fluffy flakes of snow. Wasn't that festive? Wasn't that a lovely way to return to sheep-shit Bhak?

Thank the Darkness she had a few dresses that would be suitable for the Winsol celebrations, including the red dress she'd bought yesterday. It wasn't the quality she was accustomed to, but people would be impressed that she'd lowered her standards in order to be a gracious guest and buy some dresses in Dena Nehele.

Her court would have to spread the word of her return quickly so invitations that might have been discarded in her absence could be sent again.

And if all the invitations didn't make it out, some families would be honored by her presence and the others not only would feel the social sting of their error, they also would feel a sting in their income when she, as their Queen, made a few adjustments to the tithes.

Why had she wasted so much time in Dena Nehele? Why had she wasted herself on *those* people? They wouldn't have anything resembling polite society in years, if ever. And the men! Even a standard five-year contract would have been too long to survive among them.

Could she have survived five years among them? Or would one of those Warlord Princes have honed his knife on her bones over something that should have been overlooked in the first place?

She would miss Theran. He'd made her feel special in a way no one else ever had. She would miss him for that.

She called in the jeweler's box and studied the silver bracelet. Then she vanished it again and sighed. A trinket gift that no one would notice—unless they noticed its lack of quality. How could a man live in a place like the Grayhaven mansion and not understand the difference between a gift of quality and a trinket gift?

The driver pulled up at the Queen's house. The private side, *her* side, was completely dark, including the globes that should have lit the front door. On the side reserved for the business of the court, light shone from the window of the Steward's office, and globes of witchlight lit the public door.

The driver handed her down and drove off without a courteous word or a backward glance. At least the bastard had known better than to ask her to pay a fare.

Despite the lack of welcome, she tried the private door first. Her key wouldn't open the lock, and the shields permeating the door and walls kept her from using Craft to pass through the wood.

Having no choice, Kermilla stomped to the public door of her house and pounded on it. Hell's fire! There were lights in the windows, so *someone* should be around to answer the door. It wasn't that late.

The door finally opened. A stranger stared at her. "May I help you, Lady?"

"Who are you?" she demanded.

"I'm the butler."

"What happened to the other one?" She couldn't remember his name.

"He resigned."

She took a step forward. He didn't step back. "Don't you know who I am?"

"No, Lady. You have not yet presented a card."

Stung, she blinked snowflakes out of her eyes. "I'm Kermilla. The Queen of Bhak. This is my house."

He studied her much too long before stepping back. "In that case, if you would like to step inside, I'll inform the Steward that you're here."

"Never mind that," she said, storming past him. "I'll speak with him later. Right now I want to go up to my suite and clean up. Have the cook come to me so I can tell her what I want for dinner."

"I can't do that."

She stopped short when a shield came up in front of her, effectively blocking all access to any of the rooms. She whirled to face him.

"What's your name?"

"Butler will do."

Not an answer. Before she could give him a blast of temper, she took a good look at him.

A Purple Dusk Prince. His caste didn't outrank hers, but his Jewels did.

Footsteps along another hallway. Then Gallard turned the corner and stopped.

"Lady Kermilla! We didn't expect you," Gallard said.

"What in the name of Hell is going on?" Kermilla shouted. "Why is this *male* refusing to let me into my own house?"

"Ah." Gallard looked uncomfortable. "Come into my office. There's a lovely fire in there. So comforting on a cold evening such as this. Butler? Could you arrange for another setting?"

Butler tipped his head. "I'll also inform Housekeeper that a guest room will be needed this evening."

"Thank you."

"Guest room?" Kermilla shrieked. "I want—"

"Kermilla, *please.*"

She saw it in Gallard's eyes. Nerves. Maybe even fear. Which was why she didn't say anything when the shield dropped and Gallard took her arm and led her into his office.

"There's beef stew tonight," Gallard said. When they reached the small dining table that was against one wall of his office, he released her arm. "Cook added a different spice, I think. Gives the stew a bit of heat."

"Who is that man?" Kermilla shrugged out of her coat and tossed it toward a chair.

Gallard picked up the coat where it had fallen on the floor and carefully laid it over the chair's back. "He's the butler. Considering who he reports to, it is in our best interest to maintain as amiable a relationship with him as possible."

"Who does he report to?"

"Lady Sabrina's Steward."

"Why?"

A tapping on the door. Butler walked in with a tray. He set another bowl of stew on the table, another cup and saucer, and a small plate of fruit and cheese.

Kermilla sniffed. At least Theran *tried* to set a better table. "I haven't decided if I want that for dinner."

"That's what there is," Butler replied. "If you don't want it, do without."

Too shocked to respond, she watched him leave the room.

"Sit down, Kermilla," Gallard said. "The food isn't fancy, but it is good."

She sat—and tried to ignore his gusty sigh of relief as he settled the napkin on his lap and continued his meal.

Gallard ate as if he feared an interruption would take him away from the food. She ate because she was hungry. She didn't *say* anything, but she made sure he knew she considered the meal an insult.

"That man is intolerable," Kermilla said when Gallard poured coffee for both of them. "He has to be dismissed."

"Can you afford to replace him?" Gallard asked. "He serves the Territory Queen, and his wages, along with the housekeeper, the cook, the maid, and the footman, come from her. If you dismiss any of these people, you will not get a replacement unless you can pay that person's wages. And I can tell you right now, anyone who agrees to work here will want their wages in advance."

"Fine. Then we'll pay for respectful servants."

"With what?"

"The tithes, of course!"

"There are no tithes."

She bobbled her cup and almost spilled the coffee.

Gallard's sadness spread over her like a smothering blanket.

"The court is beggared, Kermilla. I apologize for the criticism, but you spent so extravagantly when you first took over rule of Bhak and Woolskin that we haven't been able to pay all the debts."

Kermilla swayed in her seat. "Then raise the tithes. Squeeze a little more out of the damn landens."

Gallard dabbed his mouth with a napkin. "When you demanded that I raise the summer tithes in order to provide you with money you needed during your visit, I obeyed and used some of the extra income to pay down your debts. However, when I went to pay the guards their quarterly income, I discovered the village treasury had been drained. The men were given half their wages, and they all began to fall into debt because they couldn't pay their bills. You demanded more money. I raised the tithes again. When told what they would be required to pay for the autumn tithes, the landens refused to harvest their crops. They let them rot in the fields. They said that since their children were going to starve anyway on the little that was left, they saw no reason to work and sweat in order to feed you."

"How dare they!"

"We tried to keep things contained, but you didn't answer my letters, and you ignored my pleas for your return. Then Lady Darlena and Lady Sabrina's Stewards showed up to review the accounts and to personally receive the Queens' shares of the autumn tithes. They were almost buried under the complaints, pleas, and accusations from both villages."

"That's done," Kermilla said crossly. "I'm back now, and I'll fix things with the mighty Queens. What can you give me for income now?"

"There's nothing."

"Of course there's something. Household funds. *Something.*"

"There's nothing."

"Don't you have—"

He shook his head too quickly. Resentment bubbled up inside her.

"I'll see Sabrina tomorrow and fix this," she said tightly.

"Tomorrow is the first day of Winsol," Gallard said. "Except for emergencies, the Queen doesn't grant audiences during Winsol."

"This *is* an emergency!"

"No, my dear, it is not. But it is a smear on our reputations that we must all work to overcome. Everything has a price. We acted imprudently, and now we must pay the consequences."

It wasn't a smear on *her* reputation. Just because her First Circle hadn't had balls enough to keep things under control didn't mean *she* should bear the blame.

"How soon can the servants open up my side of the house?"

"You would have to discuss that with Lady Sabrina or her Steward. He closed that side of the house since it wasn't in use."

She wasn't getting anywhere with him. He wasn't saying the things he should be saying. "Where is Jhorma?"

"Jhorma is celebrating Winsol elsewhere this year," Gallard said. "Since none of us are from Bhak, everyone else is spending Winsol in their home villages. I elected to stay and catch up on paperwork—and to maintain the court's presence in the village. After darkest night, the Master of the Guard will return, and I'll go home for a visit."

"And what am I supposed to do? My house is closed up, my court is scattered, and no one seems to care that I came back to celebrate the most important holiday with my people!"

"We didn't know you were returning. Frankly, Kermilla, we had no reason to believe you would return to Bhak."

"Why wouldn't I return? I rule here."

*For now.*

She heard the unspoken warning. "I've been traveling most of the day, and I'm tired. I'd like to go to my room now. Please arrange to have a carriage for me first thing tomorrow morning to take me to the landing web. I want to talk to Sabrina before she becomes so immersed in frivolity that she forgets her duties as a Queen."

Gallard sucked in a breath, but in the end he escorted her to the guest room and said nothing.

She would talk to Sabrina and get this mess straightened out so that she could enjoy some of Winsol. And she would go home for a few days. She needed to be around people who thought she was wonderful, and she could count on her father to give her enough marks to tide her over.

# CHAPTER 33

## KAELEER

Kermilla stood at the parlor window in her parents' house and watched the snow fall. It was a roomy house, the kind typically owned by a couple who came from secondary branches of aristo families and wanted to maintain the social connections that would be an asset to their children.

Social connections were of no use to her right now. At least, not until she managed to get her father alone and talked him into giving her some help.

She should have left early on the first day of Winsol as she'd intended to do. But she'd wrangled with that thrice-damned butler in order to get access to her clothes—which was insulting beyond words—and *then* discovered most of the new jewelry and half the new clothes she'd bought before going to Dena Nehele were *gone*. Not stolen by the servants, as she'd first suspected. No, something even worse. The jewelry that hadn't been paid for yet had been returned to the jewelers. The dresses and formal gowns that hadn't been worn had been sent to shops in other Provinces to be sold in order to pay for the clothes she *had* worn.

Thank the Darkness she'd had two trunks of autumn and winter clothes sent to her in Dena Nehele. The damn nosy Stewards hadn't found *those* clothes and they never would.

By the time she'd gotten that sorted out and taken a Coach to Sabrina's residence, the Queen of Dharo was gone and her thrice-damned Steward refused to reveal her location, even when Kermilla emphasized several times that this was an emergency.

The Steward, of course, offered to hear her out.

The man had no balls, no sex, and no heart. He listened calmly, with no sign of interest or concern. He didn't respond to flirting or to pouts or any other tool that usually proved useful when dealing with men.

He listened. Then he told her what financial arrangements Lady Sabrina had authorized for Kermilla and her court.

The private side of the Queen's house in Bhak would be reopened for Kermilla's use. Sabrina would pay for the general maintenance of that house and its stables until spring. That included the wages for the butler, housekeeper, cook, maid, footman, coachman, and stable lad. No additional staff, not even restoring Kermilla's personal maid. Food for the Queen and the First Circle who were in residence, as well as for the servants, would also be paid for by the Territory Queen. Kermilla would be responsible for the expense of any entertainment held at the house.

Income? Had Lady Kermilla discussed the situation in Bhak and Woolskin with her own Steward? Yes? Then the Lady was aware that there was no income available for her use since the winter tithes had gone into paying down the remaining debts.

Insulting, insufferable man, treating her like a child who had overspent her allowance! Yes, just like that but never *ever* acknowledging that the allowance hadn't been adequate to begin with!

She'd gotten no satisfaction from Sabrina's Steward beyond him giving her an appointment to meet with Dharo's Queen the day after Winsol ended.

It had been too humiliating to go back to the house in Bhak. If she summoned her court to return, what would she do with them? She couldn't throw any parties or dinners, couldn't afford tickets to a play or a concert or any other kind of entertainment. And it occurred to her that Sabrina didn't know yet that her First Circle was short a man, and having the other men scattered would make that fact less obvious.

So she returned to Bhak long enough to pack up all her clothes, then came here to her parents' house to "enjoy the holiday as a daughter instead of a Queen."

Her father was delighted to see her. Her mother was pleased too, but Kermilla sensed a reservation there. And her brother and sister hadn't made any accommodation to spend time with her, as they should have since she was a Queen.

The parlor door opened and her father walked in. Then he saw her, realized they were alone, and started to back out.

"Father, wait." Kermilla rushed over to him, grabbed his hand, and pulled him into the room. "I've wanted to talk to you."

"Maybe we should wait for your mother."

"Don't be silly." She tugged him over to a chair, then sat on the footstool in front of him. "I wanted to talk to *you*."

He sighed, as if he knew what she wanted to talk about. But there was sadness in his eyes and more than a little worry.

"What's on your mind, sweets?" he asked.

"I need some help. Just a little," she added quickly when he shook his head. "There was a misunderstanding about the court expenses and—"

"I can't help, Kermilla. I'm sorry, sweets, but I can't."

"It's not that much," she coaxed, sure she could wear him down. He had never failed her before. Ever.

"I can't."

"But you don't even know how much."

"How much doesn't matter," he said with a thread of temper that sounded a little like fear. "When your mother found out about all the debts I'd managed to hide from her, all the debts weighing on the family now for the clothes and things you needed while you were in training . . ." He clasped his hands together tight enough to turn the knuckles white. "She told me that if I gave you so much as a silver mark without her consent she'll divorce me, and the only things I'll take from the marriage are my personal belongings and all of your debts." Now he clasped her hands. "I've got to think of your brother and sister now, sweets. They did without plenty of things these past few years because you needed so much to get established. But you are established now, ruling a village and having a Queen's income."

"And a Queen's expenses," she pouted.

He released her hands. "Then you need to talk to your Steward about court expenses, or talk to a man of business about investing some of your income to give you some profit."

"That's all well and good once the spring tithes come in, but I need something now!" Kermilla said.

"But the winter tithes were paid not more than a few days ago," he protested. "What happened to that income?"

"A misunderstanding between my Steward and Sabrina's. It will be straightened out as soon as I talk to her after Winsol, but for now I need two or three hundred gold marks to tide me—"

Shock in his eyes. Panic as the front door opened. He bolted out of the chair and almost knocked her over in his haste to get out of the room.

She heard her mother's voice—and her father's. Too low to hear the words, but she recognized the tone.

A minute later, her mother walked into the room and stood near the chair. Kermilla stood up, lifting her chin in a subtle challenge. After all, her mother might wear Summer-sky too, but she was just a witch, not a Queen.

Her mother studied her for a long moment. Too long. "We've given you all the financial help we can. It's time for you to take responsibility for yourself, especially when you've taken responsibility for so many other people's lives now. I love you, Kermilla, and I love your father. But I will divorce him if that's what I have to do to protect your brother and sister's future. I will do that."

"You won't help me at all?" Kermilla asked.

Her mother sighed. "Financially? No. There's nothing left to give, and there won't be for several more years." She paused. "Are you going to stay with us through the days of Winsol?"

Kermilla nodded.

"Good," her mother said. "It would have hurt your father terribly if you only came to see him in order to get money."

### TERREILLE

Cassidy came downstairs and paused, listening. Hearing nothing in the rooms usually occupied by the court, she went along to the kitchen, where the servants were most likely to gather at this hour for a cup of tea and a light snack.

It stung that Gray had been right to insist that she take a nap. During the first four days of Winsol, she'd visited a dozen villages in the Shalador reserves and the two southernmost Provinces; she'd listened to children in each of those villages sing the same three traditional Winsol songs; she'd toured those villages with the residing Queen or Warlord Prince to see the new loaning libraries and other improvements; and she'd felt overwhelmed by the number of people who had lined those villages' main streets in order to see the Queen known as Shalador's Lady.

A couple of sneezes this morning and Gray had started fretting that she was coming down with a chill from overwork. He'd held his tongue while she attended the performances this morning, since it was the last official function she would make beyond her home village until after Winsol, but when they returned home for the midday meal he insisted she go to bed and rest for the afternoon—and Shira had agreed with him.

Her breathing *had* felt a little raspy and her chest had burned when she coughed, so she didn't argue with them too much. Now, feeling better after drinking the healing brew Shira had made for her and getting some sleep, she wandered into the kitchen to find her court and family.

Devra looked over, then pulled two baking sheets out of the oven and set them on trivets to cool. "There you are, Daughter. You look better for the rest."

"Uh-huh." Cassidy was so focused on the baking sheets, she barely heard her mother. "What are those?" They looked like circles of dough, baked golden brown and full of . . . Was that chocolate?

"Chocolate chunk cookies," Maydra replied as she continued to blend and stir ingredients in a big bowl on the counter. "A special Winsol treat that's made in Dena Nehele."

"I brought the ingredients to make a couple of our family treats, so Maydra and I have been baking this afternoon," Devra said.

Cassidy's mouth watered.

Devra transferred the cookies from the baking sheets onto cooling racks. She glanced at Cassidy, then shook her head and chuckled. "The last time you had that look in your eyes, you were seven years old and ate yourself into a stupor." She picked up a cookie and handed it to Cassidy. "One."

Cassidy ignored Maydra's amused snort and bit into the still-warm cookie. "Oh. Mmmm."

"Lady Devra suggested that the women connected to the court each make one or two treats for Winsol," Maydra said. "Then we'll divide them up between those households. That way everyone gets variety without extra expense."

"You're going to make enough of these to share?" Cassidy asked, eyeing the cookies.

Her mother gave her a look that made her feel like she was seven years old again, so she decided it was time to sound like a grown-up. "Where is everyone?"

"Your father is with his apprentice carpenters. They've all made gifts for people and wanted his help with the finishing touches. As for everyone else . . ." Devra tipped her head. "They're outside."

"Then I'll just—"

Frannie rushed into the kitchen with Cassidy's heavy winter coat. "Lady! You can't be going out there without a coat. Not with you trying to shake off a chill!"

Cassidy eyed the young Shalador witch who wanted to work as a personal maid—and was using Cassidy and Reyhana as her training ground. The girl had potential and took real pleasure in her work—and everyone pretended not to know that Frannie had become so skilled at weaving hair into intricate braids by practicing on her father's draft horses.

"I'm just going to step outside for a minute," Cassidy said.

"Huh!" Frannie held up the coat. "The stoop is swept clean, so you won't be needing boots."

Cassidy glanced at her mother, decided the gleam in Devra's eyes meant that mother sided with the maid, and let herself get bundled into the coat and nudged out the back door.

Shira and Reyhana stood next to the stoop, watching men, boys, and Scelties run around the backyard.

"You're looking better," Shira said.

Cassidy nodded. "What are they doing?"

"Playing cows and sheep," Reyhana replied. "Eryk and Eliot are the sheep. Shaddo, Janos, Ranon, and Gray are the cows. The silver twins, Darcy, Khollie, and Darkmist are the herders. The white globes of witchlight at that end of the yard is the corral. The green globes are brambles."

"Are those little hourglasses floating near the witchlights?" Cassidy asked.

"Yep," Shira said. "Little two-minute timers. If a cow or sheep gets into the brambles, he can stay for two minutes as a resting period. If he gets herded into the corral, he has to stay for two minutes before trying to escape. The object of the game is to get all the cows and sheep into the corral."

"So who's winning?" Cassidy asked.

Shira shrugged.

"Oh!" Reyhana said. "That looks like a stampede."

The men were smart, skilled at working as a team, and had long legs. The dogs had speed, were using Craft to run on top of the snow, and were born with the ability to herd reluctant critters. The boys had an abundance of energy.

Based on what she was seeing, Cassidy figured the winners would be determined by which side had the most stamina.

*Would you bet on the men to win?* Cassidy asked Shira.

*Of course I would! Anything else would be disloyal.*

*Would you expect to win the bet?*

*Nope. So I wouldn't bet much.*

Cassidy suppressed a laugh and watched the game.

One moment everyone was running, shouting, barking, laughing. The next, men and dogs stood frozen, staring at the house. The dogs growled softly. The men, Warlord Princes all, stared with eyes that began to glaze as they rose to the killing edge. Only the boys took a few more steps before realizing something was wrong.

Then everyone was in motion again. Darcy got in front of the boys. Khollie dashed for her and Shira. Shaddo and the silver twins headed around the house in one direction while Janos and Darkmist headed around the other side. Ranon and Gray moved together, heading for the kitchen door.

Then the Scelties hesitated, and Cassidy had the impression that information was being passed between all the warriors.

*What just happened?* Shira asked.

*An alert, I think,* Cassidy replied. But what had caused it? And would she ever get used to the way Warlord Princes could change in a heartbeat from laughing, easy men to warriors rising to the killing edge?

The back door opened and Dryden said, "Lady Cassidy, Prince Ferall and Prince Hikaeda are here and have asked if you could spare them a few minutes of your time."

"Thank you, Dryden," Cassidy said. As she turned to enter the house, she realized Gray and Ranon intended to come in with her. "You don't have to interrupt your game. I can talk to them by myself."

They looked at her. Just looked at her.

Overprotective and bossy—and they managed the bossy part without saying a word.

And would fight with her and for her to their last breath in order to protect her from real or potential harm, whether she wanted them to or not.

Sighing, she went inside, shrugged out of her coat and handed it to Frannie—and pretended she wasn't worried about how to control Ranon's and Gray's response to men they knew.

She walked into the visitors' parlor with Ranon and Gray moving to flank her—Gray on her left and Ranon on her right.

Vae wagged her tail in greeting, then trotted out of the room.

Well, that explained why the Scelties had relaxed a bit. Vae had been watching the guests and hadn't given a call to battle.

What was she supposed to say to these men about being regarded with such suspicion just because they had asked to see her? Her former court hadn't behaved this way, so she had no precedent.

Yes, she did. Jaenelle's court. *Her* First Circle would have looked more casual, but they would have been just as prepared to fight.

Ferall gave her a quick glance before focusing on her men.

"Ranon," Ferall said quietly. Then he studied Gray. "Jared Blaed." Finally he looked at her. "Hikaeda and I are here on behalf of the Warlord Princes in our Province to wish you a Happy Winsol—and to thank you for the books. It means a lot to all of us to receive such a gift."

"You're very welcome, gentlemen," Cassidy said, smiling. "Could I offer you some refreshments?"

"Thank you for the offer, but with your consent, we'd like to visit the main street and the shops there," Ferall said. "Have a couple of special gifts to buy this year."

The words sounded simple enough, but Cassidy heard uneasiness in his voice. Almost fear. As if he'd just revealed something terribly important and terribly fragile, and he was waiting to see how she would respond.

She smiled. "Then I won't delay you any longer. I've gone shopping with my father when he wanted a special gift, so I know how long it can take a man to choose the right one."

Smiles and chuckles all around.

"Jared Blaed and I could use some exercise, so we'll walk over with you," Ranon said casually.

*You need some what?* Cassidy almost blurted out. Then she realized it wasn't casual at all, and felt insulted on behalf of the men who had come here in good faith.

She rounded on Ranon. "I'm sure Prince Ferall and Prince Hikaeda don't need your escort for a little shopping."

"In point of fact, Lady, we do," Hikaeda said.

She turned back to her guests, surprised to hear Hikaeda defend Ranon.

"When a Warlord Prince comes into a village, it makes people nervous," Ferall said. "And they have good reason to be nervous. We are what we are, Lady Cassidy. Predators. Killers."

"It's customary to give a Warlord Prince a local escort," Hikaeda said. "It tells the people he isn't there to hunt. Makes it easier for everyone."

"I see." Was that true in Kaeleer as well? She didn't remember her First Circle offering escort to a Warlord Prince when one of them came to Bhak. Maybe she could ask her cousin Aaron if this was typical of all courts or just a Territory Queen's. "In that case, I apologize for snapping at you, Ranon."

They all looked surprised that she would apologize at all, let alone in public.

Suddenly she wanted them all gone so she could get a cup of spiced tea and think about all the undercurrents and unspoken messages that had filled this room in the past few minutes.

"You might want to stop at Whistler's Tavern at some point," Cassidy told Gray. "I think they're serving steak pie along with some traditional Winsol dishes."

Gray glanced at the other men. "I think we'll do that."

"Gentlemen." She tipped her head, a small courtesy bow to indicate respect. "Happy Winsol."

She walked back to the kitchen and found Shira and Reyhana sitting at the table with Devra and Maydra. All of them had cups of coffee, and there were two cookies left on a plate.

"We saved these two for you," Shira said.

Cassidy took one and chewed slowly. "Maydra, could you make another batch of these?"

"We've made enough for all the households to share, Daughter," Devra said.

"I'd like to send them to someone as a special gift," Cassidy said.

Maydra nodded. "We've got enough ingredients for one more batch. I can do that after dinner tonight. Didn't make anything fancy for the evening meal, after all the baking this afternoon."

"Gray and Ranon are dining out with Ferall and Hikaeda," Cassidy said. "And Powell is out this evening."

"Your father is going to eat with his apprentices so they can keep working for a few hours longer," Devra said. "Since it's just the women tonight, there's no reason we can't cook as we please."

Cassidy took the last cookie. "That's settled then."

\*    \*    \*

"A word with you, Cassie?" Talon asked.

Cassidy turned away from the dining room. "Of course."

They went into the parlor. Now that they had privacy, he didn't seem eager to speak.

"You've got your family here for Winsol," he finally said.

She nodded. "My brother Clayton is coming tomorrow to be with us."

"You still have half the court here, so you'll be looked after."

He was tiptoeing around something. "Talon, it's Winsol. The next few days are social and fun. I don't need looking after."

"There are some who do," he said quietly. "I wanted your consent to be gone for a few days. Thing is, the mountain passes still need to be guarded, so there are still men in the rogue camps. Some of them are there because they see that as their duty to Queen and land. Some of them are there because they'd seen too much when the twisted Queens ruled here, and they haven't found the courage yet to come down to the villages."

"Oh, Talon." Cassidy's eyes filled with tears.

"Now, don't be doing that, Cassie. Don't. It's not as bad as you're thinking. And it's better this year than it's been in a long time. Thing is, I trained a lot of those boys, so I've always made it a point to spend a little time in each of those camps around Winsol Eve and Winsol."

"Then you should do that." Cassidy blinked away the tears. "Why didn't you tell me this sooner? We could have done something for them."

"It's been done. First Circle took care of it. Guess we should have told you, but you were already doing plenty." Talon smiled. "Gray made up a bundle of books for each camp. Good entertainment on winter nights. Got new blankets and other supplies to pass out. Got baked goods and casseroles, fruits and coffee. Got a bit of a feast for each camp. They'll already be making some of their own; this will add to it."

"I'm glad. Do you know how many men are still up there?"

Talon shook his head. "Some went down to their home villages for a while, then went back into the mountains. I'll have a better idea once I've seen the camps."

"You'll leave tomorrow?"

"As soon as the sun sets."

"Powell is out this evening, so I'll talk to him tomorrow morning and see what can be spared from the tithes for quarterly wages."

"Wages? For what?"

Cassidy lifted her chin. "You said they're guarding the passes for Queen and land. To me that sounds like they work for the court. And if they work for the court, they get paid by the court."

"Cassie, that's not why I told you."

"I know that, Talon. It doesn't make it any less true. If this is the work they do, they will be paid. We may not be able to give them what they deserve—not yet, anyway—but those men will be acknowledged."

He stared at her for a long moment. Then he kissed her cheek and walked out of the room.

She gave herself another minute to settle before joining the other women for dinner.

# CHAPTER 34

## KAELEER

Daemon walked into the parlor where Jaenelle was tucking the last few presents under the tree before she created an illusion spell of the brightly wrapped boxes. Most, if not all, of those gifts would be going with her to the Keep this evening, so the illusion spell would maintain this room's festive appearance.

He would tuck his special gift for her among the rest once he joined her at the Keep tomorrow for the family's celebration of Winsol.

He held out a brown delivery box. "This came for you. Special delivery from Cassie."

"From Cassie?" Jaenelle put the last box in place, frowned a little, rearranged a couple more, then nodded, finally satisfied with the arrangement.

Of course, if this package was supposed to go with the others, his darling wife could well pull them all out and start again.

He might find that annoying if he didn't suspect she was trying to figure out what the gifts were without using Craft to probe the packages.

That was considered cheating.

Besides, if challenged, he would deny having done anything similar when he'd handled packages while putting his gifts under the tree.

Jaenelle opened the delivery box and uncovered a note and a large bakery tin.

"Chocolate chunk cookies," she read. "Taste best when slightly warm." She vanished the note, opened the bakery tin, and took a cookie.

Daemon narrowed his gold eyes as he watched her slowly chew and swallow. Until now, the only time he'd seen *that* look on her face was when he was doing something especially pleasing with his hands or mouth.

"Let's see those." He reached for a cookie.

She hugged the tin, took a step back, and snarled, "Mine."

"Darling," he purred, "you're sharing."

"Why?"

"Because you like having sex with me."

She watched him out of those sapphire eyes. "You think you can give me sex that's as good as these cookies?"

"I think I can manage that."

She put the last bite of cookie in her mouth. She chewed. Swallowed. Licked melted chocolate off her fingers.

And gave him a smile that made his knees weak and his blood sizzle.

"Did you have any plans for this afternoon?" she asked.

"I don't remember."

Her smile turned a bit feral and a whole lot hotter.

She handed him the bakery tin, walked to the door, and said over her shoulder, "Why don't you tell Beale we're going to miss the midday meal?"

He watched her walk out of the room and wondered when she'd learned to do *that* with her hips.

"Why don't I do that?" Since he needed a minute before he left the room, he ate a cookie. "Damn, they *are* good." He studied the cookies—and smiled.

They tasted best when warm? Well, he'd have to see how warm he could make it when he walked into the bedroom holding a bakery tin full of these cookies—and wearing nothing but black leather pants that fit like a second skin.

TERREILLE

Winsol. For the Blood it was the most important day of the year.

For Theran, it was a bittersweet evening.

He sat in a chair near the fire Julien had lit in the parlor, his socked feet resting on a stool. Watching the flames, he idly swirled brandy in a snifter.

He'd enjoyed these past few days more than he'd expected. The first time he'd shown up at a social engagement without Kermilla, there had been an awkward silence, but word must have spread after that because none of his other hosts mentioned her absence. And because her absence meant he was free to travel to other towns, he'd spent some time with other Warlord Princes who had been friends in the rogue camps.

The days leading up to Winsol had been full. He still missed Kermilla with an ache that made him feel hollowed out at times—even when he acknowledged to himself that she wouldn't have enjoyed the parties half as much as he did, being used to things that were so much grander.

If she'd asked him to spend Winsol with her in Dharo, he wouldn't have hesitated. Would his clothes and manners have been that much of an embarrassment to her?

Probably.

She certainly would have been offended by the thought of sitting down with the servants for the Winsol feast. Since he couldn't see the cook making a separate meal just for him, he'd asked Julien, Hanna, and the others to join him in the dining room and to set the table with whatever bits of fancy the butler and housekeeper could find. Despite the surroundings and a much better quality of food, sitting with them tonight had felt more like a Winsol dinner in the rogue camps—camaraderie and easy teasing between the adults and youngsters, and laughter. A great deal of laughter and the hopeful relief that the bad times were behind them.

He enjoyed the meal and the chance to know them as people instead of just servants.

But he still missed Kermilla. And Gray. Hell's fire, he missed Gray. Not

Gray as he'd been for the past ten years, but the youth he had been before he was captured and tortured. As he sipped his brandy and stared at the fire, Theran kept remembering that last Winsol when Gray was whole and happy—when one of them wasn't weighed down by nightmares and the other by guilt.

A tap on the parlor door before Julien stepped in. "Prince Talon is here and asked if you're available to see him."

"Of course!" Theran set the brandy aside and pushed out of the chair. "Send him in."

"We don't have any of that special wine," Julien said. "Is there something else we can offer as refreshment?"

Would Julien actually open a vein and mix his own blood with red wine to make yarbarah?

Studying his butler's face, Theran realized that was a distinct possibility. "Let me find out if he wants anything." He paused, wondering if he was reading something in Julien's voice that wasn't really there. "I appreciate the offer."

Julien nodded and stepped out of the room.

A minute later, Talon walked in.

"Happy Winsol," Talon said, giving Theran a hard hug and a smile.

"Happy Winsol." Theran grinned, delighted by this visit. "Come sit by the fire. I don't think we'll have more snow until morning, but the old men who have weather aches say no one will move far from their own doorstep tomorrow."

"They're probably right," Talon replied, taking a seat by the fire. "Plenty of snow up in the mountains this year."

"You were in the Tamanara Mountains?" Theran couldn't keep the surprise out of his voice. Did Cassidy know her Master of the Guard was visiting the rogue camps?

"I always visit the camps during the Winsol nights." Talon gave him a sharp look. "You know that."

Of course he did. The past few years, he'd made those visits with the older man.

"I didn't think you'd have time for that this year," Theran said. He didn't add that, until tonight, he hadn't thought about the men who had remained in the mountain camps.

"I had time."

*Made time is what Talon meant.* Since he should have done the same, he changed the subject. "How's Gray?"

Talon smiled. "Boy's got as much energy as a Sceltie, and he's almost as good at herding."

*Is she working him hard?* Not a question he could ask out loud since Cassidy was a sore subject between them.

Still smiling, Talon shook his head. "When he wasn't working in the Queen's gardens, he was overseeing the restoration of the small public gardens and parks in the village. Since Cassie, Shira, and Vae all insisted that he balance that with quiet work, Powell put him in charge of helping villages establish loaning libraries. I've never seen him happier."

"Won't he miss having you with him for Winsol?" Theran asked.

"Nah. Cassie's parents and her brother are staying for Winsol. Along with the First Circle, he's got plenty of people around him." Talon gave him a long look, then asked quietly, "What about you? Why are you alone tonight?"

"I've attended more parties, winter picnics, musical evenings, card parties, riding parties, you-name-it parties in the past six days than I've ever seen. I had a choice of attending four Winsol parties or having a quiet evening at home. I chose to stay home."

"And Kermilla?"

He ignored the ache caused by the sound of her name. "She had Winsol commitments to fill in Dharo."

Cassidy's court didn't know that Kermilla was gone for good, and he wasn't about to say anything that would lead Talon to think that. Besides, he didn't know for certain she was gone for good. Correne's death and the reason the little bitch had died had shaken Kermilla. It would have shaken any woman with a sensitive heart. Once she had some time away, she might realize that her influence as Dena Nehele's Queen would curb the younger Queens and could prevent another tragedy like the one that had left a boy so horribly maimed.

As pleased as he was to see Talon, it was unfortunate that Cassidy's Master of the Guard had learned that Kermilla wasn't currently in Dena Nehele. Without Kermilla's presence, Cassidy would solidify her claim as Territory Queen next spring without a challenge. He still didn't think she was the best Queen for Dena Nehele, so he saw no reason to surrender the field to her until he had no other choice.

Talon stared at the fire, saying nothing. Then he shook himself out of whatever thoughts had pulled him away. "Didn't intend to disturb your quiet evening. I just wanted to stop by and give you these." He called in two wrapped packages, one large and one small.

Theran's face burned. With the way they'd parted, he hadn't expected to see Talon or Gray, hadn't expected to be remembered. So, feeling the pinch in his purse, he hadn't bought anything for them. "Talon . . ."

Talon waved a hand dismissively. "Freely given. Freely taken."

The words Cassidy used the first time she had offered Talon blood from her vein. Apparently the phrase was being used for other kinds of gifts as well.

Setting aside the smaller gift, Theran opened the larger package, then exclaimed in delight as he lifted the winter coat out of the tailor's box. He slipped it on.

Talon nodded. "You and Gray are the same size, so we thought it would fit you. There are gloves in the box as well."

Theran found them and tried them on. Fine leather. Excellent workmanship.

"I don't know what to say except thank you."

"You're welcome. The coat and gloves are from Gray and me. The other is from Cassidy."

Something burned in his throat as he removed the coat and gloves and carefully set them aside. He swallowed that burning and opened the other gift.

"A book?" He opened it to the title page and stared.

"She had the account of Jared and Lia's journey made into books so that the people in Dena Nehele would know their story. She thought you should have one."

Theran closed the book. His fingers stroked the leather cover. "I'll send a proper thank-you after the holidays, but please convey my thanks. This is . . . special."

"Well." Talon pushed out of the chair. "I guess . . ."

"Could you stay?" Theran set the book aside and looked at the man who had raised him.

"Were you lying about those parties or the invitations for tonight?" Talon asked.

"No, I wasn't lying. I really didn't want to attend another party tonight. But I'd like to spend some time with you. Maybe play some cards or a game of chess?"

"You going to serve the blooded rum at midnight?"

"I am."

Talon smiled. "In that case, let's see if you've learned anything about chess."

Talon said that every time they had played, even though Theran won almost half the time.

Theran smiled as he called in the chess set that had been a Winsol gift from a few years back.

They played until midnight, then shared a traditional cup of blooded rum to celebrate Winsol. An hour later, Talon caught the Winds and headed back to Eyota.

For an hour after that, Theran sat by the fire, swirling brandy in a snifter and staring at the flames—and feeling oddly content.

# CHAPTER 35

## KAELEER

"Lady Kermilla." Sabrina gestured to the visitor's chair before taking her seat behind the desk. "I don't usually grant audiences the day after the Winsol holidays, but I didn't think this discussion should wait any longer—which is why my Steward yielded to your request and made this appointment."

Kermilla sat in the chair. "There has been a serious misunderstanding."

"Yes." Sabrina opened the file on her desk. "That error is as much my fault as yours. I had thought that a First Circle that was experienced working together could balance the inexperience of a Queen ruling her first territory. Unfortunately, that was not the case, and too much damage was done before the problems were discovered to rectify the matter in any way except starting over."

Kermilla frowned. "I don't understand."

Sabrina sighed and sat back in her chair. "Like other Blood whose innate abilities are linked to their caste, Queens have an instinctive desire to rule and maintain the Blood's connection to the land. A Queen is born a Queen, but she also needs training in order to be a *good* Queen. In the usual way of things, you would have gone from your training with a District Queen to serving in the Second or Third Circle of a Province Queen to continue your education. Instead, you stepped into another Queen's place, acquiring her court and the villages she ruled."

"That court *wanted* to serve me!" Kermilla felt the sting of Sabrina's words because it sounded like Cassidy had handed over things the freckle-faced bitch no longer wanted instead of her *winning over* those men.

"Yes, they did," Sabrina said. "And the decision to let you rule Bhak and Woolskin was based on their experience, not yours, and the assumption that they would have the collective balls to stand firm if your inexperience was leading the court or the people you ruled into trouble. That wasn't the case."

Kermilla lifted her chin. "A friend needed my help and my counsel. Since they *were* experienced, I thought my court would be able to handle Bhak and Woolskin during my visit. I was wrong."

"Visit?" Sabrina tapped her fingertips together. "You haven't been in residence in Bhak since early summer. Being absent from the village you're supposed to be ruling for almost half a year isn't visiting a friend; it's blatant neglect of your duties—especially when you had a one-year provisional contract to prove yourself capable of ruling. If you truly needed that much time away to help a friend, you should have discussed it with Lady Darlena or me. We could have suspended your contract and reassigned your court until you returned. Or we might have allowed your court to manage the villages in your absence and had your Steward and Master of the Guard report directly to Lady Darlena."

Having Darlena or Sabrina poking their noses into her finances was exactly what she'd been trying to avoid. And their Stewards *would* have poked into everything, just like they did when they came to collect the autumn tithes and started all this trouble.

Kermilla lifted her chin a little higher. "Frankly, Lady Sabrina, I don't think Bhak is a sufficient challenge for someone of my abilities, and that was part of the reason for my absence. But I'm back now, and I'll get things straightened out."

"Things are already straightened out," Sabrina said. "And to be just as frank, Lady Kermilla, looking at the desperate situation in two villages that were happy and prosperous a year ago, my conclusion is that ruling a small village like Bhak is *more* than your current abilities can handle." She slapped the file closed and let out an angry sigh. "There's no easy way to say this.

I've given you an opportunity to voice your opinion, so let's end this dance. You failed to prove your ability to rule. At their request, the villages under your hand will be given to another Queen when your contract ends this spring. Since the villages are in her Province, Lady Darlena will rule Bhak and Woolskin unofficially until that time. You may reside in the Queen's house until spring if you choose, but you'll be living in Bhak as a resident of the village, *not* as the ruling Queen."

"That isn't fair!"

"No, it isn't fair considering the misery you've caused other people, but providing you with food and lodging and servants whose wages don't come out of your pocket is my concession, since I should have kept a closer watch on you in the first place!"

Kermilla sat back, stunned.

"I am aware that you no longer have the twelve men required to form an official court," Sabrina continued. "And I am aware of *why* you no longer have twelve men."

"I can explain that."

"No, you can't, and I strongly suggest you don't try. As for the remaining members of your First Circle, officially they're still yours to command until spring since they signed a contract of service with you. However, you should be aware that Lord Jhorma feels he is no longer able to fulfill his duties as a consort and has asked to be reassigned to escort duties for the remainder of his contract. That request was granted. The rest of your men have requested that their service to you be confined to duties in Bhak and Woolskin, whether you're residing there or not. That request was also granted. And any orders that go beyond ordinary court assignments must be approved by Darlena's Steward or Master, regardless of who gives those orders."

"So I have a court in name only?"

"Yes."

Feeling weak and dizzy, Kermilla stared at the Queen of Dharo. "What am I supposed to do?"

"It's clear now that you needed an older—and firmer—hand than Cassidy's to guide you and help you understand your responsibilities as a Queen.

It's also clear that your training failed. That gives you two choices, Kermilla. You can apply to serve in another Queen's court now, with no chance of ever ruling on your own, or you can go through the training again. All of it—repeating the lessons you should have learned in Cassidy's court as well as serving in another Queen's court for two years. At the end of that time, if the Province Queens and I are convinced that you're ready, you will be permitted to form another court and you'll be given the opportunity to rule another village."

"And if I form another court without this training?"

"You won't form another court in my Territory without that training," Sabrina said, her voice filled with cold steel.

"And if I do?" Kermilla persisted.

"The Warlord Princes under my hand will meet your court on a killing field—and destroy it." Sabrina stood up. "Is there anything else, Lady Kermilla?"

Her legs were shaking so hard, she wasn't sure she could stand, but Sabrina's dismissal didn't give her a choice. So she stood up and made her way to the door without taking formal leave of the Queen.

As Kermilla opened the door, Sabrina said, "It looks like you also need to brush off your manners, so a review of Protocol will be required along with the rest of your training."

Sabrina sank into the chair behind her desk and rubbed her temples to ease the headache. She didn't have to wait long for her next visitor. It wouldn't occur to him to keep her waiting.

Her Steward showed him into the room at the precise time she had requested. He stopped beside the visitor's chair.

"Prince Butler."

"Lady Sabrina." His bow was precise, Prince to Queen, when both wore Green Jewels. Although, with his ability to mask his rank, most people assumed his full strength was the Purple Dusk that was his Birthright.

He worked for her but wouldn't serve in her court. Not officially. A roamer who would take assignments for weeks or months to be her eyes and ears—and sometimes her knife. His credentials were as substantial as water written on wind. At least, the ones he offered contained more than a touch of fiction, and nothing was actually known about him beyond his caste and rank.

Almost nothing. Those insubstantial credentials carried the seal of the Queen of Ebon Askavi. Whoever he was, whatever he was, he was known to Jaenelle Angelline, and that was sufficient recommendation for every Territory Queen in Kaeleer.

"Please be seated." Sabrina waved a hand at the chair recently vacated by Kermilla.

Butler looked at the chair, wrinkled his nose, and fetched another chair from the other side of the room.

Sabrina worked to keep her mouth from falling open. "Is there a problem with that chair?" she asked when he'd finally, and fussily, taken a seat. "Did she pee on it?"

"It doesn't appear to be wet," he replied pleasantly, "but as a whole, I find Lady Kermilla's scent unpleasant."

*He doesn't like her.* That wasn't surprising, but it was worrying.

"I understand my orders, and I won't step outside them," Butler said, his voice still pleasant. "I am curious, though, about why I shouldn't step outside them."

"Your report first." Which would give her time to decide if she would answer the question inside his last statement.

"Lady Kermilla arrived on the first day of Winsol and met with your Steward. He made her aware of what was available for her use and what was not. She returned to Bhak and stayed long enough to pack her personal belongings—and express her outrage again over so many of her purchases being returned or sold. She spent the days of Winsol at her parents' house. Her family, by the way, is deeply in debt because of the little Queen's extravagance, so it appears her greed is a character trait rather than an error in judgment. She didn't return to Bhak, so she must have come to this meeting from her home village." He paused. "Why hasn't she been dealt with?"

"One man's bitch is another man's Lady," Sabrina said.

Butler smiled. "The wording is usually reversed. That is, if you were intending to quote the High Lord."

"The point is, despite the misery she's caused, she hasn't done anything *in Dharo* that a Queen isn't entitled to do."

"Beggar her people? Send one of her men to his death? Is that what a Queen is entitled to do, Lady Sabrina?"

"A Queen's will is the law. Where she rules, she can do anything."

"Unless someone stops her. Why aren't we stopping her?"

"I did stop her. She no longer rules Bhak and Woolskin."

"She didn't want them, so she'll feel no loss. You know what she wants and where she is going and what she'll try to do now. Why aren't we stopping her?"

*For the same reason no one asks about your credentials.* "By Blood law, I cannot interfere in another Queen's Territory."

"We could fix this before she left your Territory."

"No."

"Why?"

She studied him as he studied her. "Do you trust Jaenelle Angelline?"

"With everything I am."

"So do I. And that is your answer, Butler. That's why." Sabrina sat back. "When I met with Jaenelle and some of the others at the Keep a few weeks ago, I was ready to haul Kermilla back to Dharo. It would have been an insult to Cassidy, would have implied that she wasn't able to defend her Territory from even a small threat, but I was ready to do it. I was overruled."

Butler thought it over and nodded. "I understand."

Because he did understand, she added, "Something Jaenelle said to me in private has shaped my decisions about Kermilla and is the reason I'll stand back and let this play out as it will."

He said nothing, but his eyes asked her to share. And in all fairness, if he had to spend the next couple of months in Bhak, he deserved to know.

"Jaenelle said some people need a hard lesson in order to learn and grow—and some people *are* the hard lesson."

★   ★   ★

Later that evening, Daemon returned to his seat at the table where he and Jaenelle were playing an idle game of chess. He handed a note to his Lady. "This came from Sabrina."

"She must have had her chat with Kermilla," Jaenelle said as she opened the note.

Daemon stared at the chessboard. It would be so easy to fix this little problem. He had fixed a lot of these little problems when he'd lived in Terreille, despite Dorothea SaDiablo's efforts to control him. But unless Kermilla set foot in Dhemlan, he had to leave the fixing of *this* problem to Dharo's Queen.

Jaenelle read the note and gave it back to him. "You've had more experience with women like Kermilla than I have. What do you think she's going to do?"

Ignoring the rules of play, he picked up his Queen and set her down behind a castle guarded by a Warlord Prince.

"What do you think Cassidy will do?" he asked.

Also ignoring the rules of play, Jaenelle set her Queen squarely on the edge of the battlefield, flanked by two Warlord Princes.

They looked at each other, knowing nothing more needed to be said.

# CHAPTER 36

## TERREILLE

Theran looked up when his study door opened, then sprang out of the chair to meet Kermilla as she rushed into the room. She flung herself into his arms, her hair smelling of cold air and fresh snow. Her psychic scent filled his senses like the most intoxicating perfume.

"Kermilla," he whispered as his arms tightened around her.

"I wanted to fulfill my duties as a Queen, but I couldn't stay away." She covered one side of his face with kisses. "They don't need me. There are so many Queens in Dharo, those villages don't need me." She pulled back enough to look at him, her eyes shining with sincerity and purpose. "But you need me. Your people need me. And I need you, Theran. I missed you so much! I want to stay with you. I want to be the Queen you need for your people. I can do it, Theran. I know I can."

He hugged her, his heart so full it ached. She'd come back to him. He hadn't expected to see her again, but she'd come back.

"We'll build a good life for ourselves and our people," he said. "It will take work and time, but we'll build a good life."

"I know we will."

When she raised her left hand to touch his face, he saw the silver bracelet he'd given her for Winsol. Her wearing it now symbolized a choice, both for the woman and the Queen.

Moved beyond words, he pressed a kiss into her palm.

"We have a lot to do before spring," he said, not sure enough of what she wanted from him to ask for the intimacy he craved. "I guess we should get started."

Smiling, she kissed him softly—then kissed him again with more heat. "Tomorrow is soon enough. Today I don't want to think of anything but you."

# CHAPTER 37
## TERREILLE

Cassidy entered the kitchen, rubbing her hands. A brisk walk on a crisp morning had woken her up and made her look forward to a few hours in a warm room, even if she wasn't looking forward to working her way through the correspondence, requests, and other paperwork that had arrived like a steady snowfall since the Winsol celebrations ended two weeks ago. Just as well that the new year began in the winter season. If she was diligent, she figured she could get through all the paperwork before spring planting.

Birdie gave her a look. Before Cassidy could say anything, the assistant housekeeper made a shooing motion. "I got a pot of spiced tea almost ready for you, and I'll warm up a couple of those fruit tarts Maydra baked yesterday."

"I thought we devoured them all at dinner last night," Cassidy said.

Birdie smiled. "We put a couple aside to go with your morning pot of tea."

Grinning, Cassidy went to her office. A fire was burning nicely. A heavy shawl and blanket were laid out on the stuffed chair near the hearth, in case she began to feel chilled while working at her desk. And Powell had sorted through the new sack of mail, separating correspondence from family and friends from invitations, requests for audiences, and correspondence from Dena Nehele's Queens. There were also pens and a stack of the inexpensive paper she preferred using for notes and instructions within the court.

Sitting at the desk, she closed her eyes.

It was lovely to feel cared for, to have someone do little things like save a fruit tart or make sure pens and paper were easily at hand. It was lovely to hear Birdie and Frannie singing while they tidied up the Residence, to hear Elle and Maydra laughing, to hear the ease in Dryden's voice when he asked her to wait a moment while he instructed the young footman in the proper way to do something that involved her.

And it was a relief that her First Circle was finally learning to relax a bit. She'd notice a difference in all of them during the second half of Winsol. Oh, there was still the sharp, assessing glance whenever anyone who wasn't First Circle approached her, and her men were *always* going to rise to the killing edge when someone outside the court or the home village came near her—Jaenelle's last note confirmed *that*. But some underlying tension had disappeared. Shira also had noticed the difference but couldn't explain it either, so they'd concluded that it was something men considered private and wouldn't divulge unless given a direct order from their Queen.

And their Queen didn't see any reason to push them about something that had made them happier.

Opening her eyes, Cassidy picked up the letter opener and started on the stack of correspondence from the Queens.

It was lovely to receive these notes, to read the caution and hope beneath the stiff phrases of the Queens in the northern Provinces and to read the growing confidence and warmth of the Queens in the Shalador reserves and the southern Provinces.

Many of them were interested in sending members of their courts to learn from the two Protocol instructors she had hired to work with courts and teachers so that the people of Dena Nehele would learn Protocol and the Old Ways from people who lived by the Old Ways. Two of the cottages in the Queen's square were being repaired and cleaned for the Warlord and witch. They still hadn't decided where the "school" would be located. She'd suggested another empty cottage in the square. Her First Circle had vehemently opposed having that many strangers coming and going within the boundaries of land that was supposed to be secure ground.

She'd resigned herself to the time it would take to negotiate with her men. Hell's fire, it had taken days to get them to agree to let the instructors live in the square, and they only gave in about *that* after Gray, Ranon, and Talon met the two people at the Keep—and received confirmation that Prince Sadi and the High Lord approved of these instructors and thought they would fit in easily with Eyota's residents. What sealed the deal was learning that the Warlord came from Scelt and was used to living around Scelties and the Lady from Nharkhava, being an enthusiastic reader of the Tracker and Shadow stories, was willing to learn to live with Scelties.

Cassidy glanced at Vae, who was snoozing in front of the hearth.

*Let the Lady from Nharkhava learn on her own like the rest of us did,* Cassidy thought as she opened the last letter in that stack—a letter that bore the Grayhaven seal.

Then she forgot about Scelties and Protocol instructors, forgot about the spiced tea and fruit tarts, forgot about all the hope and promise in the letters she had already read.

She'd been so happy and so busy building a life and working to fulfill her promise to these people that she'd forgotten it was temporary—until this note from Kermilla reminded her.

"*. . . I'm sure you won't do anything to make the transition difficult . . . valuable asset to the Territory . . . treat the reserves like a Province and appoint you their Queen.*"

"To do what, Kermilla?" Cassidy asked. "Encourage these people to break their backs and their hearts so that you can buy another fancy dress?"

Vae raised her head. ★Cassie?★

"I can't do that to them. I *won't* do that to them."

★Cassie!★

She wasn't aware of Vae leaving the room, but the Sceltie returned with Powell.

"Vae says something upset you," Powell said. "What's wrong?"

"I forgot."

"I'm sorry, Lady. I don't understand."

She handed him the note.

His expression turned grim. "I didn't think Theran was really that much of a fool." Then he sighed. "The First Circle is out and about on the court's business, so there's nothing to do about this bit of information until evening when everyone has returned and Talon can join us. We can discuss it then."

What was there to discuss? In another two months, she wouldn't have a court. Just like the last time.

Her stomach rolled. Her skin turned clammy.

Was that why the men had relaxed? Had they been promised a place in Kermilla's court and had the assurance that their own status wouldn't change? Come to think of it, her former court also had been more relaxed and considerate in the weeks before they'd all walked away from her.

"Lady?" Powell reached for her. "What's wrong?"

How could he not know what was wrong?

She pulled away from him before he could touch her. "I'm not feeling well."

He studied her, and she saw nothing in his eyes except concern. "You've been working steadily all morning," he finally said. "Why don't you rest for a while?"

She pushed away from the desk. She had to get away from him before she got sick. "I'll do that. I'll go up to my room and rest for a while. Please ask Reyhana to open the invitations and review the calendar. It will be good practice for her." She hesitated, then added, "I don't want to be disturbed."

"Shall I have Birdie or Frannie bring up a tray? Or ask Lady Shira to make up a healing brew?"

She shook her head. "I'm not hungry, and there's no need to bother Shira about this." What ailed her was something the Black Widow Healer couldn't fix.

She left her office, aware that Powell followed her to the door and watched her.

Vae followed her all the way up to her room.

"I want to be alone, Vae."

*No. You are upset, and your smells are strange.*

"Leave me alone."

*No.* Vae jumped up on Cassidy's bed and growled a warning.

Cassidy studied the Sceltie's Purple Dusk Jewel. Outranked and out-toothed.

*Why are you upset?*

It bubbled out, hot and bitter. "I'm going to lose this court. I've given the best that I have, but in two months, I'll be replaced by another Queen." Again.

*You are being foolish.*

"No, I'm not. Kermilla took my court before. She'll do it again."

Vae's shock hit her as hard as a blow.

*You will not defend your males? You will not defend the other humans who belong to you?*

"Vae . . ."

Vae snarled. *When a Sceltie is given a flock to protect, she protects it. When a bad dog tries to take her flock, a Sceltie doesn't tuck her tail between her legs and run away whining. A Sceltie *fights*."

"Well, I'm not a Sceltie!"

*No, you are only human, but you are a Queen. You have shown your teeth before. Why won't you show them now and drive the bad Queen away? Your males would fight for you. Why won't you fight for them?*

"I *would* fight for them, with my last breath and beyond," Cassidy shouted. "But they don't . . ."

She stopped. Closed her eyes. Thought about Powell's reaction to Kermilla's letter.

Almost dismissive. A potential problem the men had been aware of, so it hadn't come as a surprise, but it was nothing important enough to summon the court immediately.

Kermilla's words felt like a knife twisting in her gut, but Vae's words hurt more. *Was* she giving up on this court because her former court had walked away? *Was* she giving up without even asking what her First Circle wanted? *Was* she running away, whining, instead of fighting for what belonged to her?

Would a Sceltie give up her flock to another dog when she knew the dog would hurt what she'd promised to protect?

"Do Scelties ever get scared?"

★We get scared. But we still fight.★

*Which are you going to be, Cassidy? A coward or a Queen?*

Sighing, she kicked off her shoes and approached the bed. "Move over, Vae. I really don't feel well right now. I need to rest for a bit."

When Vae shifted, Cassidy lay down on top of the covers and closed her eyes.

★Cassie? What will you tell your males?★

"I don't know. I'm confused."

Vae settled beside her, warming her back. ★That is foolish. This is not confusing. They are yours, and you will fight for them so they will not be forced to serve the bad Queen.★

Cassidy closed her eyes. Could it be that simple?


Gray stamped the snow off his boots and walked into Ranon's kitchen. "It's colder than Hell out there." He stripped off his coat and hung it on a peg, then removed his boots and called in the soft house shoes Burle and Devra had given him for Winsol. "Ranon, you got anything hot to drink?"

"I'm making coffee, and have some whiskey to go with it," Ranon replied.

Powell sat at the kitchen table with Shaddo. Archerr stayed near one of the windows, looking out at the yard—or at the Queen's Residence.

Archerr was the escort on watch today. Why wasn't the man at the Residence instead of standing in Ranon's kitchen?

When Ranon asked him to stop by the house to talk, there had been some urgency in the psychic communication, but the Shalador Warlord Prince hadn't indicated it was a court meeting rather than a personal conversation.

"What's wrong?" Gray asked.

Ranon put the pot of coffee, the bottle of whiskey, and five mugs on the table. "It's Powell's meeting."

"This came with the rest of the day's correspondence." Powell called in a piece of expensive paper and handed it to Gray.

Ranon came around the table. Leaning over Gray's shoulder, he read the letter and began swearing viciously as he paced around the kitchen. Gray read it and handed it to Shaddo, whose eyes glazed with killing fury as he gave the paper to Archerr.

"That bitch was gone," Shaddo snarled. "Talon told us she had gone back to Dharo for good."

"Because that's what Theran told him," Archerr said.

"No, Theran only said Kermilla had gone back to Dharo to celebrate Winsol with her people," Ranon said. "Talon had the impression Theran didn't expect her to return, but Grayhaven didn't *say* that."

"Doesn't matter what was or wasn't said. She was gone, and now she's back," Shaddo snapped.

"Where is Cassie?" Gray asked.

Ranon whirled to face Powell. "Is she giving up and running again? Hell's fire! What more do we need to do before she believes in us?"

Hearing grief and desperation under Ranon's anger, Gray raised a hand—and immediately felt the other Warlord Princes in the room yank on the leash to regain control of their tempers.

"Cassie isn't going to run anywhere," he said quietly. He didn't think she would run. Not anymore. But if she did because of Kermilla, he'd find her and bring her back. "Powell?"

"After reading Kermilla's letter, she said she wasn't feeling well and went up to her room. Vae went with her." Dry amusement filled Powell's shadowed eyes. "Don't worry, Ranon. Lady Cassidy isn't going anywhere without our being informed."

The tension in the room eased a little.

Powell's amusement faded. "Perhaps I was too dismissive and didn't take into account Cassidy's feelings about the other Queen."

"Kermilla is a scar on Cassie's heart, and that scar bleeds every time Kermilla brushes against Cassie's life," Gray said. "But she'll get past today's hurt and go on."

Cassie would learn to live with her scars just like he was learning to live with his.

"Is she going to let that bitch keep threatening everything we've all worked for?" Archerr asked.

"Cassie isn't letting that bitch do anything," Shaddo growled. "This mess is Theran's doing."

"There's an easy way to fix it," Archerr said. "It's not like we haven't done it before."

They looked at him, and Gray saw the same question in all their eyes. "No, that isn't the way to fix it. Not this time. When Cassie knows we've prepared for this, when she knows we're going to stand with her, she'll stand with us. She won't turn her back on her people."

"Then let's make sure she knows we're going to stand with her," Ranon said.

"I've already contacted those I could reach in the First Circle who were working beyond the village today," Powell said. "They'll contact the others, so we'll all be here around sunset."

"Fine," Gray said. "Then let's have some of that coffee before we all get back to work."


Cassie opened her eyes. Full dark outside. She must have slept for a few hours—and someone must have thrown a blanket over her and added a warming spell to it. Otherwise she would have gotten cold and woken up.

She tried to shift. The blanket grunted and yawned. A moment later, a small ball of witchlight floated near the bedroom door, lighting the room enough for her to see that she was pinned down by Scelties. Vae, Khollie, and Darkmist. Darcy, Keelie, and . . .

Catching the scent of leather and horses, she twisted to look behind her.

. . . Lloyd.

"Let me up."

They were awake and watching her. Not one of them moved.

"I have to pee. *Now.* Let me up."

They jumped off the bed. One of them used Craft to open her door. Darcy and Lloyd took up a position in the hallway, blocking access to anything except the bathroom and other bedrooms on this side of the staircase.

Vae and Keelie trotted in front of her. Darkmist and Khollie followed so close behind she was afraid of kicking them if she raised her foot for a normal step. So she shuffled to the bathroom.

Khollie followed her inside.

"No," Cassidy said. "I can do this by myself."

Khollie wagged his tail and didn't move.

"Out."

He didn't move until Vae *grffe*d at him.

She closed the door in their furry faces, but as she prepared to use the toilet, she could sense them—Vae, Darkmist, and Khollie—standing right in front of the door and *knew* those keen ears would be pricked to catch every sound.

"Back off," she growled.

She'd bet they didn't take more than one step back. And she'd bet a season's income that those ears stayed pricked.

She wasn't going to win this argument, so she pretended she had privacy and took care of business.

*Your males want to talk to you,* Vae said when Cassidy opened the door.

She wasn't sure she was ready to talk to *them*. Not that she had a choice. Darcy and Lloyd took point. Keelie and Khollie blocked her on either side. Vae and Darkmist were behind her in prime herding position.

*Cows and sheep must be terrified to see even one of them coming,* Cassidy thought as they escorted her to the big meeting room. They escorted her all the way in, then turned and trotted out, closing the door behind them.

Her whole First Circle was there, along with Gray and Shira, but Reyhana was not.

Reyhana had the kind of strength that would attract strong males, the kind of strength that would cause Kermilla to see the girl as a serious rival in a couple of years. Would Kermilla take steps to eliminate a potential rival? It was a possibility.

*And another reason to show my teeth,* Cassidy thought.

A place at the table had been left for her—on the far side, away from the door, and smack in the middle. A not-so-subtle way of telling her that she wasn't getting out of the room without going through her men.

She found that comforting, and she realized Vae was right. This wasn't confusing at all.

Gray came up to her and brushed a hand over her hair. "You feeling better after getting some rest?"

She smiled at him. "Yes, I am."

He studied her as if he'd been prepared for one kind of mood and was faced with another. Then he smiled in return. "Come over here. We have some things to show you."

He led her to her place at the table, but she felt too restless to sit down. And she wasn't sure how to interpret the men's hard eyes and grim faces since Powell had seemed so dismissive earlier.

"Powell told you about the letter," she said.

"We saw that piece of shit," Talon replied. "It pissed off the rest of us, but if it knocked your legs out from under you for even a little while, I guess it was a good ploy for Kermilla to use."

"Ploy?" Cassidy stared at her Master of the Guard.

"You bluff well enough when we play cards. I'm surprised you couldn't see this for what it is." Talon leaned across the table toward her. "Direct question, Cassie. You give us a direct answer. Are you walking away from us? Yes or no."

"No, I'm not walking away from you, but—"

"'But' wasn't one of the choices," Talon growled.

"—my contract ends in two months."

"Only if you choose to end it," Powell said. "The provisional contract was a way for us to save face if you chose not to stay with us."

That hadn't been *her* impression of what that contract meant. "Kermilla says she's going to be the Queen."

"Not without a fight," Ranon said.

Fight with words. With Protocol. By taking this challenge before a tribunal of Queens, assuming she and Kermilla both had an official court. That's what Ranon meant. Didn't he?

She looked at the men again. Warlords and Warlord Princes. Warriors who had already survived years of battles, a lifetime of fighting in one way or another.

They weren't going to fight with words or with Protocol or by arguing before a tribunal to decide who would rule their Territory. They would meet their challengers on a killing field as they had done before.

"If this turns into a fight, some of you could die," she said, chilled by the possibility.

"Some of us might die either way," Ranon said. "We're not going to submit to a Queen who cares nothing about our people or our land. We've seen what that kind of Queen can do to a Territory. And over these past few months, we've seen what a good Queen can do. We'd rather fight for you than just fight against Kermilla, but one way or another we're going to fight—and some of us will die."

"No," she whispered. For a moment, she felt grateful when Gray slipped an arm around her waist. Then she looked at him. Really looked at Prince Jared Blaed.

No longer a boy in a man's body who would be tucked away with the other young boys. This time he would stand on a killing field with the rest of the men.

"Besides," Ranon said, "just before we helped James Weaver and the other landens relocate here, he told me flat out that if Kermilla became Queen, there would be another landen uprising. So there's going to be a war one way or the other."

*No.* "If it has to be physical confrontation, it would be Kermilla's court fighting against mine to settle who ruled. It wouldn't be a war."

Talon made a rude noise. "Witchling, it's not going to stay between the courts. There's too much at stake. More at stake than we've had for a lot of years."

"You're going to give in just because some bitch tells you to go?" Shaddo growled at her.

"No, I'm not giving in, but you're talking about *war.*"

The thought of empty chairs around the table kept her arguing. "When Theran leaves it will break the court. We'll have an unofficial court going up against an official one."

"You don't know that," Talon said. "He needs to convince eleven other men to serve Kermilla, and I don't think that's going to be an easy task." He nodded at Gray. "And we've already got his replacement."

"Remember the lessons I was taking at the Keep?" Gray asked her. "I was training to be a First Escort. To be your First Escort. I'm qualified, Cassie. The High Lord, Daemon, and Lucivar all agree I can serve you and the court in this way. And the High Lord gave me this." He called in a sheet of paper and handed it to her.

She read it and landed in the chair. Hard. "Mother Night, he's not hiding his teeth, is he?"

Not a dismissal that would allow Theran to honorably accept another contract, but a kind of demotion that would have made Queens in Kaeleer take a wary look at the man if he came looking for a position of power in one of *their* courts.

"That letter is a well-phrased kick in the balls," Talon said. "It will be even more impressive once Powell copies it over and it bears your signature and seal. And the day after Theran gets that letter, you can count on every Warlord Prince within Dena Nehele's borders and in the Tamanara Mountains knowing that Jared Blaed is now the First Escort to the Queen of Dena Nehele."

Gray sat beside her. "You've shown us what's possible. We're going to fight to keep what you've given us."

Cassidy pushed away from the table, needing a little space, needing to move, to think.

She'd thought her men would step aside for Theran's choice because he was the last Grayhaven. But they were going to fight. Not just for her. She never would accept a war and the loss of life just to keep her in power. But this wasn't about her anymore. Not really. This was about holding on to the very things the Blood had said they wanted when she first came to Dena Nehele—a land that lived by the Old Ways, that held itself to the Blood's code of honor.

Weren't those the same things Lia and Jared had fought to keep in Dena Nehele for as long as possible?

*A Sceltie fights for the ones who belong to her. So does a Queen.*

She turned and looked at them. All of them.

*Everything has a price. But, sweet Darkness, don't let this price be too high.*

"All right," she said. "We fight."

Fierce pride filled their eyes, and she hoped with everything in her that she would remain worthy of that pride.

Her legs suddenly felt shaky, so she returned to the table and sat down. Clasping her hands and pressing them against the table, she gave Talon a pleading look. "Isn't there some other way?" Would they even consider bringing this to a tribunal of Queens if she could arrange to get one?

"None of us are afraid of fighting," Talon said.

"There may be an alternative to war," Powell said quietly. "Especially since Kermilla has conveniently given us justification to act."

Cassidy looked at the men, who all seemed to be weighing Powell's words on some internal scale. "I don't understand."

Talon rubbed his chin and said thoughtfully, "I doubt Theran knows Kermilla sent you that letter. Poor tactics. We've known since he met her that he wanted her to be the Queen, but I figured he wouldn't make it an official challenge until he had the men who would form her First Circle. And he wouldn't want that court made public until close to the time when the contract he signed with you was finished because that would give you less time to respond and find someone to take his place." He gave her a fierce smile. "Kermilla made the first move without having sufficient backing. Now we can hit hard and fast."

Leaning back in his chair, looking like a predator at ease, Talon said, "Powell, what's your alternative to war?"

"Secession," Powell said.

Silence.

Cassidy looked around the table and saw shock on everyone's faces.

"The Shalador reserves don't have enough land," Ranon protested. "We wouldn't be able to support the people without getting some of what we need from the other Provinces. Not for a good many years yet. And three reserves mean three battlegrounds. We don't have enough trained warriors left to lead anyone else willing to fight. Not against the rest of Dena Nehele."

"I wasn't referring to just the Shalador reserves, Ranon," Powell said. "You're not taking into account the influence Lady Cassidy has had on the southern Provinces. I think given the choice of living in a Territory called Dena Nehele that is ruled by Lady Kermilla or living in a newly formed Territory ruled by Cassidy, they will be more interested in who rules the land than what the land is called."

"You have a map of Dena Nehele in your office?" Talon asked.

Nodding, Powell called in the map and spread it out on the table.

"I had some time this afternoon to consider a few things the rest of you may not have thought about yet in terms of incentive," Powell said as Talon studied the map. "The loan Gray acquired from Prince Sadi is a loan specifically to Lady Cassidy's court, *not* the Queen of Dena Nehele's court."

Cassidy jerked in her seat. So did several of the men.

Powell smiled a tight smile. "Exactly. Prince Sadi was very precise in the wording of that loan. It doesn't transfer to another Queen. If Cassidy's court dissolves, the loan ends, and the Prince is within his rights to demand immediate repayment of whatever funds were used. However, the loan was not specific to Dena Nehele in terms of a name or boundaries. So if Dena Nehele is split between the Queens, any Provinces still under Cassidy's rule could continue to request help for their people and businesses. Provinces under Kermilla's rule could not make use of the loan and benefit from Prince Sadi's generosity."

"Oh, but . . ." Cassidy began.

"No!" several male voices replied.

"Everything has a price, Cassie," Gray said. "The Blood who want Kermilla to rule can't have you taking care of them."

He was right. She knew he was right, but she thought of the letters she'd read that morning from the northern Queens and wondered what dreams might be crushed under the weight of Kermilla's wardrobe.

"The Heartsblood River is the natural border between two Provinces," Talon said, running a finger along the map. "It begins in the Tamanara Mountains and runs all the way to Reyna's Lake on the western border. That would give us five Provinces, plus the Shalador reserves. Plenty of fresh water. Some small lakes and lots of streams and creeks for fishing.

Farmland and pastureland. Some woodlands that can be nurtured and allowed to grow back. That will help rebuild the deer herds and other meat animals."

Feeling dizzy, Cassidy leaned against Gray. "Everything south of the Heartsblood River? That's almost a third of Dena Nehele!"

"Seems fair to me," Talon said. "That's enough land to stand on its own as a Territory, but not so much it would feel like a grab without the honesty of a fight."

"It will be important to emphasize that we're doing this to avoid a civil war," Powell said. "We don't want our families or the people we have promised to rule and protect to live under Kermilla's hand. Instead of embroiling the Blood in a devastating fight, Lady Cassidy is relinquishing her claim to Dena Nehele and establishing this new Territory for the Blood who want to live by the Old Ways and want her guidance in order to do it."

"Hell's fire," Shaddo said, breaking the silence that followed Powell's words. "I'd be ashamed to fight against men who wanted that."

"I hope you remember what you just said," Talon told Powell. "I think we're going to need something in writing."

"I'll draft something," Powell said. "With the Lady's permission."

Feeling a bit battered—and wondering why they were bothering to ask her permission when they were barreling forward with a speed that left her breathless—Cassidy nodded.

"If Jared Blaed and Ranon are agreeable, I'd like them to show my draft to the High Lord and get his opinion," Powell said. "In confidence. He has a way with words, and we're trying to avoid a war, not start one."

"We can do that," Gray said, glancing at Ranon. "Once we've declared ourselves independent of Dena Nehele, I'd like Lucivar to come here for a day or two to give his opinion about what kind of defenses we need and where. No offense to you or your ability, Talon, but . . ."

"No offense taken," Talon said. "Lucivar Yaslana has been feared for centuries for what he does on a killing field. We'd be fools not to take advantage of his experience and listen to any suggestions or advice he wants to give."

"I think Jared Blaed and Ranon should meet with the Warlord Princes in the five southern Provinces," Shaddo said.

"Why?" Ranon asked.

"First Escort and the Master of the Guard's second-in-command? Your words are going to hold a lot of weight with the other Warlord Princes. You, Ranon, have always stood for the Shalador people. Jared's people. And Jared Blaed is descended from Thera and Blaed. Balanced against Theran using the Grayhaven name and being Lia's last descendant, I'd say that evens the field."

"So we move fast," Powell said. "Cassie sends the letter to Theran, stripping him of the title of First Escort, citing his failure to honorably perform his duties as the reason for the demotion. As the High Lord suggested."

"He'll start recruiting openly in response," Archerr said.

"In the northern Provinces," Talon said. "He doesn't know Kermilla showed her hand, so he'll start talking to the Warlord Princes farthest away from Eyota. Also, I suspect he's been giving those men the impression that Cassie is going back to Dharo in the spring, leaving Kermilla a clear field, and that there won't be an established Queen and court to challenge the upstart. Unless a man is truly drawn to Kermilla, he'll think twice about signing on to serve in her court when he realizes it means going up against the ruling Queen and her court."

"I think those of us who have been acting as court liaisons for the southern Provinces should head out tomorrow and set up the meetings," Haele said. "Make it an official request to meet with the new First Escort and the Master's second-in-command. It would also be good if we told them the Queens would be welcome to have an audience with Cassidy."

"They're always welcome," Cassidy said, looking at her men. This might not end up being a war, but they were still preparing for a kind of battle.

"One last thing," Powell said. "What are we going to call this new Territory?"

Cassidy looked at Ranon, who kept his eyes fixed on the table. "Ranon?" she said softly.

Obeying the sound of her voice, he looked at her.

Hope. The fulfillment of a dream. But for the first time since she'd met him, he was holding back, acting with fierce restraint.

"You and your people have dreamed for a long time that you would have a place of your own again," she said. "That you would live in a land called Shalador."

Ranon looked around the table. Cassidy's heart ached with pride as every man nodded, giving his blessing to the name.

Ranon's dark eyes filled with tears. He blinked them away. Then he said, "We have dreamed of this, but the Shalador people won't build this new land alone, and the name should reflect all the people who call this land their home." He took a deep breath and blew it out slowly. "Shalador Nehele. I would like to call our new land Shalador Nehele."

Cassidy swallowed hard to push down the lump in her throat. "That's a fine name."

"Then it's settled," Talon said, looking at her.

"It's settled," she agreed.

She'd barely said the words when someone tapped on the door. Dryden and the footman entered, carrying a tray of glasses and bottles of sparkling wine.

Seeing the number of bottles, Talon and Powell glanced at each other, then shrugged. Clearly, they had both sent an order to Dryden in anticipation of reaching an agreement.

Bottles were opened and glasses were filled.

The men and Shira raised their glasses.

"To Lady Cassidy and the Territory of Shalador Nehele," Talon said.

Their voices rang all around her. "To Lady Cassidy."

# CHAPTER 38

## TERREILLE

The next morning, the First Circle moved quietly, and they moved fast.

By the time Cassidy, Shira, and Reyhana had finished breakfast, Ranon and Gray were sitting down with Eyota's elders and Tradition Keepers to explain the court's decision to create a new Territory. By the time Cassidy and Reyhana had settled at the desk in the Queen's office to sort and review all the requests and invitations again, the liaisons for the five southern Provinces were meeting with the Warlord Princes in those Provinces to arrange a formal visit with Ranon and Jared Blaed.

By the time the messenger arrived at the Grayhaven estate and delivered the letter from Lady Cassidy to Prince Theran Grayhaven, every Warlord Prince who lived south of the Heartsblood River knew something was about to happen—and they began sharpening their knives.

Worn out by a morning of useless meetings and a midday meal that still churned sour in his belly, Theran returned to the Grayhaven mansion and found Julien waiting for him. The look in the butler's eyes chilled him because it signified another clash between butler and future Queen.

"Prince Grayhaven."

"Julien?"

Julien called in a letter and held it out to him. "After you left, Lady Kermilla went into your study and opened the mail. *All* the mail."

"Why in the name of Hell would she do that?" The words were out before he could stop himself.

"I wouldn't know." The tone said the butler knew quite well why a Queen would go through mail that wasn't addressed to her—and what happened to a man if she found something she didn't like. "When this letter arrived, I felt it was best to deliver it to you personally since it has Lady Cassidy's seal."

Shucking off his heavy coat, Theran handed it to Julien and took the letter. "I'll be in my study."

"Lady Kermilla wanted to be informed the moment you returned home."

*Should I take my time delivering the message?* That was the underlying question.

"Inform the Lady that I've returned," Theran said as he walked away.

Kermilla wanted Julien dismissed. Actually, she wanted the man banned from the town because, on his best days, Julien was barely courteous to her. On the days when memories rode him hard, he couldn't stand being around her. Since she was still a guest, she had to tolerate the butler. Once she became Queen . . .

Problem was, Julien was damn good at his job, took on more than a butler's typical duties, and by standing between Kermilla and the rest of the staff, was the only reason the other servants hadn't resigned.

Why was everyone so resistant and so resentful? Yes, she was sometimes difficult or inconsiderate, but maturity and work that made full use of her abilities would soften those edges. Sure she had a temper, but that just meant she had spine and spirit. And that spine and spirit were the reasons Kermilla was the right Queen for Dena Nehele—the one who could represent their land and people with grace and skill.

The servants grumbled on a daily basis, which he didn't understand since he hadn't seen Kermilla doing anything that justified the grumbles. He could ignore the servants for the most part, and did—as long as Julien managed to keep them from leaving. Couldn't anyone understand that it was an anxious time for all of them and the next few weeks would be so critical? Nerves were a bit frayed and tempers were sharper than they would be normally. But once Kermilla had the assurance of her place in Dena Nehele, everything would settle down.

Could he give her any assurance?

The Warlord Princes he'd met with today had listened—and had offered nothing. Not one indication that they would be willing to accept Kermilla, let alone serve her. And not one spark of interest in meeting her. There was wariness over being seen in her company because Talon had declared her an enemy of the current Queen of Dena Nehele, but there wasn't any sign of the suppressed interest he'd expected once he'd hinted that Talon's declaration would no longer apply come spring.

What was he supposed to do about that? Having the backing of at least some of the Warlord Princes and minor Queens was crucial.

He riffled through the opened mail. Invitations? Well, he didn't mind her opening those. Not really. After all, she'd be attending those events with him, so she should have a say in which ones they accepted. But the rest . . .

Uneasiness rippled through him, a warning that something wasn't good, wasn't right. Then Kermilla walked into the study, and the uneasiness was buried under his craving to be with her and use everything he was for her pleasure—whatever that pleasure might be. The uneasiness was buried, but not the anger.

"Oh, *la,* Theran," Kermilla said. "I was afraid you wouldn't get back in time. There's a delightful little party later this afternoon that I *must* attend and—"

"Why did you open my private correspondence?" He hadn't realized *how* much anger he was keeping leashed until he heard the roughness in his voice.

She stopped moving toward the desk. She lowered her head and looked at him through her lashes while her mouth shifted into its sexy pout. "I was just trying to help. And I wanted to learn. You're always telling me that I need to learn more about Dena Nehele."

"You learn by talking . . ." *Listening.* ". . . or asking. *Not* by violating someone's privacy."

"Violating?" She widened her eyes. "That's a harsh word. I just looked at a few silly old letters."

"No, it's not a harsh word." He fanned the stack of letters and the uneasiness returned. *Julien? How many letters did you put on the desk this morning?*

*Five invitations and seven letters.*

Theran counted them again, then moved them to make sure nothing was hidden.

Five invitations—and five letters.

"What happened to the other two letters, Kermilla?" he asked. Before she could lie to him, he added, "There were seven letters delivered. There are five here now. Where are the other two?"

"They were very rude." She enhanced the pout. "I burned them."

"You burned letters addressed to me?"

"They were rude."

"I don't give a damn how rude they were. You had no business reading them, let alone burning them!"

Her eyes flashed with temper. "Nothing is hidden from a Queen, Prince. *Nothing.*"

A cold fist wrapped around his spine—and squeezed. "Those letters. Who were they from?"

She tossed her head and said dismissively, "I don't remember."

His temper slipped the leash for a moment and thundered through the room, knocking a painting off the wall and sending several useless porcelain figurines crashing to the floor.

No color in her face. Fear in her eyes.

"Who were they from?" he snarled.

"Ferall and . . . I don't remember the other name. I don't!"

Ferall. Mother Night. He hadn't expected to get *any* response from Ferall. He couldn't ask the man to send the letter again. And outside of being "rude," which could mean anything, he had no idea what kind of answer he'd been given to his carefully worded inquiries. He knew Ferall wouldn't serve Kermilla, but he wanted some assurance the other Warlord Prince wouldn't actively go after Dena Nehele's new Queen.

"Don't do it again," he said, breaking the seal on Cassidy's letter. "I don't give a damn what you *think* a Queen is entitled to do. Any correspondence addressed to me is *private*. You don't open it without my consent. Is that clear?"

She pulled her shoulders back and raised her chin, the picture of wounded dignity. "Perfectly clear."

He began reading Cassidy's letter. No, not a letter. Some kind of official document that . . .

"Theran, what about the invitation for this afternoon?" Kermilla asked. "It's really important that I—"

"You bitch," he snarled. "You cold-blooded *bitch*."

"Theran!" She sounded shocked.

He rushed out of the study and roared to release some temper. "Julien! My coat!"

Julien hurried to the entranceway, holding the coat open. "Prince?"

Vanishing the document, Theran shoved his arms into the coat sleeves. ★I'll be gone for the rest of the day,★ he said on a spear thread when Kermilla rushed into the entranceway. ★Hold on to any mail or messages until I return.★

★Done,★ Julien said.

And when he returned he would put Green shields and locks around his study. Kermilla would be insulted, but better that than another error in judgment.

"Theran?" Kermilla's voice was a blend of distress and whiny-bitchy that he hadn't heard before. "Where are you going? What about our invitation to—"

"Send your regrets," he snapped as he headed for the door. "I have an appointment." *With the Queen*, he added silently.


Cassidy watched Shira remove the tangled web of dreams and visions from its wooden frame and drop the spider silk into a shallow bowl of witchfire.

"What did you see?" Cassidy asked. "Or can't the vision be shared?"

Shira looked at her for a long time. Then the Shalador witch finished putting away her Hourglass supplies before saying, "Endings and beginnings. I think most of us left in the Hourglass have seen the end of Dena Nehele—and wept for it. Some of us saw hope and a new beginning, but it wasn't always there in the visions, so we knew the end was coming but couldn't be sure if anything good would follow."

"And now?"

"I used to see orchards of honey pear trees growing out of the bodies of the men who had fallen in the killing fields."

"Mother Night," Cassidy whispered.

"Sometimes, in nightmares, I would pick the fruit off one tree. I would bite into one of the pears, and it was better than anything I'd ever tasted before. Then I would look down and see Ranon's face. The tree was growing out of what was left of Ranon."

"Shira . . ."

"Today I saw orchards of honey pear trees growing out of rich soil. Soil, Cassie. Not the bodies of our dead. And even though I couldn't see them, I could hear men talking and laughing, and I knew they were alive and helping with the harvest." Shira undid the Craft holding her hair up and let that dark hair flow around her shoulders. "You're the difference. Dena Nehele will break, and Shalador Nehele will rise. A new beginning."

"There could still be war," Cassidy said. "Those honey pears might still grow out of the bodies of the dead."

"That's a possibility," Shira agreed. "But before, it was a certainty."


*Shalador's Lady will rule this new land?*

*She will.*

*We will continue to walk the path she has shown us and reclaim the Old Ways of the Blood?*

*We will.*

*Then the people of Shalador will welcome this change, and we will strive to be worthy of the honor she has given us by naming her new Territory Shalador Nehele.*

Gray rode into the landen community with Ranon and wondered if this meeting was really necessary. Prudent, sure. But necessary? They'd used a small Coach that Ranon could handle so that they could ride the Opal Winds together. The news still arrived at the southern and western reserves ahead of them.

They were given the courtesy of being allowed to deliver their message to an assembly of elders and Tradition Keepers since they had made the journey. After their meeting in the western reserve, they were gently shooed home. Shalador's decision was made. They would stand with the Queen. Ranon and Jared Blaed should return home and tend to Shalador's Lady.

So they were back in Eyota in time to make this last visit and be home for dinner.

They rode in slowly, in part to give the guard on duty time to sense their presence but mostly because they could hear a dog barking and children laughing and squealing.

"Cows and sheep?" Gray asked, reining in before they reached the floating balls of green witchlight.

"Looks like it," Ranon agreed.

Gray watched JuliDee evade the Sceltie and dart away from the corral of white witchlight. "Wynne doesn't seem to be doing too well."

"Wynne isn't trying very hard," Ranon replied dryly. "I imagine if there was a reason to round up these 'sheep,' they'd be rounded up."

James Weaver came out of one of the workshops and raised a hand in greeting as they dismounted.

"We were all putting away our tools and having a glass of ale as an end to the day. Would you join us? Or would you prefer something hot?"

"Ale would be fine," Ranon replied. They tied their horses to a post and followed James into one of the workshops. Potter and Tanner were there. So was James's son, Rand, but the youngster got some signal from his father and excused himself.

Small glasses of ale were poured. Gray wondered if it was the cost of the ale that prevented them from enjoying a larger glass. Then he realized this wasn't about drinking. This was a ritual among them that acknowledged a day's work—and the freedom to work without fear.

"There is something we felt you need to know," Gray said. He explained the court's decision to break from Dena Nehele and form a new Territory, just as he'd been explaining it all day—and would explain it when he and Ranon met the Warlord Princes living in the five southern Provinces.

James looked at Potter and Tanner, then rubbed the back of his neck. "We thank you for the courtesy of telling us."

Ranon studied the men. "You already knew."

"In a way," Potter said. "But we appreciate you translating it into human."

Gray looked at Ranon. Ranon looked at Gray. Together they said, "Human?"

James said, "The message we got earlier today was 'We don't like the other Queen. We're keeping Cassie. So her males are going to be busy for a while marking her territory.'"

"Marking—" Ranon choked. Then he blushed.

Potter nodded. "Of course, the boys wanted to know what that meant, so Duffy demonstrated and . . ."

Gray hunched his shoulders and groaned. "How many women are mad at us?"

James grinned. "As long as you don't pee on any of the houses, I think you'll be all right."


Theran pounded on the boardinghouse's front door. Damn dogs were going to stir up the whole damn village before someone opened the damn door. How in the name of Hell could an animal that small make a noise that loud?

He couldn't see them, but he recognized the psychic scents of Archerr and Shaddo. And he felt Talon's presence.

And he felt insulted that he'd been "escorted" here by a guard.

Before he could bang on the door again—or break it down—it opened.

"Prince Theran," Dryden said too courteously to be courteous.

"I want to see Cassidy."

"If you will wait here, I will see if the Lady is at home."

"Don't give me that crap," Theran snapped, bracing a hand against the door. "She'll see me, and she'll see me now."

Dryden's eyes blazed with anger, but his face and voice retained the butler poise. "I will see—"

*Theran? Theran! You will wait in the visitors' parlor and be polite.*

Theran shoved at the door. "Shut up, Vae."

She snarled at him. A moment later, someone else snarled. Behind him.

Purple Dusk against Green? He could take her down. But he was having trouble getting a sense of the Sceltie behind him.

If it was a Sceltie behind him.

The memory of those two big cats flashed through his mind.

"Fine," he said through gritted teeth. "I'll wait and be polite."

Dryden and Vae escorted him to the visitors' parlor. Dryden left. Vae stood guard—until Gray walked into the room.

*How could a man change so much in a few months?* Theran wondered. He recognized the face because it was so similar to his own. But he didn't recognize the look in those green eyes—or that blend of power and assurance that was now part of Gray's psychic scent.

"Cassie is not available," Gray said. "Is there something I can do for you?"

It was the coldness in that voice that jabbed his temper. He called in the document and held it up. "Can you explain this?"

Gray flicked a glance at the paper. "You don't want to be First Escort. I do. You don't want to serve Cassie. I do."

Theran's jaw dropped. "You? Hell's fire, Gray. Do you know what you've done?"

"Yes, I do."

*Kermilla will never forgive him.* "You know Kermilla is going to become Queen in a couple of months. Signing on to serve Cassidy now is a slap in the face. She'll never consider you for any kind of position in her court."

"And I wouldn't consider taking one," Gray replied.

"Do you know what's required of a man to stand as First Escort? Gray, you can't do this."

"I've spent the past few months training to be a First Escort, and I'm qualified to serve Queen and court in that position. What kind of training do you have, Theran?"

*None.*

"I don't see why you're acting so pissy about this," Gray said. "You're up in Grayhaven. We're down here. You haven't fulfilled your duties to Queen or court for months now."

"I wasn't dancing to Cassidy's tune, no, but that doesn't mean I haven't been working for the good of Dena Nehele."

"That's a matter of opinion."

Stung past insult, Theran vanished the document and took a step back. Gray had made his choice, and may the Darkness have mercy on him.

"Is your position in the court official yet?" Theran asked.

Gray nodded. "I signed the contract this morning."

*Mother Night.*

"Well, I guess I'm free to—"

"You still have a contract with this court," Gray said. "You're still in the First Circle."

"Under the circumstances, I think it's best if I resign."

"You rule the town of Grayhaven on the Queen's behalf. If you ask to be dismissed from the court and Cassidy grants the request, you not only give up your place in the court, you also give up the town and its tithes."

Theran felt the blood drain out of his head. The only reason Kermilla was allowed to stay anywhere in Dena Nehele was that he ruled Grayhaven. If he lost the town, she could be driven out—or killed. He couldn't risk that. Not when Cassidy's contract would end in a couple of months, freeing him from these chains.

"You're turning into a bastard, Gray."

Gray smiled—and Theran saw the man who was comfortable around Daemon Sadi and Lucivar Yaslana—and the High Lord of Hell. Sadi couldn't have played this hand any better.

"I guess I should call you Jared Blaed from now on," Theran said.

"I guess you should."

When he walked out of the boardinghouse, the Scelties were gone. So were Archerr and Shaddo. But Talon stood at the edge of the street, waiting for him.

"I'll walk you back to the landing web," Talon said.

"That's not necessary."

"Yes, it is."

They walked halfway back before Theran spoke. "How did it go so wrong?"

"Everyone wants the same thing. They just aren't seeing the same answer," Talon replied.

"I'm worried about what's going to happen to Gray."

"Jared Blaed can take care of himself."

"Why did he have to do this now?"

"He's following his heart. Isn't that what you're doing?"

"That's not the same."

"No one ever thinks it is."

They didn't speak again until they reached the landing web.

"Take care of yourself, boy," Talon said.

"Talon . . ." What could he say to keep the people who mattered to him out of harm's way? "Cassidy isn't going to be ruling for much longer."

A long silence. Then Talon said quietly, "No, Cassidy isn't going to be ruling Dena Nehele for much longer."

# CHAPTER 39

## TERREILLE

*She looks tired,* Ranon thought as he watched Cassidy enter the meeting room and take her seat between him and Gray. Of course, they were all tired, but this past week seemed to drain spirit as well as energy from their Queen.

A week of meetings, a week of talking—a week where he'd watched strong men struggle with a fear bred from hope.

Gray had shown the steel in his spine and his potential to be a leader. The other Warlord Princes had seen it too, and Ranon wondered how much that would sway opinions.

The rest of the First Circle drifted into the room, looking alert enough, despite the early hour. Cassie had chosen this dawn meeting so that Talon could be with them and hear Powell's report at the same time as the rest of the First Circle.

Talon took his seat opposite Gray, then nodded to Powell.

The Steward looked pale but excited as he laid five letters on the big meeting table.

"The five southern Provinces have agreed to join the Shalador reserves to create a new Territory," Powell said. "All the District Queens and the Warlord Princes who are ruling on behalf of our Queen support the court's decision to break away from Dena Nehele and build the kind of life we want in a land ruled by the Queen we have chosen to serve."

The men around the table released their breath in a collective sigh. Exhilaration and trepidation. None of them wanted war, but all of them were willing to step onto as many killing fields as it would take to buy freedom for the people they loved.

"I've drafted a document," Powell said, looking at Ranon and Gray.

"We'll take it up to the Keep this afternoon and ask the High Lord to review it," Gray said.

"Until we know how Theran and his Lady are going to react to this news, everyone goes out in tandem," Talon said. "And you Ladies are to have an escort with you at all times."

"But—" Shira said.

"*All* times." Talon stared at Shira until she nodded. "We can't afford to lose either of you—or Reyhana. You'll do what we need so that we can do what Shalador Nehele needs."

"That's fair," Cassidy said, sounding too subdued for Ranon's liking. "You should remember to talk to the Scelties about helping to guard the Queen's square."

Talon nodded as if he—and every other man in the room—hadn't thought of that already. Having played hide-and-seek with the dogs in order to learn more of what they could do, the men had confirmed that no matter how well you could hide from another human, you couldn't cover yourself in shields well enough or disguise yourself well enough to hide from kindred senses unless you were downwind of *all* of them.

"Is that all?" Cassidy asked.

"Yes, Lady," Powell replied.

Cassidy pushed away from the table and walked out of the room.

"Let me," Ranon said, reaching across the empty space to stop Gray from following her.

He waited for Gray's nod before he left the room to look for Cassidy.

Wasn't hard to find her. The garden gave her comfort—even when it slept under snow.

He stood on her left side, wanting to touch her, wanting to offer simple contact. But he wasn't sure she would welcome a touch right now, so he stayed where he was.

"I'm afraid," she said. "You've put your faith in me as a Queen, and you're risking your lives and your people's lives based on that faith. What if I fail?"

"None of us know if we'll measure up to the demands of the day," Ranon said gently. "Considering what we're about to do, only a fool wouldn't be afraid of what may be ahead of us, and you're no fool. But I'll tell you the same thing Talon told me once: don't fail until you fail."

She gave him a puzzled look that made him smile. Then he looked away. It seemed easier to say the words when he wasn't looking right at her. "I was seventeen the first time I stepped onto a killing field. Warlord Princes are born to stand on the killing fields, and everything we are gives us the temper and the instinctive skills to be predators and killers. But it also takes maturity to accept what you do on those fields. I was seventeen, and I wasn't ready. Neither were any of the other boys who were training in that camp up in the mountains. But a decision had been made to eliminate a Province Queen who had gone beyond cruel in what she was doing to the people, and part of that decision was to pay whatever price needed to be paid."

"So they sent young men to support the experienced warriors," Cassidy said. "Is that why you've kept such a strict watch over Janos, kept him hidden from the Queens?"

"That's why. I didn't want him to face that before he had to.

"I remember Talon coming into the camp the night before the fight to talk to the leaders. He couldn't be with us for the attack. I think he was committed to another killing field farther north. Besides, Talon couldn't fight in daylight, but he was the best instructor we had. When he was done talking to the leaders, he took a couple of minutes with each of us. It got to be my turn, and instead of telling him I would be brave and strong and win the battle, I told him I was afraid to fail. And he said, 'Don't fail until you fail.' So I didn't. We destroyed that Queen and the warriors she sent against us. Most of us survived." Ranon hesitated, then decided not to tell her that some of the boys who survived went back into the mountains and never came down again. "There have been plenty of times in the years since then when things have looked too bleak for any hope to survive, when I watched other men fall in battle while trying to save what we could. There were days when I thought I couldn't stand to see another friend die, but I'd tell myself that as long as I could stand and fight for my people I hadn't failed yet. I don't know if that helps."

"It does," Cassidy said. "Yes, it does. Thank you, Ranon."

He touched her shoulder. When she didn't pull away, he drew her against him for a hug.

"We'll do all right, Cassie," he said as he eased back. "And since our land will be a third of Dena Nehele's size, there will be two-thirds less . . ." Suddenly dizzy, he staggered back a step.

"Ranon?" Cassidy grabbed his arm. "What's wrong?"

"We didn't think of it. I swear we didn't."

"Think of what?"

"The tithes."

She looked baffled. Completely, totally baffled. "What about them?"

"You'll only get a third of the tithes you would have gotten if Dena Nehele stayed whole." How could they have overlooked something that obvious?

More bafflement. "I know. Powell and I reviewed the accounts this week to make sure the court could still support itself, and we can, Ranon. All of you will receive your quarterly income."

"What about your income?"

"I'll have plenty."

He wasn't sure he believed her, so he'd talk to Powell. Oh, he was certain that the *court's* expenses would be paid, and everyone who was owed a wage would get the full wage. He just wasn't sure Cassidy would have a copper left to call her own. The woman was quite capable of brushing that little detail aside.

He huffed out a breath and watched it cloud the air between them. "You know, it's colder than Hell out here. I could use a hot drink and some breakfast. How about you?"

She studied him, and he had the sense that something in the past minute had shown her another point on the battlefield.

"Ranon? How do you think Theran will respond to this? Do you think he'll let us go?"

"He'll be pissed off, and I doubt he'll be the best of neighbors, but I don't think he's enough of a fool to start a war. Not with Talon backing you." But her question made him think of the reason they were risking war to begin with. "What about Kermilla? How is she going to respond?"

He looked into Cassidy's eyes and knew the answer—just as he knew the reason before she said it.

"I think Kermilla is going to be very unhappy about losing a third of the tithes, and I don't think she'll let go of that income without a fight."

Easy enough to take that stand when the bitch wasn't going to be the one standing on the killing fields.

Cassidy hooked her arm through his and headed back to the house. "Let's save that worry for another day and focus on today's worry."

"What's that?" he asked.

"Whether or not there's anything besides porridge left for breakfast."

He laughed as he opened the kitchen door and they both hurried into the warmth.

*Don't fail until you fail.*

She didn't want to fail the court or the people. And they weren't about to fail her.

## EBON ASKAVI

Prince Ranon and Prince Jared Blaed arrived at the Keep thirty minutes after sunset. That was just enough time for a man to wake up, clean up, and drink a glass of yarbarah. In Saetan's experience, young men didn't show up with that kind of precision in order to make a casual request. The fact that Jaenelle would have considered those two as Second Circle gave him even more reason to pay attention to the timing.

"Gentlemen," Saetan said as they crossed the sitting room and stopped at the precise distance that was deemed courteous according to Protocol and gave him the precise bows owed his rank.

All that precision gave him a headache.

"High Lord," Gray said.

When Gray hesitated, Saetan supplied the rest. "You have something you want to discuss, but it needs to be in confidence."

"Yes," Gray said.

"Will my keeping this confidence put anyone I care about at risk?"

A hesitation before Ranon said, "No one in Kaeleer."

Interesting answer. "Very well."

As soon as they had that much assurance from him, they both relaxed.

Gray called in a folded paper and held it out. "We'd like you to read this and tell us what we should fix. Powell said this is a copy, so you can mark it up if you want to."

Saetan called in his half-moon glasses, unfolded the paper, and read the carefully written words.

Mother Night. These children had balls.

"Are you trying to start a war or avoid one?" he asked.

"Avoid one," they replied.

Thank the Darkness for that. "Then there are a few phrases that should be reworded."

As he turned toward a chair where he could work, he felt another dark presence in the Keep. Ranon and Gray felt it too and knew who was approaching the room. Since neither of them asked him to do anything to keep this meeting private, he settled into the chair, called in a lap desk and a pen, and began rereading the document that would break a Territory.

Lucivar walked into the room. A slashing glance at Gray and Ranon, an assessing look at him, and his Eyrien son had seen enough to know this wasn't a battlefield.

Which didn't mean Lucivar wouldn't turn it into one if he decided there was a reason.

"Gray," Lucivar said. "Ranon. What brings you here?"

The question wasn't as idle as it sounded. Ebon-gray was asking Purple Dusk and Opal to explain their presence—and would get an explanation one way or another.

Since dealing with Lucivar had been a valuable lesson for all the boyos in Jaenelle's First Circle, Saetan pretended to be unaware of this particular pissing contest. He didn't want Gray and Ranon to get hurt, but he wasn't going to step in unless it was necessary because every man needed to know when to stand and when to yield.

Gray glanced at Ranon, who nodded slightly.

"The Shalador reserves and the five southern Provinces are breaking from the rest of Dena Nehele to form a new Territory," Gray said.

"That makes the Heartsblood River your northern boundary?" Lucivar asked.

"How did you know?" Ranon asked.

*Foolish boy,* Saetan thought, looking up to watch this part of the drama. An Eyrien could see a great deal from the air while riding the currents. Especially when that Eyrien was an Ebon-gray Warlord Prince.

Lucivar shrugged—and then winced so slightly no one but family would notice. "It's a natural border, not to mention a means of travel and a source of water. Stands to reason you'd want to hold on to one side of it. How many Warlord Princes on your side of the line?"

"About forty," Gray said. "That's almost half of the adult Warlord Princes in Dena Nehele."

"Adult," Lucivar said. He gave Ranon a long look. "If this gets messy, your brother will end up on the killing fields with the rest of you. You know that."

"I know," Ranon said quietly.

"That's why I'm looking over this document," Saetan said. "To try to avoid the necessity of anyone standing on a killing field because of a preference for one Queen over another."

Another assessing look at him before Lucivar focused on the other two men. "Have Talon deliver the copy of the document to Grayhaven. He's the one man Theran won't challenge."

Saetan crossed out a sentence and wrote his changes in the margin. "And be sure to have a copy of the final, signed document brought here to the Keep. Documents can be lost or destroyed in a Territory when it's convenient to hide information. Nothing can touch them here."

That wasn't quite true, but there was no one else in the room, including Lucivar, who could destroy a race so completely that all trace of them was eliminated from all the Realms.

Gray had brought a map of Dena Nehele, so while he, Ranon, and Lucivar reviewed how to make the best use of the trained warriors they had, Saetan worked through Powell's draft, making subtle word changes that would place the burden of war squarely on Theran Grayhaven's shoulders. Only a fool would start a war under these circumstances.

Of course, a man driven to serve a particular Queen could be ten times a fool. He might hate himself for it, but he'd still follow the Queen's command and be her instrument.

They would all have to wait and see how firmly Kermilla held Theran's leash.

He finished his changes, read them again, and then handed the document back to Gray. The Warlord Princes from Dena Nehele didn't linger, and Saetan thought that was wise. News would travel. Rumors would begin. The sooner the official document was in the open, the better.

When they were gone, Saetan looked at Lucivar. "Well?"

"Gray and Ranon are solid," Lucivar replied, rubbing his left biceps. "And they're a good team. You fix their paper?"

"Yes, I did. It's still possible that Kermilla can goad Theran hard enough to try to start a war, but I don't think he'll be equally successful in convincing enough Warlord Princes to join him on that particular killing field."

"I hope you're right."

Saetan waited a moment. "What's wrong with your arm?"

"Nothing."

"Would you like to answer that question again without lying to your father?"

Lucivar made a face. "It's nothing. A bruise. She didn't break skin."

"I beg your pardon?"

"Well, Hell's fire, the woman's got some temper when she's riled."

"What did you do to upset Marian?"

"I was being considerate. Don't women want men to be considerate?" Lucivar looked like a puppy who had gotten smacked and had no idea what he'd done wrong.

It took a formidable amount of self-control to convey nothing but calm interest, but he did it. "Of course they do, but wives also expect to have sex with their husbands on occasion." After waiting a beat, he added, "I take it you and Marian have resumed making love."

"I don't think there was any love in this particular bite," Lucivar growled. "But, yeah, we had sex."

"In that case, my darling, why are you here?"

This time Lucivar didn't try to hide the wince. "The village theater group is putting on a play tonight. It's a comedy. With singing. More or less."

Saetan waited. "Are you asking me to watch Daemonar this evening or accompany Marian to the play?"

Lucivar gave him a pained look.

*Everything has a price, boyo.* "What time should I come over to watch the boy?" Saetan tipped his head to indicate the clock on the mantel.

Lucivar looked at the clock and sighed. "Now?"

Saetan headed for the closest courtyard that had a landing web. "You are planning to get cleaned up, aren't you?" It wasn't really a question.

"If I can have the damn bathroom to myself, it doesn't take me more than five minutes," Lucivar muttered.

*If she really wants to see this play, she's going to clobber him,* Saetan thought. "Go. Tell Marian I'll be there by the time you're ready to leave. And Lucivar? If you're smart, you're going to give your Lady more than just sex tonight."

Lucivar went out the first available exit and launched himself skyward.

Saetan sent out a light psychic thread to the woman he considered the perfect match for his volatile son. *Marian?*

*Uncle Saetan?* Surprise turned to concern. *Lucivar was supposed to see you.*

*He did. He'll be home in a minute. I apologize for the delay, but a meeting with two Warlord Princes from Dena Nehele had to take priority.*

*And he didn't contact me because he wanted to wiggle out of going to the play tonight?*

Probably, but not consciously. Lucivar would rather crawl over broken glass than see a comedic play that included singing, but he wouldn't shrug off an event Marian wanted to attend.

*I'll be over in a few minutes to watch Daemonar. Lucivar swears he can get cleaned up and be ready to leave for you to get to the play on time.*

*So I should be understanding when he comes roaring in?*

Hearing the amusement—and the love—in the words, Saetan smiled. *Darling, make him work for it. It won't hurt him.*

Her laughter filled the link between them before she broke the thread— no doubt to deal with the husband who had just come thundering home.

Smiling, Saetan shook his head. "She used to be a gentle hearth witch before she had to deal with all of us." He felt the leash slip on his self-control and heard a peculiar sound come from behind his clenched teeth.

Imagining how well Marian would deal with Lucivar, Saetan leaned against a wall, let go of self-control, and laughed himself silly.

# CHAPTER 40

## TERREILLE

Three copies of a document that would break a land that had survived cruelty she couldn't imagine, even when she heard some of the stories about Dena Nehele's past. Three copies of a document that would change all of their lives.

*And change nothing that matters the most,* Cassidy thought as she carefully pressed her seal into the wax on the third copy—and heard the whole First Circle release the breath they'd been holding while she took this last step.

As soon as she sat back, Powell pulled the copy away and positioned it in the center of the big table, along with the other two copies.

"Done," her Steward said. "Talon?"

"I'll take the copy up to the Keep first." Talon carefully rolled two of the documents and vanished them. Then he hesitated. "Once I hand this paper to the High Lord and it's acknowledged at the Keep, the path is chosen. There's no going back."

He was giving her one last chance to walk away. A Queen's wants, wishes, and will came first, no matter the cost.

"Safe journey, Prince Talon," Cassidy said.

Her legs felt shaky, so she sat at the table while Talon and the rest of the court left the room. Naturally, Ranon and Gray were last and kept glancing at her as if trying to decide if they should stay or leave.

Shira made it simple by shoving the two of them out of the room. Before the Black Widow could close the door for a private chat, Reyhana slipped into the room.

"I want to help." Reyhana squared her shoulders and lifted her chin.

*How much death has this girl already seen?* Cassidy wondered. *How much more will she have to see?* "You serve in my Second Circle, Sister, so you most certainly are going to help." She stood up and felt reassured that her legs weren't as wobbly as they'd been a few minutes ago. "I could use a bit more to eat than the half piece of toast I choked down earlier. After that, why don't the three of us review what needs to be done?"

"Don't we first have to find out what Theran is going to do?" Shira asked.

Cassidy shook her head as she joined them at the door. "War or not, we've got two months before spring. Fields will need to be plowed, and crops will need to be sown—and the Queens need to affirm their bond to the land. We need to make sure all the Queens know how to enrich the land, we need to confirm that the villages—landen and Blood—have the plows and other tools they need for their farms and—"

"All right!" Shira said, laughing. "All right. Point taken. We have plenty to do."

Cassidy looked at Shira and knew that, for a moment, they both pictured an orchard of honey pear trees growing out of the bodies of the dead.

Then they both pushed that image aside, and the three of them went to Cassidy's study and got on with the business of living.


### EBON ASKAVI


Saetan read the document carefully. Then, assured that Powell had made all the changes he'd written on the draft, he set the document on the library's large blackwood table and vanished his half-moon glasses. "We'll make sure this is preserved. A place will be set aside in the library for any other documents or work from Shalador Nehele that you want preserved outside of your land."

"Thank you," Talon replied.

Saetan studied the demon-dead Warlord Prince who had been a friend of Jared and Lia. "This is hard for you."

"Yes, it's hard. Not so much that it happened, but the reason why it happened. Makes me wonder what I've been fighting for these past three hundred years."

"I can tell you that," Saetan said. "You've been fighting for honor and to protect what you cherish."

"I failed him." Talon shook his head. "Theran doing this means I failed him."

"You don't know that. Until he steps up to the line and makes the choice to start a war, you don't know that. And if there is enough of Jared in him, he may surprise you."

"I served a Queen before I turned rogue. She was the reason I turned rogue. I never felt the pull with her that I feel with Cassie. I don't think I could turn away from Cassie, no matter what she did at this point."

"That bond can wane or break, like any other kind of love," Saetan said. Having faced the possibility of killing a son in order to save his Queen, he knew what Talon was feeling, but there wasn't much comfort he, or anyone else, could give this man.

"It's too late in the morning for you to be traveling back to Dena Nehele," Saetan said. "I'll show you to a guest room where you can rest until sunset."

## KAELEER

A simple message was sent from the High Lord of Hell to Lord Khardeen, Lady Sabrina, and Prince Daemon Sadi. It said:

*Dena Nehele has broken. Shalador Nehele rises with Cassidy as its Queen. May the Darkness have mercy on them.*

## TERREILLE

Theran read the document a second time, then stared at the man who had raised him and loved him—and was now an enemy.

"Why?" He tossed the document on his desk. "Hell's fire, Talon, *why?*"

"It's clear enough," Talon replied.

"It's not clear," Theran snapped. "Nothing is clear. You *broke* Dena Nehele. You broke the land that survived generations of twisted Queens and Dorothea SaDiablo's hatred for the sake of a bitch who should be leaving instead of trying to take control."

"I could say the same about you. And that's the last time you get to call my Queen a bitch without blood being shed."

Sick, scared, and furious, Theran clenched his teeth to avoid saying anything more. Talon *would* shed blood. Even his.

"You can't do this. She took a third of the Territory."

"Cassidy didn't take anything. The Provinces were free to make their choice."

"And what price would they pay if they didn't make the choice Lady Cassidy wanted?" Theran asked bitterly.

"You're trying to dress Cassidy in another woman's temper," Talon said. "You're asking questions that don't fit her as a woman or a Queen, so maybe you're really wondering about someone else."

Theran rocked back on his heels, not sure how to answer that—and sure he *didn't* want to answer that. "Talon, breaking Dena Nehele isn't the answer."

"Is Cassidy going to be the Queen of Dena Nehele two months from now?"

"No, she is not!"

"Then this is the only answer that gives both sides a choice besides war."

"Choice." The word hooked its claws into him and left his heart bleeding. "You call this a choice? Kermilla will never accept this."

"She isn't the Queen yet."

"She's going to be."

"But she isn't the Queen yet. And I guess, right now, that makes you the unofficial ruler of Dena Nehele. So it's up to you to accept this."

Theran staggered back a step. No Queen. No female hand to guide them once it became known that Cassidy had turned away from the Provinces north of the Heartsblood River.

No Queen again. At least, not until Kermilla formed a court.

"I guess I'm no longer part of Cassidy's court," Theran said.

"You don't serve the Queen of Shalador Nehele, so, no, you're no longer part of the court."

So much sadness in Talon's eyes.

"Talon . . . are you really going to stand against me?"

"Let us go, Theran. We don't want a war, but if you send men against us or our Queen, we will fight. And I tell you now, boy, if we meet on a killing field I will do everything I can to destroy you."

Theran's eyes stung. He blinked away the tears. "That's it then."

"Yes, that's it." Talon walked to the study door and opened it. He stopped and looked over his shoulder. "May the Darkness embrace you, Theran."

Theran said nothing until Talon left the room. Then he whispered, "And you, Talon. And you."


Kermilla tapped on the study door and swallowed her resentment—again—about being locked out of Theran's study. That would change once she was the Queen. Yes, that would certainly change. But for now, she couldn't demand to know what had happened between Theran and that awful Prince Talon. Just looking at the man's maimed hand and the way he walked because of the missing part of his right foot made her shudder. At least she wouldn't have to consider *him* for her court, no matter how Theran felt about him.

She knocked on the door, louder this time. And this time it opened.

When she walked in, Theran was pacing, the restless movement of a man incapable of remaining still. And the look on his face . . .

"What happened?" she asked. "Did something happen to your cousin?" Not that she cared a finger snap about Gray since he'd been so rude to her, but Theran *did* care, so it was appropriate to show concern.

"He's lost his mind, that's what happened," Theran snapped. "With help, I'm sure, from that Shalador bastard Ranon."

That didn't tell her anything. "Theran . . ."

He strode to his desk, grabbed a document, and thrust it into her hands.

She read—and felt a fury rise in her unlike anything she had felt before. "That *bitch*! She's taken whole *Provinces*?"

"Everything south of the Heartsblood River is now ruled by Lady Cassidy, Queen of Shalador Nehele," Theran said bitterly. "A third of Dena Nehele is gone because of a piece of paper!"

"No! Get them back. Theran, you have to get those Provinces back!" A third of Dena Nehele? A third of the income that should be hers? Unthinkable! "You can't let her do this to us. To the land and the people who need our guidance," she amended when she noticed the uncertainty in his eyes.

"Well, they don't think they need anything from us." Theran resumed his pacing.

"You have to stop this!" Kermilla sank into a chair. That *bitch*. Should have known better than to offer *anything*. She'd been willing to let Freckledy rule the Shalador reserves, hadn't she? Wasn't much there worth having anyway, but it had been a way to show how generous she could be by letting the Queen who had been dismissed remain in her little village and be useful. Of course Cassidy, being a fine draft horse of a Queen, *was* useful.

But no. The bitch got greedy and *stole* Provinces that should have been *hers*. And that was something she couldn't allow.

That strange fury washed through her again. "You have to do something, Prince Grayhaven."

He gave her an odd look—more appreciative of this show of temper than wary of it.

Finally he stopped pacing, rubbed his hands over his face, and sighed. "There's nothing I can do, Kermilla. A copy of that document is already at the Keep. There is no way to deny it exists. They did this behind my back, not even giving me the chance to challenge the decision, but it's done now."

"Then *change* it," Kermilla said.

"How? War? Do you know what another war would do to us right now?" He shook his head. "That's not a consideration. I doubt there is a Warlord Prince on this side of the Heartsblood River who would be willing to step onto a killing field against Ranon or Talon . . . or Jared Blaed."

"So you're going to give up a *third* of Dena Nehele to *Cassidy?*" Kermilla stared at him in disbelief. How could he give up her land so easily?

"I told you, it's already done." Retrieving the document, which she'd dropped beside her chair, Theran set it on his desk. "No point chewing on a battle that's already been fought and lost. Not when we have to move fast to meet the next challenge."

"And what would that be?" She was too upset to try her sexy pout or any other maneuver on him.

Another odd look. "Convincing eleven other men to stand with me and form your court."

*Why is that a challenge?*

Before she could ask him, there was a quick knock followed by the bell that signaled that dinner was ready to be served.

Theran opened the study door and looked at her. "Shall we go?"

Wasn't really a question, so she walked out of the room—and swallowed the resentment that bubbled up again when he put a Green lock on the door.

She needed to form a court, and she couldn't do it without his help. But once she did, there would be more than one change in Dena Nehele.

# CHAPTER 41

## TERREILLE

Within three days, most of the people in Dena Nehele, Blood and landen alike, had heard some version of the news that Lady Cassidy had formed a new Territory out of the Shalador reserves and Dena Nehele's five southern Provinces.

According to the Warlord Princes in the southern Provinces, Lady Cassidy had stepped up to the line Theran Grayhaven had drawn and showed her courage by forming a new Territory that would live by the Old Ways of the Blood instead of allowing herself to be forced out by the unscrupulous Queen who was Theran's lover.

According to the Warlord Princes in the northernmost Provinces, Lady Cassidy had abandoned them without a second thought, splitting a land that had survived the landen uprisings as well as generations of Dorothea SaDiablo's machinations.

The Warlord Princes who lived in the Province on the other side of the Heartsblood River—and could wave to the guards now keeping watch along the northern border of Shalador Nehele—said nothing.

Four days after Shalador Nehele came into being, most of the Warlord Princes who lived north of the Heartsblood River gathered at the Grayhaven estate.

*Most, but not all,* Theran thought as uneasiness soured his belly. Ferall hadn't come, and because Kermilla had burned the one letter Ferall had sent to him weeks ago, Theran didn't know if there was something he could have done to convince the Opal-Jeweled Warlord Prince that he knew what was best for the people and the land.

He walked up the steps to the platform and faced the men. Less than a year ago, Cassidy had stood in this same room and selected the men who became her First Circle. Every man who was here now had been in the room that day—and they remembered. He saw it in their eyes.

Using Craft to enhance his voice, he said, "By now, you've probably all heard that Lady Cassidy enticed the Warlord Princes in the five southern Provinces to abandon Dena Nehele and form a new Territory. She did this because her contract to rule as the Territory Queen would have ended in two months and was not going to be renewed."

"Why not?" someone in the back of the room asked. "From what I hear, her court is standing strong and there have been no complaints about the Lady herself."

"I haven't heard any complaints either," someone else said. "Quite the contrary."

"Cassidy did an adequate job of starting us on the right path," Theran said, "but another Lady more suited to Dena Nehele is ready to stand as our Queen."

"Who is this Lady?" Hikaeda asked.

Hikaeda and Elendill came from the Province that bordered the Heartsblood River and would, no doubt, be reporting back to Ferall and the other Warlord Princes who had settled there.

"Lady Kermilla, who is also from Dharo in the Realm of Kaeleer," Theran replied.

Silence.

Hikaeda looked at his friend Elendill, then back at Theran. "What is it you want from us, Prince?"

"Lady Kermilla held back from forming a court here out of courtesy for Lady Cassidy, allowing Cassidy to finish her rule here uncontested. Because of that courtesy, Dena Nehele is left without a Queen or a ruling court. Our situation is a little better than it was a year ago, but the need for a Queen to rule our land remains. What I'm asking of you, Hikaeda, is the same thing I asked a year ago—that all of you offer yourselves for the Queen's consideration, and if chosen, serve in her First Circle."

"And Kermilla is the Queen you intend to have rule over us?" Hikaeda asked.

How many times was he going to have to say it? "Yes, because Kermilla is the right Queen for us."

Another silence.

"Thank you for your words, Theran," Hikaeda said politely. "Elendill and I will return to our Province and convey your message to the District Queens and the Warlord Princes who were unable to answer your summons. I am certain you will not wait long for an answer."

What in the name of Hell did that mean?

Hikaeda and Elendill turned away from the platform and headed for the door. The other Warlord Princes turned and followed, not even glancing at him to confirm that this meeting was over.

He wanted to call them back, wanted to demand some kind of answer. But there was nothing he could say to them right now—and apparently, there was nothing they wanted to say to him.

# CHAPTER 42

## TERREILLE

"Library, library, library." Ranon set those three letters on the stack marked for Gray to handle. Only a week had passed since the official creation of Shalador Nehele, and the mail coming in for Queen and court had tripled.

The day had turned cold and snowy, with a wind that cut like a mean-tempered bitch. Cassie was tucked in for the afternoon and he was the escort on duty, so he'd offered to sort the mail since Powell had more than enough to do right now. It wasn't a job he enjoyed, but he didn't mind it either, and doing something productive for the court made him feel less guilty about being warm and comfortable today while other members of the First Circle were out in that white misery fulfilling their own assignments.

"Request for a loan to repair a printing press and open a print shop and bookbindery." He frowned at that letter for a moment, then put it in Gray's stack. "Request for lessons with the Protocol instructors. Well, Gray can deal with that too."

Then he hesitated and wondered if they were dumping too much on Gray, especially since he *was* the First Escort and his first priority was taking care of the Queen.

"We really need a Second Circle to assist the First Circle," he muttered. The problem was paying a Second Circle, although Powell *had* hinted they could afford to bring in a few more people to work for the court. Well, for the time being, they would do the best they could with what they had.

Could a Sceltie learn to sort mail?

While he pondered what the dogs might be able to do with the reading skills they had, Dryden tapped on the door and said, "Prince Ferall is asking to see you."

"Me?" When Dryden nodded, Ranon set the unsorted letters at one end of the big meeting table. Nothing really confidential in the stacks he'd sorted so far, but he used Craft to make a layer of witchlight over the papers, effectively preventing anyone from reading them. "Send him in."

Ferall entered the room, still wearing his heavy winter coat and a shapeless hat.

He didn't sense any shields around the man, but Ranon instinctively put a skintight Opal shield around himself under his clothing, just in case. A warrior like Ferall usually held on to his outer gear when he figured he'd have to leave in a hurry—and that usually meant after splattering the walls with blood.

He smiled and took a step forward as if he didn't see the fury in the other man's eyes.

Then Ferall grabbed two fistfuls of Ranon's shirt and slammed his back against the wall.

"You self-serving son of a whoring bitch," Ferall snarled. "Got what you wanted so you just let the rest of us flounder, is that it?"

Clamping his hands around Ferall's wrists to prevent a grab for his throat, Ranon snarled back, "What in the name of Hell are you talking about?"

"You. This." Ferall shook him. "Didn't we work hard enough, try hard enough? Couldn't you give us a chance before you cut us loose? I almost had a life. Damn you to the bowels of Hell, Ranon, I almost had a life! A widow with two young children, a boy and a girl. Lost her husband to one of those twisted bitches a few years back. Had the courage to let me into her life and into her bed. Let me be around her children. You know what that means, Ranon. *You know*."

Yes, he knew. And he understood now about those special gifts Ferall had purchased for Winsol.

Ferall leaned in, and despite the shield, Ranon could feel his chest muscles bruising under the pressure of the other man's fists.

"I never had much of a home when I was young, and nothing you could call a *home* since I was fifteen. Do you know what it feels like to settle into a place and not have everyone look at you with fear in their eyes because they've gotten used to you, gotten used to the idea that you're there to protect them as well as be an instrument of the Queen's will? Do you know what it feels like to be with a woman who cares about you? To have a boy waiting to see you at the end of the day to play a game of toss before dinner or have a little girl snuggle up next to you wanting you to read her a story? Do you?"

"I know," Ranon said quietly. And he did know about that particular dream. He was hoping to have those same things with Shira someday.

"Then why?" Ferall pressed him harder into the wall. "You bastard! Tell me why!"

*"Let him go."*

For a moment, Ranon wondered why Vae's snarled words sounded so strange. Then he looked toward the door and thought, *Oh, shit.*

Cassie stood there, her red hair flowing down her back and her feet planted in a fighting stance. One hand held that club she'd used to defend James Weaver and his family back in Grayhaven. Vae stood beside her.

Both witches snarled at Ferall.

Pushing away from Ranon—and giving him a last knock into the wall in the process—Ferall took a step toward Cassidy, measured the wild look in her eyes, and took a step back.

"Why didn't you give us a chance to prove ourselves before cutting us loose like that?" Ferall asked, his voice ringing with frustration and lost hope.

"We weren't trying to cut anyone loose, Prince Ferall," Cassidy said.

"Then why set the line at the Heartsblood River?"

She must have heard the same leashed pain in Ferall's voice that he did because she lost her defensive anger and stammered, "It's a natural boundary, and we didn't want to be greedy."

Oh, the look of frustrated disbelief on Ferall's face.

Pulling off his hat, Ferall slapped it on his thigh and roared, "Well, Hell's fire, woman! For just once in your life, *be greedy!*"

The club slipped from Cassidy's suddenly limp fingers and almost conked Vae on the head. Cassidy stood there with her mouth hanging open, clearly shocked by the idea of being greedy.

It took her a long moment to gather herself. "If you're not comfortable having your family live under Kermilla's hand, you can relocate, move to a village on the other side of the river. There is plenty of room."

"I could do that," Ferall agreed. "But what about the other eleven Warlord Princes who live in that Province? What about the people in the towns and villages that I've been ruling on behalf of the Queen? What about the farmers who don't want to leave land that's been held in their families for generations? What about them, Lady? What should I tell them when I pack up my family and move across the river?"

Ranon watched Cassidy turn paler and paler until her freckles were the only color left in her face.

*Come on, Cassie,* he thought. *Step up to the line.*

He couldn't nudge her, couldn't urge her. She didn't ask for his opinion. Didn't even look his way for some kind of sign. Her eyes stayed on Ferall.

Then Cassidy, Queen of Shalador Nehele, squared her shoulders and quietly said, "You're right, Prince Ferall. So many people should not be asked to leave their homes. But one man should not make such an important choice for so many." She swallowed hard. "So this is my decision. Go home, Ferall. Talk to the other Warlord Princes. Talk to the District Queens who rule in your Province. If, on behalf of themselves and the people they rule, the majority of them want to break from Dena Nehele and join us as part of Shalador Nehele, you will all be welcome."

Keeping his eyes on Cassidy, Ferall called in a sheet of paper and held it out. "How about all of them?"

Ranon leaned against the wall for support. Hell's fire, Mother Night, and may the Darkness be merciful. Ferall had come with the document in hand.

Cassidy got paler, if that was possible. But she stepped up to the line. "In that case, welcome to Shalador Nehele. Prince Powell?"

"Lady?"

Powell stepped into the room. Must have gotten a sense of trouble and been hovering in the hallway. He wasn't a fighter, but if it had come down to a fight, Ranon would have locked with Ferall and Powell would have gotten Cassie out of the room.

"Please review the document Prince Ferall has brought. Then make a copy of it to add to the documents being preserved for us at the Keep."

"It will be my pleasure, Lady," Powell said. "Prince Ferall? If you would come to my office?"

Ferall studied Cassidy for a moment. "Thank you, Lady. For all of us, thank you." He followed Powell out of the room.

The moment Ferall was out of the room, Ranon leaped toward Cassie, grabbing her before her legs buckled. He pulled out a chair. She collapsed into it.

"Head down, darling," he said, holding one hand between her shoulder blades as she pressed her forehead against her knees. "Just breathe now. That's a girl."

"Ranon? What did I just do?"

"You gave a strong man the possibility of a good life." She'd done a great deal more than that, but he figured she wasn't ready to hear all of it.

When she pushed up, he rubbed her back to soothe and comfort. She had a little color in her face, but she looked like she'd had the wind knocked out of her.

He felt the same way. "You want some tea or brandy or something?"

"Yes, yes, and yes."

Suddenly realizing that Vae had been unnaturally quiet, he looked at the Sceltie, who was staring at the club Cassie had dropped. He closed his hand over the club and vanished it. A Sceltie who knew her Craft probably wouldn't have any trouble burying a club even when the ground was frozen.

As he helped Cassie to her feet, he said, "Come on, Vae. You deserve a treat too."

*Yes.*

Vae definitely sounded grumpy. Well, he'd be grumpy too if he'd come that close to being conked on the head.

He escorted his two Ladies to the Ladies' parlor. Within moments, Birdie, Frannie, Elle, and Maydra were all there, fussing over Cassie and Vae. The second time he got stepped on, he took the hint and retreated downstairs to the parlor used by the court.

By the time he'd poured himself a second brandy, he felt steady enough to consider what had happened—and what it meant.

They had Ferall on their side. Mother Night, they had Ferall, one of the most savage fighters in Dena Nehele. And they had Hikaeda, Elendill, and Rikoma, along with the other eight Warlord Princes who lived in that Province. And they had that land. That would change a lot of things, because that Province ran from the Tamanara Mountains to the western border. As the largest Province, it also meant that, landwise, Dena Nehele and Shalador Nehele were now equal in size. And the addition of those twelve Warlord Princes serving under Cassie's hand meant their fighting weight was equal or better to anything Theran could send against them.

Yes, this would change a lot of things, and he wondered how Theran and Kermilla were going to respond when they found out.

# CHAPTER 43
## TERREILLE

Theran stared at the document Archerr had delivered a few minutes ago.

Hikaeda said he wouldn't have to wait long for an answer from the Warlord Princes who lived in the Province that bordered the Heartsblood River. He just hadn't been prepared for *this* answer.

Cassidy now held the leash for twelve more Warlord Princes—including Ferall. Mother Night, she had Ferall on top of Talon and Ranon. Only a fool would stand on a killing field against those three.

And she had Jared Blaed, who had become a formidable, dominant male, even if he didn't wear the Jewels or have the power he might have had.

Now Cassidy controlled the land and income from another Province. The Warlord Princes and Queens just *gave* it to her. Didn't they have any loyalty to their own land, their own heritage?

"Theran?"

He'd left the study door open. It seemed insulting to have Kermilla scratching on the door like a servant asking for admittance. Especially today. Besides, he'd already tucked the correspondence away in a locked drawer in his desk.

He held out the document.

She read it, her brow furrowing.

"What does this mean?" she asked, handing it back to him.

"It means Cassidy holds Ferall's leash."

"Well, good riddance. He was a crude man. I didn't like him."

"He's an Opal-Jeweled Warlord Prince. I've seen what he's done on a killing field. He's no Lucivar Yaslana, but even so he was feared—and with good reason."

"Oh."

No real comprehension. He heard that truth in her voice, saw it in her eyes. "And it means that Cassidy now rules half of what used to be Dena Nehele."

*That* she understood, and those pretty blue eyes blazed with anger.

"You have to stop this, Theran. You have to get the court formed and *stop this.*"

Hadn't he been trying for months to introduce her to the other Warlord Princes and give her a chance to shine? It wasn't his fault she'd pissed off Ferall and some of the others. But she kept snapping at him because her position was still so tenuous, or she sulked over his tight control of the purse, or pouted over some real—or imagined—insult from Julien. Or wanted sex, which was becoming less and less appealing because there seemed to be less and less heart in the act.

Sometimes he wanted to shout at her to stop being a stupid, selfish girl and start being the Queen he knew she could be.

And yet, despite his growing frustration and anger with her, she still felt so *right,* and he *knew* if she could have a little more time to mature, she *would* be the Queen Dena Nehele so desperately needed.

She was right about one thing: every day that slipped away without a court forming around her made Dena Nehele more vulnerable—and made Cassidy, and her court, look better.

Over the next few days, Theran felt like a man bleeding to death from a wound he couldn't find.

Thinking that any court was better than no court, and figuring Kermilla wouldn't object since she considered these Blood acceptable companions socially, he'd gone to visit the aristo families in Grayhaven—and discovered they had *all* left town on business of one kind or another. The servants couldn't tell him where the families had gone, couldn't tell him when they would return.

The message was clear enough: The men were afraid he would require them to serve in Kermilla's court, so they had removed themselves from his reach.

When he went to talk to the Warlord Princes living in his own Province, they stared at him with bleak eyes and offered nothing.

And with each day and each failure, Kermilla became shriller and more demanding.

He sent another summons to the Warlord Princes in the remaining Provinces, demanding that they present themselves to Kermilla for consideration in her court.

This time, no one answered.

# CHAPTER 44

## TERREILLE

Ignoring her yip of protest, Gray bundled Cassidy into her winter coat and hustled her to the kitchen door.

"Put your boots on," he said. "There's something I want to show you."

Well, she needed a break from the paperwork anyway, and he looked like he could be as stubborn as a Sceltie about showing her whatever this was.

When they were outside, Cassidy lifted her face to the sun. "Not one word about my needing a hat. Not today when the air has that first scent of spring."

"Wasn't going to say a thing." Taking her hand, he led her to the sitting area under the tree.

"Oh!" Delight filled her. "Oh, Gray! Look!"

He grinned. "The first blooms of spring."

Sturdy little flowers poked up through the snow, purple and yellow and white. Similar to one of the spring flowers in Dharo, but not quite the same. The kind of flower Gray called common ground.

"Bulbs?" Cassie asked.

"Yep. There are a couple more varieties planted around the tree, but they'll bloom later in the spring."

"A couple—" Wondering how he knew that since the court hadn't been here last spring, she turned to look at him—and saw something in his eyes that left her breathless. "These weren't here last spring, were they?"

He shook his head. "I planted them this past fall. Wanted it to be a surprise."

*You're the surprise.* "Thank you."

A choice. A chance.

"Gray?"

"Cassie?"

"Could you consider marrying me?"

No expression on his face. Blank eyes. Then, hesitantly, "Really? You're not teasing me?"

She shook her head. "I wouldn't tease about that. I love you when you're Gray and when you're Jared Blaed. I want to build a life with you that spans the seasons."

"You're in love with me?" His eyes looked a little less blank, but she wasn't sure his brain was fully working.

"Yes, I'm in love with you."

"Cassie."

He kissed her with enough heat to sizzle through her body and melt bone. Then he wrapped his arms around her and held on.

"I fell in love with you the first time I met you," he said. "That's what gave me the courage to wake up and grow up. So that I could be with you." He eased back enough to look at her. "You're going to buy me a wedding ring, right?"

Happy tears stung her eyes. She laughed. "Yes, I'm going to buy you a traditional ring."

"Come on," Gray said. "Let's—"

*Gray? Cassie?*

Vae trotted up to them. She wagged a greeting, then stared at both of them.

*Cassie is crying, and you are happy,* she told Gray, her words accompanied by a growl. *Why?*

"I'm happy too," Cassie said, wiping tears off her face. "Gray and I are going to get married."

"Do you know about human marriage?" Gray asked.

*I know.* The growling stopped and the tail wagged with more enthusiasm. *Is this a secret?*

Gray laughed. "No, it's not a secret."

Vae lifted her muzzle and howled. A few moments later, Khollie howled from the other side of the stone fence. A few moments after that, Lloyd and Kief joined in. Then Darcy. Then Keely.

They heard another faint howl coming from the direction of Eyota's main street.

"Hell's fire," Gray said. "They'll tell the whole village before we have time to get back to the house."

"Then we'd better hurry."

Laughing, they ran back to the house, stomped snow off their boots, and smacked into Ranon and Shaddo, who were heading outside to find out what had stirred up the dogs.

By the time the First Circle gathered in the court's parlor and Dryden opened bottles of sparkling wine for the first of many celebrations, everyone who lived with or worked near a Sceltie had heard the news about Prince Jared Blaed and Lady Cassidy.


## EBON ASKAVI

Daemon walked into one of the sitting rooms. Lucivar came in a step behind him and immediately swung to the left to give them both working room. Their father stood by a window, looking out and smiling an odd little smile.

"Where is Gray?" Daemon asked. "You said he needed to talk to us."

"Is he outside making mulch?" Lucivar asked.

"He's outside," Saetan replied. "And once in a while he stops grinning and remembers what he's supposed to do with the piece of wood he's holding."

Daemon looked at Lucivar, who shrugged.

*I'm not picking up any temper,* Lucivar said on an Ebon-gray spear thread.

*Neither am I,* Daemon replied. But what his psychic probe *was* picking up from the boy was damn peculiar.

"Don't give him a hard time," Saetan warned as he rapped on the window. "The only reason I chucked him out there was because he insisted that he wanted to wait until he could tell all three of us the news, and he's so bouncy it was exhausting to be in the same room with him."

"Ah." Daemon smiled.

A minute later, still dressed in his heavy coat and holding a piece of wood, Gray bounced into the room.

*He's spending too much time with Vae,* Lucivar said.

Daemon stifled a laugh.

"Hi!" Gray said.

Looking at those bright green eyes and sensing the almost skin-bursting excitement, Daemon didn't need to hear the words to know the news. But he kept his expression politely interested—and noticed that Saetan was wearing the same expression.

Lucivar shook his head and said, "Give me that."

"What?" Gray looked at the chunk of wood Lucivar took from him and vanished. "Oh." Then he just grinned at all of them.

"Okay, brainless," Lucivar said. "Use words."

"Lucivar," Saetan groaned quietly.

"I'm getting married. To Cassie. And she's getting married to me. It happened yesterday. Not the getting married part. The asking part."

"Congratulations, Gray," Daemon said.

"That's wonderful news," Saetan said. "And worthy of a celebration."

Lucivar stared at Gray until the weight of that stare quieted some of the excitement in the young Warlord Prince.

"So," he finally said. "You've decided to live right up to the line."

"Yes," Gray replied. "I did. I am."

"Good for you, Gray," Lucivar smiled. "Good for you."

Draca entered the room, followed by a servant who brought in a tray filled with food and another servant who brought bottles of sparkling wine and glasses.

When told the news, the Keep's Seneschal offered her congratulations and left. Daemon opened a bottle of wine and poured while Lucivar handed out the glasses.

After the first toast, Daemon set his glass aside and called in two small jeweler's boxes. "Here, Gray. I had a feeling you were going to need these someday, and it looks like that day has come."

Gray set his own glass down and opened the first box. "A man's traditional marriage ring. Do you think it will fit me?"

Daemon chuckled as Gray admired the plain gold band. "Darling, I know it will fit you. Remember our trip to Amdarh for some of the Winsol shopping? Remember going to Banard's?"

Gray nodded. "Surreal wanted to buy a ring for Rainier, and I tried some on so you could see how they fit." He frowned. "Which actually made no sense, but at the time, it *sounded* like it made sense."

*What sort of spell did you wrap around him when you did that?* Saetan said.

*Nothing much,* Daemon replied. *And it wasn't around him, it was around my voice.*

*Ah.* "Except for a court ring or a marriage ring, the only ring a man usually wears is his Jewels," Saetan said.

"Oh." Gray narrowed his eyes at Daemon. "It was a trick?"

"A small deception," Daemon replied. "But with that little ruse, you obligingly provided Banard with your ring size. And then there is this." He flipped the other box open and held it out.

"Mother Night," Gray whispered.

When Gray just stood there, staring, Daemon tipped the box so Saetan could see the ring.

"That's lovely," Saetan said. "And it suits Cassie."

It did suit Cassidy. Amber in three colors, set in a clean design of gold.

"I can't afford that ring," Gray said.

"The two rings are a wedding gift from the SaDiablo family," Daemon said. "A gift to a Queen we admire—and to a Warlord Prince who has had the courage to live up to his potential. I hope you'll accept them."

*I trust you have no objections to the gift?* he asked Lucivar and Saetan.

*None,* they replied.

Gray took the box that held Cassie's wedding ring. "Thank you."

"Come on, boyo," Daemon said. "Let's sit down, have something to eat, and you can tell us every detail about your marriage proposal." He and Lucivar and Saetan all laughed at Gray's expression. "All right. Not every detail."

# CHAPTER 45
## TERREILLE

There was nothing Theran could do. The more he tried to hold on to the land his family had guarded and cherished for so long, the more of it fell away.

Two weeks after the Heartsblood River Province deserted Dena Nehele and gave itself to Cassidy, one of the northern Provinces that bordered the Tamanara Mountains became part of Shalador Nehele. A week after that, the other Province that bordered the mountains turned away from its heritage.

Only four Provinces left. A land that had held for centuries had been reduced to a third of its size within the space of a couple of months. Kermilla was almost hysterical in her demands that he *do* something, and he *tried*. But nothing worked.

Nothing.

When the news about the second mountain Province reached him, he didn't summon the Warlord Princes living in the four remaining Provinces.

This time, they summoned him.


They met in an old barn next to an abandoned farmhouse. A familiar kind of gathering place, Theran thought as he slipped inside. During the years when these men had fought against the twisted Queens, they couldn't gather at an inn without coming to the attention of the Queens' guards and they wouldn't gather at anyone's home and put that man's family at risk.

He knew their names, but it was understood that no names were spoken at this kind of meeting. Foolish, really, when there were so few of them left they all knew one another, but that caution had been too well trained into them.

"Prince." A Purple Dusk Warlord Prince stepped forward. "I've been asked to be the voice of my Brothers."

Theran tipped his head to acknowledge the man—and to acknowledge that these men had gathered for a discussion at least once without him. "I'm listening."

"The day after I reached my majority and my training was declared complete, I walked onto my first killing field. I've been fighting for Dena Nehele in one way or another ever since. I guess that's true for all of us here."

The other twenty-six Warlord Princes nodded.

*Only twenty-eight of us to guard four Provinces,* Theran thought. *How in the name of Hell are we going to do that?*

"I've fought for Dena Nehele," the Warlord Prince said. "My father and my grandfather and his father before him all fought and bled and died for Dena Nehele. And as much as we respect Ranon and Jared Blaed, we want to live in Dena Nehele. The Queens in our Provinces feel the same. We don't want Dena Nehele to become nothing more than a memory."

Thank the Darkness. "Then come back to Grayhaven with me. Meet with Lady Kermilla. Help me form a court so that—"

"No." The Warlord Prince took a step back. "We'll protect Dena Nehele. We'll defend the Blood against the landens, and we'll fight to keep our Provinces safe from outside attack. But none of us will serve Kermilla."

Theran's temper flared hot. "You've never given her a chance. She's young, and she doesn't have as much experience as she thinks she has, but she's not an evil woman or a bad Queen. Befriending Correne was a mistake, and I know the girl's influence on Kermilla's behavior left a bad taste in a few men's mouths, but—"

"Theran."

The breach of etiquette shocked him cold.

"We've heard words like this before, Theran. Heard them from good men who couldn't see the blood on their Queens' hands or tried to justify brutality because they couldn't live with the truth."

Theran said nothing.

"We won't serve her, and we won't stand by and let her become Queen of what is left of our land. We serve Dena Nehele, and we're willing to let the Grayhaven line stand as the ruler. But not her. Never her. If we have to meet you on a killing field and end the Grayhaven line to make sure she doesn't become Queen, then that is what we will do."

He didn't want to believe the words, but he couldn't doubt what he saw in their eyes. If he helped Kermilla set up a court, they would kill him—and then they would kill her.

"She gave up everything to stay here and be our Queen," he said, desperate to make them understand.

"I doubt she gave up anything, but you believe what you choose. It's clear enough she's your Queen; that doesn't make her ours." The Warlord Prince sighed. "Two weeks, Prince. She's safe from us for two more weeks. After that, we'll come hunting."

They flowed around him, predators heading back to the territories they claimed as their own.

Theran stood there, alone, long after the last man had caught the Winds.

Where was the promise of a new life, a better life? Where was the hope? There had been hope a year ago, hadn't there? Gone now. All gone. He didn't know how to fix it, any of it.

And he didn't know what he was going to say to Kermilla.

# CHAPTER 46

## TERREILLE

Days ticked by. Theran spent the time riding through the town. Dena Nehele's capital had too many empty houses, too many empty shops. The people who remained watched him ride by, their eyes accepting and dull.

He rode into the landen part of town and stared at the craftsmen's courtyard where Cassidy had defended a landen family against a Warlord and his two sons.

People's eyes hadn't been accepting and dull then.

To avoid Kermilla and the questions he couldn't answer, he walked around the Grayhaven estate, slogging on slushy paths and riding trails until his trousers were soaked and his legs ached. Or he'd stare at the flower beds Gray had restored, at the spring flowers that had already bloomed or would bloom in a couple more weeks, according to Julien. And more often, he would end up in front of the bed full of witchblood, remembering the day they all discovered what it was—and what it meant.

The days ticked by, and soon there would be no days left. He had to make a choice before the other Warlord Princes made it for him.

A gorgeous spring day. Sweet air and sun that gave warmth as well as light.

Theran stood on the terrace, enjoying this teasing hint of the days to come. It was still too early in the season for the land to shrug off winter al-together, but this was a day to savor.

And there, tucked in the shelter of the terrace's raised beds, was the little honey pear tree, which had survived the winter.

He heard the terrace door open and knew without turning who was there. Her psychic scent was irresistible even on a day like today when her physical presence had less than no appeal.

"Theran?"

Dredging up a smile, he turned toward the door. Kermilla was wrapped in a shawl and a sulky mood.

The shawl wasn't one he'd seen before, and he wondered if that was be-cause it was something she tended to wear in the spring or if he was going to receive an apology and a bill from one of the merchants.

"Why are you wasting time?" Kermilla asked. "Why aren't you bring-ing the Warlord Princes here so that I can choose my court?"

"It's complicated, Kermilla." He'd been trying to work out a way for ev-eryone to get something, even if he couldn't give her what she really wanted.

"It's not complicated, Theran. Just *tell* them." She walked over to the table where he'd set a few papers down. Giving him a defiant look, she moved until she could read as much of the top page as was visible around the fist-sized rock serving as a paperweight.

"I can't *tell* them anything."

Since it wasn't interesting, she gave up on trying to read the top page. "You're the darkest-Jeweled Warlord Prince in this miserable excuse of a Territory. Of course you can tell them."

He bristled, insulted on behalf of his people and his land.

Then he tightened the leash and forced himself to keep his temper out of this conversation.

"You think it's simple," he said with strained patience. "It's not."

"Keeps you in control, doesn't it?"

He stared at her. Where was that bitterness coming from?

"You control the money, so I can't buy *anything* without coming to you first," she said.

"Would you like me to show you the accounts and how much is still owed the merchants from the last time you went shopping without being 'controlled'?" he asked.

"You control access to the other Warlord Princes and the aristo families, so I can't make friends on my own or establish any bonds with other men that don't go through you."

"That's not true."

"You treat me like a child, but I'm not a child."

"Kermilla—"

"*I'm a Queen, damn you!* I'm a Queen, and I'm the one who should be controlling the purse and the men and the land! Me! Not you!" She grabbed the rock. "Not you!"

She threw the rock.

He didn't know—would never know—if her aim had been bad or if she hit exactly what she had intended to hit.

The rock missed him completely and struck the old wish pot that held the honey pear tree.

For a long moment they stared at each other.

She looked magnificent in her fury, and he wanted, more than anything, to yield to her temper and her will.

Then he looked down at the pot that was now in pieces and the honey pear tree lying in the spilled dirt, its roots exposed to the too-cold air.

"Julien!" he shouted. "*Julien!*"

When the butler appeared in the doorway, Theran said, "The pot broke. See what you can find to replace it and do what you can for the honey pear tree."

Julien disappeared.

Theran picked up part of the broken pot, a piece about the size of his fully stretched hand.

"Oh, Theran." Kermilla stood there, looking pretty and contrite. "I'm sorry I threw that rock, but you made me so angry."

He could feel something breaking inside him, and he needed to get away from her, from everyone.

She studied him. "I know you were fond of it but, Theran, it was just an old pot."

Something inside him breaking, breaking.

"It wasn't an old pot, Kermilla. It was a family heirloom, and because of who it belonged to, it was priceless."

Her mouth fell open in shock.

And a truth ripped through him and left him bleeding.

He walked away from her and passed by Julien as the butler rushed back to the tree. He didn't allow himself to think or to feel until he was safely behind the locked door of his study.

Then he set the remnant of the wish pot on his desk, sat down . . . and cried.

# CHAPTER 47
## TERREILLE

For a day and a half, Theran tried to reconcile a dream and a hard truth, but no matter how he looked at it, it came down to choosing between two loves.

*It is better to break your own heart than to break your honor.*

He finally understood Talon's words.

Kermilla mattered more to him than anyone he had ever known. But in the end, Dena Nehele mattered more. So he made his choice and wrote the letters that would bring the Warlord Princes to Grayhaven.

He still wanted Kermilla. Mother Night, how he wanted her! But every time he wavered, he looked at the two objects he'd placed on his desk—objects that reminded him of the difference between two Queens.

One was the piece from the broken wish pot.

The other was a leather-bound copy of Jared's story.

Two days later, twenty-seven Warlord Princes walked into a meeting room at Grayhaven.

This time, Theran didn't stand on a platform to address them. This time, he didn't try to stand as their leader. This time, they told him what he had to do.

\*     \*     \*

Kermilla huffed and *tsked* and made unhappy sounds as she pushed dress after dress aside. She *had* to have some new clothes. When she became Queen, she *couldn't* be seen in these old things!

And she was *finally* going to be Queen. The Warlord Princes had come. Theran hadn't said anything about this meeting, but she'd seen the men arriving. Theran would give them a stern talking-to first, and then he'd request her presence so that she could select her court. She really didn't want a First Circle made up completely of Warlord Princes—they were so prickly!—but she'd settle for it to get the court established and then select more congenial men for her Second Circle. And once she was Queen, she could select a man with better training for her bed.

Not that she wasn't still fond of Theran, but he was better suited to being a First Escort or her Master of the Guard. He just didn't have the proper skills to be a Consort—or even a lover.

So important to make the right impression this time. So important to look like what these men wanted.

But how was she supposed to do that with *these* clothes?

Alone again, Theran closed his eyes and swayed as the pain raked through him.

It was done. The Warlord Princes would help him save what was left of Dena Nehele.

Now all he had to do was fulfill his part of the bargain before time ran out.

A handful of outfits were strewn on her bed and the chairs, souring Kermilla's mood as the inadequacy of her wardrobe became more and more clear. But she had to find *something* before . . .

She glanced out one of her bedroom windows, then stopped and stared at the Warlord Princes walking down the long drive toward the landing web just beyond the estate's double gates.

They were leaving? Why were they *leaving*?

She pulled on a simple housedress, stuffed her feet into soft house shoes, grabbed a shawl, and rushed downstairs to find Theran.

Theran went into his study and gave Julien a psychic tap on the shoulder. Within a minute the butler knocked on the door.

"Lady Kermilla and I have something to discuss," Theran said. "While she is here with me, you and Hanna need to move fast."

After receiving his instructions, Julien hurried out of the room. Moments later, Kermilla rushed in.

"They left!" she said. "Why did they leave without seeing me?"

"Sit down, Kermilla." Theran waved her toward a chair. "I have to explain some things."

"What things?" She sat on the edge of the stuffed chair.

He nudged the footstool back and sat down. He didn't touch her. He didn't want her to realize he had a skintight Green shield protecting his skin, his face . . . his eyes. He felt foolish—and deceitful—doing that with her, but he couldn't ignore the warnings the other men had given him about how previous Queens had reacted to disappointment.

He sighed. "I love you, Kermilla. Everything I am wants to surrender to you. If my life was the only one at stake, I would give it to you. But I'm the last of the Grayhaven line, and I have a duty to the land and the people of Dena Nehele, and what Dena Nehele needs is more important than what I want for myself as a man or a Warlord Prince."

"What does that have to do with the other Warlord Princes leaving before I could choose my court?"

"There isn't going to be a court."

Kermilla rolled her eyes. "I can't rule Dena Nehele without a formal court."

"I know. I'm sorry. I am so very sorry."

It took her a moment, but when she realized what he was saying she drew back a little.

"There isn't going to be a court," Theran said quietly, just to make sure she understood. "You aren't going to rule Dena Nehele."

"Why?" she wailed. "Is it because you're mad at me for breaking that old pot?"

"In a way, it is about the wish pot. Not because you broke it, but because all you see is an old pot that has no value to you. And what that tells me is that in all the months you've been here, you haven't listened to anything I said about Dena Nehele. You've haven't listened to anything I said about the people or our history or what we need from a Queen."

"Well, I don't need the Warlord Princes," Kermilla said. "I'll just fill a First Circle with Warlords and—"

"If you try to form a court here, the Warlord Princes will kill you," Theran said harshly.

The color drained from her face. "They *threatened* me?"

"When one Warlord Prince makes that kind of statement, it's a threat. When twenty-seven of them say that, it's a declaration of war."

She swayed, and he wondered if she was going to be sick.

"Who's going to rule Dena Nehele?"

"It doesn't matter. What matters is it can't be you. And that's why you have to leave." *Before they come back to kill you.* He could feel his heart tearing into pieces.

"Leave?" She looked so young and so lost . . . and so lovely. "Why can't I stay with you? You love me. You said so!"

"You said it yourself the other day," he replied gently. "You're a Queen. If you stayed, you would want to rule. As much as I would want that for you, I would have to oppose you for the good of the people. We would destroy each other, Kermilla. And we would destroy what was left of Dena Nehele in the process."

She stared at him, and he wasn't sure she understood anything.

For a moment, sly calculation filled her eyes and then was gone. But he saw it, and in that moment, he saw what the other Warlord Princes had seen in her—and understood why they never would have served her.

Then the moment was gone, and she was the young woman who had dazzled him when he'd first met her. She was lovely Kermilla, the Queen whose will could no longer be his life.

She leaned forward, her lips curved in a sexy smile. "Why don't we go upstairs for a proper good-bye?" She laughed a little. "That could take a day or two."

He wanted to yield. Mother Night, how he wanted to yield!

Gone before sunrise—or dead by tomorrow's sunset. That was all the time she had left if she stayed in Dena Nehele. He shook his head. "No."

"When am I supposed to leave that we can't take that little time?"

"Now."

Shock.

*Julien?* Theran called on a spear thread.

*It's done. I'm ready,* Julien replied.

"All your things are packed and in the Coach," Theran said. "I'm going to take you to the Keep now."

"You can't do this!" Kermilla sprang away from him.

He threw a Green shield around the desk, mostly to protect the wish pot and book.

Sensing the shield, she whirled toward him, her face filled with hurt and a growing rage.

"I gave up everything for you!" she screamed. "Everything, Theran!"

He wished he could still believe her.

"I'm sorry." What else was there to say? He stood up. "It's time to go."

The hurt and rage disappeared. She was back to sexy pout. "I *can't* go to the Keep dressed like *this*."

"They won't mind." He walked over to her and reached out to take her arm.

Another change of mood. Watching her eyes, he knew the moment when she considered raking his face with her nails—and knew the moment when she realized he was wearing a Green shield to prevent her from doing just that.

Taking a firm grip on her arm, he escorted her out of his family's home to the Coach waiting at the landing web.

Kermilla huddled in the passenger compartment of the Coach with no one for company but that horrid Julien, who was giving her a smothering kind of attention while Theran, who turned out to have no spine or balls at all, hid with the driver in the locked front compartment.

She had lost. Instead of ruling a Territory for a few years and being admired, she was being sent home to *nothing*. No court, no men, no income. Nothing. Her mother was being stingy, so if she went back to her parents' house, her father wouldn't give her anything. Besides, running back home was what old Freckledy had done, and she was *never* going to be like Cassidy in any way. Never.

But she had to do something. How long would they let her stay at the Keep? Were there any interesting men who worked there? Men who could be coaxed into helping a young, pretty Queen who had been misled by a nasty Warlord Prince whose honor was, at best, questionable?

That much decided, she settled in more comfortably, had Julien bring her a plate of food and some coffee, and spent the rest of the journey considering how to turn this loss to her advantage.


## EBON ASKAVI

Theran breathed a quiet sigh of relief when he walked out of the Coach and stepped on the landing web in one of the Keep's courtyards. He'd kept away from Kermilla for the whole journey, afraid that if he stayed in that small compartment with her he would give in to her demands or his own desires.

But here at the Keep, the tug and pull of her presence faded, unable to compete with the mountain and its inhabitants.

Better that way for both of them.

He held out his left hand to her as she left the Coach. She ignored it and marched to the door. She rang the bell before he could join her, then stood there with her arms crossed and one foot tapping.

The man who opened the door had black eyes, black hair with a prominent widow's peak, *white* skin, and sensuous bloodred lips. Geoffrey, the Keep's historian/librarian.

"Lady," he said. "Prince Grayhaven."

"I'm returning to Kaeleer," Kermilla said, raising her chin. "Please summon whoever opens the Gate."

Those black eyes glittered queerly. "I'll ask the Seneschal if the Gate is available."

"How can it *not* be available?" Kermilla demanded.

"We don't let everyone into the Shadow Realm. However, if you wanted to go to Hell, that could be arranged easily."

"Geoffrey, why don't I handle this?"

Theran trembled at the sound of the High Lord's voice. *Never thought I'd be glad to see him.*

"Why?" Geoffrey asked as Saetan joined them.

"Because for some reason, you're even more pissed off with this Lady than my sons are, and I wouldn't have thought that possible."

"Maybe it's because I read history—and have a long memory," Geoffrey replied too softly.

"I, too, read history and have a long memory," Saetan replied just as softly. "But the Queen commands, Geoffrey. The Queen commands."

Tension hummed between the two men as black eyes stared into gold.

Then the tension eased and Geoffrey smiled. "In order for our guests to remain safe, she tossed your boys out of the Keep, didn't she?"

"She did. It was quite entertaining—and exciting—to watch."

Geoffrey laughed. "In that case, High Lord, I will yield and leave our guests in your care." As he turned to leave, he added, "In whichever Realm you care to have them."

Kermilla looked like she was ready to faint, so Theran cupped a hand under one elbow to offer a little warmth and support. It was damn cold up in the mountains, but when he obeyed Saetan's subtle gesture and led Kermilla into the Keep, the outside cold couldn't compete with the freezing remnants of temper on the other side of the door.

Kermilla linked an arm through his and held on as Saetan led them deeper and higher into the mountain. When they reached the room that held the Gate, Theran gently unhooked her arm from his.

She looked at him. "Aren't you coming with me?"

"No." He smiled sadly. "This is as far as I go." *As far as he dared to go.*

"May the Darkness embrace you, Kermilla. I'll never forget you." *Or stop loving you.*

He stepped back, stepped out of reach.

Saetan opened the door.

⋆High Lord?⋆ Theran said.

"Why don't you go in?" Saetan told Kermilla. "I'll join you in a moment."

She walked inside the room. Saetan closed the door and looked at him, one eyebrow raised.

Theran called in a package that was carefully wrapped in paper and sealed with wax. He held it out and waited for Saetan to take it.

"Four hundred gold marks," Theran said. "I'd like Kermilla to have it. That's a year's income for me, and she'll probably spend it in a week, but I'd like her to have it."

"Why didn't you give it to her yourself?" Saetan asked.

*I didn't want her to think it was a payment of some kind—or that she would get any more.* "It's complicated."

"I'll see that she gets it."

"High Lord? Is Kermilla going to be all right?"

Saetan stared at him for a long time. "Lady Sabrina and her Steward are on their way to the Keep. They'll see that Kermilla gets back to Dharo safely." He looked behind Theran. "This Warlord will escort you back to the Coach and retrieve Lady Kermilla's trunks."

"Thank you."

Nothing more to say, so he bowed to the High Lord of Hell and followed the servant to the Coach.

On the way back to Dena Nehele, Julien fixed him coffee and a plate of food. He didn't touch either. He sat in the passenger compartment of the Coach, breathing in Kermilla's lingering physical and psychic scents—and wondered if this feeling of being torn and broken would ever go away.

After going through the Gate and arriving at the Keep in Kaeleer, Kermilla followed the High Lord to a sitting room. He'd been awfully scary when she'd first seen him, but he *was* a handsome man. A little too old for her tastes. Older men could be so *serious* about *everything.* And they didn't have enough stamina to be fun. But the way he had handled that other strange man . . . Yes, he could be helpful. *Very* helpful.

"I'm glad Theran didn't come with us," she said, giving him a sideways glance through her lashes. "That way we can get to know each other better."

She started to link her arm through his, but when she touched his jacket, the air turned so bitingly cold it burned her skin.

He said nothing about the cold or the way she jerked away from him. When he opened the sitting room's door, she darted inside and went straight to the fireplace, hoping to warm up.

Her hands finally thawed enough to stop burning. She turned around and found him staring at her, his gold eyes glazed and sleepy.

"I was ordered to give you a gift," he said. "It was created especially for you."

"A gift?" That warmed her even better than the fire. She clapped her hands in delight and gave him a brilliant smile. "What is it?"

He stepped closer, raised his right hand, and pressed his fingers lightly against her chest.

At first it felt like a delicate necklace that rested on her skin in a web of fine metal. Then it melted *into* her skin, and threads of power flowed around her and through her, creating an odd flood of warmth that was there and gone.

Only moments passed before he raised his hand and stepped back to look at her.

"How appropriate," he said in a singsong croon.

She placed a hand on her chest, but she felt nothing.

"Look," he said. A turn of his hand, and a large gilt-framed mirror floated in the air nearby. "Look."

She looked. Then she screamed.

And the High Lord of Hell laughed.

"Don't worry, my dear. It's only an illusion spell, but it's a powerful one—and unbreakable. You'll wear that face for a year and a day. Then the spell will fade gradually over the months that follow. Within two years, you'll have your own face again and, hopefully, a great deal more."

"Why?" Kermilla wailed as she stared at a face that was even more homely than Freckledy's. Everyone would see *this* when they looked at her? "Why?"

"The tangled webs all said the same thing," the High Lord replied. "If you continue to be nothing more than a greedy little girl, you will be dead within a year. While some of us welcomed that solution to a noxious problem, the Queen decided to give you a second chance. Your pretty face was the tool you used to get what you wanted, regardless of what it cost anyone else. Now you'll have to earn what you want by proving your worth as a Queen. You're being given a chance to grow up, Lady Kermilla, instead of dying young. I hope you eventually appreciate the gift. If you don't, we'll meet again soon in Hell."

She trailed after him as he walked to the sitting room's door. Then a gleam of silver caught her eye, drawing her toward one of the small tables scattered around the room. Plenty of expensive little nothings in this room. Who would notice if there were one or two less?

The silence turned heavy and cold and peculiar.

She looked at the High Lord, who studied her with those sleepy gold eyes.

"If you steal something from the Keep, what guards this place will let you take it," he crooned. "But they will take your hand in exchange."

He walked out of the room and closed the door.

Something moved in the wall. A shadow where there shouldn't be a shadow.

Kermilla backed away from the table. Curling up in a chair, she remained there until Sabrina arrived to take her back to Dharo.


"Is it done?" Witch asked.

"It's done," the High Lord replied. "Will it make a difference?"

She rolled up the threads of her tangled web and dropped them in a shallow bowl of witchfire. "That's up to Kermilla now."

# CHAPTER 48

## TERREILLE

Frustrated and heartsore, Theran sat at his desk, his head braced in his hands.

What was the point of the other Warlord Princes making him the ruler of Dena Nehele if they weren't going to work with him, weren't going to help him?

They didn't trust him. That's what it came down to. As far as they were concerned, his bond with Kermilla had not only fouled his judgment, it had ruined the opportunities they would have had to bring in needed help for their people. And every time his efforts to restore Dena Nehele failed, he lost a little more of their conditional support.

They wanted the same things people were receiving from Cassidy's court, so he tried to approach Daemon Sadi about a loan similar to the one Gray had negotiated for Cassidy. Sadi's coldly civil reply made it clear that Theran would get no help from the Warlord Prince of Dhemlan.

He tried to contact the Queens in Kaeleer to hire Protocol instructors to teach the courts in Dena Nehele. The Queens didn't answer him at all.

He tried to talk to Cassidy, but her First Circle refused to grant him an audience. The only thing he received from that visit was an assurance from Talon that Lady Cassidy had no desire to start a war and no intention to seize any land. The Warlord Princes of Dena Nehele didn't need to worry about having Lady Cassidy for a neighbor.

No one wanted to work for him. The people in the town barely spoke to him.

And too many nights lately, he wondered if the Warlord Princes were waiting for him to fail enough for them to justify using their knives.

Julien rushed into the study without knocking and thrust an envelope into Theran's hand. "You have a visitor. Lady Rhahn from the Isle of Scelt. She said you should read the letter before you speak to her."

Theran stared at Julien. The butler looked dazed, dazzled, almost giddy with excitement.

"Read it," Julien said. "Hell's fire, man, *read*." He sprang for the door. "Refreshments! I should get the Lady some refreshments!"

He was gone as quickly as he'd come in.

"What in the name of Hell is wrong with him?" Theran muttered as he broke the black wax seal and removed the single sheet of paper.

> *Prince Grayhaven,*
>
> *I am aware that you have become the Warlord Prince of Dena Nehele and have taken responsibility for ruling your people. I am also aware that you still need a Queen who can help your people remember Protocol and the Old Ways. Therefore, I have asked Lady Rhahn to stay with you for a year.*
>
> *A second chance, Theran. If you turn away from this one, there will be no other.*
>
> *Jaenelle Angelline*

Theran folded the letter and vanished it.

Mother Night. Witch was giving him a second chance.

He straightened his clothes, ran his fingers through his hair in an effort to tidy it, and sprang to the study door much as Julien had. Then he paused.

Would the Warlord Princes accept another Queen from Kaeleer if she was associated with him? Could they ever trust her with the well-being of their people?

He opened the study door.

The answer to those questions looked up at him and wagged her tail.

# CHAPTER 49

## TERREILLE

"It was a lovely wedding, Daughter." Devra lifted Cassidy's left hand. "And that is a beautiful ring."

A lovely, dizzy warmth spread through Cassidy. "Yes, it is." Not just the amber ring's design, but what the ring stood for. Something she knew her mother understood.

She looked at the people milling around the backyard of the Residence and was glad her First Circle had declared the sitting area under the tree to be the Queen's private spot—a place to catch her breath and a moment's quiet before talking to the next group of well-wishers.

"This was supposed to be a small wedding," she said as she caught sight of her cousin Aaron and his wife Kalush talking with Ranon, Shira, Reyhana, and Janos.

Devra chuckled. "I imagine it is for a Territory Queen. You managed to limit the guest list to two Warlord Princes and two Queens from each of your Provinces, plus the elders and Tradition Keepers in Eyota, plus your court, family and personal friends. And everyone you invited accepted the invitation."

*Except Theran.* A small nugget of sorrow because of his rejection, but not for herself. Not anymore. Not when her life with Gray would be so full of dreams and challenges and work and love. Most of all, love.

Her eyes skipped over the crowd, searching for Gray. She found him talking with her father, and there was something in the way they were gesturing . . .

Devra sighed. "Can't put those two anywhere near each other before they start talking about work and new projects. I'll just go over and . . ."

"No need," Cassidy murmured, feeling laughter bubble up as she watched Lucivar Yaslana and her cousin Aaron deftly separate her father and husband, herding them in opposite directions. "I wonder. Did Scelties learn to play cows and sheep from Warlord Princes or did Warlord Princes learn from the Scelties?"

Grinning, she and Devra slipped arms around each other's waists and went out to meet the next group of well-wishers.


"Prince Grayhaven and Lady Rhahn have arrived," Dryden said quietly. "He asked to see you. I put them in the visitor's parlor."

Gray felt the bright joy of his wedding day fade. Cassie had insisted on sending Theran an invitation to the wedding. He was family, and their wedding was about friends and family, and not about courts and boundaries. So he—and the rest of her court—had yielded to her wishes, but no one had been disappointed that Theran hadn't come.

He looked over to where Cassie was talking and laughing with a group of women, including Lucivar's wife, Marian.

"Let him wait," Gray said.

Lucivar chuckled. "Grayhaven can wait until the sun shines in Hell, but Lady Rhahn is a Green-Jeweled Queen. Trust me, boyo. You do not want to keep her waiting."

The sharp warning in Lucivar's eyes had Gray chaining his temper before Ranon or any of the others caught a scent of it. He wasn't going to spoil this day for any of them, especially Cassie.

"Go meet her before you say or do something stupid," Lucivar said.

Gray handed his glass of sparkling wine to Lucivar. "Here. That way I won't be tempted to throw it in her face."

Lucivar's roar of laughter wasn't the reaction he expected, so he slipped into the Residence, more curious now than angry.

Then he stepped into the visitors' parlor.

Hell's fire, Mother Night, and may the Darkness be merciful. The Green-Jeweled Queen was a *Sceltie?*

"Hello, Gray," Theran said, sounding uncertain. "May I introduce Lady Rhahn from the Isle of Scelt?"

"I am honored by the introduction," Gray replied, bowing as he would to any Queen.

"Lady, this is my cousin Prince Jared Blaed."

Rhahn wagged her tail. *You are called Gray. You are Cassie's mate now. Are you going to have puppies?*

"Ah . . ." Was there a safe answer? He sent a psychic spear thread toward Lucivar. *You could have warned me.*

*Boyo, you have no idea yet. My darling sister sometimes has a wicked sense of justice.*

*Jaenelle* sent Rhahn to Dena Nehele?*

*Who else?*

Aware of the silence in the room, Gray looked into Rhahn's brown eyes and had a sudden urge to hide in the nearest clump of brambles.

"So," he said, "are you the Queen of Dena Nehele?"

*No. Theran rules Dena Nehele, and I rule Theran.*

A Sceltie Queen ruling a territory made up of one Warlord Prince who didn't outrank her. No wonder Theran looked like he'd gotten a hard whack upside the head.

*May the Darkness have mercy on him.*

*Rhahn!* Vae bounded into the room, dancing with delight. *You are here!*

Theran looked at Vae and turned a little green.

Gray took a step toward the door. "You two know each other?" A dumb question when the answer was so obvious.

He took another step toward the door.

*Rhahn is . . . * Vae appeared to be thinking hard. *Mother's sister.*

"What?" Theran squeaked.

"Your aunt?" Gray felt something tickling inside his belly and throat. Might have been laughter. More likely, hysteria. "Rhahn is your aunt?"

★Yes,★ Rhahn said. ★Aunt. Vae will introduce me to the Queen. Then we will play.★ She looked at Theran and growled. ★This is a happy day. You will behave and not fight with the Queen's males.★

The Scelties trotted out of the room.

"What is the 'or else'?" Gray asked. "She didn't have to say it; I heard it loud and clear."

Theran hunched his shoulders. "With Rhahn, 'bite him in the balls' isn't just an expression."

It wasn't kind to laugh, but he couldn't stop himself. "Is she as bossy as Vae?"

"She's twice as bad." Theran shook his head. "Hell's fire, Gray, when the Warlord Princes heard another Queen from Kaeleer was staying at Grayhaven, they came charging in, ready to fight."

"Didn't know what to do with her, did they?" *He looks so confused and beaten,* Gray thought, feeling sympathy for his cousin Theran even if he still felt wary of Prince Grayhaven.

"There she was, looking all furry and friendly, and before they realized *what* she was, she was charging around, issuing orders and herding them where she wanted them to go, and they just trotted along with her, as docile as lambs."

Of course, Gray thought. Why would they oppose someone who expected them to take care of their flocks and had connections to Cassie's court as well as strong courts in Kaeleer? Theran might be the Warlord Prince of Dena Nehele and the ruler in public, but the court that truly ruled Dena Nehele would form around Rhahn.

*You wanted a powerful Queen who would dazzle the Warlord Princes enough to serve,* Gray thought. *Looks like you finally got her.*

Lucivar was right. Jaenelle *did* have a wicked sense of justice.

"I appreciate the invitation, Gray," Theran said.

*You didn't get here in time for the wedding.* Cassie would have been sad about that if she'd known, but Theran's absence hadn't been obvious. Noted by the First Circle, since they'd all been on the lookout for him, but not obvious. The village was packed with personal guests and representatives from every Province and reserve, and trying to pick out a particular psychic scent among so many had been damn near impossible, especially after Lucivar and Marian arrived to represent the SaDiablo family as well as Cassie's other friends in Kaeleer.

"I figured my presence would piss off Cassidy's First Circle, and I didn't want to spoil the day. But Rhahn insisted that we come for part of the celebration."

"I'm glad you came," Gray said—and realized he meant it. He'd missed his cousin.

"I brought this." Theran called in a small box and held it out. "A token for Cassidy. It's a piece of Lia's jewelry. I thought she might like to have one."

"I know she would." Gray didn't take the box. Instead, he put an arm around Theran's shoulders. "You should give it to her yourself."

He guided Theran out the front door since Maydra had gotten snarly about people coming through the kitchen and snitching food from the platters before she got them set out.

As they rounded the corner, heading for the backyard and the guests, they heard Rhahn say, *Theran is not a bad human. He is just male and foolish. And confused.*

*Yes,* Vae agreed. *He needs you.*

Gray looked at Theran. Theran looked at Gray.

"Mother Night, Theran," Gray whispered. "You are in so much trouble."

When the two men reached the backyard, Cassie, Lucivar, and all the others saw Jared Blaed and Theran Grayhaven holding on to each other, laughing.